TWO CLASSIC TALES OF WESTERN ACTION BY THE WEST'S MOST POPULAR STORYTELLER NELSON NYE

GUNSHOT TRAIL

"So you did come after all," Latham purred. "I thought you would — you wench stealing rat!" Turbulent fires were aboil inside him, searing away the ropes of his caution, driving their robust fury storm-black across the scowling twist of his face. San Carlos was in his rage-fogged mind and this white-cheeked girl was in it too; and a pulse on his forehead was throbbing wildly. "I'll fix you!" he shouted, and fired point-blank.

TEXAS TORNADO

Marlatt pulled a deep breath and bent with both hands scraping the floor to find something he could use for a weapon, in his rage forgetting the belted gun at his hip. His search yielded nothing, but the bending saved him; for just as he stooped something thin, something glinting, whistled through the murk where he'd just been crouching. Window glass came down in burst fragments, striking the floor with a dry-paper crackle. Some fool then was letting a gun go off, filling the place with its bullets, the flame of those shots licking out like snakes' tongues.

Other *Leisure* Double Westerns by Nelson Nye:

**GUNSLICK MOUNTAIN/ONCE IN THE
  SADDLE
IRON HAND/THE NO-GUN FIGHTER
GUNS OF HORSE PRAIRIE/WILDCATS
  OF TONTO BASIN**

NELSON NYE

GUNSHOT TRAIL/
TEXAS TORNADO

LEISURE BOOKS NEW YORK CITY

For that great old gal
who edits the Cowboys Bible —
Ma Hopkins!

A LEISURE BOOK®

February 1992

Published by

Dorchester Publishing Co., Inc.
276 Fifth Avenue
New York, NY 10001

GUNSHOT TRAIL

1

LUCK RUNS OUT

Six wasted years were behind him. Six down-the-river-sold years that could not be retrieved. This crazy chase that had carried Clem Andros over forty-five hundred miles of fine-combed territory was ended—ended with the same bitter irony that had seen and watched it prosecuted. The gods could have their laugh. Dakota Krell was dead.

Upon the table by which Andros sat slack-muscled stood a bottle and a tumbler. On the wall beyond, a faded print leered down at him through the gloom of its fly-specked glass. Andros was tired of everything. It was two-fifteen when he got that message that Dakota Krell had stopped a knife in a barroom brawl across the Border. The bottle had been full then; now it was useless, empty. Six hours to kill a bottle! But Andros was not drunk.

He was, however, suddenly aware the room was hot. His clothes were clammy with sweat as he shoved away from the table, wheeling toward the window on legs that refused to wabble, driving through the clutch of this trapped heat with a sultry fury. An impatient jerk of his big, scarred hands sent the window rattling up, full open. Summer smell and town smell came in to mingle with the stuffy stench so typical of hotel rooms. Twilight's glow was leaving the hills. Soon the good clean black of night would come to hide the squalor of a town whose only excuse of being was the nearby Reservation.

Andros put his back to the window with a soft-breathed oath and drew the back of a hand across his forehead. That woman in the next room was bawling again; not easily nor loudly, but softly. A kind of choking sound as though what she cried about hurt her.

San Carlos was no metropolis. It boasted one hotel—this one. Heat came through its warped board walls. In the wall that was nearest the woman light filtered through those

5

places where the boards no longer met. "I'll be back in about ten minutes," a man's rough voice said irritably. "Be ready."

Andros heard the floorboards creak beneath the fellow's boot heels; and then the door slammed loudly.

Andros shrugged his shoulders. No affair of his. Crying, he had noticed, came easily after marriage. Kind of seemed a natural sequence. Some women took a deal of pleasure in the business. He thought the woman yonder might quite likely be of that sort.

He walked stiff-legged across the room and stood by the table grimly. He was not old, but he was not young if you put any store in faces. Experience had carved harsh lines across this lean man's countenance. Sun and the winds had darkened it, toughened it like old leather. Wrinkles were graven about his eyes which, brightly, intently blue, were bleak and cold as gun steel.

He picked up the half-full glass on the table. He eyed it, morosely considering those wasted years. There were people he supposed, who would not consider them wasted. They had brought him distinction, certainly. All up and down the twisting length of this hell-bent border country men had learned to hide their feelings, to pick their way with caution, with their hands, plainly empty, in sight when chance brought him into their presence.

It was a distinction in which he took no pride. It was to him as shameful as the fawning manner and white-faced smirks of sundry belly-crawling sidewinders with whom he'd been forced to deal.

His life these years had not been pleasant. Clues to Dakota Krell's whereabouts had not been tacked to the public signposts. The trail had been a hard one; it had thrown him into company with this country's roughest breed.

He had survived.

Contemplation of that fact put saturnine creases at the corners of his eyes. Yes—he had survived.

"Black" Andros they had called him, though whether because of his clothes or deed, he had no means of knowing. Some had packed him quarrels, all neatly stage-managed, that later they might boast of having "downed" this "king of killers." These had not "quarreled" twice.

His big shoulders lifted in restless movement. He sloshed the untouched liquor in his glass, watching how it clung with

6

an oily sleekness. With a scowl he put it back on the table.

Need of action raked him. All his nerves were screaming and that hogwash in the tumbler had no further power to relax them. He had tramped this room till he knew every crack—and *that* had not helped, either. He had need of physical, *violent* action; every sinew and muscle ached. He had to have an outlet.

His mind kept sliding into the past. There was no "ahead" for Black Clem Andros. Everything lay behind. Six years of trail dust, trickery and hate. Brush-running years of turmoil, of jerky, beans and rancid coffee; of the spat and whine of drygulch lead. Of toothpick peril—the Arkansaw kind! Pounding hoofs and choking dust; the interminable bawling of long-horned cattle thrown wet across the Border. Swinging ropes and sudden death. Murder, battle, swift oblivion. These were the things those years had accounted as his share.

And now, in one bare second of time, some fool's knife had made of those things a mockery.

The irony of it bit into him like acid.

He came erect with a smothered oath, quartering the room with heavy stride, the dying sun throwing a solid shadow against the yonder wall boards. Impulse stopped him abruptly and, as swift, he caught up his sun-greened hat, throwing open the hallway door and going through its aperture sideways.

Never before had he come within miles of this town. Chance of recognition should be anyways sixty-forty—forty no one would know him. He would do his tramping out of doors where God gave a man room to swing his legs.

He stepped into the street and checked his stride midpace. Dusk had settled, but light from the hotel windows showed four stolid, blanket-wrapped figures squatted shoulder to shoulder along the plank walk's edge. Indians. San Carlos Apaches from the Reservation. Sharp of eye and smooth of face. Short-worded, but long of memory.

He shoved his hands deep into his pockets and swung his head in a watchful arc, six years' care and vigilance breaking through the fog of his temper.

In that deeper black across the street a denser shape moved fractionally. Farther down, Andro's raking stare picked up another bit of movement; discerned the pin-point glow of a cigarette in the curdled gloom of a stable doorway. A fourth,

7

discovered among the gathered shadows of a cottonwood, sent sudden clamor through him.

Temper burned like a white flame in him and one swift step took him out of their sight beneath a wooden awning. He brought his fists from his pockets and stood there waiting for the play with his hand half curled in the darkness.

He had not long to wait.

Across the way a door swung abruptly open, its bar of light striking hungrily through the felted gloom of the dusty road. Andros saw the placed shapes stiffen as a man's big form, emerging, momentarily blocked the beam. Andros knew in that quick moment where the watcher's interest lay. His muscles loosed their tension.

But the next instant saw them stretched wire-taut again.

His chest and shoulders took a forward sloping while he called himself a fool—while he told himself what was going on here was none of his affair.

But he understood, even as he said it, what it was he had to do. The man silhouetted in that yonder doorway wore the uniform of the newly-established Forest Service. He stood for law and order—something this country had been a long time needing.

Perhaps it was ironic that a man who for six years, people said, had been doggedly bucking all kinds of law should take time out to feel kinship with it now. But Andros knew what would swiftly happen the second that Ranger left the doorway. Those men had not been posted there to while away the time.

He knew the total brashness of this thing he was about to do—the fleeting, bitter quirk of his lips showed that. But it did not stop him. He raised his voice and yelled: "Get back! Get back inside that house!"

The echoes of it slammed the street's false fronts, fell, and dimmed away. A deep stillness settled, through which he plainly heard the emboldened voices of night insects. Nothing else. The Ranger was gone from the doorway. The waiting shapes were also gone.

Andros looked across at the Indians. Their stolid forms still showed against the light from the hotel windows. They hardly seemed to have moved an inch, hunched shoulder touching hunched shoulder. They cared for no part in the white man's medicine.

8

It was a cunning wisdom. No one but a fool bought chips in a game that didn't concern him. It was Black Clem Andros' weakness—a soft streak in him. A thing he had constantly fought against, yet had been unable to conquer. Like enough it would bring him to an early grave, if his enemies' guns or a hangman's noose didn't take care of him earlier.

He shrugged. Straightening, he turned his steps toward the lights of a saloon that, up the street a little way, winked out at him invitingly. But, nearly there, he changed his mind and dragged his spurs back to a restaurant.

He slipped swiftly in and got his back hard against a wall. Then he had his look around.

A constant thing, this watchfulness of surroundings; a steadfast habit born of turbulence and grown unbreakable as the habit of taking nourishment. It was one of those things which spelled the difference between continued living and six feet of earth. With Andros, there was always the chance of recognition, and what such awareness brought in its wake. He had many enemies, not all of whom he knew. He found it well to stay prepared.

It was a bit past time for evening meals and the place was almost deserted. Not counting himself there were only three customers present. A little Mexican, folded above his plate, was stowing food noisily. Yonder at a wallside table sat a man and a woman. The woman's glance stayed rigidly on her plate; by the plate's appearance she'd been doing little more than half-heartedly sampling the heaped-up portions presented by the establishment. Her companion's plate was nearly empty. He seemed to be muttering under his breath, and kept eyeing the woman darkly.

Andros took the table next to them and chose a chair that backed to the wall. The fat proprietor waddled up, got his order and departed. With his tarnished fork Andros made meaningless ruts in the table's spotted cloth. He was not particularly hungry. Habit was what had brought him here. All his reflexes were habit; though he could remember many times when he'd wanted nothing so much as to tuck his legs under a table and keep them there till he could hold no more. This was not such a time. He had come to eat because only God knew when he'd have the leisure to do it again.

Then his hard lips twisted as he recollected. Odd how difficult it was to break yourself of habit. There was no

9

longer any reason why he should not eat when he felt like it. The chase was ended. Old habits and associations, like old shifts with their multiple dangers, belonged to the past. This was A.D.—time he was finding new purpose, new meaning to this life. Old ties no longer bound. Life seemed queer . . . a little empty.

His eyes strayed frequently to the couple at the adjoining table, remaining longest on the woman. He guessed it was the odd pallor of her face that attracted his attention—that, and the redness of her doggedly downfocused stare. Looked like she'd been crying.

He gave her a taciturn interest. She was not a woman really; just a girl, he thought, hardly out of her teens. Her tousled hair was fine-spun gold; like burnished bronze it gleamed in the lamps' mellow glow and Andros felt an urge to thrust his fingers through it. The richness of that golden hair gave her brown and willful eyes an added touch of piquancy. She was slender, pretty and golden, with lips of berry redness and a skin that gleamed like ivory and was smooth as bolted satin.

She was dressed in a ruffled white waist and blue riding skirt. Below the roundness of her chin a golden throat curved softly to the lacey collar of her waist, a covering that did little to hide the alluring contour of pointed breasts and the lithe, slim form beneath.

She must have sensed his covert study for her eyes came suddenly up at him and remained upon him searchingly. There was a strong curiosity in them and, briefly, an approval. There was intentness in that look, and a kind of troubled challenge. Then her long-lashed lids slipped down demurely and Andros, strangely disturbed, vigorously attacked the food that had been set before him.

He wondered idly if she were the one whose sobs he had heard in the hotel. She did not look like the crying kind. But a fellow never knew. Women were creatures set apart with different rules for conduct. No man could understand them, and would be a fool to try.

He was reaching for his pie when it happened. The man had said something to her, something gruff that Andros didn't catch. The girl spoke back, and he knew she was the one whose crying had annoyed him. But she had spunk; she said

10

distinctly, *"I won't!* I won't go there with you, Joce Latham, and you can't—"

The man, a tinhorn by his look and garb, showed experience in the handling of women. He wasted no words. He leaned above the table and slapped her soundly across the face.

She came to her feet with a little cry, her white cheek red with the print of his hand. Eye to eye they glared across the table, the girl pale, shaken, but still defiant; the man bent forward with a poised and threatening stiffness, a sultry anger bright in his gaze.

This was the way they were when Andros spoke. He said, very softly: "Don't reckon I'd undertake to do that any more, if I was you."

The gambler's shape swung completely round. Color livened the set of his cheeks and brash thoughts gleamed in his narrowed stare. His right hand dropped till its spraddled fingers were but half an inch from the gun that showed beneath the flung-back skirt of his coat. "Get out!" he growled with a husky slowness. *"Git!"*

He started ominously forward. Andros made no move. His soft laugh mocked the gambler's look. Latham stopped in his tracks, eyes gone bright with quick suspicion. "What the bloody hell you laughin' at?"

"You," murmured Andros, and laughed again. "You're not scarin' nobody."

A curse jarred out of Latham's teeth and his striking fingers closed about his gun. Detonation shook the walls of the place and the glint of the gambler's pistol skittered across three feet of floor. He crouched there, staring incredulously, eyeing the tingling fingers of his shocked and empty hand.

"You owe the lady an apology," Andros said, and suggestively added: "She's waitin'."

Latham's look got wild and black. He dug a knife from some place.

That was all Clem Andros needed. He let temper have its way with him. He took one forward step and struck. The blow took Latham below the ear and smashed him, gagging, against the wall.

Andros watched him, breathing heavily.

A dusty voice said at Andros' shoulder, "I guess you better come with me."

11

2

THE MAJOR MUST BE JOKING

SLOWLY TURNING, Andros saw a grim-faced man surveying him. There was a pistol in this fellow's hand and the lamp's light winked from the badge on his shirt.

With a shrug Andros said, "All right, Marshal," and, with a bow for the girl, he scooped up his hat and walked to the door. He paused there, waiting, wondering why the star-packer hadn't asked for his gun.

He could feel the pull of the girl's watching eyes, but he did not look her way again. It made no difference to him if she were Latham's wife or something else which he didn't label. It had been more the curse of his turbulent temper than interest in her that had bought him chips. There was no niche for a woman in the life of Black Clem Andros. If she were anxious to get shut of Latham she had her opportunity.

But her voice came to him softly, turning him against his will. He saw how her red lips smiled at him; nothing public or blatant, but a smile his kind of man would not miss. The curiosity was still in her eyes; the challenge was still there, too, and some other thing which he did not scan too closely.

"I'd like to thank you," she said; and her voice was like herself, desirable. "Not many men," she said quickly, "would have had the courage to brace Joce Latham; and I want you to know I appreciate it. I wouldn't have had it . . ." She broke off, her glance swinging toward the marshal. "Perhaps I—"

" 'Fraid not, Miz Latham," the marshal said gruffly. "I don't guess there's anything you can do about it." He looked at Andros and nodded his head at the door.

"Don't you want my guns?" Andros said.

"I expect you can tote 'em, can't you?"

Andros' glance narrowed thoughtfully. "I ain't wantin' any of that *ley del fuego* stuff."

The lawman met his challenging glance and the line of his lips curled derisively. "Let's go," he said, and tilted his six-gun suggestively.

12

After the door had closed behind them and they'd gone some thirty paces, Andros asked his captor bluntly if he were to consider himself under arrest.

They had continued for several silent steps before the marshal answered.

Squirting out some of his drown-tobacco then, he cleared his throat. "That depends. For a *hombre malo* you sure are long on the chin music. Now you just mosey over towards that yonder cottonwood there, an' don't bother advertisin' yourself by walkin' through the light.

Arrived at the cottonwood Andros awaited the next move. The starpacker squinted round as though he were considering. "Just keep right on," he muttered, "till you come to that vacant lot."

Andros did. At the vacant lot the marshal directed, "We'll cut on over to the other side now—an' mind you steer clear of them lights."

"What is this," Andros growled, "a parade?"

"I'll tell you. There's some fellas in this town that ain't got sufficient savvy to shake hay. They got plenty o' curiosity though. I ain't figurin' to advertise my business. Cut on over now an' step lively."

The dark section of roadway having been crossed without incident the marshal, pressing close, said: "If it's all the same to you, we'll just turn down along this buildin'. Sort of snake along, Mister, an' when you reach the back, turn left."

Andros completed the maneuver, feeling strangely like a fool. Pausing obediently at his director's sibilant *"Psst!"* he waited while that cautious gentleman came alongside.

"See them stairs?" the marshal asked with his voice hauled down to a whisper. "Well, up at the top o' them is where we're headed for. Looks like we've give them fellas the slip—but I'm not takin' any chances. Keep quiet now. Shove ahead an' mind your step."

Major Cass Bocart, the Forest Supervisor if the prospective Tonto National Forest became an established fact, was close to fifty. He had a fighting jaw, a cold blue eye. One look sufficed to show a man his silver hair was not attributable to age; more like to be a memento, you'd say, of some of those occasions which had graved those deep-creased lines in his ruddy face. And you'd have been right.

Bocart had been selected for this post at that time last year when Theodore Roosevelt had kicked the legislature into action about the need for water in this country. He had proposed setting aside this vast Salt River watershed as a National Forest. That it had not yet been so proclaimed was the fault of neither the Major nor the President; both were fighting for it tooth and nail.

The Major's face, as he sat before his battered desk, was couched in somber lines. Big teeth champed savagely at his pipestem and the lips that curled about them were as tightly grim as his thoughts. He was bucking a stiff proposition; none realized it better than himself.

"Come in," he growled to a sudden knock, and lowered one hand beneath the desk's edge.

A tall and black-clad man came in and stood with a poised directness that took into account with one sweeping glance every detail of the room. The marshal, coming in behind him, closed the door and, eyeing Major Bocart sourly, said, "I see you got the shades drawed. Guess you ain't so hard as you put on to be. You want I should stick around?"

"What for, Tom? You reckon I'll be needing assistance?" The Major's eyes showed a fleeting twinkle. "Rather have you circulate. Like to keep that badge in people's minds."

The marshal spat at a knothole. "This fella," he said, "has been doin' his best t' commit suicide. You recollect Joce Latham, don't you? Well, this guy just busted hell out of him." He turned to the door, spoke over his shoulder: "Kinda figured you'd want to see him." He went on out. The door closed softly.

Settling back in his chair the Major folded burly arms across his chest and regarded the stranger frankly. He saw a black-haired man with a dark, burnt skin pulled tight across high cheekbones. The man's eyes were like smoky sage, indeterminate of hue but alive with a hard skepticism he did not bother to conceal. Tight-pressed lips cleaved this fellow's face above a coldly saturnine jaw, and the hat shoved back from his forehead was of the horsethief type, battered, faded. The whole look of him patterned on that hat and the Major, shrewdly studying him, decided this appearance was no paraded toughness but a thing very much a part of him—as real as the guns in the thick black belt that was buckled about his hips.

14

There was weight in this man. But it was a distributed weight, carefully balanced and obscured along the broad flats of his shoulders, in the sinews of his chest and arms. There was an unsmiling coldness in the directness of his regard; yet the Major slowly nodded, entirely pleased with what he saw.

"So you been bracing Latham, have you?"

The man took the time to turn those few words over, but he gave no answer to them. "First time," he said, "I ever heard of the Service walkin' in on a private quarrel. Must be plumb hard-up for trouble."

"Plumb hard-up," the Major admitted, "but not, by God, for trouble. I got more of that than I can handle. Sort of a stranger round here, ain't you?"

The black-clad man didn't answer.

The Major tried another tack. "Familiar with the Four Peaks country?"

"I've been there. Am I supposed to be under arrest?"

"You wouldn't be hunting for a job, would you?"

"First things first. I'm interested right now in findin' out where I stand." The shape of his cheeks changed slightly. "If I'm under arrest I want to know it. If I ain't I'll be sayin' goodnight to you."

"You're not if you take this job," Bocart said.

"Like that, eh?"

The Major smiled. "Are you taking it?"

The stranger said, "I'm not a fountain-pen man, Mister."

"The job I've got in mind don't call for any fountain pen." Major Bocart poked tobacco into his pipe with a stubby finger. He struck a match. He drew the flame down into the bowl of his pipe with a noisy sucking sound. He exhaled a gust of smoke, then said. "This job calls for a lot of nerve. And lead," he added softly. "I want a man who can use his think-box; who can put his lead where it will do some good."

The stranger grinned. "An' you think I fit that description?"

"It'll be no bed of roses," the Major said as though the man had accepted. "You'll need a lot of luck to cut it. But—"

"I didn't say I was interested—"

"You will be. And you're going to take it—"

"What is this job you keep harpin' on?"

"Undercover work." Major Cass Bocart said frankly: "No glory and no credit. If you slip, we don't even know you. If

15

you get in a jam you'll have to get yourself out. You'll be on your own without backing. The pay is good, but your biggest compensation—if you're the kind of man I think you are—will lie in the satisfaction of seeing a worthwhile chore done to the best of—"

"Brother Jones," the stranger drawled, "will pass around the plate."

Major Bocart scrubbed his jaw and grinned a little sheepishly. "Just the same—"

"The floral offering is received with thanks. Let's get down to brass tacks now."

The Major gave him one quick sharp look then turned his glance to the ceiling. For several moments he puffed in a reflective silence. Then he said, "The situation's this. Here in Arizona—in New Mexico, too, far as that goes—a number of usually antagonistic interests have lately amalgamated to put a stop to the creation of further Forest Reserves. This combine is a powerful one; it's made up of sheepmen, the big cattle kings, the lumber and railroad interests—it's got a hell of a lot of influence. You can easy see what more Forest Reserves will spell to the last two. To the stockmen such reserves are an even greater danger when considered in the light of present range methods. It is claimed they'll bring about the end of the open range—no more free grass, in other words. Neither sheep nor cattle will want to see that. They thrive on the present feudal system where might is all that's necessary to insure a lot of profit.

"Chief Forester Pinchot claims sheep are destructive to grass; he's pulling strings to get them barred from the preserves. Sheep need a lot of territory; they've got it now and they mean to keep it. The sheep kings work on a hundred per cent profit. They don't want to *buy* range so they're fighting us for all they're worth.

"The Combine's doing a deal of lobbying up in Washington; greasing palms and that kind of rinkydink. But the President's got his eyes open. He's lived out here. He knows that if present conditions are allowed to continue another five years the farmers and small ranchers haven't a snowball's chance in hell; Teddy knows they'll be put out of business by the capital back of sheep and beef. Forest Reserves won't ruin the big fellows —they've plenty of cash to buy range; but Reserves will save the small independents. The only thing that *will* save 'em—"

"Very interesting. But what's all this got to do with me?"

"I'm getting there. All this fighting ain't being done at the Capitol. The worst of it's going on right here in Arizona. And, bad as it's been, what's happened already won't hold a patch—"

"Suppose," the stranger drawled, "you get down to plain facts. It ain't my habit to go into things blind. I'll want a few names an' figures."

Bocart nodded. "You'll get 'em when you give me the word—and when I'm convinced you're the man I want. So far you haven't said you'll take the job. Been a rancher, haven't you?"

"I've run cattle."

The Major looked at him shrewdly. "You've got the look of a Texas man. How many folks on your backtrail?"

There was a visible temper about this dark stranger that gave, the Major had noted, a certain color to his ironies. But his look had undergone a change; was stiff now and darkly inscrutable. "I guess," he drawled, "you better leave that to God an' me."

Poking the dottle in his pipe the Major struck another match, put a cloud of smoke about him. He said, speaking through it, "Do you want this job or don't you?"

"I'll reserve my say till I've heard the rest—till I've seen a few of your facts."

"For a brash looking man you're pretty cautious."

"Not cautious. Say rather I'm not in the habit of playin' things blind—"

"You'll be playing this blind regardless of how much I tell you," the Major said sharply. "I don't have half the facts myself. That's one of the reasons I need you. I can say this much—these sheepmen and their allies are prepared to go the limit. They mean to control that Four Peaks country and all the range above it. They don't want it made National Forest—" He broke off. "If you're hard enough to suit my book I'll confide a little more."

"Did you say *hard?*"

"I did." The Major got to his feet. "I've got to be damn sure of you, Mister. You've got to be bold to cut this."

He lifted a big Colt pistol from the drawer and stood with it in his hand, eyeing the stranger closely.

17

"Shoot if you must," that gentleman said, and the look of his grin was like granite.

But the Major's face stayed sober.

"You're pretty proud," he observed. "But how are your guts? Have you got enough for this?" He laid his pipe down carefully. His stare was bright as he explained with an added dryness. "The tests of the man I'm looking for, all other considerations satisfied, is simple. I take all the cartridges out of this cylinder but one—like this," he murmured, shaking four out and standing them up on the desk top. "Since there were only five in it to start with, that leaves one still ready for firing. The applicant for this little chore of mine picks up the pistol, puts its muzzle against his right temple, spins the cylinder and pulls the trigger."

He held out the gun, butt forward.

3

"YOU PREPARED TO BET ON THAT?"

THE STRANGER'S glance was very bright.

"Your gall should take you far," he said. "Put a loaded pistol to your head an' pull the trigger, eh? Think you'll find a man fool enough to do it?"

"I've found two. Unfortunately, both times the hammer dropped on the loaded chamber."

The room got very still. These two men looked each other over while locust sound in the night outside rose three full shades in loudness. The stranger's eyes were steely slits. His interest was cold and wicked.

"I'm wonderin'," he said, "why you haven't taken on the job yourself. Man with the kind of stuff runs in *your* veins—"

"I wish the hell I *could!*" Bocart said. "I'd take it in a minute!" The flash of his eyes showed a grim regret. "I'm too well known in this country. Can't hardly waggle my elbow without the length of Salt River knows it. Sheepmen's spies're every place. Why, only tonight—but no matter. Man who handles this can't have any connection with the Forest

18

movement. And a set of cast iron guts is only the first requirement of such a man."

Leaning forward the stranger put the flats of his hands whitely upon the desk. "I can savvy that part all right. But how can you tell but what *I'm* one of these sheepmen's agents?"

The Major's eyes were brightly cool. "I can't. That's one of the reasons for this gun trick. Red Hat's men are tough, but not *that* tough I imagine." Again he held the pistol out. "Well?"

The man grinned bleakly. "You've a rare persuasion, Major." He accepted the proffered gun, stood turning it over in his hands, professionally hefting its balance. "Nice taste in sixshooters. This your iron?"

"It was the pistol packed by the last man I tried to hire for this job." The Major knocked the dottle from his pipe, stood eyeing for a moment the few flakes of half-burned tobacco still clinging to its bowl. "It's yours . . . if you get the job."

A remote smile briefly curved the set of the stranger's lips. He twirled the gun by its trigger guard. "All right," he said, "I'll call you on that," and put the gun to his head.

No muscle of that lean hard body rippled as he met the Major's eyes. His own were cold as gun steel. Without blinking he lifted his left hand leisurely and twirled the weapon's cylinder. With a devil-may-care derision he set his finger to the trigger. The hammer clicked back with a loud, clear sound.

And then the hammer fell.

The Major's breath was a quick-drawn thing across that brittle stillness. He said abruptly, "I congratulate you," and bending, shoved the drawer shut.

The stranger returned the four removed cartridges to the emptied chambers of the pistol. He put the pistol in the waistband of his trousers. "Let's hear the facts," he said.

The Major's probing eyes were bright. He shoved a hand through his silver hair and a queer consideration darkly tightened the line of his mouth. "The Combine," he said rather gruffly, "is not satisfied merely to block the proposed extension of Forest Reserves; their lobbyists are prepared to filibuster all suggested changes to the present grazing laws. Pinchot, as I've said, is trying hard to get sheep barred from the Forests; that's one of the changes they'll probably get shelved. Meantime the Combine is maliciously set on getting more and more territory set aside for the use of sheep. This, with them, is a protective measure, just in case the bill gets by them. The easiest way to make land sheep range is by way of showing a previous use, by sheep, of such ground as they wish to take over. This way, of course, means gun-trigger trouble, but a few dead men mean nothing to them; they've been hard at it ever since they discovered our intentions with regard to this Salt River watershed. This long drought and the Combine together have just about spelled finish to the small rancher in this region. Those who've had the courage to fight back have pretty near all got the worst of it. They've been shot, they've been jailed and they've been lynched. This Combine," he reminded dryly, "represents real capital."

"I haven't heard any names. Ain't you got any idea who's back of it?"

Bocart nodded. "To mention a few, this Joce Latham you just tangled with is representing the town men of Long Rope; he's also repping for the lumber interests. He runs the biggest saloon and gambling dive in the country and bosses most of the tough-hombre gentry. We haven't been able to uncover, so far, the man who's watching the railroad's ante. Nor the cattle crowd's man. The sheep trusts are backing Talmage Vargas, better known as 'Red Hat.' "

"No big spreads in that Four Peaks country?"

"Only one—the Half-Circle Arrow. Operated by a man named Barstow. You'll meet him."

The Major let several moments pass while he puffed in a thoughtful silence. "I'm going to leave things pretty much up to you as to how you handle this. You'll have to decide for yourself what steps you can or can't take. I want the small ranchers protected and I want that bunch of plug-uglies cleaned out of Long Rope. That's about all for the moment, I guess."

The stranger was inspecting his calloused palms and said nothing.

"Here," the Major went on, removing a roll of bills from his desk, "is some expense money. Use it," he said, smiling wryly, "any way you see fit. Now aside from what we want accomplished, there's just one fact for you to bear in mind. Any jam you may get into is your tough luck so far as this

Service is concerned. Is that clear? Good. What name do you care to go by?"

"I've always used my own," he said. "Just write 'Clem Andros' in your book." And the smile he showed the Major's stare was a thin, cold thing; and sudden. " 'Black' Andros, if you prefer."

"Black Andros!" the Major cried, and jaw agape stood staring. He blinked and took another look. "Black Andros!" He repeated the name amazedly and shook his head dumbfounded. "That's a hard thing to believe, sir. . . . And yet—" He pulled himself together. "Some of the tales—"

"Yeah. I expect so—"

"But we've thought of Andros as a younger man—"

"How old do you think I am?"

"I'd say thirty, anyway."

"I'm twenty-three," Clem Andros said; and the way he said it settled it so far as the Major was concerned.

"By grab," he said, "I couldn't name a man I'd rather have, boy! With a rep like yours you're cut to order. No one will ever think to connect *you* with this Department!"

Color flashed suddenly through his cheeks and he said hastily: "What I mean is—"

"I expect I could guess. Don't—" Abruptly Andros stopped his talk. Head canted he seemed to listen to something beyond the Major's hearing. He was like that, standing stiff and off-balance, when a door behind him came violently open.

Three men slogged into the room with metal flashing in their hands; a fourth showed in the hallway's gathered gloom behind them.

The smell of sheep was acrid.

Bocart was never quite sure in his mind of just what happened after that. One moment Andros had his back to the door; the rest was a blue-smoked blur with Andros crouched above blazing guns. The smash of those two big pistols was a thunderous pulse in the room's jarred air.

Lamp flame swayed and shuddered. One man's hoarse scream went buffeting into the rafters. The tumultuous echoes slashed around long after the firing ceased.

Just inside the door were two crumpled shapes; across its sill another lay with yellow curls damp-plastered to its forehead. Down the hall's dark planks was a trail of blood.

"You'll do," Major Bocart said.

21

Sun's heat and furnace-driven wind had turned this Four Peaks country into a region bare as the desert. In the beds of long-dry washes sparse clumps of galleta grass showed, but these were but a mockery to the stark, lethargic cattle Andros saw from time to time. Waterholes were infrequent, and those he encountered gone dry as bone—as the bones that bleached the sands of the barren wastes about them. On more than one occasion he had distantly observed dismounted cowboys swinging axes in this killing heat; chopping down the tiny-leafed palo verdes while drearily ringed by a gaunted circle of lowing, wall-eyed cattle. These critters staggered up as though on stilts each time the thorny verdure fell. It must have been painful nourishment, but they followed the axe-swingers round like dogs.

Yet, grave though they were, it was not of the cowmen's troubles that Clem Andros now was thinking. His mind was fixed on the pistol he had got from Bocart, the gun inherited from the Major's second candidate. The one he had taken his test with.

It was a nickeled, long-barreled Colt's of forty-five caliber. It had bone grips inlaid with mother-of-pearl; a first-rate weapon of balanced weight and fine precision—as Andros had reason to know.

The gun had belonged to Dakota Krell.

Andros took it out and regarded it, in his eyes a morose glinting while his mouth was a tight-clamped slit. He presently put it away again, rolling it up in his slicker which he relashed behind his cantle. He rode then with his lambent gaze grim-searching his dun surroundings.

After awhile he was skirting a canyon's rim, toilfully climbing up into the uplands where the hot wind shouldered him roughly and the smell of scorched grass was a familiar, remembered bitterness.

A hundred feet below him, back down on the grassless plain, a rider was felling a giant sahuaro, stoic cattle indifferently watching him. The great thorny cactus toppled, bursting wide in the blistered wash. The cow brutes, gathered like stage props, dropped heads between bony spraddled legs to munch at the bitter pulp. Melon smell and the pungence of turnip drifted up on a gyrating dust devil.

With bitter thoughts Andros wiped streaks of sweat from his gritty cheeks and kneed the tired pony on again. Since noon

22

he had counted sixty carcasses; all that was keeping these cowmen going was such gruelling work as that below, a chore no self-respecting hand ordinarily would perform. Not a solitary calf, alive or dead, had Andros seen. He cursed, reflecting that there were none. If the sheepmen came this year it meant the end of these small cattlemen. If it had not been for sheep in the first place these punchers would not be having to chop cactus; there'd have been graze enough along these upper ranges to have carried these dying critters through.

Slanting sun dripped down like melted copper, throwing its final and fiery glow all across the land. The hush of desolation lay over the dust of this empty waste, gripping alike each skeletal spire, each gulch and bastioned rock-ribbed peak.

Long Rope was a huddle of bleached, false-fronted structures brooding in the dust of a gloomy gulch that cracked these timbered mountain flanks; eleven rude frames whipsawed from the neighboring pines and weathered to a drab and uniform gray. It included one hotel, one saloon replete with a grand miscellany of gambling devices and a trio of painted hussies still trading on the glories of a vanished past, one general store, a marshal's office, one stable and a blacksmith shop. All else was a sun-warped clutter of glassless windows with weeds and cactus growing up between the twisted planking of roofless porches. By daylight this was cow town, but with the falling of the sun other interests took it over and more upright men found it a place to keep away from.

It was dusk when Andros urged his pony up its wide and single street.

A seated man rose quietly from the hotel's shadowed veranda and faded through the door. By the blacksmith shop an idler cuffed his hat across sharp eyes and dropped one hand to his sagging belt. Night air pulsed a coolness down this street, acrid with the smell of the blacksmith's forge.

Andros' regard was quick and keen as he bent the gelding's course toward the stable and swung his head neither right nor left when a burly man rolled out of its doorway and gave him a stiffly searching look. Brief was that look and impatient was the gesture of this fellow's hand as, abruptly, he turned and vanished down an alleyway between two farther buildings.

Bleak humor touched Andros's wide thin lips. For this was history repeating itself as it had a thousand times during

23

his six-year hunt for the man-killer, Krell. He was being sized
up. Later there would be further developments. These things
made an unforgettable pattern and, though occasionally their
sequence differed, were as familiar to Andros as the stitching
in his boots.

He swung down before the stable and after some moments
its proprietor came out. A slender, leather-faced man who yet
lacked that definite gauntness so generally characterizing the
men of this high region. He lighted a lantern he was carrying and carefully hung it from a hook above the doorway.
Nothing in Andros' face gave away his cognizance of the
motive that had swayed the man. Andros' face gave nothing
away—not even when the stableman turned and casually bent,
lifting one of the gelding's hoofs.

"How are the folks at Quinn River Crossing?"

Andros was curling himself a smoke when the man's soft
words drifted up to him. His glance stayed on his building
smoke till the cigarette was completed. His gaze came up then
coldly, sharp on the stableman's countenance. He could not
place the lean-bodied man. This was not strange for in six
years of wanderings he had met a lot of such hombres.

But the man knew him—had known him instantly.

"I thought Dakota Krell was dead," he said.

And so Krell was, said Andros' mind; and saw in that tight
moment what part he'd have to play in this town if he was
to survive and aid the Forest Service. Only fear could serve
him here—fear of his deadly guns. He could no longer hope
to hide his identity; he was committed by this man's words
to make the most of it. Quinn River Crossing was in north-
western Nevada, within stone's throw of the Oregon line. If
a man from that far place were here and recognized him, there
might be others here from other places. And these would also
recognize him. Once seen, Andros was not a man to be
forgotten.

He stared at the stableman gravely. "I'll be stoppin' here
a spell," he said, and walked away.

Where the saloon's bright lamps cut a bold path through
the gathered murk and spilled their gold across a restive line
of racked range horses, a group of men had gathered.

Andros turned that way.

Approaching, he observed two central figures plainly; these

24

were the dominant factors in that group. All others were merely watchers.

He came to a pause by the edge of this group, stopping by a pot-bellied man. Light from the nearby windows showed the two principals clearly. One, a confident, swaggering fellow, stood baiting a person half his size, and by his look deriving a deal of satisfaction from the process.

Andros' wheeling shoulders abruptly stiffened and he went shoving through the group with a rude directness. There was a dark look in his cheeks as he came to a stop before the pair.

The slender person was a girl. The burly man laughed. "Hell," he scoffed, "you ain't got a waddy on your payroll with half enough salt to teach me——"

"You prepared to bet on that?" Andros murmured.

4

A MAN'S COLD WAY

THE BIG man turned with the quick, lithe speed of a cat. It was the first good look Andros had of his face. Under a low-crowned, wide-rimmed hat the fellow showed good features; a face probably thought very handsome by any number of impressionable women. Even Andros would have owned to the man's good looks at another time or place perhaps. He had black hair—black almost as Andros' own, and beneath the wide, cleft chin his hat straps were fastened through a silver concho. A second concho held the dangling ends of the lavender scarf pulled tight about his throat. His shirt was of gray flannel tucked into corduroy trousers. These were protected by chaps as scarred as Andros' black ones. Good range boots peeped from under them; range boots with silver spurs.

Yet plainly this was no cowboy.

About his heavy waist were strapped two sagging cartridge belts, scuffed and dark like their holsters. Pliable, well-oiled leather. Like the smooth and mellow ivory of his gun grips these told a story.

He had smooth cheeks that were sleek and suave and, just

now, a little critical. His derisive eye picked Andros over and he winked broadly at these avid watchers hemming them.

"Sorry, pilgrim—I'm a little hard of hearin'. Mebbe you better ride that trail again. Say it louder—"

"Is this loud enough?" Andros said; and, swaying forward, drove a smashing blow to the fellow's chin. The big man's head went rocking back and his bigger chest went rocking with it, and suddenly he found himself with his back in the yellow dust.

"You swivel-eyed snake!" he gritted. He got an elbow under him; hunched forward and got a knee beneath him and blurred a clawed hand beltward. Fast! Steel rasped leather and a bright flame tore from his thigh. Gun thunder jammed the street and rolled against the building fronts.

But Andros, experienced in the art, had flung himself aside. The big man's finger was clamping down for another shot when Andros' boot sent his pistol flying.

Andros' eyes were blazing slits. "You fool!" he said. "I ought to break that cutter across your head! Never throw a gun on me again—never! *Is that plain?*"

The man got up with his lips in a laugh. But he was breathing hard and the laugh did not match the look of his tawny eyes. "I expect it is," he answered. He backed up, bent, and retrieved his pistol. He shoved it back in his holster and stood a moment, tight-lipped, watching Andros darkly.

"I guess you're the Rockin' T ramrod—the *new* one," he said fleeringly. "Nothin' to get so proud about; she hires 'em reg'lar once a month an'—"

"Does she?" Andros said with a quick step toward him. Temper burned like flame in his eyes and the slant of his cheeks showed to what uncaring rashness the proper words might goad him. This was his weakness; this red rage-fog that, quick as a wink, could close his mind to danger. It was closed right now. He stopped with his chin a scant hand from the other man's. "You aimin' to insinuate somethin'?"

The twisted sneer got off the man's mouth. He found himself backing away from this stranger, moving with a foreign care, moving haltingly, step by cautious placed step until he felt his horse behind him. His left hand made a groping upward move for the horn. He revealed an extreme reluctance to remove his gaze from Andros' face.

"No." His voice was a curdled sound. "No," he said huskily;

26

"I guess not." He paused, big shoulders stiff, his gleaming eyes on Andros with a taut and straining watchfulness. "You're sittin' high an' feelin' proud. But it won't last—"

"Don't waste no dinero on that bet."

Andros' scarred brown fists hung loosely at his sides. "I gave you one warning. Here's another: Never let me catch you on range controlled by Rocking T."

He turned then, ignoring the man's malignant glance. To the girl he said, "Come on. If you got your shoppin' done it's time we was gettin' back."

That smooth he carried it off. He tossed one cool quick look around, noting its effect on the watchers' faces. Lamps' shine revealed their expressions stony.

The girl put a hand on his arm and her fingers closed on it tightly.

From his seat in the saddle the big man called: "I'll be rememberin' you!"

"I'd be some put out," Andros grinned, "if you didn't."

Night's meshed blue had thickened to a deeper shade and all these surrounding shadows had rushed together closely, crouching low like opaque walls, before the girl or Andros spoke. And then it was the girl, this belted boss of Rocking T, who broke their riding silence.

"You've made a bitter enemy," she said; and then her low voice stopped. It was strangely husky when she spoke again, suggestive of deep inner turmoil. "There are times when even the most sincere of thanks sound trifling—almost farcical. This is one of them. That man has bothered me before. You've done yourself no good by helping me. Grave Creek can nurse hate like an Apache."

Andros' eyes showed a grim amusement, but they sobered swiftly as he said, "He'll be more like to take his spite out on you, I'm scared."

"It's my quarrel though. You needn't have become mixed up in it."

"I'm in it now. Don't worry about me. Just count on me."

"But you don't understand what's back of this. That man is Grave Creek Charlie. He's boss of Red Hat's gun-throwing sheep crowd. They just about *run* this country," she said vehemently. "They moved in on us last year and, from the look of things, they're figuring to sift through here again."

He marveled at the low, gritty rasp of her quick-said words.

27

It was as though she hated these sheepmen personally; each nameless man of their outfit with a hard and gathered anger. He wondered what reason they might have given her for such bitter animosity. He wondered, but he did not ask.

He probed the night with a watchful interest. Summer's smell and greasewood's pungence came with the wind whipped off the desert. A late moon flung its argent haze across the black rim of yonder hills; and Andros rode without thinking, content with the night and pleased with the feeling of riding in this quiet girl's company.

The trail ahead was a vague ribbon gleaming through the murk of shadows. The stillness of vast distances was thick upon this country; the feel of it stirred him, renewed his strength and, someway, hope was reborn in him and some of the ingrained harshness of the past years fell away from him, and he rode with his head bowed, grateful.

Yet, after awhile, looking round he said, "A lonely land."

"But home to some of us," she answered. "To strangers it may not look like much—all they can see is the harshness, the barren bleakness of it. You have to live here to understand the worth of it. I couldn't begin to put it into words, but when you own a piece of the land your values change."

He nodded. How well he knew. "Ground gets in a fellow's blood," he said. "It's something tangible; something you can taste and smell and touch if you've got a mind to. Something a man can build hopes on. . . . A man that's got any," he added.

He rode then with his glance ahead, broad shoulders hunched a little as he thought of Dakota Krell whose gun was rolled in the slicker back of his cantle. He thought also of that Long Rope stableman who had known him at Quinn River Crossing. Some things didn't change, he told himself. They just grew scars and festered. Sometimes a man's past was like that. Looking back was not good medicine. If a man had a chore to do, he *did* it. He didn't stop to procrastinate, to count cost or a hundred other things—not if he was a *man*, he didn't. You had just one life to live. You lived it according to your lights.

He mused for quite a spell, gone moody, yet he did not think it queer to find himself beside this girl whom he hadn't known an hour ago—whose name he didn't know yet. That was all right; she didn't know his name, either. Perhaps if she

28

had he wouldn't be here. It was enough that he knew she owned a ranch; had been having foreman trouble.

He said with his shoulders twisting. "About that ramrod's job, ma'am . . . That Charlie pelican let on like you might be in need of a range boss. Might be I could fill—"

"The job," she said, "isn't open."

That was pretty plain. They rode without talk for another half hour, then Andros said abruptly: "Mebbe you could use an extra hand then. I could use the work—"

She said, not mincing words, "I haven't the money to hire anyone. I've four punchers working for nothing now, and a range boss, too, far as that goes. The punchers haven't drawn even smoking money for over six months. The Rocking T's got its back to the wall. If the sheep come through here again this year, you can have it for the taxes."

"Mebbe they won't come through—"

"They'll come." She said it hopelessly. There wasn't even a sob in her breath.

"What about the other outfits scattered through these hills? Reckon any of them would be hirin'?"

"No."

"Bad, eh?"

"Next year there won't be a cow critter in this country."

"What's happened to the cow crowd's guts? It use to be that a cattle spread would fight for its rights—"

"Fight!" In the moon's risen light he could sense the intensity of the look she flashed at him. He could not make out her features clearly nor catch their expression really; but the sound of her breath was expression enough—that and her stiff-set, back-thrown shoulders. Her words struck bitterly across the quiet.

"Listen! Last year sheep came through here. There wasn't much browse along the trails so the herders turned them up the hillsides, spreading them out. When they left, this range was stripped to the roots. Some of the ranchers got a little riled. They rode down into the sheep camps primed for trouble and ready to start it. The sheepmen palavered; they were slick with their lingo. And all the time the ranchers stood jawing the herders were pushing their sheep deeper into this country's best grass. It was too late to do much by the time we discovered it."

29

Andros rode for awhile, grim thinking.

"No," he said, "I guess talk never did solve much. There's some guys don't understand fair talkin'. Any of these Four Peaks ranchmen packin' irons?"

"They were packing irons last year." Her voice was choked with feeling. "Jack Broth killed a couple herders up on Tonto Creek. The sheep crowd pooled a lot of money and hired a lawyer to get Jack the limit. He got it. They sent him to Yuma and finally hung him."

The creak of riding gear, the clink of metal and the soft, steady drubbing of the ponies' hoofs were the only sounds to disturb a silence become physically uncomfortable.

Andros eyed the girl very briefly and turned his glance on the trail again. The girl had pluck—she had a lot of it. She had seen and felt the sheepmen's power, and like most others who had lately confronted it could find no weapon she could use against it. Bocart was right. They were going too far.

"What's happened to the calf crop?"

"There wasn't any."

"This drought?"

She shrugged. The bleakness of it held no hope. The cow crowd of the Four Peaks country were beaten—beaten badly, and they knew it. The prospect before them was one of ruin. They still hung on because it wasn't in a cowman's soul to ever quit; but they knew already what the end would be.

"You're pretty sure they're coming back—the sheep, I mean?"

"They bragged of it last year when ninety thousand sheep went north. Grave Creek boasted round they'd take the desert for a starter. Then, he said, they'd take over the good range up along the Verde. They took both. The only graze that's left this country that amounts to half a button is our higher range; the stuff we save for wintering. It's Grave Creek's brag they'll take that coming back."

"How about a deadline?"

There was no mirth in her brittle laughter. "Last year, we tried it three different places. Like slapping a bull between the horns."

"If they ain't stopped soon," Andros ventured, "looks like they'll gobble the whole of Arizona."

She said indifferently, "They'll gobble it. Most of these small

30

ranchers round here have seen the Writing. They'd be glad to sell and get on out. But who'd be fool enough to buy?"

"The sheepmen might," Andros mentioned.

She said indignantly, "I'd rather give it back to the Indians! Even if they *could* the sheep crowd wouldn't buy. Why should they? You know well as I do all our graze is public domain. It's the start of every sheepman's argument—it's their God and Bible!" she said with her lips curled back.

The things discovered in her voice left Andros somber. Her outlook was so markedly like his own had been these last six years. Depressed, he rode with shoulders hunched, cheeks etched in moody lines of bitterness. These people knew too well what they were up against. The thought of it was defeating.

After awhile he said, "If you all bunched up and stood against them—"

"We've tried that, too. Barstow had that notion. He said if enough of us would get together on the thing the sheep crowd's legal machinery would jam. They convicted and hung Jack Broth, he claimed, because we had no organization. Together we could do something.

"It sounded good. We tried it. We met them at the river and we turned them back. But it wasn't any good. They crossed below. We had a little good beef left then and kind of figured to keep our eyes on it. But we found we couldn't watch every place."

Her voice had grown tired. She was weary. Her shoulders had a sag to them now and Andros felt conviction himself. But he wouldn't give in to it. Of course this was tough! It *had* to be tough to bother a man like Bocart.

"Ever try again?"

He saw her hat dip briefly. "We stopped another bunch ten days later. Grave Creek said we'd let him or he'd order camp right where he was and sheep that side clear to ledgerock. Barstow guessed mebbe it was better not to fight them."

"This Barstow," Andros said. "Who is he? Where does he come in?"

"Reb's the biggest rancher in these parts. He runs the Half-Circle Arrow—covers the whole far side of Diamond Mountain and spreads out north for twenty miles."

"Guess the sheep hit him pretty hard, eh?"

"They went around him."

31

Andros said: "Went around him, eh?" and after that a silence gathered. The girl seemed strangely embarrassed and just a little resentful. This displeasure became more marked when Andros suggested softly, "Didn't folks find that a little odd?"

"Why should they? He owns his own range; it's purchased, paid for, recorded. Reb's father was Constantine Barstow—the Pork King. The Half-Circle Arrow was a hobby with him; it is with Reb, far as that goes. He don't have to work for a living. He sided up through sympathy."

"I see," Andros said. "Kind of fancies playin' champion to underdogs. Expect he lent you men, eh? Lent you money too, I guess likely."

She eyed him sharply. She didn't reply immediately, and when she finally did there was reluctance in her voice.

"No-o-o . . ." She said it slowly, with her eyes straight ahead, and appeared to go on thinking.

Andros didn't. He said brusquely: "Advice, mebbe."

"Yes." She took a deep breath. "Yes!"

It was ten by the stars when, in a valley spread below them, Andros got his first clear look at the ranch headquarters of the Rocking T. Timbered hills hemmed its platter-like hollow and he nodded his head with approval. A well planned place —well built, too; and situated in such a way that winter winds must pass it by. The moon's blue slant struck silver sparkles from the eighty-foot tank between the house and the other buildings. All of these structures were made of logs long seasoned by the elements. Lamp's shine was a sheen on the bunkhouse windows. There was also a light in the ranchhouse, and Andros thought to catch a surprised look on the girl's stiff cheeks; then their ponies were taking them down to it swiftly.

The bunkhouse lamp winked suddenly out. Shadows stirred by its darkened front. A challenge ripped the pound of hoofs: "Who's there?"

The girl pulled up. Andros' horse stopped, too. Dust came up and touched his face. Suspicion was a stealthy feel in the dappled shadows of this waiting yard. There was a familiar something in the challenger's voice that evoked old scenes in Andros' mind; time-blurred, half-forgotten pictures, vague as the fragments pulled from a dream. He was not even

32

certain if it was the voice itself or the intonation that jumped his mind back into the past.

With both hands rested across the pommel he sat unmoving, but his eyes were watchful.

The girl said, "It's all right, Sablon."

Ahead the shadows flattened out. A light came on in the bunkhouse. At a walk they put their ponies forward, the girl in the lead. She stopped by the porch. In the open door a man's still figure made a big and burly shape against the light. His lazy drawl reached Andros softly as he told the girl, "Was beginnin' to get a little worried about you—didn't have no trouble, did you?"

The girl said "No," and turned to Andros. They sat their saddles in the pooled gloom of the porch roof and neither could see the other's face with any clarity. Light from the man-blocked doorway did not touch them. Some walker's nearing progress scraped the flowing shadows back of them. She said: "You'll stay the night, at any rate. Since you're set on dumping your bedroll here I'll try and think up something. Thanks again for what you did. I'll talk with you in the morning."

The man who had followed them across the yard came up. It was the fellow, Sablon, who had challenged them. His half-remembered voice was gruff. "I'm wantin' to see you, ma'am. Right now. It's about that—"

"In the morning, Sablon—"

"No—right now. When I got something to say, I say it. I'm tellin' you now. Barstow better be hearin' this, too. We'll step in the—" He stopped abruptly, staring past the girl at Andros.

A cold suspicion thinned his words. "Who's that? What's *he* doin' here?"

Sablon's shape was stiff where he stood beside the girl's off stirrup. Through the dappled sway of foliage branches Andros saw his hand slide down and spread above his gun.

Her words striking out with a measured clarity, the girl began: "You may be rodding this outfit, Sablon—"

The man's rough voice plowed across her talk. Insistent, probing—like the feel of the peering eyes that stared from the shade of his hat brim.

"Who is he? We can't hev strangers round this spread. Them sheepmen got their spies—"

Andros said, very soft with his words, "Do I look like a sheep spy?" He swung down out of the saddle and stepped full into the moonlight. "I guess you know me, Cranston."

The sound of the man's shrill in-sucked breath was a plain thing in that stillness. The small pale blob of his poised gun hand gyrated nervously. It stiffened, rose a full six inches. His boots took him back three crunching steps.

The quiet increased, grew brittle. The man in the doorway lazily said, "What is this, anyway—some kind of play?"

Time was a nerve-strain plucking their sinews while wind made a down-draft and no one spoke.

Impatience lifted Andros' shoulders. His voice cut a cold lane through the shadows. "You're done here, Cranston. Pack your duffle."

The man-blocked doorway was suddenly empty. Light slopped out across the porch, its refracted radiance spreading like water, driving the dark back, showing the groupings of those stiff shapes. Each ear was strained for Cranston's answer. That it would come in gun flame no one doubted.

It did not come. The man left his gun deep-shoved in its holster, abruptly wheeling away with a curse. He crossed the yard with the lurching wallow of a man gone blind.

The other man reappeared in the doorway. "Come in— Come in," he muttered gruffly.

5

GUN PLAY

THEY MOUNTED the steps, the girl and Andros, and passed in with their dragging rowels cutting tinkles of sound from the frozen quiet. Tiredly the girl went up to the mantel, shucking her cartridge belt and pistol, placing them on the stone's cool surface by the faded picture of a gaunt old man.

She turned then. No expression blurred the pattern of her features. "I'm Flame Tarnell," she said; and her lifted brows put a question the rule of this land forbade her asking.

Flame! It suited her well, Andros thought; and had his

34

good long look at her then. Quickened interest roused his blood and rushed it through him turbulently, the challenging directness of her level glance disturbing the accustomed run of his thoughts.

He looked more closely.

Tall, she was, and slender—willowy. She was like some proud, commanding goddess. Her beauty was a vital thing, as real as this room or the other man's scowl. There was flame in every clean-etched inch of her as, impatiently, she waited his answer. Her eyes were the blue of surging oceans. The dark mass of her hair was black as midnight and her lips were the red of ripe crushed berries against the warm ivory of a flawless contour.

She stood poised, still asking her question; and, within him, Andros shrank from answering lest knowledge of his name and bruited repute change the look on her face to one of loathing. Temptation gripped him.

It was then the man spoke who had been in the doorway. His voice cut an easy slur through the quiet. To Flame he said: "You're wonderin' who this fellow is. A *man* could tell by lookin' at him. Just another drifter like that tinhorn, Sablon. I advise you not to have any truck with him. Easy come, easy go. I know his kind. He's got no interest in your troubles— all he's interested in's himself. You mark my words. He's a leather slapper. Keepin' him here will just promote more trouble."

Andros pulled his look from the girl reluctantly.

He turned a cold, quick-searching glance upon the speaker of those words.

The man was big. A solid looking hombre with the store clothes clinging snugly to his stocky, muscled figure. He made no move at Andros' turning; did not move the burly shoulders from their rest against the mantel. But his sleepy lids rolled slowly up, disclosing amber eyes whose measured glance indifferently brushed his own and turned back to the girl again as though the reaction of this man to what he'd said was of no import.

Andros said with a thin tranquility. "I guess your name is Barstow, ain't it? You seem pretty handy givin' advice."

The big man's cheeks showed a faint surprise, like an elephant might if a mouse stepped on him. His eyes came back to Andros' face and a pale glint touched his arrogant stare.

"Certainly I'm Barstow."

His lambent glance raked Andros' garb and an amused grin tugged the corners of his mouth. "Who'd you think—"

"Mr. Barstow," the girl said hurriedly, "owns the Half-Circle Arrow—"

"Which bestows on him, I reckon, a God-given right to jerk the plums from his neighbors' pies."

Saying which, Andros' left hand fished the makings from a pocket of his shirt. The same hand smoothly rolled his smoke and his tongue licked a wet line across its flap while his stare lashed color to the big man's cheeks. "I've met a lot of Barstows in my time. None of 'em ever amounted to much."

He let that lay while he got a match from his hatband, briskly raked it across his chaps. He said around his cigarette: "I don't expect this guy will, either."

Barstow's lip corners lost their smile. Quick-flaring anger changed the set of his cheeks and his lifting fists were bunching when he suddenly shrugged. A wry grin crooked his heavy mouth. He said, "You're probably right," and turned to the girl, ignoring Andros.

"About that matter we were discussing yesterday . . . Expect you've made your mind up—"

The slow and negative move of her head stopped his talk in mid-sentence. "No," she said, and two small lines showed across her forehead. "No." There was a quick appeal in the look she gave him. "Reb, I've got to have more time—"

"Time!" A scowl cut an angular path through the twist of his cheeks. Compressed lips showed the run of his thoughts. He swung broad shoulders roughly, yet checked the gesture with a savage impulse and darkly eyed the open palms of his beefy hands. He rubbed those palms across the coarse blue weave of his trousers with a slow and circling motion while his frowning stare traced the carpet's pattern. He brought his head up restlessly. A quick half-turn shoved his big hands deep and brusquely into the pockets of his coat. They bunched there, knuckles showing plainly against the bulged-out fabric.

The things that were in his mind abruptly got the best of him. "By God," he growled vehemently, "you know the way to keep a man afire! I don't *want* to be held off! I want my answer now!"

"Don't press me, Reb." There was a softness and a pleading

in the timbre of Flame's voice. "Don't insist on having your answer tonight. Let me have more time, Reb—"

"*Time?* Does it take a woman forty-eight hours to make up her mind if she wants a man?"

She stood there with her lips apart, her quickened breathing lifting her breasts, her eyes upon him gravely, appearing to study the half-crouched shadow his shape threw against the wall. His large, cream-colored Stetson was shoved far back from his forehead showing the rebellious tangle of his thick and sandy hair.

"It sometimes takes a great deal longer, Reb," she answered quietly. "Love doesn't always come like the crack of a pistol; quite often it is a slow, steady-growing process, careful to find its true measure in a man's real worth. It's not just a question of whether I want you or not—you know that. There are other things to consider. Things I've got to get clear in my mind."

Barstow scowled at her, saying nothing, roan cheeks showing the sultry turbulence of his thoughts.

"After all, Reb," she said reflectively, "we've know each other a pretty long while. Until just recently we've not found the need to speak of—"

"When I make up my mind to a thing, I *want* it!" he said loudly. "I want *you!* An' I want you *now!* By God I don't propose to stand twiddlin' my thumbs—"

She said: "Reb!" and waited till, with the anger plain on his cheeks, he stopped. "Where is the need of all this rush? Why must I give you my answer now? Why won't tomorrow do just as well?—or next week? If I loved you now, don't you think I'd love you as much tomorrow or the next day?"

He looked at her, a film of caution slowly crowding the anger out of his glance. But his cheeks still showed the sullenness of him and arrogance was a white-rimmed line in the surly twist of his lips. Her spunk seeemd at once to anger him and to please him. Yet resentment was the greatest force bottled in him at the moment. Few persons had had the temerity to balk his known designs.

"You know how it is with me," he muttered, coming as near an apology as his nature could ever let him. "It ain't that I've any doubt of you—it's just that I ain't no hand for waitin'. Never had to," he added belligerently. "I always been

37

strong for doing things right now. Bred to it—my ol' man was hell for settling things in a hurry."

A thought kicked over with suden clarity in Andros' mind. The look he fixed on Barstow showed a keen and close attention. He did not speak; but a risen interest was apparent in the hunching of his shoulders.

Neither of the principals noticed him. The girl said, "Yes, I know. You've told me that before. But it happens I'm just not built that way, Reb. You'll have to wait until—"

"*Wait!*" Barstow ground the word out, the anger in him heating up. "I've waited too long already. I'll have my answer *now* by God!"

He said it flatly and his face took on a harsher cast, his ruddy skin showing heightened color. He was palpably a prideful man and one who had got his own way too long to care anything for the wants of others. This girl's stubbornness was a thing to be crushed; she must learn he was master of all he surveyed. His eyes said so plainly. It was in the harsh snarl of his words.

"No Barstow ever begged for a woman's favors. I'm takin' my answer! Yes or no?"

Andros bent his head and went out the door. His spurs, dragging over the planking, etched jingling sound in the silence behind. He gathered up his pony's reins and struck out for the black outline of a yonder stable. Abruptly he stopped and came wheeling round. He retraced his way to the hitchrail. He paused by Barstow's horse and put a swift hand across its flanks. He looked at the hand with lips curling. Afterwards he turned and went back to the stable.

The night was now black and thick as velvet and the soundings of nocturnal insects were like tiny flutes in the stillness. He tramped along, grim locked in his thoughts, quick mind stabbing questions at this discovery he had made about Barstow. He gave no attention to where his boots took him; he went plowing along with all his accustomed care relaxed.

He reached the stable and, still intent on his problem, went tramping inside and peeled the gear from his horse. With the same abstraction he rubbed the animal down and put an ample measure of grain within its reach. Then he quit the place and headed for the bunkhouse.

That building's lamp flung oblong patches of yellow brilliance into this enfolding darkness, relieving it somewhat in the immediate vicinity and elsewhere made a vagueness of the night-black shadows. Against these light lanes Andros made out the silhouetted shapes of loitering men. He saw enough to understand their eyes were focused on him. These, he guessed, must be the punchers Flame had mentioned. They were men who would judge another by the things that other did within their sight. Experience with their kind had taught Clem Andros that peculiar wisdom.

He wheeled his shoulders toward them, swift to cross lamp's brightness where it spilled from the open doorway. A streak of flame bit instantly toward him from the yonder gloom. Cat-quick he whirled his lean shape slanchways as a pistol's clamor stilled the insects' chorus. One blurred flip spun his gun to hand. He drove his lead through the slatted outline of the corral's peeled poles and straightened as a stifled cry sheared through the dimming echoes.

Against those denser shadows by the corral gate a dark shape tipped forward, supported by the outflung arm that gripped a corral bar. Andros, striding forward, held his fire, but his spurs clanked harshly as he crossed the yard.

When there were but ten paces between himself and that bent shape he stopped. "You cut your string a little close that time, friend."

Cranston's jaw was clenched. His teeth shone palely between parted lips and his eyes were bitter with the fury of his balked intention. He said: "By God——" and fell with Andros' bullet in his chest.

6

LONG ROPE

THE SCREEN door banged at the ranch house. Barstow's shape came plowing through the gloom, came stamping from the shadows, striding savagely toward the crumpled figure by the gate. Someone else came, too, stopping a little way behind. Andros' shoulders impatiently stirred, and he wheeled his torso half around to send a raking look across that halted person.

It was Flame Tarnell. She had no hat and her hair was tumbled by the wind. Her look was on him with a strained attention. Her breasts showed disturbed by a quickened breathing and she had one hand upflung before them as though to fend off something ugly. "Who *are* you?" Her whispered words were choked with feeling.

He had his moment of hesitation then. He guessed the expression of her face would be in his head forever. But he could not regret having killed the saddle tramp, Cranston; the man had made his play and Andros had called it. It was that simple. Life or death. You had your choice.

He slid his pistol back in leather and twisted his shouders to where his glance might follow Barstow's moving shape. He watched the big man pause by Cranston's booted feet and stand there, stilled by a rigid interest. His soft-snarled oath reached Andros plainly; and then he was turning striding across the yard again, his big shape swinging a grotesque shadow, his flat roan cheeks inscrutably set.

Andros had no need to guess what answer Flame had given this fellow. The revelation of her decision was in the sullen cast of all his features, it was in the traveling swing of him, in the jerk and leap of his muscles.

Andros caught Flame's lifted voice again. She stepped from the murk beside him, one white hand reaching out to fall upon his sleeve and instantly stop him. "Who are you?" she repeated. He read wonder in that quick-breathed phrase; wonder and anxiety, and a something else that stirred his pulses oddly.

Her upturned face was ashine in the lamp's refracted glow. He stared long at her and the leaping blood slogged through him with tremendous acceleration. It was a vivid, compelling moment that got beneath his guard, stirring up long-dead emotions, jarring him loose of that cold implacability with which he had gunned Cranston. He had no thought of Cranstone now. He almost forgot Reb Barstow.

But not for long.

Barstow's heavy tones growled: "Yes! It's time we had a handle to you!"

Andros turned. The move was entirely unhurried. Every enquiring line of his face was coolly tranquil. "Getting nervous?"

"Nervous?" Reb Barstow scowled. "It'll take more'n any dead saddle bum to make *me* nervous, bucko. I don't like

40

havin' strangers round—particularly the gun-packin' kind that don't dare let their names out."

"I'm not scared of my name. Andros is what I'm called; Clem Andros. Sometimes known as *Black*."

Something bleak and frantic rushed the rancher's whitened cheeks and was instantly blanked by a lifted, watchful vigilance.

But Andros had seen. Sardonically his glance reached out to Flame Tarnell. But her expression had not changed. "Black Andros" was just a name to her, just an ordinary name without any connotation. Relief bathed Andros in a blessed wave— until he caught the thin-lipped smile that was twisting the rancher's features.

"I'd best have the boys unfurl the flag. This is quite an occasion, bucko. Ain't every spread can boast entertainin' the *king of gunslicks*."

Andros' smile matched Barstow's own. "I don't think yours'll be able to. Generally I aim to steer plumb clear of rattlers' nests an' polecat burrows."

Barstow's cheeks surged bright with color. His smile peeled thin and an ugly glitter crept into the stare from his down-squeezed eyelids. "I don't like that—"

"I guess you know what to do then." Andros grinned at him, teeth coldly bared in the moonlight.

Barstow's shape whipped clear around. "You get rid of this fellow, Flame, right now! Get him outa here! He's nothin' but a stinkin' *Texas man!* Havin' him round'll be just shoutin' for trouble—"

"*Who's* trouble?" Andros chuckled.

Flame said, "You'd better be going now, Reb. You've quite a ride and it's getting late. When I want advice—"

Barstow snarled, "You'll want it, all right! An' *need* it!"

"Then," Flame told him with lifted chin, "I expect I can find it closer to home. Goodnight, Reb."

Barstow gave her one long dark look and went storming off, the clank of his spur rowels harsh as a jay's call, the twist of his features a pale mask of hate.

Flame said to Andros abruptly, "I'll see you in the morning. Goodnight."

Andros put no trust in the bunkhouse, nor in the sloe-eyed punchers who so silently had planted Cranston. He carried

41

his blankets into the felted gloom of the pink-barked pines and squatted long moments there on his bootheels, watching the moon through the sighing limbs, before at last he crawled into them.

He was up before the sun crossed the peaks and swam for a cold five minutes in the icy waters of a gurgling creek that fed the eighty-foot tank in the yard. Then he climbed back into his wrinkled black garb and buckled the scuffed black chaps on over his dark-checked trousers. He buckled on his gun belt, too, and carefully inspected the big, sheathed pistols that sagged its greasy holsters before he started for the mess shack where cook's triangle was banging the call to chuck.

He entered the shack prepared for anything, well knowing his knack for making enemies and alive to the likelihood that there might be one man here who drew some portion of his pay from Barstow. There was last night's shooting to be considered, also; Cranston may not have been a popular man, but he'd been their boss—it might add up to something.

If it did he found no betrayal in the schooled looks of these punchers. They were all here. Three of them were eating and the other, an older man, was busy with the steaming pots on the stove top. There was a dogged method in the way these men kept shoveling the food to their faces. They maintained an adopted silence and kept their eyes on their plates. He was made to feel his place as an outlander; and by their manner these men showed what welcome they extended. He could, Andros mused morosely, have put it on his eyeball and never felt the pain.

But he was hungry. He attacked his food with vigor. The same old fare—plain beans and bacon and sourdough biscuits washed down with hot black coffee. But it tasted good to Clem Andros with his feet beneath a table.

He had his meal half finished and the punchers, shoving back their chairs, were getting out the makings when Flame Tarnell came in through the open doorway and stopped in the lamplight's pale effulgence to call a brief goodmorning.

The punchers grunted, nodding their heads, and got promptly busy with tobacco and papers. The girl showed the strain of a sleepless night. She raised one arm toward Clem Andros. "This is Andros, boys—the new range boss." Her look pointed out each in turn to him: "Curly, Pecos Jim, Tom Flaurity, Coldfoot Dan."

42

The men looked up at him briefly and went on rolling their quirlies. They neither spoke nor nodded. Nor did Andros acknowledge their acquaintance. He went hard on with his eating. He had sized these fellows up when he came in and their names added nothing new to the score.

They were a typical crew; lean-hipped, bold fellows with the mark of the saddle on them and the marks of the sun and wind. Their like could be found on forty outfits in this wild Arizona country. An average group. One thing stamped them for what they were—the bold, dark look of their faces. The basic difference that sets the range man apart from his fellows is that individual liberty, that lawlessness that a wild land inculcates in a man, that tough adherence to his own set notions and standards, that scorn of all other conceptions. He is impatient of rules and enforced restraint; he makes his own code and abides by it.

The men tramped out when their smokes were finished.

Andros concluded his breakfast and sat ruminatively smoking himself while he waited for Flame Tarnell to get finished with hers. He felt no particular jubilation or pride as a result of Flame's proclamation.

He did feel a little curious though to know what had changed her mind. He had his own suspicion; but mostly he was concerned with how his job as foreman here might effect his agreement with Bocart. It might make its fulfillment either more difficult or easy according to what pattern events might take. But he knew one small satisfaction; this job of ramrod for the Rocking T gave him reason for remaining in this Four Peaks country.

Last night he'd found it good to be in this girl's company; it had seemed in some measure completeness. This morning his mood was different. He got no ease from her presence. She was too vivid a personality, too personal a factor. There was dynamite in her, disturbing to the accustomed run of a man's cool thinking.

Putting down her fork she shoved her chair a little way back from the table and turned her head to look at him. "You have my thanks," she said, "for what you did in town last night. In payment of that score I've put you in as foreman here. You wanted that job and you have it. Understand though, I'm not condoning that affair with Crans—"

"What I did for Cranston has nothing to do with your affairs."

"Oh!" Her eyes showed suddenly angry. There was deeper color in the curve of her cheeks. "Then let's have it understood right now you're not to pack private quarrels here—"

"I didn't pack it here—"

"Must we bandy words? You deliberately killed the man you call Cranston!"

"Yes, ma'am. I reckon I did. I most usually figure to kill a snake when I find one—particularly one that tries to bite me. I'm makin' no apologies for it."

Flame's quick stare was sharp and cold. She had lived too long in the West to be shocked by Andros' blunt words or by the code that prompted them. But she was angry—mighty angry, Andros thought; and something else was there in her stare. Scorn, perhaps. He had no time to convince himself, for just then Flame said bitterly: "So you're what Reb Barstow said you were—what he called you to your face! A hired-gun hombre!"

Andros shrugged. He made no remark. If she chose to think that, let her. Might be best all round—certainly best for her. There was no place for a woman in the life of Black Clem Andros. He felt no regret for having killed Cranston. The man was a plain damn horse thief; Andros knew this of experience, and that same experience had proved the man a double crosser as well. Five sheriffs were hunting Cranston's scalp. The country was well rid of him.

Flame said abruptly, gravely: "I had too much to think about to do any sleeping last night. Talmage Vargas—you had better know this—will be bringing his sheep back through here again. He's due most any time now. It's going to mean the end of the Four Peaks cow business . . . if he's permitted to get away with it."

But she was fair. "That's putting it pretty much up to you—"

"That's all right—"

"But it isn't—not really. It's not your fight; it's not your land or your country."

"I like this country," Andros said. "It's got room for a man to stretch himself—"

"Not any more, I'm afraid. It used to be like that. But now it's just got room for one thing—sheep."

44

Her stare met Andros' straightly. "I've changed my mind. You can't be my foreman. I've got no right——"

"Shucks," Andros said, "don't waste your breath. It's up to you whether I boss this spread, but wild horses couldn't drag me out of this country now." He paraded his tough-hombre smile for her. "Why, ma'am, this thing comin' up is just what hired guns comb the border for. You'd better have me with you than teamed up with someone against you."

Her indrawn breath made a quick, sharp sound. She sat stiff as if he'd struck her. "You——"

"Go on," he said, "let's hear the rest."

Her glance stayed on him a moment longer; bright, ice cold, disdainful. Then it wheeled away. She said a trifle stiffly, "There isn't any rest."

"Of course there is. There always is in things like this. Vargas had you on the hip last time. You had some cattle left, didn't you? All right; that's why he beat you. You had property you were scared of losing. Kept you on the defensive, didn't it?"

Her glance came back with an odd, searching thoughtfulness. "Yes."

"But you've lost your cattle now," he said. "The drought an' sheep have ruined you. What steers you got left wouldn't bring a dollar a hoof at the glue factory. They're nothin' but hide an' bone. I've seen 'em. So now you can roll up your sleeves an' give Vargas your full attention. Can't you?"

"I can't do much by myself——"

"You can *try*."

Andros rolled up another smoke while he left her to think it over. "Nothin's so bad as you think it is. These Four Peaks ranchers need organizing; they've got to be talked into fighting Talmage Vargas solid. No single one of you could do a thing against him. You've got to trot out some teamwork. You've got to fight him together—all for one and one for all."

"You make it sound very convincing——"

"It's a cinch," Andros said. "All you need is a leader."

"Yes. That's all." She pushed the hair back out of her eyes. "We found that out when the sheep came last time." She stopped then, stared at her booted feet for a moment. Then her eyes came swiftly up and she said: "You're sure you want to do this?"

Andros chuckled. "I wouldn't be here if I didn't."

"Very well," Flame said. She swung from her chair and paced the room. "If you lick the sheep you can have half this ranch—"

"I'm doin' this 'cause I want to—"

She faced him with her throat a tight line. "You'll fight on *my* terms or not at all."

"Okey," Andros said picking up his hat. "Many thanks for the grub—"

"Where you going?"

"That depends. Comin' down off your high horse?"

Her brown eyes stared at him very bright. "I think I hate you, Andros."

"That's all right. A lot of folks do." There was little humor in Andros' grin. "I never play the other man's game. I call the turn where I hire my guns. An' there'll be a couple strings to it, too. Have you got your mind made up yet? About what you'll do if the sheep come?"

"If the sheep come back I'll fight," she said.

It was Andros now who threw cold water. "With what?"

"With the last gasp of life left in me!" She meant it, too.

Looking into her eyes he could not doubt it. He considered her with a probing interest. "You know how long you'd last agaist Vargas?"

"That's one of the reasons I'm hiring you."

He let that pass. "Can you trust these punchers?" He ignored the cook's look. "Would you trust them like you would a brother?"

"I—" She hesitated, then said with her chin up: "Certainly."

"And what about these other small outfits? Think they'll throw in with you?" He rested one hip on the table.

She looked doubtful. But she said, "They might."

"Which ones?"

She stared at the cupboard; stood considering. "Flowerpot would—I'd bet on them. And Spur and the Boxed Q—they'd help, too." She bit her lip and a frown showed how desperately she tried to convince herself there were others. She said, "I think Lazy J and Tadpole might come in if we talked fast and the chances didn't look too terrible against us. But that's all, I guess. There's others, but I'm afraid they'll do their cheering from the sidelines."

"Or," Andros said with his cynical smile, "they might not cheer at all. Ain't that it?"

Her nod was reluctant. "I'm afraid so."

"Those spreads you named—how many men could we count on from them?"

"Sixteen, perhaps. Not more."

"Say twenty, counting yours."

Andros got to his feet, crushing his cigarette out on his plate. "I'll see what I can do," he said. "But make no mistake. I'll have to have full rein here. No half-way stuff will cut it."

He watched her grimly, wrinkles cracking the hat-paled smoothness of his forehead. "We've got to have this plain right now. When I make out to run something, I aim to run it—all the way. Is that clear? I'll not be hounded with questions. I'll not be stopped with recriminations. I'll do whatever I have to do an' you'll have to trust my judgment. There'll be times when you're not going to like it."

Once more her nod came. Slowly. "I guess I can stand it." She gave him a moment's probing scrutiny then, but whatever her thoughts he could not read them. He had his wistful moment, seeing what this girl could mean to a man big enough to win her—to Barstow, maybe, if at some later time they patched their quarrel. He tried not to scowl as he thought of that.

Sun's glow lay warm along her cheeks and the sheen of her hair was a midnight black. The nearness, the desirability and the vivid fullness of her grabbed and pummeled him, tore beneath his guard and turned him harshly savage.

The cook went out and Andros took a half step toward her, then pulled up suddenly with the knuckles of his clenched fists white as far-North snow.

He said roughly, "I better get along," and wheeled out past her, ducking his head as he went through the door.

The idling punchers were by the corral. Three of them appeared busily whittling; a task they continued. But the fourth, a redhead, looked up coldly as Andros stopped.

Andros said, "If a man was figurin' to air his views before a choice assortment of this country's neighbors, where'd he do his talkin' if he didn't want the sheep crowd hearin' it?"

"Flowerpot," Coldfoot murmured. He kept on whittling.

"All right; I want Boxed Q, Lazy J an' Tadpole notified immediate that Rocking T is holdin' a powwow there tomorrow night. Scatter."

A couple of the boys half-heartedly picked up their ropes. But the gaunt, rehaired Tom Flaurity kept his place on the opera seat. He looked down at Andros stolidly, shifted his quid and spat. "Them Miz' Tarnell's orders?"

"They're *my* orders," Andros said, and yanked him off his perch. "You git in a saddle pronto."

It was noon with a hot sun smashing fury when Andros rode alertly into Long Rope's daytime somnolence. Its single street lay stark in the sunlight, playground of dust and fluttering rubbish. There was no animation on it save for the flight of an occasional paper and the restive shifting of the six tethered ponies racked at the shadeless hitchrail fronting the big saloon. He tied his own bronc there with the feel of malignant eyes upon him. With stiff-held head he stepped upon the scorching walk, and off it onto the saloon veranda, as deserted now as the street it flanked.

With a quick sideways move he was through the slatted doors and sweeping one raking glance the length of the dim, near-empty room. A shirtsleeved man whose pear-shaped middle was hid behind a dirty apron was behind the bar spelling out the text of a week-old paper. Two men in range clothes midway down one tabled side sat with their heads above a bottle. There was no one else in sight.

Andros crossed the sawdust sprinkled floor and stopped with an elbow on the bar beside the reader's paper. The barman's glance came up and abruptly widened. The end of a pink tongue crossed his lips. "My Gawd," he murmured, *"Andros!"*

A cold amusement briefly laid its glint across Andros' glance.

"Morning, Turly. I'll take two fingers of the best," he said; and wondered at the strong uneasiness of the barman's manner. He had casually known this man five years ago when Turly had run a gambling dive at Ogden. There'd been no particular enmity between them; nothing to account for this queer unease that so markedly was bothering Turly now.

Then he caught a blur of movement in the back bar mirror; a woman's face coming swiftly toward him—a face he remembered with quickening pulses.

Her lips were red in the back bar's mirror and curved in a look of pleased surprise. He saw in her eyes things he'd rather were not there; saw the touch of warm color that brushed her cheeks. It was the girl in whose behalf he had antagonized Joce Latham in the San Carlos hashhouse.

48

Plainly she remembered him. With tightening lips Andros turned to face her.

"Oh!" she said. "So it's really you! I'm glad! I—" she stopped; and all the light and eagernes fell completely from her features, leaving them twisted and haggard with startled fear. Andros' stabbing glance caught the face of Barstow hugely grinning from a window that opened out onto the veranda. He heard in that instant the opening creak of the batwing doors.

He stood with all his muscles screaming and thought how his fate ever followed patterns; how each thing at its appointed time dropped snugly in place to mock and trap him.

With a sideways leap he flung his torso clear around. Stillness stretched like a wire in this place. Joce Latham was coming in on the balls of his feet with one white clamped fist tightly gripping a gun stock.

7

"YOU'RE NOT A CLEVER LIAR, BISHOP—"

ANDROS stood beside the girl and watched cool reason crawl away. He stood with brown fists dangling empty and knew it had to be this way. He could not explain this girl to Latham. Blood would tell—blood and the things in a man's hot head. Desire for revenge was a still white flame in the gambler's stare.

"So you *did* come after all," Latham purred. "I thought you would—you wench stealin' rat!" Turbulent fires were aboil inside him, searing away the ropes of his caution, driving their robust fury storm-black across the scowling twist of his face. San Carlos was in his rage-fogged mind and this white-cheeked girl was in it too; and a pulse on his forehead was throbbing wildly. *"I'll fix you!"* he shouted, and fired point-blank.

But rage's red flare played hell with his aim. Andros, braced, took the impact of that shot without leaving his tracks. He seemed to lean a little forward as though he might be welcoming it. All saw the dust jump out of his vest.

49

He straightened slowly.

"You fool!" he said; and flame was a white streak that jumped from the pistol some unseen magic had conjured to his hand. Latham's eyes sprang wide in shocked unbelief. Wind off the hill-slopes crossed the room, swirling the stringers of blue smoke round them. The girl was like a statue—tranced. The men beyond hung tense by their table, their startled looks gone stiff and frozen. A shudder ran through him and Latham dropped. Like a tall, sleek aspen to the bite of steel.

Time stretched and thinned. Andros stood immobile, hunched shoulders set, his vacuous stare seeing all before him while the big gun gaped its menace from his hand. He watched, for this was a care ground into him by all those years of turbulence Krell's death had made a mockery. It was a care he could not put away though weariness tugged every nerve and muscle and that pain in his side was a sharp, barbed blade some devil was twisting, twisting, twisting.

First to break the tableau, he moved at last and turned his head toward that window where Reb Barstow had stood and grinned at him. Barstow still was framed in it but his grin had gone twisted—ludicrous. Gone was all of his displayed enjoyment. The heavy slant of his stiff roan cheeks obscured his thought; but changed ideas, a new perception, had thrust haunted shadows beneath his eyes.

A last flare of anger had its way with Andros. Barstow had known Joce Latham was coming—had probably egged him on. That was Barstow's craft. Andros' stare was brightly wicked. "You wantin' to pack this on from where Joce dropped it?"

Oddly, Barstow displayed no anger. He stood coldly still and shook his head. In the roan of his cheeks was a strange perplexity. His amber eyes held lifted caution. He had the look of a man uncertain, a man slow groping toward an unwanted conclusion.

His shoulders stirred with abrupt impatience. "Not me, bucko. I can wait for mine," he said, and wheeled from the window, the stamp of his boots growing fainter and fainter.

One moment longer Andros watched the window. Then his glance came round, raking the look of those men by the table —searching the still white mobile face of that one lone girl who stood so stiff in this room's frozen quiet.

A curious numbness crawled over Andros. His will would

50

not function; his sight was grown hazy. He could not understand why the place was so cold, or his veins were like fire, or his pistol so heavy. The pain of his side was grown monstrous, ugly.

He became suddenly aware that the girl was moving. She was coming toward him. Her eyes were funny and her features twisted with a plain emotion he could not account for. Anxiety—yes! That was it—anxiety. Perhaps, after all, she had really loved Latham. But no! Anxiety was for the living; the dead were beyond it—and she was looking at *him*. He could not understand it. She had one hand hard against her breasts; the other stretched toward him—a queer, unfathomable gesture.

Ed Turly's voice came strictly grave. "The king is dead. Long live the king."

Crazy thing to say!

Andros, with his straining gaze on the men by the table, said: "Turly! Come out from behind that bar where I can see you!"

He heard Turly moving.

The light was bad, was failing rapidly. It was a haze, like smoke, all run together. The men by the table were vague-placed shapes, uncertain as ghosts in this ghastly gloom.

In the vaulted quiet he could hear the shuffle of Turly's feet as the barman came from behind the mahogany. He saw the gray mass of Turly's soiled apron move against the white wall.

He wondered angrily why Turly did not light the lamps.

He swept a glance at the girl and shook his head from side to side. But it did not help. Her face was a blob, one pale smear against this gloom. It seemed to be floating. Her legs—Why, she hadn't any legs! Her face, in the haze, kept swimming closer.

He put one hand before him to stop it, to fend it off "That's far enough, ma'am. Just stop right there." He brought the muzzle of his sixgun up; or he meant to. But someway his hand was like lead. It was heavy and numb and he could not move it.

And that cursed fire in his veins—it was burning him up. His lips were stiff, they felt cracked and feverish. His tongue wouldn't move.

He peered toward the men he had seen by the table. Two

dark lumps that seemed curiously bent forward as though they were about to fall over.

He commanded his wabbly legs to move and was childishly pleased when he found they obeyed him. Still watching the lumps by the table he backed to the bar. Still facing the room he hooked his elbows over it. He hung there that way with his knees all turned to water. With a straining care he watched the two lumps that had once been men beside a table.

Outside a wagon or something went by and filled this big room with its clatter and rattling and the smell of its dust got into his nostrils.

He wondered why no one had come to find out about those shots he'd fired. No—he'd only fired once. That was right. Latham had fired an then he had fired. Two shots in all. In this dead town that should have been aplenty to bring men running. Maybe they'd moved; gone away to some better place. That kind of tickled him. He thought they'd not have to look very far to find one.

Damn the light anyway. It was so dark now he could not see the rear of this place. He could not see the lumps any longer, or Turly's apron. Even that girl—he could hear her breathing—was but a vague silhouetted shadow.

As from miles away Turly's voice came dimly. "Don't you reckon, Clem, it's gettin' time we racked the chips?"

Andros' mind could not shape an answer. A strange weird peace was stealing over him. He felt quaintly drowsy as though he'd been sitting too long in the sun. It was only by the sheerest effort he kept his eyes from closing and his sagging chin from hitting his chest. It took a world of effort.

His thoughts became disjointed and held no bearing on the thing in hand. They took him back along the trail to things he'd done in other times. And then he had no thoughts at all and everything about him was a solid black and he found the peace he sought.

The Upland road that, going by Barstow's, led to the country beyond Diamond Mountain, crossed Rocking T range within mocking bird's call of the Tarnell ranch house. A hoof-stamped trail that strangely twisted, following meticulously in its dips and windings the lazy meanderings of the curling creek.

Flame Tarnell had watched that road since five o'clock

52

this evening. It was nine and the moon would be soon coming up now; and Clem Andros had not returned.

Flame Tarnell was restless, and she was not a restless girl. A vague uneasiness had crept upon her and she could not cast it off. She told herself again, more firmly, that her range boss' absence had no least part in it; but intuition said she lied. She turned from the window and crossed the room aimlessly, and there wheeled and came back without lighting the lamp. Yes; she admitted it; Clem Andros' nonappearance *did* have considerable to do with her strange uneasiness.

She was filled with a bleak foreboding.

There were men abroad in the dark of this night. Furtive riders. Dark shapes crouched with their hats pulled low, with chests down-bent above their saddles. This was a little used trail of late, and yet she'd counted six men riding north since dusk.

Abruptly she backed with a quick catch of breath. There a seventh man went, right now, slipping by without sound in the curdled shadows!

She caught her lip between her teeth and crouched there with a pounding heart. This stealthy traffic held implications. There was something sinister in those vague-seen shapes.

Flame was twenty-two and all her life had lived in this hard land: had lived and watched and learned, to some extent, to gauge this country's moods. Intangible stealth flowed darkly through this silent night, and the vagrant wind soughing through the pine tops was dreary and dismal. A soul in anguish.

There was light in the bunkhouse, low turned and dim.

Straightening presently she pulled up a chair and sat down by the window where her anxious eyes could continue their vigil. She was acting like an idiot, and told herself so, tartly. It did not help much. She thought of Andros.

She had thought about him many times. He was the kind of man she'd dreamed of in the loneliness of this wild solitude. He was some way different, unlike other men she'd known. He was capable; efficiency was in his every gesture. Yet he had a quietness and deference which she had secretly found attractive. She liked to listen to the soft Texas drawl of his talk, to watch the clean white flash of his teeth behind the lazy smile that sometimes briefly curved his lips. His arrival, she thought, had changed things somehow; had shifted values

53

and given her the first real sense of security she had known since her father's death.

She stood up and, crossing to the table, lit the lamp. She drew on her riding gauntlets and paused a bit uncertainly beside the table, finally to pull off the gloves and toss them indifferently on the lounge. She turned then, hesitantly, and paused, surveying the sleek and empty blackness of the window on which were superimposed reflected portions of the room behind her.

She shrugged, turned away with affected nonchalance and strolled aimlessly about examining various trophies hung upon the walls, the oak-framed Remingtons, the Navajo blankets, that Mexican sombrero with its silver threads and tiny bells and band of gleaming conchos.

She went to the fireplace, her eyes on the border rifles crossed above it. She wondered idly if perhaps a little fire might not improve her spirits. She did not build one though. Her glance roved across the mantel, came to thoughtful rest upon the deep-seamed features of that tough and gaunt old man in the beaten silver frame.

Her eyes grew soft and wistful and she forgot for a moment the most of her fears. She smiled at the pictured face determinedly. She must show him she was not afraid. She *wasn't* afraid. A little moody maybe—daunsy, as the cowboys said; but not afraid. She put the thought into words. "If the sheep come again I'll fight, Dad. It's been rough round here, but there's a man on the spread that'll back me now. He six feet tall; he's slim and sometimes he's handsome. But mostly he's got an odd, tight look—like you used to have when things got to crowding. I wish you could meet him, Dad. You'd like him. . . . Things are going to be different now with him around."

A floorboard creaked and she whirled with paling cheeks. But no intruder was crouched behind her. There was no one in the room but herself. She thought: "Just the old house settling," and laughed a little, flustered.

She went back and paused by the window. She pressed her face against it, with her hands cupped by her cheeks, and saw three men come out of the bunkhouse. They squatted down in the moonglow with their backs to the bunkhouse wall. She watched them dig out the inevitable makings. She could not hear what they talked about, but moments later she thought to raise the window a mite and she found they were talking of horses.

She felt soothed some way, quieted by these familiar things. She pulled her chair to the table; picked up and opened a book. But in this mood no printed page could hold her; the masterful figure and dark commanding features of the range boss kept coming between it and herself.

She wondered where he was tonight. He had gone, she thought, to town. He had not taken her into his confidence. Well . . . that was the bargain. No questions.

Strong interest and her feminine pique of riddle drove her into speculation concerning other things about him, just as it had a thousand times since his coming. Where was he from? Who was he? She had sensed on more than one occasion the deep streak of bitterness that was in him. It excited her curiosity. What thing from a hidden past still held the power to torture him? What had he done that was so grave that even now it must color his actions? Or was it something that another had done . . .? Who *was* he? Who *was* Black Clem Andros? That he was a man of import was definitely proved. She had seen Reb Barstow's face when he heard that name.

Andros was cool, quick-thinking, dangerous. She had been around men long enough to know. Her mind went back to the look in his eye when, tapping Grave Creek Charlie's shoulder, he'd taken up the sheepman's challenge; to that darkly tranquil slanting of his cheeks when last night Barstow in this room had likened him to Cranston; to the saturnine curling of Andros' lips when to Barstow's face he'd disparaged the Barstow tribe. Yes, the man was dangerous; the cut of his mouth and the slant of his jaw were certainly not those of a pacifist.

She recalled other things about him. The softness of his step. The sure quick way of his shoulders. The steadfast directness of his gaze. Queer how great a claim he'd made upon her thoughts.

She remembered him as he'd looked in town the night she had first seen him—could it really have been but last night? A black-haired man with dark, burnt skin pulled toughly across high cheekbones; a man whose eyes were the color of smoky sage. She could see, as though he stood right now before her, the grim lips cleaving that wind-whipped face above his cold and saturnine jaw. She saw with an awakened clarity how that battered hat shoved back from his bony forehead clearly typified her whole impression of him. A thing of service, unostentatious and uncared for, it yet displayed with an odd completeness the brash and mocking confidence of the man.

He was tall, lean, sure. He had a physical toughness that characterized each tiniest shred of gesture; not a blatant swaggerer's toughness, yet nonetheless impossible of concealment. He was one who stood full head and shoulders above the level of his fellows, a man who had heard the owl hoot. A vital, colorful figure.

And so Flame sat and mused. Not the display of animal brawn, but the sturdy character to be read in Andros' features it was that so swiftly had captured the girl's imagination. Those features told of experience beyond his years; they told that well, but they told more—in them crouched strong hint of their owner's staunch, unswervable viewpoint, the adamantine quality of purpose that would send Black Andros clear through hell before he'd lay aside or be balked out of completing any chore he'd put his hand to. This trait shone like a thread of silver through the cynical mockery of the look with which he viewed his enemies.

He made a long, efficient shape in his scarred black chaps and flannel rider's shirt. His confidence was like an impregnable rock; yet, combined and toned with that quiet deference he showed her, this very quality, she felt sure, must be the uncarriable barrier against which all her troubles would beat in vain.

The thought was tremendously reassuring.

But Andros was no man of iron; she knew him to be very human, as prone to likes and dislikes as any other. He had his prejudices—strong ones, sudden ones; they were plain in the swift impatient stirring of his shoulders. She had marked that habit more than once.

Moreover, he was a man who made mistakes, and had made others in the past. Could one forget or ever miss the caustic bitterness which was so much a part of him? And the rash, quick-striking temper of him that could lift like a flare of light!

These were his weaknesses and—

Her reflections and evaluations of Clem Andros were suddenly scattered by the whooming, hollow boom of horses' hoofs across the bridge. With one hand caught up to her throat she straightened tensely, throbbing premonitorily to the rush of yonder horsemen and their stop before the bunkhouse.

A definite alarm took her hurrying to the window. She crouched with face pressed against it, recognition of those riders touching her instantly. They were men from the Half-Circle Arrow; Barstow's foreman, Bishop Torril, and one other—Bronc Culebra. Excitement ran their lifted voices; her men showed an avid interest. Fragments of that talk came to her, swinging her round with whitened cheeks and pushing her throught the outside door.

"Got 'im, all right, I say. Plugged 'im—"

"Yeah. He shore looked like the wrath of Gawd with them elbows hooked to the bar that way an' them damn eyes of his a-borin' holes through me an' Bronc, here, over the muzzle of that hawglaig!"

"Downed 'im, eh?" That was Flaurity's voice, with satisfaction—the last Flame heard as she pulled the door shut after her. The stiff night wind shoved against her face, roughing her hair and whipping her skirt out gustily as she made for the dark group by the bunkhouse.

She came hurrying up unnoticed just as Torril said, "An' served him plumb right, if you're askin' me—the goddam meddler "

Flame caught at Torril's stirrup; cried breathlessly, "What is it, Bishop? Are you talking about my range boss—about Clem Andros? Oh! what *is* it? What has *happened?*"

Culebra shifted his chaw and spat. Bishop Torril said, "Ain't nothin' to get up a lather over." And Culebra leered at her wickedly.

Tom Flaurity got up and came over to her, taking off his wide-rimmed hat. "Now, Miz' Flame, ma'am," he said soothingly, "this yere ain't nothin' fer you t' bother yore purty haid about. You jest leave this business to us an'—"

But the queer squinted eyes under Torril's hatbrim had been watching her alertly. Now, with neither regard for Flaurity's opinion or for the fact that Flaurity was talking, he put the crux of the matter bluntly:

"That top screw of yours, if you want to know, has got himself another piece o' steak—*see?*"

57

Flame turned a puzzled look to Flaurity. "Whatever in the world—"

"He means," growled Flaurity harshly, "that yo'r friend has killed another guy."

"My— You mean *Andros?*"

"Yeah. *Andros,*" Torril mocked. "Tonight, just now, he killed Joce Latham."

Plain to see in this moonlight was the startled dismay that paled Flame's cheeks. All caught that sharply indrawn breath —the involuntary gesture that sent one hand to her breast.

Tom Flaurity looked away; but Torril, spurred on by an evident malice, said smugly, "I was there in Latham's place when it happened. I seen it all—an' Bronc did too; he was right there with me. Your range boss was a-shinin' up to Latham's woman an' Latham come in an' caught him. This Andros yanked his gun—Joce didn't have no chance a-tall."

Flame looked at the man with hard, straight eyes. "You're not a clever liar, Bishop. Andros isn't the kind to waste his time on a gambler's woman—"

"I guess," Torril said, scowling away the dark look of his cheeks, "that's what-for he's staying' so long in town, ma'am." He smiled then with a look of amiability. "I expect that's why he's in a back room now with Latham's harlot."

Flame Tarnell's lips came open and she stood that way, eyeing Torril with the hurt bewilderment she might have shown had he slapped her across the mouth. She backed away a stumbling pace, the knuckles of one hand jammed hard against her teeth. With the harsh, crass laugh of Bronc Culebra in her ears, red-cheeked she whirled, making blindly for the house.

8

THE POT CALLS THE KETTLE BLACK

THAT STRANGE peace into which Andros had descended did not, in reality, last longer than a short ten minutes. He regained consciousness in a different room from that in which he'd fallen. There was a strong medicinal smell about him

58

and just over him stood a shirt-sleeved, bearded sawbones. This was a room much smaller than the barroom, but that pale-cheeked girl over whom hostilities had started was still close by him. She was tearing some white, flimsy garment into thin strips and watching him with her wide dark eyes across the medico's shoulder.

The doctor straightened with a grunt. "Guess that will— Oh! so you've come out of it, eh? Hurt much? How's your head feel? Kind of light?" He nodded sagely. "You'll get along. You can't kill these damn ranch hands," he told the girl as he pulled the cuffs of his shirt sleeves down. "This boy's got a constitution like an ox."

He looked back at Andros, grinned at him encouragingly. "You'll be all right. Never mind the dizziness—that's a pretty cheap price to pay for the kind of brashness you showed. They tell me you never even ducked. Must think your hide is armor! Stay in bed two weeks and—*What?* You'll do nothing of the sort! You'll stay right where you are, young man, for *at least* two weeks or I'll wash my hands of you. Scowl all you want—I *mean* it!"

Andros got an elbow under him and, despite the doctor's voluble protests, swung to a sitting posture on this couch where he'd been laid. The thing did considerable creaking and he groaned once or twice himself as pain knifed along his ribs again with renewed energy. But he could stand it, he reckoned. He *had to*. There were things that needed doing.

The medico, horrified to see his patient getting up, came rushing over with spluttered wrath, but Andros waved him off.

"No use, Doc," he muttered, fumbling with his shirt buttons. "I know how you feel an' I'm a heap obliged to you. But I've got chores to do an' they ain't waitin' on no blasted two-weeks vacation."

The bandage was a little bulky but he got the shirt buttoned round it. He stood up, reaching a hand to the wall to steady himself. He dug some greenbacks from a pocket and tossed them on the table. "You're fortunate in your patient, Doc. You're goin' to get a lot of advertisin'."

The doctor's stare was incredulous. "Good God, man! You tryin' to underwrite the undertaking business? Do you realize—"

"You bet! That's what I'm gettin' up for."

"You keep flat on your back for the next two weeks or you'll be buried before the first week's over! The human body—"

"Sorry, Doc. The body's mine."

He turned a twisted smile at the girl. "I'm sorry about your trouble—but you saw the play, ma'am. I only did what I had to. You've got your chance now. Go on back East an' leave this country to nuts that are fool enough to like it."

He picked up his cartridge belt and buckled it about him. He took the two big pistols from their sheaths and looked them over critically. He shook their cartridges onto the table and replaced them with fresh ones drawn from his belt.

"You've lost a lot of blood—"

"Sure. Andros returned his guns to leather. He said to the scowling medico: "Nice, meetin' you an' all," and with a ghastly grin shakily started toward the door.

It came open before he got there.

The man behind it was Grave Creek Charlie, boss of the fighting sheepmen. He stopped with his mouth wide open. A glassy look sheared across his stare. And then his eyes bulged frantically.

"Lookin' for somebody?" Andros jeered.

The man seemed frozen in his tracks. Incapable of speech he looked. He shook his head like a pole-axed steer and commenced an impetuous backing.

Andros' cheeks were set and sultry. He dropped his stare to Grave Creek's boots. There was brittle frost in the look he brought up. "Too bad. Your luck's out, sheepman. The bullet ain't been cast that'll send me where you're wishin." Come you're catchin' different notions now's a damn good time to prove it. Turn loose your howl, you sheep dog."

Grave Creek's look was a paralyzed thing. He stood stiff-placed beyond the door; his shadow made a rigid shape across its sunlit sill. There was no motion in him. His eyes clung glassily to Andros' face. He seemed there to read some threat that shook all thought of action out of him. He stood there stunned, gone breathless.

They made a grim, unforgettable picture poised there in this tautened stillness. There was no sound, no movement, in all this plank-walled place.

The tableau was rudely broken.

The swing of slatted doors scratched a harsh sound across the stillness, and a man came in without his hat, one lock of

60

hair between his eyes, his sweating cheeks coarse-streaked with dust. "Rockin' T's callin' a meetin'—"

That many panted words spilled from him before he stopped with jaw loose-hanging, his startled eyes fixed blankly on the smiling cheeks of Andros.

But he was quick. He grasped the play on the instant, and nervously backed three halting steps, his boot-sound like dropped plates in the stealthy quiet. His tongue darted across his dry lips and his desperate glance jumped from Andros' face to Grave Creek's.

"That's quick work," Andros drawled approvingly, and his displayed smile made this newcomer wince and back away another step. "Accurate, too—you're to be commended, Grave Creek, on the speed that keeps you posted."

Then he looked at them derisively. "Make the most of it," he said and wheeled across the room, striding between the rooted sheepmen and crossing the saloon without turning.

He loosed the gelding's reins from the hitchrail and, with the animal in tow, strode down the dusty street with the smashing sun hot upon his back and with shoulders hunched to the pain in him.

He came to the stable and turned in there and dropped his reins to the straw-littered floor. He considered the tall, lean-bodied man who stared at him from the shadows. The man, stepping forward, put his back to a stall post and, from that position, eyed him reticently with his folded arms well away from his belt.

Hay smell and the smell of horses was an acrid thing in this air. It buoyed him. A familiar tang that felt good in his nostrils. He shrugged abruptly. He said to the watching stableman, "This afternoon I had to kill a man. A chore I take no pride in—but a necessary one. You were at Quinn River four years ago. I'm afraid I don't remember you."

The stableman's face showed stolid. "Does it matter?"

"I think it does. It's not often I forget a face." The corners of Andros' mouth grew tight. "Who are you, friend?"

The man's lips showed a thin and reluctant smiling. "They called me Gallup John, them days."

Light broke lines across Andros' cheeks. "The Quinn River marshal!"

The stableman said, "We didn't have very much in common."

"No," Andros said. "I guess we didn't," and felt the stable-man's glance trekking after him through the door.

There was something urgent Andros had to do. He felt a need to get in touch with Major Bocart. He had just recalled this gun the Major had given him—this gun rolled snug behind his cantle which had once belonged to Dakota Krell—had belonged, so Bocart had said, to the last man attempting the gun trick which was Bocart's test for applicants.

Andros found it hard to believe Krell could have met his death in two different places, and on two different dates, at that. There was a chance the Major had watched Krell die. If he had not—But, of course, someone other than Krell might have used that gun in the Major's office. Either way, Clem Andros had to know.

From his long knowledge of Krell, and Krell's character, Andros did not think the Major and Dakota Krell had ever met. He was not the kind the Major would hire, with his shifty eyes and cat-thin lips—with his slitted dead-snake stare. It seemed to Andros a deal more likely that some way another man had come into possession of Dakota's pistol, even as Andros himself now had it.

One vague disquiet tightened Andros' cheeks. Despite all evidence to the contrary the man *might* still be alive.

But what Andros wanted badly to know right now was whether or not the man who had brought Krell's pistol into the Major's office with him had been given the same information concerning the Forest movement which Bocard had given him. If he had, it explained a lot of things. The Forest movement's adversaries appeared particularly well informed—which, to Andros' mind, was in no way a healthy condition.

He thought of that dusty hatless man who'd barged into the saloon with the knowledge of Rocking T's called meeting. It had not been later than this very morning that he'd sent the Tarnell punchers out to gather the men for that meeting. If the sheep crowd, knowing when, where and why that meeting was to be called, didn't figure to do something about it, also, there was sure enough something almighty rotten in Denmark!

A new set of plans must be formulated at once. Andros reflected morosely that he was not feeling up to planning much; that nagging pain in his side was engaging too much of his

62

attention. It was sapping his energy, too. It was getting worse again.

His thoughts swung back. It was not like Dakota Krell to go risking his life so foolishly by trying any tricks with a pistol. Even if Krell was alive and mixed up in this infernal sheep-cattle-lumber-railroad-National Forest business, it was not in his character to have done himself what easily he could have hired someone else to do. The man had never been given to the taking of unnecessary risks. He had never been the kind to do *anything* he could get another to do as well.

Dakota Krell had sense.

Andros crossed the windrowed dust of that sun-smoked street and mounted the scarred board porch of Long Rope's lone hotel. Sun-warped, a weatherbitten shack it was, thrown together of native pine whipsawed from the vanished yesterdays. It was garnished with a tall false front intended to convey an impression of three full stories where but one existed in solid fact.

He stepped through the open doorway, getting pen and ink and paper from an observant and reticent proprietor. He went to the table shoved against the farther wall of the small and dusty lobby. The buzz of flies was a steady drone as he eased himself into a stiff-backed chair. He sat awhile there resting, with canted head upon an elbow-propped hand, endeavoring to corral his scattering thoughts.

He roused at last and, staring morosely at the cheap, lined paper, picked up the scratchy pen and began laboriously scrawling hen-tracked words. But the effort of this was tremendous and his thoughts did not come easily. Halfway through he abruptly stopped. The Major would not like this. The last thing Bocart had told him was: "Any jam you get into you can stay in, far as this Service is concerned."

Andros realized then the crazy thing he'd set his hand to. He was not in any jam just yet—but he quickly would be if he tried to post this letter in any town in the Four Peaks country. The new Forest movement's adversaries, Bocart said, had spies all over this country. These men would never permit a stranger's notes. . . .

He tore the letter up and thrust the fragments into a pocket. The hotel keeper's glance was blandly disinterested when Andros went heavily past him, turning out upon the street.

By his shadow Andros saw the time was hugging five

o'clock. His head felt strangely light again. His skin was clammed with sweat as, feeling the pangs of hunger, he saw a restaurant's sign and willed his rebelling body toward it.

He went in. A long, gaunt place this was, with on one side a clean but fly-harassed counter. The other side was flanked by two long rows of scrubbed-white tables garnished with stiff-backed chairs. There were no customers present when Andros swayed to a stool at the counter.

A man in what once had been a spic-and-span white apron got up off his elbows, laid his cigar on the counter's edge and limped up to get Andros' order.

Andros, when the man had gone, cupped calloused hands to his heated face. There was a faded sign on the wall across from him which said: "Gents learning to spell are politely asked to use last week's paper." He stared at this till the man returned with his supper. Its only merit was heat. Andros ate lethargically and, now that he had got it, without appetite; but he finally cleaned his plate and, leaving the price beside it, got up to go.

He had just climbed off the stool when a shadow fell across the floor and a whiskered old fellow stood peering in. Locating Andros he said: "Miz' Latham wants to see you. She's over at the saloon."

Andros rubbed one hand along the smooth edge of the counter. "Tell Mrs. Latham," he said wearily, "I'll see her next time I come this way." He stood there thoughtful while the old man left, after which he cuffed his hat down over his eyes and tramped out after him. The stabbing pains in his side were worse. He lurched against the restaurant wall and hung there, groggy, till he got his breath. If his enemies had come for him then they could have taken him without resistance. It was all Andros could do to keep himself erect and moving when, finally, he went lurching toward the stable. He staggered like a drunken fiddler, but with jaw grim-set he made it.

The shadows of approaching dusk were thick inside the stable murk. Gallup John came out of the gloom. His glance combed Andros' cheeks intently. He said, "I'll get your bronc. Wait here."

Andros still was waiting when, above the sounds of the stableman's labor, a quick, springy crunch of footsteps wheeled him round to face Grace Latham.

Slanting rain poured earthward from a black and cloud-tossed sky. Through this steady drench of water rode a pon-choed solitary horseman who urged his dark bronc down the last steep pitch of Diamond Mountain and out upon the running flat where huddled the soaked adobes of Half-Circle Arrow's headquarters. It was not two hours since a moon had ridden these heavens; but the roof of the world lay hidden now behind dark layers of curdled cloud, and the still-ness of these limitless distances was crammed with the mono-tone purr of rain, was jarred by the rolling oaths of thunder, was seared and blanched by the threat of lightning's whiplash. The soggy pound of this animal's hoofs was lost in the roaring maelstrom—was found and again torn away by the flapping skirts of a rising gale.

The solitary rider pressed on, unperturbed by rain and wind-lash, indifferent to storm's blustery outbursts, cautious only to catch first sight of other storm-bound travelers.

He swore presently and jerked his horse up sharply, wheel-ing him into a catclaw thicket and clamping quick hand across the swelling nostrils. For there came other riders, forward-hunched above their saddles, splashing from the yonder lane that led to the outfit's largest building.

When lightning's flare had dimmed away and storm's full darkness had rushed like a wave across the puddled flats, the lone rider turned his mount behind three willow's interlaced branches and there remained until successive flashes proved the flats deserted.

He came then from their cover, a careful man who gave no edge to risk, and swung his own horse into the lane vacated by those other riders. He jogged this trail at a sloshing pace till the heavier blackness of the big house's angles imposed their outlines stark against night's thinner dark.

He pulled to a halt beside the veranda, swung dripping down and dropped his reins. He crossed the porch planks then and sideways passed through a door held open by his own left hand. Barstow, with glance lifted from his cluttered desk, showed a deeper dark in the roan of his cheeks. He came out of his seat with a jarring oath. His bull-throated yell sailed against this man like the flat of an ax. *"Where the hell you think you been?"*

The man's teeth gleamed in a twisted grin while his shoulders made an arcing gesture and his insolent stare quartered Bar-

65

stow's face with a cold amusement. It was the only answer Barstow got.

"I told you to get here *yesterday! Didn't I?*"

Barstow took two forward steps. His fists were clenched and his lamp-thrown shadow was a monstrous blotch against the wall. A huge and lumbering beast he looked as he crouched there with his face contorted and tried to make the other quail. "You cocky bastard!" The hurled-out words were ugly, gritted. "I ought to smash that goddam grin down your throat!"

With lips still curved the man, without fear, drew the makings out of a dry vest pocket. When the smoke was rolled his glance came up. He leered at the Half-Circle Arrow boss knowingly.

"Y'u got fists," he drawled, "could hammer a man 'most near to death, I reckon—if y'u c'ld ever git 'em on 'im. But don't put on no dawg with me. Y'u couldn't cut it, Barstow."

Breath rushed shrilly through Barstow's teeth. His livid cheeks were mottled, bloated. He showed the desire so rampant in him, the hot wild lust to maim and batter. But he checked his impulse, held his place; rooted there by the man's indifference.

The newcomer chuckled. He kicked the door shut, put his back against it while rain from his poncho pooled the floor about his muddy boots.

He was tall—very near as tall as Barstow, but without the rancher's brawny bigness. Rather, he was lithe, slim waisted, quick and sure in all his movements. Brash were the eyes beneath his hatbrim, hard was the mouth above his rakish jaw.

He crossed the room toward Barstow coolly, helped himself to a cigar from Barstow's pocket, snapping his own smoke into a corner. Glaring, Barstow strode quick after it, stamping it out with visible venom. The other man's eyes looked after him, mocking.

He bit the end from his purloined smoke and snapped a match alight on his thumbnail. "Y'u wanted me here for somethin' besides glarin'. S'pose y'u spill it."

Barstow's temper had cramped his style. It had thinned his broad features and squeezed the stare of his amber eyes to pale and wicked-glinting slits. But he could not cringe this man with anger; he had tried before and been derisively laughed at. This dripping man enjoyed his rages. "One day you'll go too far!" he snarled.

"But not today," the fellow chuckled.

With tremendous effort Barstow smoothed his cheeks into some semblance of the other's grin. "I guess we understand each other—"

"C'mon—get at it."

Barstow's scowl was black. "I had a meeting here tonight. If you had—"

"Meetin's bore me," the other man said. "Long's yore backers pay off, I'm for y'u. When they don't I'll find somethin' else. I ain't much worried. Y'u'll see they pay me if y'u value yore health." His smile was malignant. "We savvy each other all right."

But Barstow was not to be tripped again. He kept the hatred off his cheeks and put his mind to his need of this man. The storm had quit, gone rampaging elsewhere, but wind still plucked its cold shrill whine from the swaying trees.

While Barstow shaped his thoughts the dripping rider whistled the dust from a nearby chair and eased his lean wet form down into it. Muddied water marked his trail from the door. Barstow's glance morosely eyed it.

He said gruffly, "The sheep'll be back here in three-four weeks. Was kind of scared till we got this rain; but they'll come now. Soon's the grass gets up—what they've left, I mean. Talmage allows they'll be crossin' over ninety-five thousan' head through the Four Peaks country. Says it looks like Roosevelt'll lick us on this Forest business; it's in Talmage's mind to clean these two-bit brush-poppers out before the bill goes through."

"I coulda guessed that much without comin' down here," drawled the visitor fleeringly, and pulled back his poncho to puff on a star that was pinned to his vest. He polished the metal with the tail of a curtain. "Some of your brush-poppers is goin' to fight—I s'pose y'u know that? Y'u an' Talmage an' some of them others has whittled this country down to where it ain't got much left to lose. They'll git their backs up this time."

"They've got their backs up now," Barstow said. "I got the word not half an hour back. Rockin' T's called a meetin' at the Flowerpot for tomorrow night. They've sent invites to Boxed Q, Tadpole, Spur an' Lazy J."

67

The man in the chair merely shrugged indifferently.

Scowling, Barstow said, "Which'll be when we smash 'em." He purred with satisfaction: "We'll hit that meetin' like a load of logs! Grave Creek's camped with twenty men just north of town; with them an' my fourteen we'll give hell some helpers. I want you to stay in town where—"

"'D y'u get me out here to tell me that?"

"I got you out here to show you how to run your job."

The lean star-packer sneered. "When I take lessons off'n y'u—"

Barstow snarled, "The way you gallivant about this country it's a whoppin' wonder you ever *do* know what's goin' on! For a marshal you sure don't grow no moss around Long Rope! The Rockin' T's got a new range boss—"

"That ain't news; it always gettin' one. Reg'lar as clockwork, every month."

"The one it's got now is news," snapped Barstow, "an' don't you doubt it! This guy blew Cranston's light with just one puff. This noon he killed Joce Latham in his own saloon. God only knows what he's doin' now!"

But Long Rope's marshal was no longer listening. Straightened in his chair his look was suddenly intent—pleased and thoughtful and wholly busied with something in mind. His eyes showed a lewd and febrile gleaming. He ran a moist tongue across his lips and, getting up, cuffed his wet hat to a rakish angle.

He grinned. "I guess that leaves Joce's woman—"

"You leave that damn slut out of this! You listen to what I'm tellin' you!" Barstow swung the words at the man like cudgels. "You'll get hamstrung by a dame yet, damn you! But you'll do it on your own time—*get me?* You lose us this game—"

"Ahr! Get on with it," Long Rope's marshal told him. "Jest strip it down an' never mind preachin'. What about the Rockin' T squirt?"

"I kinda thought you might mebbe know him. His name," Barstow said, "is Black Clem Andros."

The marshal went dead still in his tracks. His face went pale as wood ash and he looked at Barstow and never saw him. All the cocky confidence was gone clean out of him. He seemed to age ten years in that moment.

He spoke no word; and Barstow said: "I see you do!"

The marshal jerked and his eyes were frantic. Hoarse, blasphemous oaths came tumbling out of him and he paced the room like a captured tiger. He was cursing still when the door shoved open and Bishop Torril came sloshing in with Bronc Culebra.

A watchful glint colored Torril's stare. "How are you, Krell? Long time no see. How's the star-packin' business comin' these days?"

Culebra sneered. "By the look of his pan someone's swiped his star—or mebbe his woman! That *would* be good! The biter bit!" He laughed uproariously and all by himself. The sound quit suddenly as Krell's tall shape went into a crouch.

Culebra cried hastily: "Wait, Krell—wait I meant no off—"

"One mo' crack outa y'u an' I'll put y'u in a coffin!" Like the glint of his teeth, Krell's voice was wicked. "Y'u two bums come in here fo' somethin'—spill it an' git!"

Smoothly Bishop Torril said, "Andros got nicked in that shoot-out with Latham." He directed the words at Barstow, adding: "Thought mebbe you might want to know that."

Barstow nodded. His mind was still on Krell's strange conduct. It was the first time he'd ever seen Dakota Krell scared.

"Well," Torril said, "we figured they'd be plantin' him, come mornin'. Grave Creek rode up an' when he heard about it he allowed he aimed to 'go in an' spit in the face of corpse number two—meanin' Andros. He grabbed open the door an' liked to die of shock. Me, too! There was this Andros up on his hoofs an' comin' towards us like the wrath of Gawd! Right then, Bill Lovin' come bustin' in all lathered up an' spoutin' about that meetin' Rockin' T's called at the Flowerpot. He stopped, quick's he seen Andros standin' there. Andros says: 'Make the most of it!'—"

"All right," snarled Krell. "Y'u've spilled yo' guts. Now dust."

Torril, in the quiet that crept about them, pulled himself two inches straighter. His turning gaze was soft, misleading. But that brown and drooping mustache neither concealed nor in any way glossed over the long and tight compression of his mouth.

"Playin' this game," he drawled, "is bound to brush a man's elbows again' a pretty broad stripe of skunk—but he ain't obliged to take lip off'n 'em."

It was Dakota Krell's glance that slid away.
"Git out! Git out " he gritted.

9

COMPLICATIONS

IN THE stable gloom Andros faced the girl.

He could see the surge of her breasts against the fabric of her tinseled bodice and in the hush her breathing made a hurried, husky whisper. He could glimpse the drawn expression of her cheeks, and their high pallor. Then she was close against him, one hand tightly gripping his arm.

"Andros!" she breathed softly. "Andros—don't leave this town tonight. Don't go!"

"They're expectin' me at the Rockin' T, ma'am—"

"Of course. I know. Of course they'll be expecting you. But don't you *see*? Those men that were in the saloon—they'll lay for you on the trail. They were Latham's friends. They—they'll kill you!"

"I reckon not."

"But they will! I saw it in their eyes!" she wailed. "You're sick—you're hurt—you wouldn't stand a chance! *Please!* For my sake, Andros— *Andros!* My God, boy, don't . . ."

Even through this gloom Andros could see the redness of her lips, the starry, widesprung darkness of her eyes. A mighty handsome girl she was, intelligent and sensitive. Andros could not blame Latham for his jealousy.

But he shook his head. "I'm sorry, ma'am—sorry for everything. But I've got to go—"

"No! *No!*" she cried, and her glance was frantic. "You'll be—"

"I'll have to chance that, ma'am."

Her hand fell from his arm. A great weariness bowed her pale bare shoulders; he could feel the courage drain out of her. She stood silent, with all her muscles slack and with her stare gone helplessly through the open window into night's collecting shadows. It was as though unavailingly she had tried to grasp and hold some thing she knew she could never capture. Her breasts were stilled. She was beside him,

70

scarcely breathing, and Andros saw with a sudden clarity the bitter nature of her aloneness.

They stood a bare three feet apart. The girl had pluck; it was a remembered quality he recalled discerning at San Carlos the night he'd knocked Latham down in the restaurant. She had pluck; but it was now a conviction of her helplessness that stirred him strongest. He wanted to comfort her, to reassure her, but stood silent, abashed by the knowledge that a single word from him would do it—a word he could never give.

Her voice reached out to him softly. "Isn't there anything—?"

He shook his head. "I couldn't do it, ma'am; it wouldn't mean anything—you wouldn't want it that way. You'd hate me an' I'd hate myself. A man's got to live according to his lights."

She stood there, still as death, looking outward into the thickening gloom. She appeared to be pondering his words. And then she whipped around; stood facing him. In her lifted eyes was a strange intentness. It might have been the reflection of some hard and reached decision. Abruptly, inexplicably, looking up at him that way she smiled. "People *are* queer, aren't they? Shall I tell you something? That first night —that night I saw you in San Carlos; remember?—I said, 'Here comes the man I've always dreamed of. . . .' Odd, isn't it? When I was a little girl I lived on a farm in the Missouri bottoms. I used to climb an old tree there and sit and think for hours. What air castles I used to build! I had grand notions; I was going to be a circus queen!"

She laughed a little, wistfully; and Andros smiled.

"I used to dream that some day I would meet the finest man— a tall man, lean and handsome, who would come and woo me like some knight of old and carry me off on his big roan gelding. And, finally, I met a man. Tall, and in his way quite handsome . . . and very artful. And he *did* carry me off. I ran away with him and married him and . . . when I woke up I *hated* him. He made my life a hell for months. Until you came, and killed him, and I realized, too late, it was you that I had dreamed of."

Wistfulness, a forlorn mad passion, lay dangerously near the surface of those final soft-breathed words. Andros could feel the tug and vibrance of her. It was on his lips to say

71

something about Joce Latham when he saw the turn of her shoulders loosen, saw her shrug as Joce himself might have done; a gambler's shrug, concealing much or little.

No words would come to Andros' call when he saw her rueful smiling.

Perhaps she expected none. "Well, thanks for listening," she said abruptly, and took a long, deep breath, as though putting that part behind her. "I thought I'd got all over daydreaming."

She moved closer, near enough for him to have put quick arms about her. The firm, warm pulsing of her breasts was against him briefly. She said: "Andros—do you really care so much for her?"

"Mebbe you better ride that trail again, ma'am."

"Flame Tarnell, I mean. You're working for her—they say you're Rocking T's new range boss." Her glance was grave, and melancholy was a shading in her voice that touched him with a deep despair. "You were a fool to cross Grave Creek Charlie. Tell me true; do you find her so attractive, Andros?"

Andros' cheeks felt hot and flushed. "Why, ma'am," his tone held protest, "you're sure imaginin' things—"

She shook her head. "I'm afraid not. Did I imagine I heard you telling those men no more sheep would cross this Four Peaks country? You were crazy to have told them that. That you should have wanted them stopped I can understand; but to *warn* them that way of your intentions— Red Hat will never rest till he has driven you out or killed you. I know him, Andros. Is Flame Tarnell *worth* such terrible risk?"

Andros had no answer to that and his glance strayed uncomfortably toward the thickened gloom of the stable's rear. It was high time Gallup John was getting done with that saddling. He felt a mighty wish the man would hurry. This girl kept talk beyond his depth. It embarrassed him that she could be so personal. Frankness ceased to be a virtue when shoved that way at a man.

Nor was she done. Her voice came softly, pleading; her hand pulled him round to face her. "Andros!" It was a wail almost, the way she said it. "What has Flame Tarnell to offer that I can't give you better? What—"

He said in desperation. "You're talkin' wild-like, ma'am. You've got this whole play figured wrong. Flame Tarnell owns the ranch I'm roddin'—there's nothin' between us personal!

72

How *could* there be? I'm nothin' but a crazy, driftin' gun-packer—a Salt River ranny with no past a man could talk about an' a mighty sight less in the way of prospects. I'd have no business travelin' double harness even if I was the marryin' kind—which I ain't. Get that foolishness out of your head. This is just a chore—"

"Do you always put such energy into your chores?" she cut dryly. "Is it your habit to let men shoot you and then, when you'd ought to be flat on your back with fever, to go hunting up more enemies so as to give them on a platter the chance . . ." Her voice trailed off with bitter hoplessness. Abruptly, soft and completely pleading, she said: "Oh Andros—"

"Ma'am," he blurted, "you oughtn't talk like that!"

Change ran its darkness through her eyes. She swayed as though whatever cane she'd used to bolster courage now had snapped. Haggard lines of weariness marked her cheeks. The dull indifference of her listless voice depressed him immeasurably. "Why don't you say it?" she asked drearily. "Why don't you tell me I'm a no good slut?"

To hear such talk from this young girl's lips, to see them twisting so bitterly, was more than he could stand. Her words had bitten deep into him and, hardly himself knowing what he meant to do, he was starting toward her when she whirled and, with a queer, choked sob, plunged blindly into the night.

With glance unutterably miserable, with the planes of his high cheeks gone dark and taciturn, Black Clem Andros let her go. There was vast pity in him and a wealth of sympathy, for he understood what was in her mind. But such things could not be, with him. There was nothing he could do for her. Too well he knew that, bitterly.

Gallup John strode from the blackness with no expression on his face and handed him the reins of his saddled horse. He thrust them, unspeaking, into Andros' hands and wheeled away immediately.

Andros stared uncomprehendingly after him, feeling dissatisfied with himself and little knowing what to do about it, and at last got into his saddle.

In the living-room of Barstow's ranch headquarters, these four men for some while stood absolutely still. Krell's dark face was demoniac. He raised his shaking fists. "Get out! God damn you—*git!*"

73

One longer moment Torril eyed him, then turned upon his heel contemptuously and started, with Bronc Culebra following, toward the door.

Krell's hand was one streaked blur of light. Down and up it leaped, and flame jumped from the gleaming tube that showed beyond his knuckled grip. The shot's report rose huge and thunderous.

Torril's spinning body jerked. The hinges of his knees collapsed and dropped him in a crumpled heap.

A hot breath hissed through Culebra's teeth. His slitted eyes were glittering cracks of hate and wild, hot anger. With ash-gray cheeks his body crouched with clawed hands spread above gun butts.

But the feline sneer on Krell's thin lips was mad and wicked as the glow of his eyes. He had one hand still whitely wrapped about the stock of his leveled gun; its gaping muzzle was fixed point-blank on Culebra's chest.

"Are you wantin' some?" he jeered.

* * *

Andros' eyes came painfully open on a room he had never seen before; a room entirely unfamiliar. A single window, dead before him, poured in a flood of warm and lazy light that dappled the sparse and roundabout furnishings with spots of gold that, by their placement, proved the time to be late afternoon.

He was not out of his head, though he had for a moment thought so. His faculties were sufficiently clear to tell him he was in a pine-slat bunk, and its position against one rough log wall was proof he was in a cabin. Some line rider's shack, was his natural thought.

He heard no sound of movement and guessed that he was alone in the place. He lay there quiet for many minutes, absorbing such details as came to view; striving to piece together the forgotten acts that had brought him to this situation.

The dusty floor showed scuffed boot tracks where the litter of broken and discarded gear left any place for foot room. A warped table in the corner held a miscellany of things, the sort of stuff rannies cram in their warsacks; wrinkled underwear tangled with a washed and unwashed smear of socks, a shaving outfit in a leather case, a latigo strap draped over a pair of go-to-hell shirts, a dog-eared tally book, a spool of

74

thread and a packet of rusty needles. An old hat drooped from a peg on the wall.

There was a door at the room's far end and, like the window before him, it stood open. The view disclosed was of shadowed pines with, beyond, the sharp pitch of a timbered slope.

But this told him little, for there was plenty of that kind of country roundabout, he guessed. He saw nothing from which he could compute a notion of his whereabouts.

His faculties were closely taken up with this, for he keenly felt the need of knowledge; but there was a portion of his mind rather irritably striving to connect his being here with what had gone before.

He remembered leaving town. It had been dark at the time. It was almost dark again; therefore it must have been yesterday that he left the ranch to ride into that gun-smoke trouble with Latham. But he had left town; he could plainly recall riding out of it after that embarrassing talk with Grace Latham. He remembered that, and the shot that had whistled past within feel of his ear just after he'd put Long Rope behind. He had ridden and ridden for what seemed hours; but he must have dozed or have been but partly conscious, for this recollection was a hazy thing—disjointed. There was much that had happened after for which he could not account. He had seemed to have been burning up; his veins had writhed with some strange malignant heat, and his limbs had got unwieldy. He remembered how the moon had fled. He recalled the steady roar of the rain, the grateful feel of it soaking him and its impotence to quench the conflagration in his veins. He had a dim thought he must have fallen from his horse.

And that was all.

What events had shaped after that he did not know, nor how he had come here, nor where this was.

He pondered it for quite a while with the buzz of circling flies for accompaniment and the tang of the pines smelling good in his nostrils. Then he saw his clothes on the floor by the table and realized he must be undressed. He hoisted the blanket and peered beneath it to find that another bandage had been added to the one the Doc had bound on him. There was an unpleasant smell to the blanket. Some odor he knew but

75

could not place. He judged this might be a nester's shack and, conjecturing, he dozed.

When he woke again his head was clear. His mind was sharper and a deal of the pain had gone from his side. He felt hungry now and thought considerably about getting up and pawing round to find what sort of food was here. But he slumped down off his elbow quickly. The sweat of that exertion took a long time drying.

He was not as tough as he had figured. And this was odd. He'd been shot plenty times before and never felt so kitten weak.

But he was definitely awake now and his mind got busy. Sunlight, smashing through that window with a renewed brilliance, proved this morning. Another night had gone down the back trail.

He had not been alone all the time he slept, for the yonder door was closed now and there was a spoon and a greasy dish upon the floor nearby. Evidently someone had fed him some kind of broth. Broth! They must believe he was pretty sick. His roving glance observed a bright and cared-for rifle, a .30.30, now standing against the table.

These things he noted subconsciously. His mind was busy with other matters. Such as how he'd better be sending someone to warn the Flowerpot; and how Flame Tarnell would sure be wondering where he'd gone to.

And, thinking of Flame, he thought of other things concerning her! the lithe and supple shadow that she made against the sun, the sound of her voice through changing moods, the courageous spirit and that rugged honesty that shone so patent from all her features. He loved the play of the light in her hair, its midnight blackness and sleek blue luster. It was in his mind some man would win a precious thing in her.

He mused awhile, thus dreaming.

Somehow then his shifting thoughts wheeled his mind to the girl, Grace Latham. A gambler's woman. Grace Latham . . . She had pluck, and something finer he would not let her waste on him. He regretted that it was not in him to be of any use to her, that his capacities did not include the chance of his ever loving her; for he had sensed in her a fullness and strong possibilities for betterment if the right man mated up with her—but he was not that man. They traveled different

76

trails, she and him. A matter of mental viewpoint, perhaps. Each sought a goal beyond attainment; this was what they had in common—the only thing. It was not enough. He saw with clarity the forlornness of her hopes and his, the crass futility of their strivings. Man was born to a course laid out before he was conceived. That which was to be would be; what was not written, no man's efforts could persuade. This was the truth Black Andros had learned from twenty-three years of living.

He sighed, knowing the attraction he possessed for Grace; and sighed the harder for knowing where his own wish lay— for knowing, too, how little could ever come of it. Better far that he and Flame should never meet again.

He had set his hand to violence and could not cut loose of it now. A king of hammer-bangers whom a lesser breed took joy in hunting, when it dared. That members of that glory-loving tribe seldom found that much pure courage, was beside the point; he was a pistol-grabber who was almost legend, and was so marked. He could take no woman into that kind of life. Yet he could not swerve his thoughts from realization that Flame Tarnell would one day be the end of some man's trail.

She'd be the end of his, he knew well enough, if he didn't get her out of mind. You could not mix day-dreams and gun-play.

His thoughts were abruptly terminated by the sound of a crunching boot. It came from beyond the door and, looking that way, Andros saw it open, letting in a gush of sunlight swiftly blocked by the man's black shape. The man stepped in and lounged there eying him. A man in boots and chaps that showed hard usage. There was a scraggle of beard on his hard, burnt face. He wore a low-crowned, broad-rimmed hat and packed a sixshooter in tied-down holster.

He had the look, but he was not a cowman.

Andros knew in that short moment what this smell was on his blanket.

THE MESSAGE

FLAME TARNELL, despite herself, thought much of Andros in the days that followed his departure and Bishop Torril's harsh indictment. Again and again Flame told herself Clem Andros was not the kind of man who had been painted by Barstow's foreman. One fact, though, could not be gotten round. If Andros had found no attraction in the Latham woman's charms why hadn't he returned? He might at least have sent some message. Even a lame excuse, she told herself, was better than none at all.

Day followed dragging day and no word came from him, nor of him. She was too proud to seek out word of him in town; her own men might have given some explanation of his absence had she not been too self-conscious of the feelings he had roused in her to ask. Time crawled and the work got done, but Rocking T was not the place it had been. The glow was gone clean out of it.

Two days ago, determined that Andros had indeed forsaken the job that he had asked for, she had made Tom Flaurity range boss. Tom had joined the outfit just before her father's death. A top hand in every sense, his extreme taciturnity had not made him over-popular and he had got the name of living beneath his hat. There was this, and there were other things that made her doubtful of the wisdom of promoting him. The odd way he sometimes regarded her when he figured she was not looking. There was the toughness of his way with the other cowboys . . . the way he handled horses. Yet, in him, there were attributes of leadership; and so, while not completely trusting him, she had—lacking stauncher stuff—named him boss in the departed Andros' stead.

But all Flame's thoughts were of the absent man. She could not help, looking round her, comparing the place to the way it had been during Andros' so-brief tenure. Andros' presence had brought a new and siren song to her; had colored all her actions and thrust a strange exhilaration upon her that was like some heady wine; it had brought her out of herself and into a vivid, exciting world she had not known existed. Somehow, it seemed, he had shown her how to live, had given her an awakening glimpse of the joy that from true living might be gotten. About the man was an atmosphere, intangible yet intriguing; lusty—a veritable tonic that toned up sluggish blood and filled one with a keen pulsating eagerness, endowing the most forlorn of hopes with the gay regalia of certainty.

He was like some great retaining wall that, soaring into the heavens, kept out the clouds and was impregnable as the secrets God had stored in Davy Jones' locker. In Andros she had sensed that tremendous, unassuming confidence that complements completest knowledge of the frailties of humankind and of oneself, the kind of wisdom locked within an old man's heart.

She had read into some of his actions the taints of callousness, of cynicism and contempt; yet deep within the man himself she had sensed better things convincing her at soul he was a vital force for good—or could be, if he had someone to point the way. She was convinced of the sterling qualities he had screened behind that shell of cynical toughness he presented to the world. That calm tranquility he so usually showed, the very bitterness that seemed so strong a part of him—these combined to reveal him in her mind an extraordinarily colorful, dynamic figure.

The low and muted thud of hoofs from some place yonder presently pulled her from her thoughts. Glancing up, looking out across the wind-ruffled surface of the tank, looking past its farthest edge of cracked and hooftracked gumbo to where the range stretched seared and yellow, she saw the rider. A faint frown put pinched lines between her brows as she watched his leisurely progress. He was riding slow, being careful of his horse in the furnace heat of this midday sun. She was certain she did not know the man. He did not look like a grubline rider. He came with a purpose she was sure, and unaccountably, as she watched him ride in past the tank, there crept over her a premonition of disaster.

She glanced worriedly toward the bunkhouse. None of the crew was in sight, but Tom Flaurity's big bay stood saddled before the foreman's shanty and Flame breathed easier for knowing she was not alone.

Beside the porch the rider stopped. He did not trouble to remove his hat but sat there looking down at her with the thoughts behind his sloe-black eyes inscrutable. He was a little man whose swarthy face was adorned with lean, pinched features.

She left her chair and crossed to the porch-edge, facing him. She looked to read the brand on his horse and saw the man's tight lips quirk faintly. His pony bore no brand; there was dried sweat upon its flanks beneath the crusted dust.

Flame studied the man's face thoughtfully.

He said, "I guess y'u are Miz' Tarnell?"

She nodded.

"I got a note fer y'u," he grunted, fumbling in a pocket. The hand came presently to sight again, and he held out to her a soiled scrap of blue-lined paper obviously torn from someone's tally book.

She took it nervously and read it. With throat gone dry she read again:

Am bad hurt and holed up some place south of Boulder Mountain. Send some food if you can by man who brings this message. Don't come out yourself.

There was neither heading nor signature, but sick at heart Flame knew at once whose hand had scrawled the message. Her cheeks were hot, her veins like ice. She put a hand out weakly to support herself against a post lest this sharp-eyed rider see the shaking of her knees.

"Who gave you this?" she asked when she could trust her voice. "Describe him."

"Well—" the fellow hesitated, rasped a hand across his stubbled jaw. "The gent wasn't givin' out his handle an' he wasn't the kind y'u'd ask such things of. He was sort of tall, a long-geared ranny, kinda wide across the wind. High, flat mug about the color of my saddle. Smoky eyes an' tough as they come—y'u might think a little tougher." He rubbed his jaw and said: "Flagged me over an' said I was to give this note to y'u. Personal. Don't y'u know who sent it?"

His eyes were on her slyly; and she turned her flushed face thankfully when Flaurity came up. The strange rider could not see him, but he said swift and soft, admonishingly: "Leave that fella out of this. I'll wait y'u on the Edwards Park trail where it dips towards Boulder Creek. Don't forget the grub . . ." His voice trailed off as Flaurity stopped beside the porch.

Flaurity's voice was unfavorable as his look. "What's this hombre wantin', ma'am?"

The man turned in his saddle then and said with a cool contempt: "What'd y'u think I'm after, eh? Her money or 'er life?"

"I ain't thinkin'. Spill it quick an' hit the trail."

"I'm in no hurry. I want a job—"

"You'll get no job around here. Pull out."

The rider's lip curled fleeringly. His mean little eyes peered at the girl. "What's this stinkin' scissors-bill—"

"Mosey!" Flaurity said real soft.

The swarthy rider turned his mount. He said across his shoulder: "I wouldn't shame my hawse by bein' found on this spread."

Flaurity stood, a wiry, angular, menacing shape against the sun's bright slanting. He watched that way with stiff-set cheeks till the stranger dropped down into a wash. To Flame he said then, "This country's needin' a clean-up bad; all sorts of riff-raff runnin' loose—"

He stopped, amazedly finding himself alone when he looked round for her. Scowling he eyed the half-closed door leading into the house. His cheeks showed sultry color. Then he shrugged and spat and headed, growling beneath his breath, for the harness shed.

Flame, from back of a window, watched till he went inside. She emerged then, softly, swiftly crossing the porch and, skirting the tank's near side, hurriedly made her way to the mess shack. From the stealth with which she entered it one would never have guessed she owned this ranch and everything upon it. Very softly, with an immense and foreign care, she closed its door. She meant to follow the rider's orders to the letter. Flaurity, the man had said, must not be brought into this.

She left the mess shack ten minutes later with a bundle under her arm. She went to the stable and got her horse. The saddling gave her difficulty; she seemed all thumbs and everything appeared to be conspiring to delay her. She undid her bundle, disclosing neat-wrapped packets that were hurriedly thrust in her saddlebags. She was leading her pony toward the door when sound of voices pulled her up.

Leaving the horse on grounded reins she crept to the door, paused there tensely while she listened with hammering pulses.

Flaurity's voice said suspiciously: "What you wantin' her for?"

Someone laughed. A man's hard tones said roughly: "Get her out here an' quit arguin' with the law!"

The law! Flame felt faintness stealing over her. She fought it back with all her will—with every resource of her strong young body. They must be after Andros; he had killed a man in town—a gambler, Bishop Torril had said. If, somehow, they had discovered that Andros, hurt and somewhere hiding, had sent that stranger to ask her aid, she would need all her wits about her. She must be careful; a single false move might cost Andros his life. They must not guess the tumult their presence here had roused in her. She must rid the place of them swiftly so she could get this food to where the man— Lord God! if she should miss him . . .

She stifled a shudder—dared not think of that.

She stepped out into the sun's hot smash, striving to appear indifferent to the three men sitting saddles yonder insolently eying Flaurity.

From a corner of her eye she caught the sudden turning of their heads.

Flaurity called: "There's some rannies here to see you, ma'am. They allow their business is a heap important. Mebbe you better talk to them—but don't if you don't want to."

She turned then, fully, looking quietly toward them as though constrained by nothing stronger than an idle curiosity. She hoped the three men thought it that, and fought to still her nerves and oust the fluttering that was in her, to calm her agitation lest they see and guess her secret. She tried to face them as Clem Andros would, at ease and coolly tranquil.

Seeing she meant to come no nearer they swung their horses toward her with gaunt Flaurity at their stirrups, belligerence disturbing the set of his freckled features.

They stopped ten paces from her, holding their horses with commands from their knees. From this closer vantage she could see the grip of an excited admiration suddenly coloring and focusing the brash gaze of their leader.

She felt new warmth steal across her cheeks and the leader

grinned. He muttered something about being 'born to blush unseen' and his two companions sniggered.

Flaurity snarled: "That's packin' it far enough, Krell. You've had yore fun. Get down to business or get yore plug-uglies outa here." And he set one hand upon his belt where its fingers brushed his holster.

Krell, a tall lean man with a star, ignored him. His look, and the sleek, quick grace of his movements were remindful of a mountain cat's. His mouth was hard above a rakish jaw and his chin-strapped hat was cuffed at a swaggerish slant across one saturnine eyebrow.

He caught her glance amusedly and doffed the hat with an impudent flourish, bowing low above his saddle. "I'm Sheriff Krell," he said with broad smile, "an' y'u, of course, are Flame Tarnell. I blush to think we've not been acquainted sooner. But a sheriff's duties—" and here he sighed— "sure keep a fella humpin'."

"Of course," she said; and wondered at the evenness of her voice. "Won't you come in and rest awhile? I'm sure the cook—"

"Why, ma'am, that's downright handsome of y'u," Krell said smoothly. "Happens, though, I'm here on business and ain't got a heap of time. We'll leave that pleasure for another day—y'u bet I won't forget it." Still smiling he swung down from the saddle, left his horse on trailing reins.

He looked taller now—tall, almost, as Clem Andros. Thinking of Andros that way helped to calm her trepidation, but she kept her glance upon him, daring not to look away lest he should sense the fright and dismay she was trying so hard to hide from him. "Business . . .?" she said it doubtfully as though she'd no idea what business he could have with her. "I'm afraid we haven't any cattle for sale—"

"It's not that kind of business that's brought me out here, ma'am—an' no one could regret it more than I do. But I've got my duty an' I sure hev got to do it. A complaint has reached me, ma'am, that y'u folks here been stirrin' up trouble, been figurin' to keep the sheep from crossin' back this summer. I been told y'u been connivin' with Spur an' Tadpole, with Lazy J an' some other spreads to organize a vigilance committee."

The glance he put on his deputies brought each man's head around to nod in solemn agreement.

"Things like that cause trouble, ma'am. Y'u ain't cravin' to see blood flow, are you? 'Course y'u ain't—no more than me. I can savvy how y'u been feelin' about these sheep. Blasted nuisance. Ruinashun of the range, they are; I feel the same myself about 'em. But law is law, an' right is on their side jest now. Ain't nothin' we can do about it—y'u nor me nor nobody else. Them sheep got as much right to the grass—"

"As a sheepherder's got in heaven," Flaurity said with comprehension.

A lazy grace marked Krell's slow turning, "*Yo'* chance of heaven is súre goin' to be mighty certain if y'u don't shut that mouth."

He swung back, smiling easily, the rolling of his shoulders reflecting his low opinion of the Rocking T range boss. He continued smoothly, "Like I was saying, ma'am, we can't hev y'u folks stirrin' up no trouble. Election's comin' on, y'u know, an' honest folks is goin' to be needin' all the votes we can get 'em. Range wars is dam bad medicine—ruin business, knocks politics to hell, an' gets wound up with a lot of faces missin'. Y'u know what come of tryin' to buck sheep last year. We don't want no more of that.

"Now I been told yo' foreman has been shootin' off his jaw in town. Said the Rockin' T was takin' measures t' see that no more sheep crossed through here. That talk's plumb crazy! Y'u couldn't no more stop 'em than the devil could make a snowball. Likewise, it's been pointed out to me that y'u hev called a meetin' at Flowerpot."

Krell's cheeks showed bland and smooth as silk. "I'm warnin' y'u to call that meetin' off right now."

Flame eyed him hotly, all her fears forgotten in her sudden indignation. "You know very well there'll be no meeting called at Flowerpot!" she charged bitterly. "You know that ranch was raided and burnt four nights ago—the night that meeting was supposed to have been held. Only Andros' disappearance kept those plans from going through; if that meeting had been held there'd be a different story going the rounds about that raid! Teal's two hands would be alive tonight and Teal would still be round here instead of run off into the brush!"

"Shucks," smiled Krell, "y'u are gettin' all het up, ma'am." He eyed her with a gleaming mockery. "I ain't surprised yo' foreman pulled his pin fo' other parts. I been huntin' that ranny a right long spell an' over consid'rable country. 'F he sets any value on his hide y'u shore hev seen the last of him."

Flame drew herself up stiffly. "Clem Andros is no outlaw. If he were here you'd not dare call him one!"

Krell laughed. "I won't be callin' no lady a liar, ma'am—special one as pretty as y'u are. Shucks! Long as he keeps away from here y'u'll hev no quarrel with me."

He sobered then. His glance rested on her searchingly. "That Flowerpot raid is sure news to me. Seems like folks hereabouts does all their behavin' when I'm round, an' quick's I ain't makes ready to lift hell plumb off its hinges. I been away the las' two weeks on business; been up Ashdale way to see a couple fellas—"

"About a horse, I guess!"

Her scornful tone appeared to bother Krell not at all. He grinned broadly, showing his teeth. "Well, yes, it was. A sorrel horse," he added and the two men with him guffawed.

"If you'd been here tending to your duty—"

"Y'u are dead right, ma'am. I aim to be, from here on out. I sure feel some constrained about that Flowerpot business. I'll be lookin' into it, y'u bet, though I don't guess I can do much now."

"As if you ever *would* do anything to help an honest rancher!" Flame saw the change film across his glance and would have shut her lips on further talk but for the hot resentment pushing her. "That star you pack does not deceive the honest people round here; we know you for the railroad's spy! A man don't have to run with sheep and cattle kings to show which side of his bread is butttred. Not since you've been in office have you once lifted hand to favor a small independent! Everything you've ever done has been an abomination!"

Rash words were those and fully meant. Flame's eyes blazed her scorn of him. Krell's look was coldly saturnine, bright with malicious humor.

It infuriated Flame beyond discretion. "If you weren't backed by the Pool," she accused, "how could you be holding down two star-packing jobs at once? How could you be Long Rope's marshal and Gila County's sheriff?" She took a long, deep breath and said: "I think I'll ask Reb Barstow what he thinks about your politics!"

"That's a right smart notion, ma'am," Krell drawled. "Yes,

sir," he said, swinging up into his saddle with a feline grin, "Y'u do jest that, ma'am, will y'u? Meantime I'll be leavin' these two deputies on yo' place to see y'u don't go to startin' somethin' that might jest mebbe someway embarrass Reb— or get yo'self in trouble."

11

RED HAT

FLAME bit her lip as she stood there staring after him. She was a fool to let her temper drive her into hurling such rash words at him. She had put the man on guard. She had made an enemy of the man who represented all the law there was in this country. A man who would not forget—the timbre of that laugh proclaimed it.

She put a hand to her forehead wearily; it was a worried gesture that pushed back her hair. What was the use of all this grubbing toil?—in this never-ending turmoil that began anew each day? What purpose could there be in a life that held so little of joy and took that little away?

She stiffened, abruptly recalling Clem Andros' plight and the note his messenger had lately brought. A covert glance disclosed Krell's hard-faced deputies unsaddling. Her shoulders stirred impatiently. Her turning glance caught Flaurity watching her; caught his odd, quick-masked expression. The sound of Krell's laughter was still in her ears, and some reflection of its malevolence seemed to have lodged in Flaurity's cheeks. Then he smiled a little, and there was in the curving of his lips a gentleness and reassurance she had not seen there before. Somehow this look of him helped her; she found it good to know that here, at least, was one man she could depend on. She thanked him with her eyes.

Her thoughts flew back to Andros who had such urgent need of her, who was waiting out there somewhere cunning-hidden in the hills—waiting in some brush-choked park or canyon, hiding, hurt—sore in need of this food she had not sent. Needing a woman's care, perhaps!

She felt a renewed surge of fear. What if his messenger

86

no longer waited! What if he had gone and left the meeting place deserted without sign or indication of where she could find Andros!

The accelerated beating of her heart drummed one word frantically: Hurry! Hurry! Hurry!

But she must hide away from Flaurity the hurry she was in —the man had bade her gruffly leave Tom Flaurity out of this. Recalling words and look she almost doubted her new range boss; it were as though they did not trust him . . . But that was absurd! And yet—this man had come from Andros . . . She dared not risk it. She must get the food and go alone.

"Hurry! Hurry! Hurry!" an inner voice kept prompting. "Hurry ere it be too late!"

With impatient move of her shoulders she surveyed the yellow distance; her glance gone narrow, thoughtful. She remarked the depth and color of the stretching evening shadows; the afternoon was nearly gone. Another couple hours or so and night would send its curdling dark to hide this land away complete.

She said: "I think I'll ride," and started for the stable.

Flaurity demurred. "Better wait till after chuck. The boys'll be in—"

"Nonsense! I'll go—"

"Don't seem like you had ort to, ma'am," he argued, following. "Them two deputies Krell left won't be a heap in love with the notion. He put 'em here to watch us. Was they to see you streakin' off—"

He quit as she whirled angrily.

"Well," he shrugged, and said sarcastically: "I'm only the range boss round this place."

He saw at once how ill-timed was that reminder.

Flame's cheeks went gray and she swung lithe shoulders clear around and passed without an answering word inside the stable's doorway. She came out with her saddled horse.

Flaurity's eyes went bright and narrow.

Flame gripped the horn and with one cold look got grimly into the saddle. She whirled the bay, sent him drumming across the yard. The deputies shouted and, with a curse, caught up the gear they'd just stripped from their own broncs.

The bay took the Park trail going fast.

Andros' glance, from where he lay on the pine-slat bunk,

87

had fastened with a definite awareness upon the low-crowned hat of the smiling watcher. If he held scant knowledge of his whereabouts, at least he knew into what hands he'd fallen.

The man who lounged at smiling ease complacently eying him from the open door was the dreaded sheep king, Red Hat!

Red Hat grinned. "You're lookin' better. I thought you'd pull around."

Andros studied him with a taciturn interest. Talmage Vargas, he had heard, had started life under a Red River cart, and thereby learned at a tender age to make the most of everything. He was famous for the definite and unvarying order which he gave his men: "Feed my sheep!" He did not tell them how, nor little cared; he supplied them each with a pistol and a .30.30 rifle, and after that it was up to them.

This revealed the caliber of the man, his insight and his vision. He had learned the pitfalls of other sheepmen and shaped his plans accordingly. No plodding, stick-carrying walkers did their watching over Red Hat's flocks. He hired Chihuahua Mexicans, than whom there are no tougher breed; men who for long, lean years had labored in the yoke of rich hidalgos. He gave them modern weapons, good food and plenty of it, mounted them on swift and enduring horseflesh and did not scorn to toil beside them; and by these things discovered his *pelados* would cross any deadline cowmen set. Their years of slavery and hunger had shaped them well to Vargas' ends; their crowning desire was to kill someone and Vargas' plans gave them plenty of practise.

All this Clem Andros knew from hearsay and, seeing the man before him, believed it. There were no scruples on that dark face. Tall and spare was Talmage Vargas, a man of unpredictable actions, brash of opinion and ready always to fight or carouse at the drop of a hat or the bat of an eyelid. His creed was his own and he flaunted it openly. God, he said, grew grass for the sheepmen and cattle were run by weak-minded fools. The scraggle of beard on his hard, burnt face had never concealed the iron squareness of a jaw that heralded guts and stubborness. He had both; and his chin-strapped hat with its silver concho was symbol of the hardbitten trails his boots had traveled.

Vargas' gaze was long on Andros with a cool and careful probing.

Abruptly he roused and stepped inside. He rested his back

against a wall and from his vantage, with big thumbs hooked in cartridge belt, he chuckled softly. The sound was rich with a real, rare humor.

They were a lot alike, these two.

"So you're Clem Andros, black wolf of the wastelands. I've heard some about you these last few years."

"I've heard a few things of you," Andros said with a frosty twinkle aglint in his stare.

Vargas nodded. "So now you're backin' these two-bit cow fools. For *what*, will you tell me? It's too damned bad. I could go a long ways with a ranny like you. . . ." He paused suggestively and Andros smiled.

But he made no answer. He had burned his bridges. Talk couldn't change it. Nor would Clem Andros if he had the chance.

The sheep king rubbed big shoulders against the wall and stood considering. After some time he said: "You're a fool to take chips in a game like this—to back that bunch of fourflushing nesters. Them cowmen ain't got an earthly chance. Even the cattle barons are backin' me! We got a pool. . . . You've mebbe heard of it?"

"I'm willin' to listen," said Andros grimly.

Vargas waved a hand. "No matter. There's big int'rests backin' us. We got this thing in a nutshell; these shoestring brush-poppers has got to go. Hell, it's progress, Clem—progress. You ought to see that—you been around."

"I can see your point all right."

" 'Course you can. Cattle have always lost to sheep—"

"I grant you that," drawled Andros smoothly. "But this is another time, friend Talmage. Another deal. Things *do* change, you know; it's a part of that progress you been mentionin'."

Vargas' growl was harsh, intolerant. "Dont talk like a rattleweed-smokin' Hopi. If them crazy cow-prodders fight we'll give 'em another dose like Flowerpot. If they're smart they'll pull stakes an' drift. This is day of the sheep. You can't git around it. These droughts have licked the cow crowd for us."

"Why waste time retailin' that to me? I'm just a white chip in a no-limit game."

"You're that all right. You got a rep, too—for fightin'.

89

You couldn't hold out, but you could make this bloody. What's the use? Sheep'll win in the end anyhow—why go an' get yourself planted? These two-bit squirts in this Four Peaks country will bank on the luck of havin' you with 'em; they'll figure your guns to pull 'em through—*an' they can't!* You ought to know that, Andros. A lot of damn fools'll just get 'emselves killed an' you'll not have a goddam thing t' show for it when the fumes an' the gun stink blow away."

Andros with a somber gravity drawing its shadows across his cheeks thought it over, his mouth grim-etched, turning dour and moody. "The probabilities," he finally said, "sure camp on your words. There's a damn good chance you can cut the mustard. But there's one little item you're overlookin'. Most of these rannies you been callin' fools came into this country when it was a heap more wooly than you'll find it now. They were pioneers in the Salt River watershed. They fought the redskins for what they've got; they fought drought an' storm an' wind an' sun. They battled rustlers and range-hog ranchers. They've had plenty of practise; an' when a man fights for somethin', it gains in value. These small spreads ain't countin' their cattle in whopping herds. What little they've got they've nursed along; but it's the land that's really got in their blood. That's somethin' for you to remember, Vargas. The land. It's a part of them—the part they'll die for."

Vargas snorted. "Sure they'll die for it—an' you along with 'em!" He brushed back his mop of red hair with an impatient gesture. "Quit bein' a fool!" he said exasperated. "I've put sheep in cattle country before. A lot of these nesters'll have to be killed—you're right about that; but it's been my experience the bulk of 'em'll roll their tails for other parts without ever waitin' to pop a cartridge. They may love their land but when it comes right down to the pinch they'll love their lives a whole heap better!"

"Then you're goin' through with it?"

Talmage Vargas laughed. "Did you reckon I was just cuttin' a rusty?"

"Well," Andros sighed, "I expect we understand each other. I'm no cut-an'-run hombre, neither." Relaxing on the bunk's pine slats he eyed the big sheepman somberly. "What was it you said about Flowerpot?"

Vargas chuckled. "It's been gutted, bucko. That's how much

90

good your called meetin' done you. The two hands was killed an' Teal himself has run off in the brush. That's just a sample to what we'll give 'em if you go on encouragin' these fools to fight."

Hard set and inscrutable were Andros' cheeks. He lay there eyeing the red-hatted sheepman with a dark smooth glance that gave away nothing.

Vargas said, "You're a large-bore gun, bucko. Plenty large. But one gun ain't enough, as you'll find. I've got this country good as licked right now."

"Time will tell."

Vargas grunted, swung away from the wall. But ere he could speak boots scuffed the planks of the open door's threshold. The man who came in loosed a sneering laugh. "Goin' to spend the whole day argyin'? Bash in his head an' be done with it! Hell's fire— *I'll* do it if you' gone chicken-hearted! I owe that bastard somethin' anyhow!"

Andros said to him, "That's right, Charlie. Why don't you try it?"

Grave Creek stiffened. "You think I couldn't?"

"Oh, I guess you're tough enough to kill a sick man—"

"Why, you—" Grave Creek snarled and his face went livid. He swelled and showed his raw cheeks bloated. He snatched out a gun and started for Andros.

"I'll handle this," drawled Red Hat coldly.

Grave Creek's swiveling eyes were like agate. "You been handlin' this for the past six days an' he's better now than he was when we found 'im! What game are you playin'? This skunk'll git the whole damn range—"

"What he gets is my business—an' the game is, too. You're just a cog in a big wheel, Charlie. You best keep it in mind," remarked Vargas softly.

There was in his glance some dim-seen thing that stopped Grave Creek where he stood and rooted him. The shadow he threw seemed someway shrunken. Color changed in his cheeks and to Andros it seemed that for all his talk this tall, chesty gun fighter was soft inside him, less sure of himself than he'd have men think—an intricate bit of oiled machinery over which dust had settled thickly.

Something then turned Andros' mind off Grave Creek Charlie with a clean abruptness. That unsent letter he had

91

penned to Bocart was in his chaps pocket—torn up, but there to be pieced together and read if these fellows should happen to find it!

His narrowed stare raked Vargas' face. In that moment he almost groaned, for his wheeling glance failed to find his clothes on the floor by the table where he'd formerly seen them. If Red Hat got that letter——

God! Would he never do anything right in this business?

He said in a voice held coolly tranquil: "If you've got no objection I'll sit up for a spell; I'd like to get shut of this blasted dizziness——got to be gettin' my strength back some-time. My side's feelin' itchy so mebbe it's mendin'. Where'd you put my gear?"

"Never mind yore clothes," Grave Creek sneered. "You ain't goin' no place."

"No," grinned Red Hat. "No harm in your sittin' up though, if you want to. Wrap that blanket around you."

It would not do, Andros knew, to balk. He got shakily up on an elbow, paused there, resting, with sweat plainly shining across his forehead. He was not half as well as he'd hoped he was; but he swung his feet to the floor at last and pulled the blanket around his shoulders. He leaned back, closing his eyes, feigning a weakness far in excess of that he was feeling.

"I guess," Vargas said, "you'll not be needin' them duds for awhile."

Andros was thinking of that gleaming .30-30 leaned against the table. He kept his eyes shut for a good three minutes and hoped his face looked pale and drawn. He stared blearily round, trying to simulate the dizziness he had claimel to feel. If he could only get his hands on that yonder rifle . . .

Grave Creek stood curiously watching Vargas who was busily scribbling in a dog-eared tally book. At last Vargas stopped. His lips shaped a grin as he looked it over. He tore out the sheet, put the rest in his pocket. "I guess that'll do."

He looked at Andros. "Last chance, bucko. Throwin' in with me or ain't you?"

Andros didn't bother to answer.

With a snort the sheep king tossed the note to Grave Creek. "Have the cook take that to the Rockin' T. He's to give it to the Tarnell skirt—nobody else. Savvy? I want the girl to come back with him; tell him to read it an' use his head."

Grave Creek, reading, sniggered. "This'll bring 'er all right."

Vargas said, eyeing Andros: "Some gents take a lot of learnin'. I'm goin' to show you, bucko, that when Red Hat wants a thing, Red Hat gets it. Give him a peep at that note, Charlie."

Grave Creek moved to Andros' side. Still grinning, he held the note where Andros could read it. He did. He said to Vargas with curling lip, "You're wastin' time, Mister."

"We'll see."

"That thing won't fool—"

"It'll fool that Tarnell dame—wait an' see. It'll bring her out here quicker'n hell."

"She won't know who it's from—"

"Don't be so modest."

"She won't come, anyway. You've told her not to."

"You don't know much about women, do you?"

Dull color darkened Andros' neck. It took considerable to hold his temper. "You're overratin' her interest, Vargas."

The sheepman grinned. "I don't overrate things. She'll guess it's from you. She'll come out here, too."

"What good will it do you? I give you more sense than to try kidnappin' her, or holdin' her here against her will. What's the answer?"

But Vargas just grinned. "Give the cook the note," he told Grave Creek. "An' when you come back bring Andros' clothes. I kind of got a hankerin' to see what's in 'em."

12

THE CARDS ARE DEALT

FLAURITY knew the need of quick thinking.

Krell's deputies were plenty mad as they dashed for their horses. He didn't blame them much; he was peeved himself, her lighting out that way. There were several alternatives plainly before him. He did not cotton to any one of them.

He shrugged and spat and made after Krell's men.

"No sense gettin' all lathered up, gents. She's jest gone for a ride."

The biggest man swore. "I'll ride her when I get my hands on her!"

"Stow it," the other man growled peremptorily. He led his recaptured horse from the corral. "Slap on your saddle an' let's get goin'."

The big fellow growled but got to work.

"An' *you*," the short deputy said to Flaurity, "had damn' well better be round here when we git back!"

Then they were riding, ripping up the Park trail's yellow dust.

Flaurity waited till they'd gone from sight. He turned then and sprinted for the saddled bronc he had cached behind the foreman's shanty. He caught up the reins, lammed a boot in the stirrup. An instant later they were out of the yard, running hard toward the mountains.

Gallup John Murac, ex-marshal of Quinn River Crossing, made a rigid shadow against the rough adobe of his stable wall. He sat with both calloused hands in his lap and stared toward the wind-scarred front of the late Joce Latham's Golden Ox Saloon. He had held this posture for over an hour, with his hat pulled low to shade his eyes and his dark cheeks showing strictly enigmatic.

Sounds of argument, rising on the heated air, drifted to him from a dive across the road. Yet his face's grim contour showed no change; nor did it when, a little later, he saw Grace Latham leave the Golden Ox and, glancing quickly in either direction, move abruptly toward him. But his pulse stepped up as it always did when this girl came near, and there was a vast approval in the eyes that watched her clean-limbed stride.

She came into the stable and he rose to greet her. There was a heightened color in her cheeks that he knew came not from meeting him this way. Nor was it a thing of the hot sun's doing. Her searching scrutiny met his own gaze steadily.

"John." No hesitation marked her tone. "I've—" she said, and paused then plainly hard put to shape the rest of it. As she stood that way he read the diffidence in her bearing, the troubled light of her dark, level glance. "No," she said before he could speak. "I've no right to ask——"

"I told you once," he reminded gently, "to pass the word if you had any need of me."

"But this——"

"After all," he said, "I'm counted old enough to know my own mind."

They stood that way, silent for awhile, each busied with his own patterned thinking. He showed a faint touch of embarrassment beneath her long, continued scrutiny. He spoke with a voice that was not quite steady. "I—I'd do a lot for you, Grace."

A sharpness and a quick inquiry jumped into the glance she gave him. One hand came up a little uncertainly. Then she took the plunge.

"John— I've discovered where Andros has gone to!"

It was out. She stood there with her agitation evident; not noticing the deepened look of the lines about his firm-lipped mouth. Nor seeing the sudden stillness of his hands, or the hint of pallor raced across his cheeks. She was young and her mind was on her problem.

"There's a man inside the place—" Her shoulder gestured toward the Golden Ox. "A sheepman, I think. He's been talking with the barkeep, bragging. He's pretty drunk—been taking it on since noon. Red Hat's holding Andros prisoner! At the camp near Boulder Mountain!"

She moved a little nearer; said intensely: "John! We've got to do something—we've got to get him out of there!"

Gallup John got up. He stood there looking down at her, then sent his glance out across the range where it showed, framed dark, through the stable doorway. "Yes. I'll saddle up."

"I'm going too—"

"Better if you didn't, mebbe. I might have to unravel some lead."

"I'm going," she said; and followed him back toward the stalls.

The shadow of the tree trunk on the wall was three inches higher ere Grave Creek's returning boots crunched the gravel outside the door. He came in and tossed Red Hat a rolled-up bundle. "There's his clothes. The cook's on his way to the Tarnell place."

He leaned against the door jamb then, watching curiously as Vargas spread Andros' things on the floor and, squatting by them, began his search, systematic and careful.

Andros, looking ahead, could easy see where this was headed for. When Vargas found and repieced the fragments

95

of that letter to Bocart a crisis would be instantly at hand. In such an event his chance of continued life would be slight. If they did not kill him at once, the very least he could look forward to would be close watched incarceration till this question of National Forests was settled for once and for all.

It was in no way a pleasing prospect.

He said, "And where's my hat gone? What'd you do with it?"

"Forget it," grinned Grave Creek. "Where you're goin' they don't need hats."

"Don't be too sure of that," Andros countered. Hunched lower in his blanket he pulled its folds up about his chin.

Vargas frowned. "Go get the hat."

Reluctantly his gun fighter shoved free of the door jamb. He flashed Clem Andros a malevolent look.

Vargas called after him: "When you locate it bring it straight in. I'm doing the hunting." With a grin at Andros he picked up the chaps.

"I can't figure," Andros said, "what you think you're lookin' for. Don't seem like you could be so flat you'd take to robbin' a sick man's pockets. Sheep business must be lookin' mighty daunsy."

But Vargas, still with that faint half-grin, just grunted and kept on hunting. Seconds later his lips stretched wide in a saturnine smirk of triumph as he brought a handful of paper to light. Torn scraps, this was; the letter written by Andros in the hotel to Major Cass Bocart!

"The sheep business is lookin' up," Red Hat said with his grin turning sharp. His squatting figure bent a little forward then and he began ranging the bits of paper in a pattern on the floor.

Sunlight, slanting from the open door, shone full across the sheepman's face, making vivid each tough, a-grin angle, blocking out the square mass of his chin.

Swiftly, Andros knew, this crisis would be shaped for the payoff.

Hunched upon the hard pine bunk he considered this, briefly thinking back to other times when he had known this feel before. This was a little different though. The wound in his side, though nearly healed, was not without certain twinges of pain; and his faith in his abilities was not so great as it had been. He was weakened by the lack of food and the time he'd

96

spent upon his back. These things were dead against him; but worst of all was the definite fact that he had no kind of weapon.

There was this one chance:

Vargas, intent upon his scraps of paper, was forward bent—to all appearances unmindful of him. Grave Creek Charlie was outside someplace, hunting the hat for Vargas.

The will to live was strong in Andros and in this fix, knowing Bocart's need and the trust the Major had placed in him, he would have taken chances greater than these. The need was urgent; it forced him to revalue the odds.

With glance hawk-bright on Vargas crouched in profile but five feet away, he got his legs beneath him and, snail-slow, lowered the blanket. He made no sound. But suddenly Vargas' head swung round. He was reaching for his hip when Andros sprang.

The encompassing hush of limitless space lay like the smash of sunlight all across the Half-Circle Arrow when Barstow opened the ranch house door to a frantic, hard-knuckled pounding. Immediately his burly shoulders tensed, and the voice that pushed his words out was a gutteral, rage-choked snarl. "What are *you* here for?"

Tom Flaurity said with an equal anger, "I've a hunch I'm bein' double-crossed! What was the idea sendin' Krell an' them damn' deputies—"

"Damn you!" Barstow shouted. "Have I got to take it up with *you* every time I make a move in this thing? If I'd got a man instead of a tinhorn to do the chore I give you, I'd of had no need for sendin' Krell! If you'd do your work an'—"

"I planted old Tarnell, didn't I?"

"An' was damn well paid for it, by God! Krell would of done that trick for less than half your price!"

"Tough you didn't think of him sooner!" Flaurity flared. "It's Krell this, an' Krell that till I hate the sound of the bastard's name! You must think a heap o' Flame Tarnell to be sendin' that damn stallion—"

"You shut your caterwaulin' mouth!" roared Barstow, starting for him with big fists clenched. "Another crack like that—"

"Take it easy, Barstow." Flaurity did not back a foot. "Lay paws on me an' I'll see a rope wrapped round yore windpipe, bucko! What I know of your skunk tracks is plenty—savvy? An' I got it down in writin'."

Barstow paused in his forward reaching and with a bitter scowl put down his fists. "So you've got it down in writin', have you?" He stood there stiff, the bully cast of his big roan cheeks inscrutable. "So you've got it down in writin', eh?" His shoulders arched in a left-off shrug, and he swung them round as though to go back inside.

Flaurity's arm shot out to grab him back; and like that he was, with one arm reaching, when Barstow's burly shape came round with his teeth white-showing like a crack of light. One powerful fist smashed Flaurity's jaw with a sound that slapped clear across to the bunkhouse.

Flaurity dropped like a sack and lay loose-stretched on the yellow earth.

When, with a groan, he got one elbow finally under him, Barstow bent and yanked him up. He held him till he got his balance then shoved him at the waiting horse. "Git on that horse an' git back to your ranch, an' quick's you get there tend to that chore! You get him this time or *I*'ll get *you!*"

13

"APOLOGIZE—AN' DO IT QUICK!"

EVEN as the force of Andros' hurtling body struck and smashed the sheep king backwards, Andros discovered what mistake he'd made in estimating Red Hat's character. Vargas was not slow; he was faster than chain lightning. He came up off the floor like a cat. One slashing fist smashed Andros sideways; a second, quick-following, struck his jaw. He lost his balance, crashed against the wall with both arms spread. But his waggling knees had no chance to drop him. Vargas' third blow did it for them. He went down the wall like a busted kite.

One folded knee struck braced and stopped him. He shook his head like a hammered bull and had barely clawed to a half-crouch, blear-eyed, when Vargas closed, intent on the kill. The pummeling of those rock-hard fists drove thought and all conscious action out of him.

The floor was dropping. He clutched at Vargas' middle and hooked clawed fingers in the sheepman's belt and clung there crazily while star after star exploded across the blackness of his mind.

Vargas, breaking the grip at last, backed off. On wabbling hands and knees Andros saw him as the only stationary thing in sight. With the punch fog and the roaring thinning Andros got a leg beneath him. He came upright without hearing any sound save the tempestuous pant of his own gasped breathing.

"You got enough?" said Vargas, grinning.

Andros watched him and could not control the trembling of his punished body. He found these moments of inaction precious. Standing off this sheepman was like tangling with a pile-driver.

But he would not quit.

Vargas saw that. "I'm goin' to put you back in bed, bucko. All set? You're askin' for this," he grunted. He closed in with his long back arched, putting his feet down like a cat.

Of a sudden he leaped with a slashing drive.

At the final moment Andros dropped his lean form slanchways and the sheepman's caroming body pitched over him, tripped upon that outstretched leg. Red Hat hit the wall with a force that shook the entire cabin.

Andros clawed unsteadily erect. He wheeled a whipped-out look at Vargas. But Red Hat lay unmoving. There was bright red blood in his tangled hair.

Andros' head throbbed madly from the punishment of Vargas' blows. He felt weak and sick and dizzy. There was a palsied shake in every limb. But he dared not waste a second. Where Grave Creek had gone he had no notion, but the man would not be away much longer. When he came back it behooved Clem Andros to be ready for him.

He caught up his trousers, pulled them on and buckled his chaps over them. He stamped into his boots while he buttoned the shirt across his chest.

He was reaching for Vargas' pistol when the scuff of boots crossed the boards outside. He dived for the gun. His fingers were just touching its grip when Grave Creek appeared in the doorway. Grave Creek yelled and slammed for leather.

Andros' spinning leap was lightning. Even as Grave Creek fired flame seared from Andros' pointing hand. One shot and, instantly, another pounded the room with sullen thunder.

Dust jumped from the front of Grave Creek's shirt. He staggered. One flailed arm tried to catch the doorframe, but it did no good. The hinges of his knees let go and spilled him backward down the steps.

He stayed where he stopped and did not move.

Andros drew a shaky breath. He came erect slowly. His cheeks and neck were agleam with sweat. All his muscles were slack and jerky. He quit looking at the man, wheeling to learn if Vargas had stirred.

Vargas had not. The blood was beginning to clot in his hair; aside from that there was no change apparent in the sheepman's posture.

For seconds longer Andros eyed him warily with eyes gone somber, the lines of his face completely grave. After which he turned away and rummaged the shack for his belt and guns. He found the belt and its scabbards but the pistols were gone. He ran over its cartridges quickly, then strapped it snugly round his waist and holstered Vargas' sixgun.

He stared once more at the shape on the steps. He could look back now and see that it had had to be this way; ever since that first encounter on Long Rope's street he had known sometime he would have to kill him. Grave Creek's injured vanity, his towering egotism would never have let it stop at less.

Andros wearily shook his head. The ways of a man caught up with him. Like Grave Creek he had lived too long by the gun to think different. Some place, some time, Black Andros too would meet a man whose hand was just that trifle faster —a man like Latham, but whose aim would be surer.

Well, so be it.

Then his shoulders stirred impatiently. He had better be getting out of this.

He picked up the .30-.30 that was on the floor by the table; cast a final glance at Vargas. The man was still out—probably would be for some time. He must have hit that wall with his head, Andros thought. But he would come to presently, or some one of his men would be along and find him.

It would not be good if he found Clem Andros.

Prudence counseled he tie the man, but he was too impatient to linger longer. Flame Tarnell was in his mind—and Red Hat's trickery. He must find her swiftly. Even now she might be riding —decoyed by the cook and that lying message.

100

The nails of Andros' clenched fists bit his palms. If she cared at all Flame would read that note as a challenge. Every instinct of her clean young life would be outraged by the picture painted by Red Hat's note. She would . . .

He closed his mind against that vision; and hurried out.

The sun smashed hotly across his shoulders—a blessed feeling to a man who for six long days, and six longer nights, had lain flat on his back, inactive, beneath a sheepman's blankets.

His side was sore and his bones ached badly, but his one concern was Flame Tarnell. He glanced at his shadow.

It was four o'clock.

This was enemy country. Red Hat's men must know he'd been prisoner; they would shoot on sight. An instinct—an overpowering need—of self-preservation warned him to be careful and he sent a long, probing look about him; at those ridges cutting the skyline yonder, at the brooding bulk that was Boulder Mountain, at the yellow earth and its seared new grass.

All the ways of his life had taught him caution; he stood awhile, stiff-placed, absorbed—gleaning impressions from the things he saw. There were many horse tracks on this ground; no sign of sheep. Bootprints were here in plenty with their heels deep-driven in the soft adobe. Some led toward a spring, others made a beaten path to the corral off yonder beside the alders.

There were broncs penned up in that pole enclosure. His own was there, but he dared not rope it out quite yet. Another cabin stood off to the left; there might be a man, or men, inside. He had to know. And he wanted one look for Bocart's pistol—the one Andros knew had belonged to Krell. If it was there to be found he'd no intention of leaving it.

The door was ajar. He shoved it inward with a kick of his boot and stood, gun drawn, awaiting action. But nothing happened. He stepped inside.

The shack was deserted. Cook shack, looked like. He looked round swiftly. Rusty stove. Rickety cupboard. Empty pail and unwashed dishes piled on a bench. Nothing here. Whoever had found him that night on the range had probably stolen the gun and slicker. He thrust a hand at hip pocket. They'd got his wallet, too.

He stared around outside for Vargas' and Grave Creek's horses; but he saw no saddled broncs in sight. Evidently they'd pulled off their gear and put the horses in the corral with the rest. There was a kak-pole yonder with three saddles on it. One was his own. He shouldered it, opened the corral gate. He dropped his hull, strode inside, shaking out a loop.

Six days of inaction had slowed his hand. He was awkward from the battering Red Hat's fists had given him. Accepting these facts, his face showed grim. Three minutes it had taken him to catch and saddle this pony. A man's ways caught up with him. . . .

He gathered the gelding's reins in left hand and reached for the horn—stopped taut as a bowstring. Rough wind shouldered across the flat, throwing its soughing through the needled pine branches. Faintly through it rolled the muffled drumming of distant hoof-beats. Loud, then soft, then loud again—coming nearer.

Two horses. They were running fast.

He waited no longer. He piled into the saddle and sent the gelding into a beaten trail that angled north-westward through the pine stand.

Flame Tarnell rode worriedly along the dipping, twisting humus-covered trail that swung its circle south of Boulder Mountain. Many times as she urged her horse after Andros' dour messenger her anxious eyes lifted to scan the four peaks that, yonder, darkly thrust themselves against the cloud-flecked sky. She was filled with a strange, oppressing restlessness; vague apprehensions that would not be shaken off.

She studied the night-blurred back of the man before her with a deepening curiosity. Strange messenger for Andros to have sent, she thought; but then recalled he had probably had no choice. The man had come within hailing distance of his hideout and Andros, knowing not when chance might bring another, had been forced to use him.

This was convincing logic, but someway it did not satisfy her.

The man ahead brusquely said, "Gettin' tired?"

"I'll make out."

He muttered something which the wind whipped away and a moment later increased the pace. They galloped steadily for twenty minutes. A fringe of trees loomed dark before them. She saw his hand raised through the murk and his horse slowed

102

down, dropped back beside her. "We'll walk through this. You'll be talkin' with this guy pretty quick now."

She ought to feel glad, exultant, she thought. Her resentment of Andros' neglect had vanished when she read the note. He hadn't been able to get in touch with her. She understood his silence now.

Yet his messenger's words brought only dread.

She could not guess why this should be. Apprehension gnawed at her. Unaccountably she was filled with foreboding.

She tightened her grip of the reins and shivered. She slowed her horse until a larger interval stretched out between herself and the man ahead. For moments she lost sight of him. Then she rounded a bend in the tree-lined trail and found herself in a ghostly basin—a pocket whose pallid floor was studded with the red-tipped wands of ocatilla. Her escort was waiting by a Joshua tree.

He said: "Stick close—we turn here. The trail's—"

She said, "This looks like Ballantine Can——"

He cut her off with a heightened curtness. "We ain't takin' the Ballantine trail." He turned his horse. "Come on," he said.

"Are you heading for Little Pine Flat?"

That wheeled him square around in the saddle. "Bring that horse up closer."

She kneed her horse. The man's hand shot out and caught its cheek strap. The animal snorted—danced three sideward steps. He forced it round till its saddle was beside his own. His beard-stubbled face showed with greater clarity. She saw the gleam in his narrowed, squinting stare.

"Yes?" Only her will kept that single word free of tremor.

"I'll take yo' gun," he said; and before she could move to stop him he had lifted the pistol out of her holster. Then he settled back, thrusting the weapon inside the waistband of his trousers. "Y'u'll be able to keep up better now, I reckon. Ride a lot lighter without that hogleg."

With deadly calm she asked, "What was your idea in doing that? Am I a prisoner——"

"If y'u are," he jeered, "y'u've got no kick. I told y'u plenty that y'u wasn't wanted—but y'u *would* come."

Flame drew one quick, taut breath and stared at him.

The man laughed. "No sense gettin' riled. Y'u're here now —better make the best of it. Yo' been cravin' to see that fella,

103

an'y'u're goin' to. We've got him holed up in Red Hat's sheep camp."

He chuckled smugly. "Andros said that note wouldn't fetch y'u. Red Hat knowed—"

He swayed in the saddle, wildly clutched for the horn as Flame's spurred horse drove into his own. Flame's slashing quirt cut whistling sound that stopped at his face. He cringed, wild, swearing. Then swore again—ripped the quirt from her hand. "By Gawd," he snarled, "I'll learn y'u somethin'!"

He was grabbing a violent hold on her when a cold, flat voice said:

"Apologize—*an' do it quick!*"

14

THE BOARDS OF A CABIN FLOOR

FLAME felt Andros' messenger stiffen. Through the ghostly gloom she saw the rolling whites of his startled eyes—saw the livid marks of her quirt on his cheek. His insucked breath was a chill-clawed sound. He let her go with a hoarse-snarled oath and rocked back into his saddle with his right hand streaking hipward.

"If you're faster than Grave Creek keep on reachin'."

Flame Tarnell hysterically stifled an impulse toward laughter. The stiffness of the man's stopped shape was ludicrous. She watched him slowly turn in his saddle, slit eyes peering for the speaker's shape.

She knew that voice—it belonged to Andros. She could see that this man, too, suspected it. His edgy turning showed a visible caution. His eyes were stretched wide and his face was chalky.

A wild exultation rushed through Flame. It crammed her lungs and threatened to stifle her; but she was *glad, glad, glad!* She knew a mighty joy. Black Andros was free and very much alive; and all the world was filled with glory!

Cold fear blanched the cheeks of the man before her. If there was glory about him he saw no part of it. He cringed like a dog and his hands were shaking. Flame reveled in the

104

knowledge. Black Andros had a way this man could understand!

She did not turn to seek Andros out; she watched the pseudo guide with an alive, malicious interest. She would not let Andros shoot him, but she meant him to think Andros would to the last. It was a fate he richly deserved and had merited.

No motion swayed the man's stiff shape. His hand still hung where it had stopped by his belt. His upper body was forward crouched and his frightened gaze watched Andros fixedly.

"I'm still waitin' for that apology, mister."

"I—I'm sure beggin' the lady's pardon—"

"For decoyin' her out here?"

"For decoyin' her out here—"

"An' for takin' her gun?"

"An' for takin' her gun—"

"An' particular for what you was just fixin' to do?"

"Yeah. F-For what I w-was fixin' to do—*Gawd, yes!*"

"That satisfactory, ma'am?"

Flame nodded, too filled with the tumult of this thing and of her thoughts to speak.

But Andros seemed to understand.

"All right, friend. Drop that gun," he ordered; and a feel of change lashed across the gloom.

The man licked dry lips. His eyes jerked round in searching stabs that seemed to hunt for some way out. All the brashness seemed drained out of him. He was filled with desperation.

The night, Flame thought, seemed abruptly colder. She wondered what things the treacherous messenger read in Clem Andros' look. She watched him gingerly take the gun from his holster.

"Throw it into that pear thicket," Andros bade quietly.

The man's hesitation was plainly apparent. Flame guessed how much he wanted to turn the pistol in his hand till its muzzle eyed Andros. But he didn't dare. With a raking groan he tossed it from him.

Flame looked at Andros then.

He stood so near she could almost have touched him. He stood tipped a little forward. His haggard cheeks showed no emotion. But his gaze was smokily hot and bitter and all his weight seemed to rest on the balls of his feet.

"Climb off that horse."

Awkwardly the man obeyed. He stood beside the pony nervously, tight of lip and watchful. Slow lights burned in his glinting stare.

"What y'u fixin' t' do?" he blurted.

"What do you think I'd ought to do?"

The man had no answer for that. Flame saw him tremble.

"I'm goin' to send you back to Vargas," Andros told him. "You seem pretty handy at deliverin' messages. Tell Red Hat this: No sheep will cross the Four Peaks range. Get goin'."

It was not till Flame saw the sheepman turning that she remembered he still had the pistol he'd taken away from her. It was too late then—*his shoulders were swinging in a vicious arc*.

Her scream and the shot rang out together.

It was Andros' gun that threw the flash; she saw the glint of his teeth in the gun's explosion.

The little man staggered. He reeled three steps and hung there, swaying. He was trying to speak but no words came though the groan welled out of him. And suddenly he was down, a dark still shape beneath the Joshua.

Flame felt the tug of Andros' glance but she would not look at him. Deliberately she turned her back on him.

His voice reached out gruffly. "What's wrong? Good Lord! You don't think I engineered that, do you?"

Flame said stiffly: "Yes. That's exactly what I think!"

He said impatiently, "Don't be a fool!" and she heard him coming toward her.

She could have hugged him three minutes sooner. Now she was coldly furious, convinced it had been his intention all along to kill the man. She said, bitterly resentful, "Don't come near me!" and turned her face to show him her opinion of a man who would do the contemptuous thing she believed Black Andros had done.

"I've no intention of coming near you," he said; and whirling, she saw that he was approaching the dead man's horse.

His lifted glance regarded her gravely. "You can start on back. I'll be right with you. I think that fellow has my slicker. By the look of them clouds I'd say you'll be needin' it pronto."

She answered icily: "I've one of my own, thank you." But this time, despite the scorn of her tone, she did not turn away. Curiosity compelled her to watch his movements.

106

Her glance stayed on him while he unfolded the slicker behind the dead man's cantle, while he shook it out and examined it. She caught the slight compression of his lips, so close was her own horse to him.

Andros, after looking it over, draped the slicker across an arm and bent above the dead man's side. Presently he rose and Flame could see the glint of something in his hand. She saw him fling the thing aside with an impatient gesture and at once make off toward the pear clump into which the pseudo guide had flung his pistol.

A little grimly she wondered if he were not touched, or something. It would, she thought, be fitting retribution. Why should he be poking into the thorny maze of that prickly pear? Was he hunting for the dead man's gun?

Apparently, he was, for a moment later she saw him straighten with it. She heard his grunt and wondered why he should be staring off into the night with that painfully hunted pistol unregarded in his hand.

Andros wheeled with an impatient lift of his shoulders and came striding back to the dead man's horse. He stood still before it, then caught up its reins and looped them about the saddle horn. Stepping back he slapped the animal smartly, watching as it moved off down the basin.

He put the slicker on and gave a peculiar whistle. His horse loomed in the yonder darkness and came trotting up like a well-trained dog. Stiffly Andros climbed aboard.

"All right," he said.

"Aren't you taking a lot for granted?"

He stared sharply at her, shrugged and swung his pony's head to the backtrail. "Look," he said. "I'm not likin' this any more than you are. But when a chore's to be done there has to be some ranny game to do it. I told you that when I took this job. I said no halfway stuff would cut it."

He regarded her morosely, parallel wrinkles upsetting the smooth pallor of his forehead. "I told you right at the start you'd have to trust my judgment—I said there'd be times when you wouldn't be likin' it none. This is one of them times. I got to play this as I see it. I guess I'm stubborn; but when I take on a job of work I rattle till it's finished."

"Was Joce Latham's woman a job of work?"

She saw the color that bit his cheeks, but his words were

smooth enough. He said, "I guess there's some would call her one." Then, harsh, intolerant, he growled: "Mind tellin' me the name of the polecat that's been packin' tales—"

"I certainly do. I'll not have any more murders on my conscience—"

"So you've got a conscience, have you? I been entertainin' some doubts of it." His glance stabbed across at her darkly. "Let's get this straight. I went into town on business. Joce Latham jumped me and I—" The pause was slight, but it was there. He finished doggedly: "I had to kill him. Leavin' town I was feelin' kind of weak I guess—"

"I don't believe I'm interested," Flame said with lifted chin. "I expect Joce Latham's woman would find—"

"Yes," he said, "I expect she would." Then, savagely: "What do you take me for? You ought to know I've been held prisoner. By Red Hat's crowd. That note—"

"Oh! So you sent that note to me, after all! I might have—"

"If you think I wrote that note—"

"I *know* you wrote it! You proved it when you killed your messenger! You were scared the man might tell me!"

Incredulity was in Andros' look. His gaunt face went suddenly dark. "Okay," he said, "I sent the note. Where do we go from there?"

Flame said, "I'm going *home;* where you go doesn't interest me."

"That's good. I'll trail along then."

Flame wheeled her horse in bitter wrath. "You'd better go back to Latham's woman—you seem to understand her kind."

"I can see I'll never understand *yours!*" Andros said.

They sat their saddles, resentment like a blade between them.

Andros said with a lift of his shoulders: "Probably just as well, at that. A hired hand's got no time to waste thinkin' about his boss—"

"You're not wasting any time of mine. Your name came off my payroll the day you rode in to see Grace Latham—Tom Flaurity's giving the orders at Rockin T these days."

"You seem to have already forgot one of the main things I been tellin' you. I'm the kind of guy that sticks. When I hire on I don't get shucked till all the steers been counted. You can put Flaurity back in the bunkhouse. Or," he finished maliciously, "I'll put him back myself."

He heard the sharp intake of her breath. If she'd had her quirt she'd have struck him sure. "You *gun fighter!* I'm sorry I ever crossed your trail—"

"No sorrier than me," he growled. "You'll have reason to thank your stars I *am* a gun fighter before this thing is finished." He took his resentful look at her. "If you're all through pouring in the broadsides now I expect we better get along. Happens in my hurry gettin' shut of Red Hat's camp I forgot to loose the remuda. So if you ain't hankerin' to see me carve another three-four notches on my guns you better start layin' tracks."

They were near to gunshot of the Rocking T, still riding in the grip of turbulent thoughts, when the first big flattened drops struck down, lashing up the yellow dust, creating sullen mutter in the dim-seen tracery of hemming trees. Flame did not make of this rain an excuse for speech. Clem Andros rode in a black, tight quiet that proclaimed if any talk were started she'd be the one to do it.

Wet horse smell was in his nostrils and the legs of his pants were soaking water where the drip ran off his chaps; but he would not break this riding silence if he never talked again. The things she'd said still rankled, still raked him with their unjust spurs. There was no understanding a woman—the sex was hell any way you took it!

That was a good enough conclusion; but getting Flame out of mind was something else again. It amazed and shamed him to find what hold she still had on his thoughts. He felt meeching as a yellow hound to think he could still feel interest in a girl who had used him so. What kind of pelican was he that his pride could stoop to such admittance? Did girls affect all men like this? A sorry world if it were so!

His bitter glance took in the slicker-covered shape of her; and he went suddenly stiff in the saddle. The recollection that had come to stop him that way in his tracks was staggering. *That note to Bocart!* The torn scraps of it were still where the fight had left them—littering the boards of the cabin floor!

LOW EBB

It was after midnight when the girl and Andros came in sight of the Rocking T. The house was dark, but from the foreman's shanty a light gleamed pale and mistily through the curtain of rain.

"Might's well settle this right now," Andros told himself, and sent his horse across the sloshy yard. He stopped it in the veranda's gloom, swinging down, aware that Flame was wheeling after him.

He strode beneath the dripping eaves, boots squelching on the spongy gumbo, and stepped upon the porch's wet planking. There was measurement of his temper in the way one booted foot sent the shut door banging open.

The place was empty. There were crumbs and an unwashed cup on the table. The coffee pot still held its warmth.

It reminded him of his search for Krell. This was the way it had always been; never once had he come upon a place with Krell still there. Many times he had missed him by this fraction.

Now he was missing Flaurity. There was irony in it for him.

His wheeling shoulders put him face to face with Flame. There was something odd, he thought, in her glance. "So he isn't here," she said, and he'd have sworn that she breathed easier. What had she been afraid of? That he would kill the man? Yes; that was it.

Under his close look her wet cheeks took on color. Resentment raised her chin, and he read nervousness into the gesture with which she pushed the damp hair from her eyes.

He wiped the water off his nose, took off his hat and shook it. This girl's attraction hit him hard. He had to fight it, for her nearness was an unsettling thing. It had the power to make him forget his rancor; it dug up hungers he hadn't known were in him.

She said, "I guess you'll know me next time."

"Did you think I'd ever forget you?" The words came

roughly. Emotion shoved him toward her; and she looked up with a catch of breath when, close, his arms closed round her, crushed her close against him. The wild fragrance of this nearness was too much and he kissed her savagely, exultantly, wild tumult slogging his arteries.

He let her go abuptly, stepping back and suddenly conscious she had offered no resistance. His nerves tingled in this brittle silence; but there was nowhere in him any least regret. He said gustily: "I reckon you won't be forgettin' me, either—"

Her eyes were bright as diamonds. She said, "You *fool!*" and drew a tremulous breath. "Get off this ranch and don't come back here ever!"

The cynical curl of his lean wide lips was the only answer Black Andros made. He went past her through the door and crossed the dark veranda to his horse. He came back with a .30-.30. "See this?" He slapped the dark blue barrel. "You've given out you'll fight if Red Hat's sheep come back. This is Red Hat's answer." He slapped the gun again and said, "You're goin' to find out how they put Old Home Week on in hell. Them Chihuahua gunslicks he's imported—"

She said, "I'm not interes—"

"You better *get* interested! You made your brag you'd fight an' I've played the hand accordin'." His grin was cold and sudden. "You're goin' to fight an' like it!"

"All right, I'll fight—but I don't need any help of yours!"

"You're gettin' it anyway. I told you I was the kind that sticks—"

"Yes. When it comes to forcing unwanted attentions on women you shine with real determination."

The rise and fall of Andros' breathing was the only sign of movement in him. He stood there silent, somberly watching the play of light across her scornful features and wondering how a room could get so cold so quickly.

Fatigue etched heavy lines beneath his bloodshot eyes and brought up in dark shadows across the hollows of his cheeks. A slogging bitterness was in his stare.

He squared his shoulders then. "I'm stickin' anyhow," he said, and wheeled his silver spurs around her to stop suddenly in the doorway, listening, his glance gone into the night with cat-quick vigilance.

111

But all Flame heard was the purr of rain on the roof over-head. It obtruded on the restless quiet, lifting its sullen mumble to a full attack upon the puddled yard, then dropping to a duller mutter through which at last she heard the pound of hoofs.

A cold wind ran the valley. The slogging hoof sound rose in volume. Premonition touched the girl with icy fingers. Where were the sheriff's deputies? Was this the sound of their returning? Where had Flaurity gone to?

Her glance at Andros was sharp with worry.

Time crawled, and through the rain the hoof sound crept ever nearer and nearer.

Andros' grunt was a plain command. "Douse that light an' close the door."

She killed the lamp and stood there looking to where his lean form made a dark, crouched shape against the night's drenched black. It seemed aeons before her straining eyes picked out the blur of advancing horsemen. They had slowed to a walk; the reach of their wind-driven voices was sharp and harsh with anger. They were arguing. One—she believed it the voice of the biggest deputy—growled: "Don't I know a light when I see one?" Another voice snarled, "Where the hell is it now then?"

Then the horses stopped. Some vagary of the wind now dropped the riders' tones to an incomprehensible muttering. Flame said to Andros softly: "You better sharpen up your gun-cutting knife—there's two more notches waiting out there," and was instantly sorry.

Andros' voice ran the murk with a reckless temper. "That's far enough. Sing out your handles—quick!"

She saw then that, dismounted, the deputies had been sneaking forward. They were under thirty feet from the fore-man's shanty when Andros' shout sailed out and stopped them. They crouched in the rain-soaked gloom and seemed to be peering round them uneasily. Then one of them growled: "Who's talkin'?"

"I'm wantin' those handles," Andros said. "I'm countin' three—"

"Shane an' Hodders. Deputy sheriffs."

"Deputies, eh? What are you doin' out here?"

"Sheriff's orders. We got word this crowd was— Say! You ain't seen that female, hev you?"

Andros' voice was grim and earnest. "Climb back into them saddles—"

"What for? We spent half the goddam night—"

"You leavin'?"

"No. By Gawd—"

From the veranda's edge a streak of flame bit wickedly into the rain-soaked dark. Echoes flattened against the buildings hemming the yard. A curse, a squeal and the sloshing splut of sprinting boots swift rose to mingle with the startled snorts of the frightened broncs.

The men had plainly reached their saddles. The big deputy's sulphurous tones sailed back in muttered threats. Once again Andros' lifted rifle put muzzle light across the dark and retreating hoof sound slapped the night. Andros sent his shout ringing after it. "Tell your boss this spread ain't needin' his advice. Next one of you I catch round here will be needin' a coffin though—remember it!"

Andros tried another match to the limp cigarette that hung from his lips and, swearing softly, dropped them both and ground a boot heel on them. A good two hours had passed since Flame had stormed from this cabin, yet Andros' jaw still showed its stubborn angle. The breach between them was grown beyond repair, and it were better so. He could put his mind to the business now. He'd been telling himself that for the last two hours but his mind didn't seem to hear him. It took note, though, of the sudden draft that struck across his neck.

Cat-quick he slewed around to find the door wide open.

Framed against the slanting rain big Flaurity stood with his shoulders pushed grotesquely forward. Water dripped from his sodden coat and he was breathing heavily. Maliciousness was bright in his stare. He said, "You're goin' to stay here *this* time!"

TEMPER

ANDROS' muscles cocked themselves.

Tom Flaurity was on the edge of murder!

Fact and purpose were shouted from a thousand details; that curious posture and balefulness of feature, his parfleche-taut skin, the white-knuckled tenseness of his widespread hands and the undulant flame that redly flared in the vacuous eyes watching Andros. Far too long had Black Clem probed life's hazards and conned the obscure shifts of men to be mistaken now.

Flaurity aimed to kill him, to gun him in cold blood.

Andros sat with twisted torso, held rigid by the knowledge that his slightest move would be, to Flaurity, the signal for unraveling lead. Flaurity's placement had him at a wicked disadvantage. He had turned in his chair at the feel of that damp air, wheeling his head and upper chest to get this look at Flaurity, and so had brought his hands to the left. He wasn't wearing his own two guns, for Red Hat's crowd had taken them. He was packing Red Hat's pistol, and it was holstered on the right. Might as well have been in Frisco for all the good it was like to do him. And besides all this he was still in the chair.

Every twisted nerve yelled protest. But he dared not move.

Rain beat loud on the yard and roof.

He shoved blunt words at Flaurity; sharp breathing packed the words with hurry. "What you doin' here? Where are the men? Where the hell has Red Hat got to? Speak man—don't stand gapin'! Speak up quick!"

The questions pummeled Flaurity like the blows of a blunted crowbar. You could sense the urgency of them battering at his consciousness—could feel them skidding across the armor of his fixed desire.

The copper of his gaze was curdling.

Andros followed his advantage, swearing like a man bad

used. "Damn you, Tom—speak up! Where are those blasted deputies? *You get Latham's note?*"

That last was a touch of genius, for Latham, of course, was dead. But Andros was shouting anything that came to mind; caring little what it was or that it made any sense at all, so it tangled Flaurity in the maze of his slow reactions.

And it worked!

Flaurity's jaw fell open and his eyes showed a stunned bewilderment. Andros jumped to his feet still cursing; and Flaurity, on the defensive and wondering where and how he'd erred, clean lost his advantage and never knew it till, suddenly, Andros grinned.

Andros said, "When you aim to gut a man, do it quick an' get it over—don't stand around swallerin' hogwash."

Flaurity got it, then. His head jerked down and he hit a crouch, and the fingers of his right hand spread; and color spread up from his neck, making wicked stain on his waxpale cheeks.

"Your chance has went," drawled Andros. "You ain't got nothing but a busted flush."

The gnawing agony of choice put twitching lines in Flaurity's face. But he had guts. He said: *"We'll see!"*—and lost his nerve on the instant, for there was Black Andros, gun in hand, with his pistol's muzzle aimed dead center on the dripping third button of Flaurity's coat.

Andros' laugh was softly mocking. Then brashly, recklessly, he twirled his gun by the trigger guard and dropped it back in leather. "Go on," he murmured—"shuck 'em!"

To Flaurity his look seemed cold as ice. He could feel its chill in his own veins, freezing. Short moments gone he had entertained notions—violent and bloodthirsty purpose. He had meant to murder Andros where the fool had sat with his back to the door. That had been his fatal mistake; he should have done it from the rain-drenched darkness of the puddled yard.

The will to murder was in him still, but something balked the nerves of his hands; they would not do what his brain commanded. Desperation's courage had brought him to the brink, but it could not take him over. That bravery was gone, suddenly and completely whelmed in the sweat that bathed his back.

He stood stiff legged and forward tilted—rooted. He could

no more have dragged the heavy gun that sagged his belt than he could have flown. Fear—cold fear had clutched his muscles.

The girl, pistol in hand, peering white-faced through the shack's side window, could see no menace in Andros' pose; it was, in her eyes, the epitome of studied carelessness.

But she was not looking into Andros' eyes. She could not see that rising, falling, wanton flame that was defying, taunting, daring big Flaurity to touch his gun's wet handle.

Flaurity knew himself outsmarted. Andros was not bluffing now. He had it this time, cards and spades.

Spades! The thought made Flaurity cringe.

He writhed at the ease with which this grinning outlander had turned the tables, depriving him of his sure-thing edge. He had thrown the game away by striving to make sense of foolish words that had none.

Cursing himself for that folly he shivered to think of facing Barstow with this tale—then abruptly realized the scant likelihood of ever having again to face Reb Barstow with anything. He roused from his abysmal dread to find Andros plying him again with questions. He stared at the outlander sullenly. A crick in his back ached viciously, but he dared not mend his posture. He hardly dared even draw his breath. And then—but no! He could not believe it! A trick! A sneaking, scurvy, tinhorn trick! A ruse designed to trap him! But he could not choke his quick words back. *"What's that?"*

"Said you better talk fast if you're aimin' to get out of here whole."

It was the first token Flaurity had that Andros might be disposed to let him off without reprisal. Reaction hit him like a backhand blow; relief came near unhinging him. He reached a shaking hand to the doorframe; sagged against it weakly.

He licked dry lips. "A-Ask again—ask that over, will you?"

"Who told the sheep crowd I was callin' a meeting?"

"Not me—not *me!* I'll swear it wasn't me! I—"

"Did you tell Barstow?"

Flaurity hesitated. He darted anxious glances round, but found no comfort. There was no assurance any place. "What was—"

"You heard me. Come on—get at it."

116

Flaurity's glance licked round again. It brought up suddenly, shocked, at the window. He'd seen a white face briefly there—the steely glint of a pistol's barrel.

It left him limp. New sweat stood out on his forehead. Stiff-lipped he whispered, "I—I told him . . . yeah."

Andros' glance got keen and searching. "It was Barstow got you on here, wasn't it? How'd he work it? What'd he tell old Tarnell about you?"

The words came like the stab of a knife. They bugged Flaurity's eyes with terror. Dread closed like a rope about his throat. Too clear he saw where this trail led.

His nerves were scraped too raw for craft. He stared at Andros numbly.

"Come on—I want the truth."

But softness was a mask with Andros; it could not deceive Flaurity further. The glove was off, the hand revealed. Flaurity tore the collar of his shirt open, panting. He could not get rope's feel from his neck. He cringed away from Andros' stare.

Andros dropped a hand to his holstered pistol. "The choice," he said with summer's mildness, "is entirely yours, Mister Flaurity."

Flaurity broke.

Contempt curled Andros' lips. It was not a pretty thing he saw.

"Come! Get it over, man! Barstow got you this job here. He was pretty thick with Tarnell them days. He wanted Tarnell out of the way—"

"I didn't savvy that till later. He said—"

"I don't give a damn what he said! The truth is what I want from you, Flaurity. Regardless of the details, you killed Flame's father—"

"It's a lie. I never!" cried Flaurity hoarsely. "Swear to *Gawd* I didn't!" His face was like a gaub of putty. "It was Dakota!" he whined desperately. "Dakota—I can *prove* it was Da—"

"Don't bother."

An odd look showed in Andros' stare. It went through and beyond big Flaurity; it was as though the man weren't there. And Andros' voice was even more strange. "Get aboard your bronc an' make tracks—far apart ones that'll take you places. Don't linger an' don't stop."

Like a whipped cur Flaurity left.

Long moments after the last dim echo of Flaurity's leaving had been drowned in the slogging rain, Black Andros stood there, chin on chest.

But presently he roused and set about the cleaning of the gun he'd taken from Red Hat's holster. He got a box of cartridges from the cupboard and filled the loops of his gun belt. An edgy restiveness marked all his movements.

"Dakota, eh? So Barstow's got a Dakota on his payroll. And Bocart had a Dakota's sixgun. Hmm . . . Dakota. I expect we better see," he murmured, and slid broad shoulders into his slicker. He pulled the brim of his soggy hat down low across his eyes and stepped through the open doorway, so full of what he was thinking as to be oblivious to the danger of that lamplight back of him.

At veranda's edge he paused, confronted by an unexpected figure. "What you doin' out here in the rain?"

It was Flame Tarnell. He could see her shiver. By the refracted glow from the shack's lit lamp he could see how pale, how drawn was her look. There were circles under her eyes, dark smudges; and her glance was strange—oddly different. He could feel the shake of her hand on his arm.

"Clem . . ." Her voice was husky. "Let's be friends again."

He stared at her sharply. She seemed to mean it. For that one instant exultation gripped him. He forgot all rancor—his just resentment; remembering only the wild warm feel of her lips against his.

She said, "Let's put away our differences; the mean things we've said. Let's go back to where we left off the night we met."

The thrill of remembrance fell away from him. This was his curse—this need for detail that must ever probe beyond spoken words for the thing that was back of them, the motive or impulse that gave them birth. He paused, considering; and shook his head.

"It's a little late for that."

"But Clem—"

"A man can't go back. He can only go forward—or stand still and rot."

Wheeling, he reached for his saddle.

"Where are you going?"

118

Her sharp words swung him round. He said bleakly, "I'm takin' care of a chore—"

"You're going to Barstow's!"

"You called the turn. What—"

"But you *can't!* I won't let you! I heard what Flaurity told you and—"

"Eavesdropper, eh?"

He caught the flash of her eyes—her wild anger. "I own this spread and I've a right to know what's going on!"

"You know now."

"No thanks to you!"

"I want no thanks." Again he turned, reaching up for the saddle; but she whirled him round.

"Aren't you satisfied? Haven't you done enough? You can't believe those lies about Barstow— Surely you . . . Why, he's all I've left to turn to!—the one person who's stood by me from the start. If you hadn't come that night and got me all stirred up with your talk about his help I'd be married to him now—"

"An' still regrettin' it, like enough. The man's a crook," said Andros bluntly. "Why don't you quit this damn play-actin' an' face the facts He's thrown over all his small-fry friends; he's playin' in a big game now—playin' to win. I'll give him benefit of doubt—say he was an up-an'-comin' square-shooter once. But he's a hell of a long way from bein' one now! A gila monster could waddle right over him an' never touch! He's got one virtue—the determination of a mule. That's the most I can say for him."

"Do you always talk about people who are not around?"

"Call this a rehearsal; I'll tell him to his face. The man's rotten to the core! Why d'you suppose the sheepmen have kept their woollies off his grass? Because they're 'fraid of him?—because he's got more hands than you? Don't make me laugh! It's because he's a part of the Pool—that's why! The politics pool; the Big Interests' pool. The sheepmen, lumbermen, railroads an' big cattle barons that want to spike the Salt River watershed—the crowd that's fighting the National Forests! Barstow's the cattle kings' rep in that bunch!"

She didn't believe him; and said so, hotly. Her blue eyes flashed and she said: "I don't believe a word of it!"

"How much of this range do you own?" he said grimly.

119

"Two or three hundred acres—"

"Patented? Got title to it?"

"Certainly."

"How much range do you normally run on?"

"Ten or twelve miles, I suppose, most generally—"

"But you've got title to around three hundred acres? All right," Andros said, "I'm going to tell you somethin'. Your fine Reb Barstow's after that title."

The brittle sound of her laugh was derisive. "Are you *crazy*? Reb's got more range than he can use right now—"

"Right now, mebbe. But it's the title he's after. Else why would he be in such a sweat to get married? Didn't he go stormin' off like a wet potato when you wouldn't up and marry him—"

"I don't care to discuss that," she said disdainfully. "Your manners—"

"Manners be damned!" Andros flashed, and stopped. Flame looked as though she were going to slap him. "Go on," he said. "Mebbe it'll make you feel better. Has your fine friend been around since?"

She wheeled away from him—but not before he had seen his answer. "I see he ain't," he said, darkly satisfied.

She came square around. "He's been here twice!"

"Fine! But he came to do some more arguin'."

He could see by her face that Barstow had. He said, "I guess I better tell you a few. 'Twouldn't be brotherly to let you tie up to that kind of lobo without—"

"I won't listen to your vicious lies—"

"I'll tell 'em anyway." There was a stubborn jut to Andros' jaw. "Ordinarily I ain't much of a hand for—"

"Don't you think," she threw her protest at him, "I'm old enough to judge for myself what is best for myself?"

He didn't; but he was beginning to realize argument was useless. He eyed her dourly. With a shrug he sighed. "All right. Go ahead. It's not my funeral. If you're bound an' determined to ruin your life—"

He stopped when he saw the curl of her lips. He stopped and stood there irresolute, thinking back to the night of their fateful meeting. Much had happened in the time since sped, but little of aid to the small rancher's cause, and nothing at all toward the winding up of the chore Bocart had set him.

And there was that cursed note that he'd left in the cabin; Vargas, ere now, would have patched it and read it.

His shoulders stirred and changed thinking ran its darker shades across his cheekbones. His lifted glance caught Flame's regard. She was stepping closer with one hand toward him and lamp's light bright on her rain-wet face.

"Is fighting Reb really necessary, Clem? Can't you find some other way—"

He said morosely, "I told you once. I'll do what I have to do—hell or high water."

"Are you sure it isn't just plain, mean spite?"

"Spite!" He laughed shortly. "I've got no spite against Barstow. He's swimmin' in water that's over his head. I'm goin' to warn him out while he still can get out."

"You're sure it's not just me that moves you?"

"You don't enter into it, Flame. You cut no ice one way or the other."

It was Andros' unhappy faculty to rub her ever the wrong, rough way. And her pride was strong—as strong as his. But she humbled it. "Clem, leave Barstow out of this. For my sake, let it drop."

"You think a heap of that bull-headed Dutchman, don't you?"

So careless he was with his words—so roughshod. So blind he could be in the grip of temper.

She pulled her chin up, bitterly watching him. "Will you?"

"No!" he said curtly; swung up in his saddle.

Her voice was a whisper, but strong to reach him. "You better take the advice you left Flaurity. Don't come back. There'll be nothing for you here."

He showed her a twisted smile.

"At least," he said, "there'll be men to kill."

17

JOLT

A LUMPY COUCH draped with a faded blanket was shoved against one wall of Barstow's ranch office. He was seated on it, scowling. A contributing cause to his ill-humor was the

121

amount of good hard money he had frittered away without getting one inch closer to the goal that spurred his every ambition. First there was no small sum he'd given Flaurity for getting old Tarnell out of the way—and he was far from certain it was Flaurity who'd done it; then there was the extra cash it continually cost him to keep the fool on the Tarnell payroll so that he might keep informed of what went on there. There was the money, too, that Cranston had cost him. Good hard cash thrown down the spout. Flame was still putting him off—still stalling. And he had just made an astounding discovery: he was actually becoming *interested* in the girl!

It was phenomenal in a man of his cold temperament. He had never felt the desire that actuated Krell, for instance. Krell's many and varied affairs had only curled his lips in scorn. He'd told Krell more than once to quit mixing women and business. And here he was in Krell's own stable.

It was incredible!

Particularly when he thought of how she'd turned him down three times hand-running! *That,* of course, was Andros' doings! She was nuts about the fellow—and him too dumb to savvy!

He poured another drink from the bottle. Damn bad habit, whisky.

He drank, and his scowl grew blacker as he thought of Andros. Things had been going sweet till that damned drifting gunslick had stumbled in. Why had he come here? Why did he stay? What was there in it for him? Flame Tarnell hadn't hardly more than enough to keep her taxes paid. She couldn't be paying the man in money. . . .

He jerked straight up of a sudden, jolted by a nasty thought. So *that* was the way of it, was it? His cheeks took fire from the fury in him. The tumbler cracked in his hand and with a curse he hurled it from him. Sell him out, would she? By God, he'd show her! He'd get her ranch and he'd get her, too!

It was commentary on Barstow's character that he no longer thought of marrying Flame. He would get what he wanted and afterwards it might be amusing to see what Krell would do with her. Krell had a way with women.

Barstow smiled a little, wickedly. All dogs had their day. Andros' luck should cost him high. God, how he hated that drifting gun-packer! It was the man's cool, easy imperturbability that first had roused his antagonism; but he would

122

think of a way to humble him. If Krell and Flaurity between them weren't sufficient to rid him of the fellow, some other means should be found.

He thought of several ingenious tricks himself, but discarded them as being too hard or too risky of accomplishment. There was a deterring influence in the remembered look of Andros' stare. Not that he was afraid of the man—*Hell, no!* But there was no getting around the fact that Andros' eyes were the coldest he had ever seen. They had a way of getting inside a man's guard—of turning his boldest resolves to water.

Barstow polished off the bottle and set it down with care. There was a nervous flutter got loose in his chest; he was suddenly taut-strung and short of breath. There was a shake to his hands and he braced them, scowling. And still he listened, hunched like a mouse on the couch, eyes darting.

He saw nothing, heard nothing. The storm lashed down with an increased loudness, and the cold of this room crept into his veins. There were eyes upon him—hard eyes probing. He wrenched his chin around and stared.

Bronc Culebra grinned from the doorway.

Temper blazed from Barstow's eyes. *"Knock* when you want in, damn you!"

"Feelin' proddy, ain't you? Mebbe you ain't sleepin' well—"

"Never mind! What do you want here?"

Dark, lean-carved, Bronc Culebra stepped inside with a panther grace and booted the door shut after him. He got his back against a wall without taking his glance off Barstow. Hooking thumbs in his cartridge belt he regarded his boss with the confidence of one who knew his position well.

"I been doin' a mite of thinkin', Reb. This thing won't last. Gov'ment'll step in sure; if the Pool gets licked we'll get licked too. You been diggin' in on Rockin' T, an' this guy, Andros, won't be likin' it. You got too many irons in the fire."

He shifted his shoulders to a greater comfort. "Been thinkin' about death, mostly, an' how one thing's led into another; an' how Tarnell got killed, an' Cranston, Latham an' Bishop Torril. This range is sure a heap onhealthy."

Barstow's shoulders expressed impatience. "How much longer you figurin' to rant?"

"Not much. I'm buildin' up something' for you, Reb; I'm wantin' you to get the picture." Culebra's eyes showed a fleeting irony. " 'Mong other things I been thinkin' how you got Flaurity switched to the Rockin' T—an' how Tarnell cashed his chips quick after. I'm thinkin' a lot about this Krell that you got made a sheriff around here; an' how you've sudden got sweet on Flame— But mostly, Reb, I been thinkin' it's time I got a raise."

Ruddy color crossed Barstow's face. He surged to his feet.

Culebra smiled coldly. "Of course," he said, "I'm appreciatin' how you hev elevated me to Torril's place. But eighty bucks is chicken feed to a guy that's got a mind like mine. Kinda strikes me, Reb, I'd be a pretty good ranny for you to keep around."

"You tryin' to blackmail me?"

"I don't see no call fer ugly words," Culebra said.

Barstow watched him a minute, darkly. "Suppose I don't— Why, you damn' whelp! I'm payin' you more'n you're worth right now!"

"That's a matter of opinion." Culebra set one hand on the handle of his sixshooter. "I could trade notions easy with the Rockin' T—with this guy, Andros. With the Gov'ment, mebbe —I expect they'd be some interested in you. I ain't no fool, Barstow! There's somethin' on that Tarnell spread you're wantin' mighty bad, I'm allowin'. What one guy can find, another can, too. Better think my proposition over."

Barstow's breath was a harsh-pulled sound. "How much?"

"How much you got?— Well, hell," Culebra's grin was a cool, bland thing, "I ain't no plain damn robber, Reb. I expect five grand would do . . . fer now."

Barstow's stare glittered ominously. "For now, eh? An' tomorrow, I guess—"

"I wouldn't be worryin' about tomorrow, Reb. You mightn't be round tomorrow."

"You mightn't yourself. I'm not payin', friend." Barstow grinned across his folded arms.

Culebra also smiled a little.

Rain made the only sound in the room.

Restlessness tugged Barstow's lips. Culebra's shifted posture laid its restraint on Barstow. Culebra said, "You'll look pretty good in striped canvas."

A sigh welled out of Barstow. "I was only funnin', Bronc. I'll pay you, of course." He wheeled off toward a desk in the corner. "I've got the money right here now—"

124

He'd got his left hip out of Culebra's sight. He was reaching for it lightning-fast when a whisper of breath from Culebra stopped him, turned him, stayed his hand. His glance jarred after the other man's. All the color fell out of his face.

Andros lounged in the doorway watching them.

18

"I SHOOT TO KILL!"

WITH AN impatient curse Vargas wheeled from the rain-lashed blackness of the window and crossed to stand bitter-faced above the table where paper fragments made a lettersize square, white against the dusty wood. He grimly gathered the scraps and stowed them in a pocket of his shirt and stood a while longer, scowling. He worried a snatch from some doleful tune. A tough man, Vargas, and one quick to recognize that fibre in his fellows.

A vaquero-garbed man stamped in, dripping water. "We'ave buried—"

Vargas said, "Send in that new ranny—that fellow, Bandera."

The man touched his forelock and left without words. The sound of his bootsteps squelched away.

Vargas lay down on the pine-slat bunk and thought of the message on the torn-up letter. The door groaned protest and brought his glance up to the man who stepped uncertainly in. Vargas said: "I gave Sandoval orders to kill Cass Bocart. Why hasn't he done it?"

Bandera twirled his hat uneasily. He shrugged and presently told of Sandoval's trap and how that devilman, Andros, had shouted warning as Bocart stepped out. He recounted their later attack on the office, and vividly described the black-clad gringo crouched above his flaming guns. He told it with the ring of truth. He was the man who'd trailed blood down the hall.

Wryness disturbed the set of Vargas' mouth. "Send me Duarte Salas," he said, and the ends of his tawny mustache cast moving shadows across his teeth.

Vargas got up when the man went out. He roved to a pause

by the window, throwing his bleak gaze across the yard and fingering the paper he'd stuffed in his pocket. He was that way when Duarte Salas came in with a man behind him who shut the door.

"Who's this?" Vargas asked.

At a sign from Salas the man pulled a damp scrap of paper from inside his poncho. Vargas took it and, without dropping his glance, said: "Where'd this come from?"

The peon shrugged. Salas answered. "It was stuffed in a gun tied on Klauson's horse."

"Klauson? You mean the cook?"

Both men nodded.

"Where's Klauson now?"

Salas put a black cigarette between his cracked lips and smiled.

Lamplight put a gleam of copper about the rims of Red Hat's eyes. His left hand gestured. Salas' companion went out. Vargas' glance met Salas' searchingly. Salas shrugged.

He was a rawboned man with a scraggle of beard on his seamed brown face, and deep squint wrinkles about his black eyes. His clothes were brush-clawed and his bare arms scratched. There was something about him though that spelled efficiency. It was the wicked care he took of his pistol.

"There's rotgut in that cupboard," Vargas said, and watched Salas fetch it. He poured himself a good stiff tumbler. He had known, Vargas thought, better days; he was no cheap greaser to guzzle from a bottle. He drank it neat and when he set the glass down empty his schooled face displayed no reaction. Salas asked, "Have you read it yet?" and his watchful eyes were brightly amused when Red Hat shook his head.

"I don't have to," Vargas said. "There ain't but one man in this country with guts enough to down a sheepman and advertise it. I don't need to read no messages from him."

He put his big hands grim into his pockets and all their knuckles showed against the fabric. "I'm goin' to get that ranny," he promised softly. "But if things were different . . ."

Understanding was a look in Salas' eyes. A remote smile touched his lips and he nodded.

Vargas studied him somberly. Grave Creek's showmanship had ever tended to obscure Salas' virtues. Grave Creek had been the swaggering kind, flamboyant in taste, spectacular in action; Salas' work was done with a quiet efficiency evoking no comment—unnoticed. How much of Grave Creek's success, wondered Vargas, had depended on this man's unseen co-operation?

Far back as Vargas could recall, he'd always thought Grave Creek the man indispensable. But now, with Grave Creek gone, he recalled the many chores given Salas, tough and homely tasks so well concluded Salas' quiet worth had passed unnoticed.

"The men," Salas said, "is getting tired potting rabbits," and looked at Vargas carefully. Through the blue haze of expelled smoke the hush held its own understanding. The steel in Salas' holster shone. It matched the glint in Vargas' stare.

"Round up the boys," he nodded. "We're goin' up after them sheep."

Andros lounged with an easy confidence, empty hands loose-hanging at his sides. His soft voice contrasted mightily to the harsh, wet set of his cheeks. He said, "Mebbe I'm interruptin' something. You were going to shoot that fellow weren't you, Barstow?"

Barstow scowled with a palsied fury. But he jerked his hands away from his belt. He dared not risk a look at Culebra. It seemed that only in the locking of his gaze with Andros' could there be any safety in this for him. Andros had heard some part of their talk; it was plain in his stare that he understood it—the black rage in him was apparent, too. It was there in the tautened lines of his figure, in the far-apart way he's got his feet planted, in the curdling of smoke that was in his gray stare.

Someone's breathing in this quiet room made a raucous sound that sent the pounding of Barstow's pulse to tumult when he recognized it for his own.

Andros said, "I understand there's a fellow on your payroll called Dakota."

Barstow gave a start and stiffened. Shifted thought flashed through his stare and a heightened caution reshaped his cheek-bones. "You been misinformed," he grunted, and still dared not look toward Culebra. Desperately he prayed the man would keep still. He spoke again, less certain, more worried. "May be one in the country some place; but there ain't none hangin' his hat round here."

He could almost feel Culebra's grin. But the man did not speak and Andros' stare stayed hard on Barstow.

A cold repression got into his voice. "I think you're lyin', Barstow. The man I'm talkin' of has a bad way with women— most particular with other folks' women. Knowin' your interest in Miz' Tarnell . . ." He let the rest trail off, but Barstow read what was in his mind. He was wheeling to pick up the bottle when Andros said: "It may interest you to know that Flaurity's no longer on the Tarnell payroll."

A sudden chill stopped Barstow stiffly. He stood, locked still, with cheeks gone wooden when he saw that Andros was watching him. "He's not on yours any longer, either," Andros said.

"He never was on mine!" Barstow shouted.

But his voice had a stifled sound even in his own ears; and the remote smile gleaming in Andros' stare did nothing to comfort him. "If he said he was, he lied!" Barstow gritted.

"This country's sure plumb full of liars."

"You don't have to stay here," Barstow blustered. "There's other places—"

Andros nodded. "You'd be well advised to start lookin' 'em over. You got a phone here, ain't you?"

Barstow stared. He nodded, silent; then grudgingly added, "Over there by the desk."

"I'm usin' it," Andros said; and crossed to the phone box ominously. He ground the crank, got the operator and gave a San Carlos number. Putting the receiver back on its hook he stared at Barstow grimly.

A silent cold enveloped the room. Culebra stayed against the wall with cheeks expressionless, pale eyes glinting. Andros sat with seeming carelessness upon a corner of the desk.

Barstow stirred uneasily and moved his hands in a nervous motion against the fabric of his coat. The phone shrilled then with startling loudness. "Yes," Andros said, receiver to ear. "Give me Cass Bocart—*Bocart!* Yeah. . . . Well, get him there right away."

Barstow found the wait oppressive. His mouth got sullen and there came a strained look about the edges of his stare.

Andros said abruptly: "That you, Major? . . . Andros talkin'. Yeah. . . . I'm at Barstow's Half-Circle Arrow— Not any more, it don't; Red Hat's wise." He seemed to be listening for several seconds while the gibbering receiver etched rasps of sound across the silence. "Yeah; I'd clean forgot about it. Red Hat

128

. . ." Then Andros said distinctly: "No matter, don't worry about that. I'm all through here—this country's goin' to bust wide open. Yeah. You heard me right. I'm resignin'—*quitting!* Right now!"

He banged the receiver on the hook and wheeled a bright, hard look at Barstow. His voice drove at Barstow wickedly: "You tell your Dakota he better clear out—an' I got a word for *you!* Keep plumb away from the Rockin' T!"

Barstow glared.

"I'm wise to that Long Rope play with Grave Creek. I'm wise to plenty an' I'm onto your game! You keep clear away from Flame Tarnell!"

Rage tore wild words out of Barstow. "You ain't tellin' *me* what I can do! I'll go where I damn well please, an'—an'—"

It stuck in his throat.

The cold, brash gleam of Andros' stare struck terror through and through him. He cringed, and then, in a last access of rage and hate, he snarled: "I'll get her, goddam you, *an' I'll get her ranch!*"

"I've warned you." A sudden smile curled Andros' lips. "And I shoot to kill. Remember it."

19

"THE PLACE'LL RUN PLUMB RED!"

THE ROOM was dark with the shapes of men when Andros entered. He closed the door and put his back against it, eyeing the gathered brush-poppers with a hard, appraising glance. These were the men—these and their outfits—that must form the nucleus of his wild bunch; these must bear the brunt of the Pool's black anger when it was learned what Andros was up to. Others would direct them—hellbenders he had known along the Trail, pistol slammers. But here in this room were the men who would have to do the work.

He saw Dane Quirt, and Shiltmeyer of the Spur, and Hernbarger, and Trane, the boss of Tadpole. And then he saw a face that sent hope surging through him, the face of a tall, lank man, sun-scorched like an Indian's. This face was back in

129

the shadows, but Andros saw its flash of teeth and felt the years roll off his shoulders. Sam Hackberry, one of the four he'd sent for, a tough and reticent rider who'd seen more misery in his time than all this Four Peaks country together.

Andros murmured, "Howdy, Sam," and saw the grin on Hackberry's face grow broader; but he remained back there in the shadows.

Andros' glance swung to front again, to the wondering faces of these Four Peaks cowmen. "I guess we all know what we're up against," he said. "If the sheep come through again we're licked—an' they're comin'. Vargas has gone after 'em."

"How do you know that?" Quirt said in an utter quiet.

"Vargas," Andros told them, "has been camped south of Boulder Mountain. I been over there. He's not there now. He's headin' for White Mountains—may be on his way back now. The trail I cut was six days' old."

"You're sure 'twas Vargas?—Red Hat?"

"It was Red Hat. He's been lookin' out the lay of things. He's with the Pool, of course, an' the Pool sets considerable store by takin' over this country. The Pool don't want no National Forests, an' they got no use for two-bit cow-nurses. It's Vargas' job to run us out."

There was a sullen rumble of thickened voices. Through this cut a high-pitched groan. In a nasal twang somebody said, "Boys, this is terrible bad."

"Bad!" Andros said with anger. "If the whole damn push of you don't get back of me to do something about it this range is finished!"

"Don't see's there's anything we kin do about it," Quirt said dubiously, and Shiltmeyer shook his grizzled head. "There ain't, Dane. This country's seen the last of cattle. We've fit Injuns, rustlers, drought an' hoemen. We can call all the critters we've got by name."

Old Hernbarger muttered, "In der Vatterlandt dey vould nod stand for dis. Vere iss your pragged-of vreedoms, hein? Py Gott, we ain'dt got noddings pot plood und pullets!"

Andros' gaze whipped hard to Trane. Trane shrugged his saddle-bowed shoulders. "We ain't got the dinero to see this through even if there was sense in it. It takes hard cash to wad a gun." He shook his head without anger. "Was we to try toughin' it out against these sheepmen, it would be like askin' what they give Jack Broth las' year. Jack was a heller, but

130

short on savvy. Reckon there'll be a mort of us pullin' out next two-three days. . . . I'd sure like t' see it diff'rent, but . . ." He shrugged; held out his hand. "I'm wishin' you luck, stranger."

"Yellow, eh?"

Obe Trane scowled and the tips of his ears changed color. He looked down at the hand he'd held out, and gingerly rubbed it across the frazzled corduroy of his pants. "Them's fightin' words, friend. I've seen the day——"

Cold frost rode Andros words: "When the rest of the stove-up has-beens has pulled their freight an' said good night, the rest of us'll get down to business."

No one moved nor, apparently, did anyone resent that tone; nor the fleering curl of Andros' lips. "Okey," he drawled. "Tuck in your tails an' get to your slinkin'——I'll manage to make out some way. But I wish to Christ there was a couple of *men* in this locality! I ain't askin' for any real double-actin' engines —just a couple one-armed swampers is all I need to get by on."

Quirt flushed. "Y'u got no call to——"

"A-ah!" sneered Andros, "get to hell on outa here—— *all of you!* I got a couple rustlin' friends I reckon'll help me out in this!"

"We tried——" Shiltmeyer started to bleat; but Andros cut him off with a snort.

"You wouldn't know a try if it kicked you in the pants!"

Sam Hackberry spoke from the shadows. "What you got in mind, friend?"

"Nothin' you'd be interested in. No use my wastin' any more breath. It's more'n a fellow should expect to get a show of spunk from a bunch of sod-turnin' squatters——"

"I don't take that kind of yap off *no* man!" Trane blazed hotly.

"Don't make me laugh! Go on—clear out, you bunch of frayed-out scarecrows! I'd rather have your room. I'll get me some Digger Injuns!"

"Well, spill your guts," Quirt muttered. "We'll listen a bit——"

"I don't need no audience—what I want is *fightin'* men! Som——"

Trane snarled: "Say what you got us here for!"

"My plan's to scatter," Andros said, still scowling. "Scatter an' peck at these Pool outfits till they——"

"Raidin'!" jeered Quirt, disgustedly. "Might's well pop at 'em

131

with a fly-swatter! I thought you had some kind of *plan!* Why, they'd larrup us off this range so quick we'd never know what struck us! C'mon, boys; let's git home."

Straight and solid Andros blocked the door. "Go on," he said. "I couldn't use you no how. This is *men's* work—an' I guess I savvy where to get 'em—"

"You'll get no men round here," Quirt snarled, "that's fool enough to back you in no such damn foolishness as—"

"I'll get Rockinstraw, Ed Tailman, New River Ned, Sam Hackberry, an' Kid Badger!"

The hush that gripped these ranchers showed the power of those five names. They were the five most wanted gun-fighters on any sheriff's list. Outlaws all—notorious from the Panhandle to Nevada. Rewards on them, if paid would have run to fabulous figures. They were the worst of the Border Riders —men close associated with the bloody histories of the Southwest's unhealthiest sections. Names to be feared and whispered.

"God A'mighty!" Obe Trane cried. "You'd bring them *here?*—them *hellions?*"

"I've sent for them."

"Caesar's ghost!" breathed Quirt, his voice pitched like a prayer. "Might's well turn red Injuns loose an' be done with it! You gone stark ravin' mad?"

"Mad enough to give that Pool a dose of its own damn medicine! I'm goin' to give 'em what they gave Teal's Flowerpot. There's just one way to beat this bunch—it's a way I'm goin' to take!"

Lamplight piled the shadows darkly across his tautened cheeks. He stood with thumbs hooked in gun belts, regarding them with bitter eyes. "It's not a thing I would or *could* do if I was hooked up with the National Forest movement—or any other kind of accepted law. But I'm not; an' this is cattle country! By the grace of God I'm goin' to see it stay that way!"

"Hell's fire!" Quirt snapped, "they'll never come. An' if they did—"

"They won't! What could he offer 'em?" another growled.

"I'm offerin' them nothing," Andros answered. "Sheep put those men where they are. Sheep will bring 'em back—"

Shiltmeyer shouted. "You're crazy as a loon!" And Quirt buttoned his coat and looked at Trane significantly. Trane nodded, pulling on his gloves, and turned bent shoulders door-ward.

Andros cursed them bitterly. "You fools! Sam Hackberry's here right now!" He flung his glance across their heads to a flash of teeth in the shadows. "For God's sake, Sam, help me talk sense into 'em!"

Sam Hackberry's voice came dry as dust.

"Clem's right, the boys will come," he said. "Needn't to worry about that part. We been waitin' too all-fired long t' git a lick at them sheepmen."

Stillness stiff as a drumhead followed.

A man's spurs harshly rasped the floor. Old Hernbarger's. He stopped beside Andros solidly. "Py Gott," he wheezed, "you god some pullets for mine gon?"

"I'll buy you a cartload," grinned Andros tightly; and kept his look hard upon the crowd. Here and there a man's glance sheepishly slid away.

Quirt's uneasy look said he did not like it. Trane said with the solemn care of a man deep-thinking: "Let's have the rest of it."

"Get your kids an' womenfolks some place safe. From here out this is goin' to be wolf eat wolf. Cut loose of everything; there'll be no holds barred. My way ain't goin' to be easy, but it's the only thing there's left to do. Them that rides with me ain't goin' to have no time to look out for belongings.

"You'll have to let your spreads take care of themselves. Some may get burnt; but as things stand right now the sheep-men'll get 'em anyway. Cut an' run, is my plan—hard an' fast. We've got to band into bunches an' I'll pick the leaders. I'm pickin' Sam Hackberry here, an' New River Ned, Art Rockinstraw, Tailman an' Kid Badger. Them as don't like it can pull out now an' take their chances. Anyone quittin' later will get plugged sudden."

Shiltmeyer swore aghast. "Them hellions will pull this country plumb apart! Nothin'll stop 'em—*nothin'!* This country'll go clean up in smoke—"

"But it'll still be ours. The sheep will go up with it."

Shiltmeyer stared. "Good Christ, the place'll run plumb red!"

Andros said, "I hope so."

133

COIN OF THE REALM

Experienced in the ways of big outfits with smaller competitors, it was not at all hard for Andros to understand the dread in which these cowmen held the Pool. No luke warm measures had built it. Only by the speedy piling of disaster on top of disaster could the Pool be licked.

Andros' plans were brief and simple. The money Bocart had given him was swiftly converted into pistol and rifle fodder. Had Vargas thought to search his hat that roll would have gone the way of his wallet. But Vargas hadn't—or rather, he hadn't had time to once the thought struck him. Sam Hackberry proved invaluable with shrewd suggestions. Andros avoided Flame Tarnell whenever he could. He had not forgotten her parting words that night he rode to Barstow's.

His meeting with the small-spread cowmen took place on the night of August's last Tuesday. By Wednesday night all his owlhoot riders had come in but Tailman, and they had word of him. Kid Badger had brought six friends along, tough and reckless Texans who considered this business a lark.

With twenty men Andros set to work. Saturday night the first blow was struck; northwest of Mocking Bird Pass, in the heart of the timber country.

Lamplight, spilling from the windows of the super's office and from the low rough shanties flanking it, filtered through the shaggy pines, driving golden rays through the crowding dark flung down by a moonless night. Dark-garbed riders statuesquely sat their ponies in the screening brush and studied the clearing without comment.

Sixteen sawmills whined and snorted. This was headquarters camp for the great Southwestern lumber syndicate which in whirlwind strides had already denuded twenty miles of ranching country. It was the largest timber interest in the Pool.

Sam Hackberry, watching the screeching sheds, said, "Got a mort o' ridin' starin' us in the face tonight, boys. Take them sawmills first. Then the shacks. I'll handle the Super's office. Watch out fer the women an' brats. Cold Water Crick an' Dry Cimarron next." He sent a last raking glance across the open, shifted his cud and spat. "Let's get at it."

The eastern sky was brushed with pink, the land's dark contour shoving against it like the hackles of an angry dog. A long file of horsemen drifted down the rimrock toward where a group of cabins vaguely showed through the thinning murk. The ponies moved on muffled feet and only the rhythmic creak of chaps and saddle leather disturbed the morning's stillness.

A faint down-draft from the tumbled hills carried the smell of lifted dust, and sheep—thousands of them—covered the valley like a soiled gray blanket, a fuzzy huddle against the earth. There was a dozing horse before the largest cabin; if it heard or sensed the approaching riders it gave no sign.

In a great thin circle the dark horsemen wheeled, quick spacing their broncs, taking what cover offered as Hackberry rode up to the cabin where the horse stood. Brightening day gleamed dully on the barrels of lifted carbines.

Hackberry's .45-.90 drove a slug through the cabin door.

Men spewed forth like angry wasps to blink and halt confused midstride when they saw the ring of watching riders. "Figurin' to move them sheep?" asked Hackberry casually, and the sheepmen's eyes went slitted.

"You're goddam right we are!"

"That's fine. We're here to help y'u," Hackberry said. "Jest turn them blatters round an' head 'em back through the Pass." He jerked his rifle nozzle north.

The sheep boss laughed. He was pretty tough. "You go to—"

Flame licked out of Hackberry's rifle. The sheepman licked his lips. "There's a law in this country, hombre—"

"Y'u bet!" said Hackberry. "Gun law—it's lookin' y'u spang in the eye!"

There was a shifting in the sheepmen's ranks. But they knew the courts were back of them. The sheep boss snarled while his hombres eased hands beltward. "The courts—"

"Will be a leetle mite late t' do y'u fellas much goods," drawled Hackberry. "Ed, get this outfit's burros packed. Jack, y'u an' two-three the other boys get them blatters movin'. 'F

135

they don't move fast enough mebbe y'u better burn some powder."

The sheep boss scowled. He was over-gunned at the moment; and he knew well what his owners would say if he let these cowpunchers shoot his sheep. He glared at Hackberry poisonously. "We'll move 'em. I was on'y funnin' any—"

"Me, too," drawled Hackberry drily. "I'll be funnin' a dang sight harder if I catch y'u comin' back."

Horse Mountain was a blaze of heat and sun's glare bright upon its crags when three men rounded a bend in the trail and pulled up under a towering pine that stood forty feet from a ranch house. The leader of this trio dismounted and hammered a white piece of paper to the tree's bole with his pistol butt. While he backed, inspecting it, his companions sniggered.

A swart and stocky man came off the veranda at a lope, and an angular man came after him, throwing talk back over his shoulder. The strange riders completely ignored them. Shoving forward, the chunky man stared narrowly at his tree's new sign. With a lurid oath he jerked about and shouted: "Keal! Stafferd!" He flung a brash look at the strangers. "What's the big idea?"

"Read, can'tcha?"

"No slat-eyed Mormon bastard is goin' to move—"

"Ain't this the Keyhole horse spread?"

"No!" the chunky sheepman snarled. "Not no more, it ain't! We done taken it over. This outfit's a holdin' of the Kelsadine Sheep Cor—"

"A part of Vargas' outfit, eh?"

"What about it?" The chunky man paused, took another look at the short man facing him. "Say, ain't you the squirt they call Art Rockin—"

"I reckon y'u know me, Kelsey. Get yo' traps together."

"You—" The sheepman made as though to step backward. He stopped with a gun barrel digging his belly. Few men lived who could whip a gun from leather quicker than Art Rockinstraw. Fear beaded Kelsey's brow with sweat; he threw a tortured look at the lanky man who had come with him off the veranda. But the lanky man was earnestly directing his attention at the cloudless sky; he was not interested in things mundane.

Kelsey's bloated face was purple. You could almost smell the rage in him. He said gratingly, "You can't get away with this, Rockinstraw!"

Perhaps it was the hurried pound of booted feet that made him brash and belligerent in the face of Rockinstraw's pistol. He slammed his words like the flat of an ax. "By Gawd, you'll never cut it!"

Two men came round a corner of the barn. There were pistols in their lifted fists. They were a pair of Kelsey's sheep hands and they sized things up at a glance.

Kelsey clawed for leather. Four guns roared out at once and Kelsey, with his gun half drawn, lurched round and fell like a pole-axed steer. One of Rockinstraw's boys dropped forward across his saddle cursing, and was dragged off by his pitching bronc. Rockinstraw struck the hammer of his triggerless gun again. The ball went through the head of the nearest sheepman; he crumpled up by the toolshed. His companion whirled with a choking scream and tried to get behind the barn again, but Rockinstraw knocked him down in his tracks.

There was something fierce and blazing in the look Rockinstraw gave the lanky man who still stood with his hands straight up. Gun sound rolled around the yard, smashed like ball bats against the buildings. Rockinstraw said: "Git goin', fella—git goin' quick."

The lank man's lips writhed whitely. His face was like bleached paper. "But—I can't!" he groaned. "The sheep—"

"Y'u want a bullet through yore guts?" Rockinstraw did not wait for an answer. He struck the hammer of his gun. "Let's get at them goddam woolies now!" he said to the man still with him.

Andros thought it would take Vargas' men another two days to get the main flocks down from the mountains onto the Cottonwood. Assured of this he had sent his raiders far afield, scattering their activities from the Prescott ranges to the White Ledges below Soldier Creek—and north as far as Long Valley.

Always the sheepmen's comings and goings had been timed to the rains and the coming of grass. Feed brought up by the winter rains had been gouged to the roots by sheep working northward into the White Mountains. Now with fall just

137

around the corner, Vargas' men would ease these sheep back, feeding off what grass these recent storms had pulled from the stubborn earth.

Andros was right; but he miscalculated Red Hat's speed.

This morning, backed by a crew of nervous Four Peaks cowmen, he had ridden to the flanking hogback above the Cottonwood, and there had left them to hold it just in case the sheep came early. "Dig in here an' if the sheep come, fight—but hold this ridge till I can get some men in to help you. Whatever you do don't let them sheep pass." He had gone off then with New River Ned; and hardly had he gone from sight when the sheep hit Asher's Basin.

The move showed Vargas' foresight. He had expected that hogback to figure in Andros' plans and had cunningly avoided it. He had crossed Salt River away up yonder and had run his sheep through Brown's place, feeding it down to the roots. And now their dirty white ribbon was snaking through the pass from Asher's Basin—a stinking, blatting stream of gray—a flood that spilled across green-carpeted uplands with the appetite of starving locusts.

Band after band surged bleating from the pass. The sound of their cropping teeth and cutting hooves made little more noise than the wings of buzzards sailing round above them, waiting for the guns to bark.

Andros' cowmen left the hogback when the first sheep smell came down the wind. They cut for the timber with quirt and spur, dragging out with stunned minds reeling before the crashing fragments of their useless hopes.

But deep in the midst of the sheepmen's laughter, a big and high-powered rifle spoke. The bullets came from such distance only a faint popping sound reached the sheepmen's ears. But the bullets came with plenty of force. One swarthy sheepman sprang to his feet with a frightened curse as lead ripped the skillet out of his hands. The bunched sheep made a splendid target, a target the rifleman was quick to spot. All across the bedground sheep dropped. The rest scuttled frantically downslope as the cursing herders sprang to saddle. The flocks ran wild and no one stopped them; that man with the rifle was too fine a shot. The herders flew to protect their own hides.

The X.O.G., a cattle syndicate that months earlier had

138

taken over Ed Tailman's range, was holding a large gather of beef in the vicinity of Spaulding Spring, fattening up for the approaching fall market. It was eleven P.M. and only the smoldering embers of the cook's dying fire illumined the starless night. Around the wagon a score of men made dark shapes in their blankets, their rising snores giving testimony of a day hard spent at work.

A crash of gunfire roused the night. Belching guns shot streaks in the sky. One instant later every steer was up, afoot with snorts and frightened bawlings. Dust swirled about them, and muzzleflame sheared at the bedground from thirteen points southeast of camp.

The beef herd lifted tails and ran. Shrill screams, hot lead and high-pitched whoopings hustled them into a lumbering gallop.

Faster and faster the wild hooves pounded. The terrified steers with lowered heads went humping for Leonard Canyon in a crazy charge that could not be turned nor ever stopped.

21

"I'M COMIN' FOR YORE HIDE!"

ALL ACROSS three mighty counties men scarce dared to draw their breath for fear of stopping ambush lead. Word from a dozen places reached the Barstow ranch of havoc wrought by raiding horsemen. The Four Peaks country flew with rumor that Black Clem Andros was fighting the Pool.

Badly shaken, Barstow stayed in his ranch house brooding. From the San Carlos Reservation in the east, to Mormon Flat in the west, clear north to the Tule Butte range, war guns were cracking and the song of lead drowned out all others. The Limestone Hills were splotched with blood. Bloated carcasses were polluting the waters of Twenty-Nine-Mile Lake. Sawmill had seen fighting. There were no buildings left at Schoolhouse Tank. Leonard Canyon was filled with dead cattle. On Wildcat Hill three men dangled stiffly on hempen ropes attached to tall pines. A surveyor's party from the railroad had bucked ambush guns and were left where they'd fallen. Cave Creek Village was a ghost town after a five-minute raid by a dozen masked horsemen. Tortilla Camp was a buzzards' rendezvous, acrid and nauseous with the stench of dead sheep. There was talk of calling in the soldiers—only those who needed them most had no excuse for the calling.

Red Hat Vargas was raising hell. Already two larruping horsemen had come pelting to Barstow with messages from him. He demanded to know why Barstow was holding back. His far-flung flocks were being scattered by the slashing forays of Andros' raiders. The Pool was strong as ever, he said, but he needed more men and he needed them *now*. The first of that Barstow would not believe; he believed the last part too well. He told the messenger his crew had quit him. Quick as he could get others he would hasten with them to Red Hat's aid—that was what he told the first man. To the second messenger Barstow explained, exasperated, that he could not get men at *any* price; that, perforce, he must stay and guard his ranch.

Culebra, after this last man left, strolled grinning from the bunkhouse for a look at Barstow's face. "Next time," he taunted slyly, "It'll be Red Hat comin' himself. You better decide what you're goin' to say to him."

To which Barstow said not a word. He clamped his lips and tramped inside and slammed the door behind him.

But Bronc Culebra was proved a true prophet within the next five hours.

Barstow had himself in hand. He nodded curtly when Vargas strode in; he ignored Culebra's sly smile entirely. He pushed a bottle across his desk and Red Hat knocked it flying. But Barstow got his talk in first. "I was sure relieved to hear you got them brush-poppers licked," he stated. "Looked for awhile like you mightn't cut it."

"Happens I ain't *got* them licked." Vargas' smile was completely unpleasant. "I want to know why you refused to send help when I asked for it—an' why you got ten fellas posted around outside with rifles. A guy ain't short-handed when he can afford that many ornaments."

"Them men are there," Barstow said, "to protect my property. They're men I've just now hired—which I was goin' to bring up to stiffen your hand just as quick's you got another messenger here so's I'd know where the hell to take 'em."

140

"I always figured you for a belly-crawlin' snake, Reb," Vargas told him. "Nothin' you've said makes me change my mind."

Barstow's ears showed a risen color. His head tipped a little slanchways and threw one look at Culebra who was stiff against the left-hand wall.

"You're the kind," Vargas said, "that figures to let some other fool rake your chestnuts out of the fire for you."

"You can talk," Barstow gritted thickly. "You ain't got money tied up in buildings—"

"I've got *sheep,* by Christ!" Red Hat bellowed. "An' I been seein' a hell's passle of 'em shoved over canyons an'—"

"Exactly!" Barstow grunted. "Think I want to see my cattle—"

"It's too damned bad about your cattle! You're in this or you ain't, by God! If you are, I want your help—*right now!* Am I gettin' it or not?"

Barstow's face showed a strong dislike. "You're gettin' a little brash, friend, ain't you? I'm as much in this Pool as you are—more, I shouldn't wonder. If this was any other time I'd be tellin' you to go plumb to hell. As it is, I'm sidin' the Pool," Barstow said, "like always."

Vargas nodded. "This is a damn good time to prove it. We've got Andros' crowd bottled up in Hell's Hip Pocket. You can back up your good intentions by collectin' them outside rifles an' ridin' up there with me—now."

Culebra's chuckle crossed the silence; and when he saw their wheeled expressions he guffawed, loud and heartily.

"What's so funny?" Vargas said.

"This whole damn' business." Culebra grinned sardonically. "Ain't y'u found out yet Reb's great intentions is things to be *aired,* not acted? Ain't y'u savvied all he's wantin' is Tarnell's Rockin' T?"

Vargas looked at Barstow carefully, a strange glint in his half-closed stare. "All the old man owned is three hundred acres. What would Reb be wantin' with that? Goin' to take to gardenin', is he?"

"He's got a mighty itch for land, Reb has," Culebra told him. "Partic'lar that land. He's spent more nights pokin' round there than a feller could shake a stick at. He's—" Culebra broke off suddenly, shoved free of the wall. One bunched fist burst above his holster. There was danger in his tense, splayed fingers. Danger to match the rage of Barstow.

The cowman's bloated face was livid; but if Culebra couldn't share the wealth, he was determined Barstow should not, either. "This bastard," he said, looking straight at Reb, "has found *oil* on the Rockin' T!"

There was brutal fury in Barstow's snarl. His hand made a white streak slapping hipward. Outward flame leaped, blue and wicked.

Culebra's face went a haggard gray and all the lines of it stretched—contorted. He swayed in the lamplight, trying to trigger. But Barstow's payoff lead had tagged him. His bent form broke at the knees and toppled.

Barstow's gun was covering Vargas. The lust for blood blazed out of his stare. *"You* wantin' some?" he snarled at him thickly.

Vargas said "No," softly, and did not move so much as an eyelid. "Comin' with me, are you?"

Sweat was a shine on Barstow's forehead and madness still glared bright from his eyes. "I'm through with your goddam Pool!" he snarled. His gun motioned Vargas toward the door. "One word o' this an' I come for your hide! Now get out, by God, an' don't come back!"

22

CUPID BUILDS A LOOP

PARTING with Ed Tailman Thursday morning on the assurance that all his raiders were working overtime, Andros rode south from Shake Tree Canyon and moved on down Deer Creek toward the stream's intersection with Maple Draw. Rocking T was in his mind and he strove to plan some decisive blow that should smash the Pool at one fell stroke. But Flame Tarnell was before his thoughts and he only knew that, somehow, it had become terrifically important that they bury the hatchet and be friends again. It made no difference that time and again these last few days he had called himself all kinds of a fool ever to think they could be friends again. He was going to see her anyway; something stronger than himself was shoving him ranchward.

He reached headquarters just after noon. Three punchers lounged by the bunkhouse with .45-.90s across their laps. Coldfoot grinned. The other two held their cheeks wooden and watched him warily. Andros swung down. "Better work a little bit farther out. Spur was burned to the ground last night."

He trailed his reins and walked to the ranch house. At the porch he wheeled abruptly and crossed to the mess shack, passing straight through to the kitchen back of it. No one was round, but he found what he wanted and carried it to the table in the outer room.

He gulped the food in hungry haste and was clearing his throat with a swig of cold coffee when a shadow crossed the mess-shack floor. His quick swing found Grace Latham in the doorway, sun's glare outlined her limber figure. "What you doin' here?" he asked ungraciously.

Her lips framed a twisted smile. She said, "You sure are glad to see me," but no resentment looked out of her eyes. She came toward him leaving the door standing open.

She stood for a long time staring down at him. Her voice was thoughtful—just a little protesting, when she said, "I guess you've seen me about all you aim to . . ."

He looked up then. She met his glance defiantly. "I didn't come here hunting you—Gallup John brought me out last night. Seemed to think it wasn't safe for me in town." She smiled a little, wistfully.

"Where's Gallup now?"

"Off raidin' with your crowd, I guess. Soon's he got me here he went tearing off with three-four others—I think one of them was the man they call Kid Badger." She said with some obscure thought lighting up her eyes, "Folks are beginning to learn that you're around. They're saying in town if you keep this up another week all the two-bit ranchers in the country will get behind you. My gamblers are placing odds of five to one you'll break the Pool."

"Gallup John," Andros said, "thinks a powerful lot of you."

The brightness left her eyes; left an odd expression in them. She rested one hip on the table and her dangling foot made tiny motions in the air. She said rebelliously: "If I'd wanted Gallup John I could have had him long ago. Why don't you use your eyes for a change?"

143

She leaned abruptly forward, pointed breasts swaying two sharp patterns against the fabric of her blouse. "Why can't you like me?" she cried miserably. "Aren't we both lone wolves? Why can't you see in me what it is you're after? God knows I've plenty to give a man—why don't you *want* me?"

He didn't immediately answer. A stillness fell between them. He pulled a long breath into his chest and got up. "It's not what I want or don't want, Grace; it's the way things have got to be. It's facts we've got to reckon with and they've got me pegged for a killer. You don't want that kind of man."

"How do you know what I want?"

"I know what wouldn't be good for you. A man can't go behind the record of six years. The things a man does catch up with him. When the things I've done catch up with me, I'll face 'em by myself."

"I'd be glad to share them, Clem—"

"It won't work, Grace."

"What about Flame Tarnell?"

He stared and felt his cheeks go hot. He said angrily, "I ain't askin' her to marry me!"

Her laugh was harsh. "You know better! She wouldn't wipe her feet on you—do you know what she calls you? *Gun fighter!* She hasn't the sense to know you're takin' God's only way to save her range! Her and her Sunday-school mind! What does *she* know about love? Do you think she could really *love* anyone? Don't be a fool, Clem Andros!"

She looked at him boldly, willfully. "I can give a man what he wants—"

Andros said with taut, pale cheeks, "Love ain't a thing you can shift at will—" and her tinkle of laughter mocked him.

"I've read that in the copybooks, too." She put a hand on his arm; leaned toward him. "Don't you know it's sheer animal magnetism that backs nine out of every ten marriages? What could Flame Tarnell ever bring you? Why, you'd play hell every time you—"

He slapped her hard across the face, his cheeks dead white with anger. "Don't speak her name again!"

Then the rage fell out of him. He looked at her, shocked. She was actually smiling. She swung off the table, leaned forward eagerly. He felt the bulge of her breasts against him, the pull of her arms. "Oh, *Clem*—" It was the whisper of Eve, and Eve's spell was on him.

With an oath he caught her arms from around him, forced them down. "Flame's puttin' you up here, ain't she?"

"What of it? She'd do the same for a dog—I owe her nothing for that!" She broke his grip. Her arms went round his neck again, pulling his head down with all her strength, forcing his mouth hard against her own.

He got the flats of his hands against her shoulders and was bracing himself to shove her loose when a shadow blocked the open door. Across Grace's shoulder he saw Flame's white face. One moment he saw it and then she was gone.

The sound of an oncoming horse finally roused Andros. Grace Latham was against the table and he stood, not seeing her, with shoulders bowed. The horse sound stopped in the yard outside. A rider's boots struck dirt and skidded. The door burst open. A wild-eyed rider stood peering in. He cried affrightedly: "Sam Hackberry's dead!"

Andros stared at him numbly.

The man said, "God sakes! Can't you *hear* me? Sam Hackberry's dead on Methodist Mountain—near cut in two! An' there's six of his boys layin' riddled there with 'im!"

23

BARSTOW

VARGAS tossed his reins across the peeled pole fronting Latham's saloon and stepped inside with his hat cuffed low. If he enjoyed the way all talk fell off at his appearance he did not show it. A barman hurried forward to serve him. Vargas asked for Barstow and the barman's thumb indicated a back room. Vargas crossed to the door and went in, kicking the door shut after him. Barstow was there and Krell, the sheriff, leaned against a wall at the room's far side. A single lamp shed sickly light. Vargas said, "You wanted to see me?" and Barstow nodded. He shoved a note across the table silently, his glittering eyes on Vargas' face.

Red Hat picked up the note and read it. "I've found out what you been wanting with the Rocking T. Better leave that oil alone." A single name was signed to the scrawl—*Andros*.

Vargas, lifting chin, saw Barstow watching him. The glint of Barstow's eyes had changed. Trouble feel was in this place. Krell was shifting weight with a straining care. Vargas said, "You don't think *I* told him, do you?"

"Somebody did!" Barstow gritted; and the hand on his gun butt showed white knuckles. Krell leaned a little forward.

Vargas said, "I see you've told Krell. Mebbe Krell told Andros."

Krell said wickedly, "Yeah—an' mebbe he *didn't!*"

Red Hat's lips showed a faint kind of smiling, and he put the flats of his hands down gently on the table. The room felt cold and brittly taut as though this stillness were stretched beyond endurance.

Barstow stooped. "I got a way with sidewinders." When he straightened there was a gun in each hand.

Fury was bright in Vargas' eyes. One hand whipped under his coat and came out. Detonation bulged the room. Smoke was a blue fog swirling crazily. It was thick round Barstow's low-crouched shape. It curled from the gun in Krell's lean hand. Not a shot ever left Vargas' pistol. He fell with its hammer still at half-cock.

Less than a minute later Barstow came into the barroom through the swinging doors of the big front entrance. The barman who'd directed Red Hat looked up and his face went grayly blank. His swabbing hand left off all movement. Some of the customers who'd been inquiringly staring toward the back room's door, looked around.

Barstow said with a cold thin smile, "Seen anything of Vargas, Halpin? He sent me word to meet him here. Where is he?"

The barman stood like a blight had struck him. He jerked his head at the back room's door. "He—he went in there, Mister Barstow."

Barstow turned on his heel and went coolly down a room gone quiet, watched by the customers' completest attention. He did it well. He went to the door and tried the knob. "Huh —locked!" he muttered, and pounded its panels with peremptory fist. He waited a moment, then banged again. "You sure?" he said across a shoulder—"sure he went in here?"

The barman nodded. "He—he sure did. I saw 'im, didn't I?" he appealed to the custom.

Barstow, grunting, drew back one shoulder. "No sense

146

bustin' the door down," a voice said quietly. "There's another door round at the back."

Barstow looked at this man coldly. "Mebbe you better go an' try it."

The house man went out.

Barstow looked at his watch. He said to the putty-faced barman: "If Red Hat's in there, tell him I'll be back. I've a chore down the street—won't take but a minute."

Saloon lamps drove yellow bars across the street's blackness. Andros, facing Latham's hitchrack, stepped out of the saddle and looked to his guns. Sheathing them he stood for a moment among the shadows, eying the gaunt shack's dust-grimed windows. Ten-fifteen, Barstow's note had said. It was ten-twelve now. He could recall every word of Barstow's message. "Meet me at Latham's at ten-fifteen. I believe we can end this feuding pronto. If you fail to come, responsibility for all further killings will rest with you. I'm doing this account of Flame."

Andros had come account of Flame, too. He well knew what danger might conceivably attend his open appearance on any town's street. Barstow's note had the smell of a baited trap. But he had to make sure—this thing *might* be straight. Barstow, now that his oil grabbing scheme was exposed, just *might* be tricky enough to swap sides. He might hope to smooth things over and get that oil by marriage.

Andros' shoulders stirred impatiently. He would damn soon know.

He mounted the steps to the saloon veranda. A buzz of excitement came through the batwings. He pushed through them swiftly—got his back to a wall. Latham's custom was congregated about some intensely interesting thing on the bar. Andros could not see what this was; but he noticed one man who was not with the others. A tall wasp-waisted man with his face shaved so close his blue jowls shone: He stood at one end of the polished bar. A smaller man held the other end. Both watched Andros with a sly regard. Then the little man started toward him. He said, "Howdy, pardner. Hev y'u got the makin's?"

Andros saw the Durham tag dangling from the man's shirt pocket. From the corners of his eyes he saw the tiny shifting of the tall man at the bar's end. With left hand he reached for the sack in his own shirt pocket while he rubbed his jaw with his other hand slowly. "Yeah," he said, and knew there was no change in this pattern. He had stood this way many times before and seen other troubles shaping up toward gunsmoke. He had guessed right. Barstow's note was a trap.

He smiled at the little man thinly and tossed the man his tobacco. His wheeling look caught the tall man in the act of moving forward. The tall man stopped under Andros' look —lowered his lifted foot with solemn care. A scowl swept fleetingly across his face. Andros grinned at him toughly.

One cat-quick step took Andros to where the back-bar's mirror showed the batwings back of him; and he laughed when he saw the face framed there—Barstow's face, black scowling.

The little man had rolled his cigarette. He had it between his lips now with his left hand bringing up a match to light it. He puffed and, grinning, tossed the sack back to Andros. Andros let it fall unheeded. That trick had whiskers that would need a lawnmower. He knew the men before him now —they were Shane and Hodders, the sheriff's deputies—the men he had driven off the Rocking T. He appreciated the gleam in the shorter man's eyes.

Hodders, the tall man, abruptly spoke. "We're arrestin' y'u, Andros. Git your hands up."

Andros stood stiffly planted, unmoving, the planes of his high cheeks bleakly angular. He drawled at Barstow's mirrored reflection. "You won't ever learn, Reb, will you?"

Barstow sneered. "Your goose is cooked."

Andros sighed when he saw the little man's shoulders settling. At the bar's end steel rasped leather. All bets were off; to stall any further would be sheer suicide. Andros drove his right hand legward.

The crash of guns rushed against these walls. Blue fog choked the room and bit men's nostrils. Powder smoke swirled about Andros' bent figure and frantically whipped through a half-raised window. And when it cleared little Shane lay dead; and against the bar the tall man, Hodders, sagged, sobbing curses, both elbows shattered.

Andros turned with a look cold as death. He said dustily, "You can't catch a wolf with skunk traps, Barstow!"

148

His eyes smashed the burly ranchman backwards. "You started this. Now suppose you finish it."

Barstow stared like a man demented.

"You been itchin' to see me planted ever since I hit this country," Andros said. "Quit starin', tinhorn, an' drag that gun!"

Venom flattened Barstow's roan cheeks. But he shook his head. "Not yet, friend. Not just yet."

"Why not? What you waitin' for? Have you always got to see a man's back before you dare put finger to trigger?"

Cold sweat stood on Barstow's forehead. "I can wait for mine," he gritted doggedly.

"Wait till I turn my back, you mean?" Contempt was plain in Andros' look. "I don't think even a polecat would eat from the same plate you use!"

24

"COME A-SMOKIN'!"

FACING his men in the ramshackle cabin at Tournament Flat Andros said: "What we've done we've done pretty well—but it ain't enough. We've got to work faster an' hit a damned sight harder if we aim to smash this Pool."

"Brass tacks," Kid Badger suggested.

"In plain words," Andros said, "the Pool's commencin' to get its breath. They've got more gun fighters an' their riders outnumber us ten to one. We've got by thus far because they've not been organized. We've had the jump on 'em. Fast as they'd lam reinforcements off to some isolated spot, one of our gangs would come down on the place those men were taken from.

"But that's all over; they're set now and our system's pegged. Way they trapped Sam Hackberry shows it. We got one chance left to bust 'em. An' one chance only."

"Let's hear it," said Rockinstraw, clearing his throat.

"We've got to hit at their strongest point. We've got to smash Reb Barstow flat!"

New River Ned whistled softly. "Barstow's got more'n thirty

riders—all tough hands from who laid the chunk. They'll be watchin' for a play like that!"

There were other grumblings. Rockinstraw said, "The whole country will."

"That's why we've got to do it." Andros minced no words. "It's the surest way to crack this Pool. If we can carry it off there won't be enough nerve left in that bunch to pin up a baby's diapers with! You fellows," he looked them over, "used to have pretty hard reps—but nothin' like this Pool will pin on you if they come through on top. If we quit now, or lose, they'll have posses huntin' us from hell to breakfast. What's more they'll have the whole Southwest laughin' at us for a bunch of fool kids that thought we was tough."

That brought them up as nothing else could have. They *were* tough; but not so tough they could stand folks' laughter. Andros said: "Barstow's on the skids right now."

"That don't make me feel no better," New River Ned said scowling, "about bein' made food for the posies tomorrow. Crackpot stunts I'm ready to try; but a stunt like that—Hell! we could never cut it."

"Barstow's shaky," said Andros harshly. "He's scared of his shadow. Three-four of his best men's left him—pulled out complete for other parts. There's talk around his bunkhouse of more of 'em pullin' out. There's others wants to hook up with Vargas' fightin' Chihuahuans—an' Barstow knows it. He can't trust a one of 'em."

Ed Tailman said slowly, "How d'you know this, Andros?"

"What do you think I been doin' these nights? Twiddlin' my thumbs an' playin' mumblypegs?"

These were good men and tough that were pushing this fight for him, but suggesting they brace Reb Barstow's Half-Circle Arrow was asking a powerful lot. Barstow's outfit had its roots in the ground, and Barstow's name meant power the entire length of the Canadian. Andros could not blame these boys for pawing dirt; but he had to swing them round to it if he would see the Pool disintegrate. No other way was possible. Barstow must be smashed, his power made a thing for ridicule. Bocart had given this chore to him. Bocart was expecting results.

National Forests were the only answer to the two-bit rancher's problem, and it was this Pool that was blocking the government's efforts at every step. In this section Barstow

150

and Red Hat were the Pool's chief agents. Red Hat was dead, but Barstow remained untouched. The Pool was beginning to breathe again. Shortly it would band its interests and stamp Andros' raiders into final oblivion—unless they smashed Reb Barstow now.

At that moment one of Kid Badger's Texans came in. He handed a note to Andros. "Lady at Rockin' T ast me would I git this to yo'."

Andros tore the envelope open.

Come to the ranch right off.
Grace Latham.

Rockinstraw read it across his shoulder. "I guess that Half-Circle Arrow raid is off."

Andros hurled the crushed paper from him. "Go get your broncs. We're headin' for Barstow's pronto."

Three nights later Andros sat glumly in a lonely cabin at the head of Alder Creek. The raid on Barstow's had been pretty much of a draw. Barstow's men had repulsed the raiders, had fought the flames and saved most of their buildings. Both sides had lost a few men. Andros' boys had gotten away with seven thousand head of prime beef, but the coup had fallen dismally short of the results he had hoped for.

His men thus far had scored many victories. The Southwest Lumber Syndicate was broken and bankrupt, its sawmills burnt and its men scared out of the country. Salmon Lake Basin had been freed of sheep; so had Horse Mountain and the Sierra Anchas. Asher's Basin had been retaken and the ranches northwest of Pius Draw had been reclaimed from syndicate riders and returned to their owners. Mormon Flat, the Tule Butte range and the Limestone Hills had been cleared of Red Hat's blatting flocks, and Tortilla Camp was strewn with dead sheep. Cave Creek Village, a sheep stronghold, was deserted. Pool interests at Sawmill and Schoolhouse Tank had been soundly thrashed. All across the country syndicate riders were quitting. Three railroad survey parties had been brought to a standstill and twenty miles of markers ripped from the ground. The Rincon was retrieved and Table Mountain cleared. Fifteen of Red Hat's Chihuahuans had been killed at Apache Hill, and the syndicate ranches west of Curry Basin had all been gutted.

But this was not enough.

Against it, Red Hat's men had beaten them at Sombrero Butte, killing eight of Andros' raiders. At first Andros' successes had attracted other small ranchers to his side, but since that trap in which the sheepmen had dropped seven other of Andros' men—including the famed Sam Hackberry— no more owners had thrown their weight behind him. His money that Bocart had given him was gone—spent to the final penny. Red Hat's Chihuahuans had badly whipped the raiders at Pueblo and Sugar Loaf Mountain. Kid Badger had been killed in the raid on the Half-Circle Arrow and his Texans had promptly departed for safer places. New River Ned was down with a bullet in his groin, and Hernbarger and Obe Trane both were dead. The soldiers he had expected to come after that fight at Barstow's had not appeared, their officers no doubt bought off by syndicate money. Andros had counted heavily on getting those soldiers down here; their presence would have stopped all warfare and spiked the Pool's retaliation—which could be expected now at any moment.

Three weeks of blood and gore, and so far Andros could see the Pool was just as solid as ever. Its resources were illimitable. It was throwing hired guns into this fight three times faster than Andros' men could kill or scare them off.

He let his breath out in a dismal sigh. It had been a desperate hope, this play of Bocart's; doom-slated from the outset. He didn't blame Bocart for getting him into this. Bocart's back was against the wall, his hiring of Andros a final expediency. But the Pool was too strong for them; the two-bit ranchers had been right from the start. They had never had a chance to smash that outfit. They never—

He was like that, scowling, when a lean white hand flung the door back.

"Clem!"

It was Grace Latham's voice. He reacted to it sluggishly, the fatigue that was upon him showing visibly as he wheeled. His glance picked her up and it was not gallant.

"You don't have to eye me that way!" she lashed. "I didn't come here for myself!" Fierce strain lay across her features, reshaping them to a face he did not know. "It's Flame!" she

152

cried. *"Flame Tarnell!* They got her yesterday—arrested her and carried her off—"

"What's that!" Three swift strides got Andros' hands upon her shoulders. *"What was that?"*

She grimaced at the pressure. But her eyes were level, frightened. "Flame's gone!" she whispered hoarsely. "I warned you something was up three days ago; I told you to come to the ranch—"

But Andros' grip was off her. He was whirling toward the door.

"Wait—*Wait!"* Grace cried. "I'm going with you—"

"No you're not! This—"

"Well, *I* am!" Art Rockinstraw stood in the open door.

"Then you better come a-smokin'!" Andros said, and whipped past him into the night.

25

WHEN A MAN FIGHTS

NIGHT was far advanced when Andros saw the lights of town. He came in sight of them alone, Rockinstraw's horse having gone lame and dropped him out of this six miles back.

With jaw tight clamped he passed the gaunted outlines of Long Rope's forgotten shacks. Light streaming from the batwing doors showed a pair of broncs standing hipshot before the saloon, and locust sound filled the gloom with jerky rhythm.

His saddle creaked as he swung to the ground. Skirting the broncs he went softly through the hock deep dust and, with an equal softness, mounted the steps. Floorboards skreaked as he crossed the veranda; another step and he was through the batwings.

Behind the bar Turly's head jerked up and all the color went out of his face when he saw who stood before him. They had the place to themselves. Andros leaned on the bar and hooked one thumb to his gun belt. "Never mind the rotgut. I'm not drinkin' tonight. I'm huntin' Barstow an' the sheriff."

Turly appeared to have trouble swallowing. He fumbled

153

a letter from his pocket and put it on the bar's gleaming surface. "For you. It—it come this mornin'."

His tongue made a frightened lick across his lips and he stretched his hands flat down on the bar. "Look! I—I ain't in this—see?"

"I never thought you were—"

Andros broke off as a man came in with his hat awry and his blue eyes popping. He did not appear to see Andros. He looked at Turly unbelieving and said: "Good Christ! you heard what's happenin'? They claim this thing's all over but the kissin'—they say the Pool's gone smashed all over! Busted! Beat! Barstow an' Red Hat riders is bustin' a blue streak towards the Border. Hossflesh can't get 'em out here quick enough! They say four of the Pool's biggest outfits is under the hammer—"

Andros' voice cut through to say: "Never mind the wild rumors, Turly—I'm wantin' Barstow an' the sheriff! Where are they?"

It looked like Turly had to prime himself to speak. "As Gawd's my—"

That much he said, and got no farther, stopped by Andros' lifted hand.

From the back room Barstow's voice came swearing—and a girl's voice said: "I won't! I won't!"

The bones showed up like castings through the skin of Andros' face. He left the bar, and the two leaning on it, and walked to the back room's door and opened it.

A lot of things came clear to him then; he understood what he saw immediately. *Krell wasn't dead!* He never had been! For there Krell stood against the wall, short steps removed from sheepman Duarte Salas. And a few paces nearer the door stood Barstow facing a scared-looking parson, his left hand tight-locked about Flame's arm.

But it was Krell that Andros watched. He saw Krell's muscles leap and stiffen—saw him take one backward, groping step. He'd have taken more if the wall hadn't been there. The wish was plain in his frantic stare.

"Clem!" Flame cried, and crushed the back of a hand against her mouth.

Barstow's ruddy cheeks jerked round.

Andros said cat-soft, "If you're ready, gents—" and let them finish the rest for themselves.

154

The parson groaned. Color was two wicked splotches on Krell's gray face. Barstow loosed an oath, big shoulders tipping. Salas stooped. He raised with the gleam of a gun in his fingers.

And still Andros waited. That had ever been his greatest danger—the weakness of this soft streak in him that would give every man the benefit of doubt. If the sheepman fired, the rest would slap leather. Andros knew that, yet waited for it stubbornly.

Then Salas fired, and the light went out in a shower of glass. Even as his guns slid clear Andros wondered why Salas had not sent that shot at him.

Then all was pandemonium, with lead ripping through this gloom and the thin wall rocking to the pulsing blasts as gun after gun made the smoke-reek fiercer. He saw the lean bright flicker of Barstow's pistol and drove three slugs in that direction instantly.

The neckerchief at his throat gave a jerk, something quick slapped his vest and his hat jumped back. He heard Krell yell, "Y'u damn' coyote, where are y'u?"— heard the smash of a slug biting wood beside him. He caught the scrape of someone's feet, and a long, shrill breath he could not place. A door slammed suddenly, and the muffled sound of Salas' shouting came to him from the alley. "Andros! Give 'em hell! I got the girl out here with me!"

Andros knew his safety depended on his staying where he was and holding his fire as much as might be till he got a definite target. No one would expect him to remain by the door.

So he stayed there. No sound came from Barstow, and Krell had gone cautious. Quiet crept among the dimming echoes—a hush so vibrant Andros dared not fill the empty chambers of his pistols. But he'd plenty left. He would make them do.

Then, abruptly, he could stand the wait no longer.

His left hand felt for the handle of the door. With a flick of the wrist he turned the knob. He took a long stride right and yanked the door open.

Light from the barroom showed Barstow down; he was over in the corner with his head between his knees. Krell was staring from the opposite doorway, lank and crouched, face twisted with hatred. He said, "I'm tired of yo' goddam follerin', Andros!" and jerked-up his pistols to rake the shadows.

He was firing when Andros' bullet pushed a hole between his eyes.

Andros stepped across his body and lurched into the alley's coolness, pulling the clean sweet air deep into his tortured lungs. He keened the night with red-rimmed stare. "Flame!" he called. "Flame Tarnell—where are you?"

When no one answered he punched the empty shells from his guns and reloaded. He stumbled through this murk to the street. He stopped there, breathing hard. Flame stood by his ground-hitched horse. Lounging beside her stood Salas.

The sheepman elevated empty hands. "Nice evenin'," he said dryly.

"Salas, why didn't you gun me when you had the chance?"

"For why should I gun you? This thing is over—*es verdad;* the Pool is busted. Smash' complete."

"But why—"

"*Quien sabe?*" he drawled; gave a Latin shrug.

"I can't make you out," Andros sighed.

"Let it go like that." Salas grinned a little at Flame Tarnell. "I got a girl who is wait down below the Line. If you're through with me—"

"Go with God," Andros said, and shook his hand.

"Flame—" Andros said and stopped, at a loss for words to use with this girl who meant so very much to him.

But she seemed to understand. She said, "I know . . . Grace Latham told me after you had gone. She—she's going to marry Gallup John. Clem, somehow I can't help feeling sorry for her."

He nodded. "John'll be mighty· good to her, though. I reckon he plumb worships that woman, Flame." He paused then, wondering how he was to speak his thoughts, to explain himself to her—to say what had to be said. Course the only thing he'd ought to say was "Good-bye"—and say it quick, but—

He had to find out how she felt.

"Guess I better be gettin' my truck together. If what's bein' said about the Pool is true, I reckon my job's plumb ended here."

She backed off from him, looked up at him anxiously.

Her lips seemed about to protest. Instead, they said; "Ain't you wantin' to ask me somethin' first, Clem?"

"My record's too damn' black!" he blurted miserably. "Besides, you wouldn't want me; I been married before! Krell—"

"As if that could make any difference!"

And then she was in his arms.

Minutes later he recollected the letter Turly had given him. He got it out of his pocket. Flame ripped it open for him because he had his arm around her. The document inside was very official looking. It was written on crinkly paper. It said:

Clem Andros
Long Rope, Arizona

CONGRATULATIONS! The National Forest Bill went through! You can name your job.

Cass Bocart.

THE END

157

TEXAS TORNADO

ONE

FRAGMENTS of the shattered adobe wall dustily skittered off his hatbrim. Kane Marlatt knew then with what gullibility he had swallowed the notion Tularosa's men had quit. Tularosa's men would never quit while life and breath remained in him who, of all Craft Towner's enemies, could alone bring ruin to the rancher's plans.

He was tall, this young Kane Marlatt, with a cool, dark, highboned face very easy of remembrance. The lash of the wind lay plain seen on it, and the sun's bright fury and the turbulent ways that had shaped him. Peril's sharpness was in each gesture, in his laugh, in his shout —in the quick flash of teeth that showed through his tight streaked smile. A penniless fool, he had oft been called —a soldier of fortune whom none dared trust because of the wild high courage that enlivened his acts and spoiled the pattern of the things men would have used him for.

Kane Marlatt, crouched, whipped a lean and desperate look about. The crumbling wall at his back was all that was left of some Mex woodpacker's shack—poor shelter against the rifles of Tularosa's riders. The fringe of timber between him and the mountain slopes he'd just come down would be filled with those riders, dismounted now and fanning out to trap him. They would probably do it.

He was afoot, and this was a country strange and new to him who had come from Texas. He had lost his horse in a treacherous slide some ten miles back in the Santa Ritas, an hour and a half out of Greaterville. They had told him there to ride straight west and he'd come to the Santa Cruz Valley. There it lay right now, below and before him like a gray-brown sea, stretching vast and lonely to the far blue crags that would be the peaks of the Tucson Mountains. Somewhere north, between here and there, would be the famed walled town of Tucson, home of the wild and the free—home to the tinhorns and brothel touts, to the stage-boot robbers of the Spanish Trail, to the hired-gun hombres of the last frontier.

Marlatt doubted he could make it.

Not that he was scared of that far a walk—he would gladly tramp twenty times that far if only the gods would let him. But the gods were having their horse laugh now. Two hundred and fifty odd miles he'd come—all the dusty way from Hachita in the heart of the Grant County cow country. All those broiling miles he had come with the truth about Craft Towner, that later he might return to send the cattle king's grand schemes toppling; to expose him for the man he was—the elusive, night-riding "Kingfisher."

Kane Marlatt had thought when he got to Greaterville that he had given Towner's men the slip. That had been his one great foolishness. He had underestimated the dogged tenacity of Tularosa, Towner's range boss. And now he was apt to pay with his life, if Tularosa had any say in it.

The smell of danger was a tang in the wind that plastered Kane Marlatt's curls back. And his grin was tight as he dropped to the ground and, snail-like, wormed his way to the wall's far corner whence a glimpse of Towner's men might be had—or at least a glimpse of the powder-smoke puffs that had to lift every time a Winchester whanged.

The corner reached, he dragged off his hat and had his quick look; and was mighty thankful it had been quick. If it hadn't, the lead that kicked grit in his face might have grabbed the range for a second neat shot that would have smashed him between the eyes.

He lay still awhile in scowling thought while the sun's heat pulled the sweat from his pores and time ran on with no further sound from the timber-hid men whose plain, grim purpose was to see that he left his bones in this place, along with the secret he had wrenched from them.

It looked, Marlatt coolly thought, as if this were to be

the end of him. He didn't particularly mind being afoot, or even in a strange land, as far as that went, for God's open had always been friendly to him and he could easily have made out had these been the only threats to his safety. But Tularosa, he had learned, could not be ignored; nor could his gun-slinging, cow-stealing riders. Particularly now, when he'd just discovered his cartridge supply was exhausted. He had what few shells were still in his weapons, and not one cartridge more.

The sound of his watch was a very loud thing in the sultry quiet of the surrounding space. A mocking thing it seemed to him, inexorably ticking the time away till Tularosa, grown impatient, should cast caution to the winds and stake his all on a clean-up charge that would wind Marlatt's rope round his picket pin.

It was not in the man to wait much longer. It was high tribute to Marlatt's marksmanship that he had countenanced any wait at all. Tularosa's way was a headlong way—brash and reckless as Marlatt's own. None knew this better than Marlatt, who had worked two months with the man. He was frowning with the somberness of that thought when Tularosa's yell came sailing downward from the dappled shadows of the timber. Quick and hard, it was; intolerant and demanding.

"Marlatt! *Marlatt!* You still there?"

The solemn turn of Marlatt's lips grew faintly mocking. He made no answer. Nor did he move.

He heard Towner's foreman curse—heard the swift speculations of Towner's men. Then Tularosa's lifted voice said: "Damn your soul! Come out of there! Come outa there pronto, with your paws up, or, by Gawd, we're comin' after you!"

Marlatt chuckled. "Any time you're ready, boys."

Tularosa's men went silent. The feel of this thing got tighter and tighter. Marlatt turned his head, inch by slow inch, and raked a look behind him. The squat thick brush of a burro weed was a sturdy green against the yellow earth. It was three feet back of him.

Marlatt looked at the adobe wall again. Its crumbling

contour, tapering toward the corner, where he lay rose a bare two feet in height. He tried to recall what degree of angle the timberline might have; how much elevation at that distance would be needed to spot him above the wall's rough rim. Not much, he thought, were he by that weed.

He turned over with infinite care and, with his rifle flat against the ground, gripped it by the barrel, edging it outward till its stock stopped against the weed's gnarled trunk.

Nothing happened.

Marlatt's grin showed a cool bleak humor. That Tularosa's men had not seen his rifle stock was scant insurance the would not see him. The were bound to see the weed's bush top. It was ten inches high; and he meant to have it even though certain they'd catch its blur when he pulled it loose. With the weed in his hat and his hat on his head, anyone who sought to pot him as he looked above the wall would very likely be considerably surprised.

He pulled back his rifle. He dragged off his hat and edged around until his booted feet were solidly against the the wall, with a fervent hope that it would hold the exerted pressure. He felt his shoulders scraping outward toward the weed. One outstretched hand abruptly touched it. He lay slack then, slowly tightening his hold on it.

He was all set to yank it loose when his narrowed glance intently scrutinized a thing he had not thus far noticed. Instead of dropping sheer and direct to the far-down floor of the Santa Cruz Valley, the tip of a juniper gently waving beyond the lip of the land just yonder seemed to indicate that the slope fell away in more easy stages.

Kane Marlatt lay awhile thinking hard. The plateau's brink was forty feet distant, beyond the burro weed in his hand. But if he could reach it and the slope *did* descend in easy stages—or if it but had a ledge he could get his feet on, there was a sporting chance that even yet Tularosa's chase might be made to end futilely.

There would be risk, of course; grave risk in plenty. But risk and Marlatt were old bedfellows. He would be seen, and the Towner guns would play grim music. Yet it was something else that held Kane Marlatt moveless with the burro weed still clenched in his hand and his eyes grim-squinted in the sun's hot light. The plateau's brink lay forty feet distant. His rifle lay by the adobe wall. Should he risk precious moments to fetch the rifle or rush for the slope without more thought of it?

He'd about decided to leave the saddle gun when Tularosa's growl came down the wind. "All right, boys!" Tularosa snarled; and hard on his words came the crashing of brush that told they were coming, and coming fast.

Marlatt's reaction was characteristic. He yanked out the weed and rolled for his rifle. He snatched up his hat, stuffed the weed in its crown, clapped the hat on his head and cinched up its chin strap. Beneath his knees the ground was trembling to the booted rush of the headlong charge as, utterly calm, Marlatt picked his rifle.

He thrust its barrel across the wall and raised himself till his glance could follow it. From three different angles slugs tore through his hat; and the Towner men loosed savage yells as they bent to their triggers, wild to drop him.

Marlatt sighted and fired, as cool as a well chain. One bent-forward runner at the extreme left of the converging charge stopped running with one foot still raised. His rifle struck ground with an unheard clatter. His arms flailed wildly and he turned half around, spilling sideways as his knees let go.

Marlatt fired again. A lanky man, dead center of the charge, reared back as though an ax had struck him, then jackknifed forward with his face plowing sand.

Marlatt's face and hat front were brown with adobe dust and his eyes burned fiercely from the flung grit in them, but he held his place with inflexible calm. It was uncanny, unnerving, that a man dared hold so steady in the face of such fire. It was meant to have, and had its effect.

Tularosa's charge was stopped. Ludicrous in their amazed bewilderment, Towner's men triggered frantically, their aim gone haywire. Slug after slug had jerked Marlatt's hat, yet still he was there, teeth flashing derisively, levering a fresh shell into his Winchester.

Marlatt's rifle picked up Tularosa's gaunt figure; he centered its bead on the man's checked shirt. But just as he triggered Tularosa whirled, leaping sideways, and tore for the timber. The final bullet from Marlatt's rifle kicked dust on the backs of his bounding boots.

Marlatt swung the warm barrel for another target. He had no shots left, but they couldn't know this. Nor were any waiting to discover the fact. Like their boss, Towner's gun hands were scuttling for shelter.

Marlatt dropped the Winchester and raced straight west for the plateau's brink. Reaching it, he stood crouched there, and cursed bitterly. There was a ledge beyond—but it was fourteen feet down and hardly three feet wide; and after that the slope dropped sheer for eighty feet to the rock rubble piled on the valley floor.

But he had to go over—there was no choice now. If he stayed where he was he'd be dead in ten seconds. And there was no time left to get back to the wall. Already Towner's men had swung around and were firing. The sound of that lead was a shrill high fury as Marlatt dropped to the earth and swung his legs over.

Spattered grit from their shots stung his cheeks, bit his forehead. With all his weight on his elbow, he twisted his head for one down-flashing look, and that way, still looking, he felt the lip crumble.

And then he was dropping-swiftly plunging through space.

TWO

ONE final harsh regret brought a frown to Marlatt's face as he felt the lip break under him. He should have killed Tularosa while he'd had the chance. All thought was then dashed out of him—shocked from him in that fierce and headlong impact with the ledge. He struck on his feet but could not keep his balance. The fall's force and sudden stoppage doubled him, thrust him outward, and he staggered, desperately reeling. He got one backthrust foot beneath him and knew in that same moment there was naught beyond but vast, immeasurable space and, finally, the rocks of the valley floor. Instinct flung both arms out in a frantic windmill sweep and he felt something brush an elbow. Clutching fingers told him it was an out-thrust branch of the juniper, and he closed the hand round it savagely. With both feet hard against the rock-sharp rim of the ledge, he swayed far out to the springy give of the bending branch. With a long-drawn groan it abruptly snapped—just as Marlatt's right fist grabbed frantic hold of a crevice-bound root.

He was still hanging on, but that was all. And the root's brittle creak was a fearsome thing as Marlatt's boots skittered off the ledge and dropped all his weight clean and hard against it. Sweat was cold on the back of his neck and the palms of his hands were slippery with it. He tried to dig the toes of his boots in, but the shale of the cliffside wouldn't hold him. And all the time the protesting creak of the weight-strained root told how short was the time *it* was likely to support him.

He dropped the branch his left hand held and grabbed for the trunk, catching a hold low down on it. He let go the root and, wildly swaying, with a tremendous effort got his right hand, too, round the juniper's trunk and hoisted his knees until he got his boots on the ledge again.

With the pounding of boots stamping earth above him and the Towner men's shouts growing loud, triumphant, Marlatt knew a desperate need for haste ere those running reached the brink and looked over. One look would be plenty. They would shoot on the instant.

Hand over hand he pulled himself upward, with the juniper groaning and crazily swaying, till at last both his knees were firm on the ledge. He let go his hold of the tree and with arched back dived for close contact with the roughly eroded plateau's wall. With back hard against it and taut nerves vibrant, he heard Towner's men on the brink above him.

He reached for his pistol and found it gone—shaken loose, no doubt, by his recent exertions.

He was trapped again!

His soft curse was harsh. But more bleak still was the glint of his eyes as he flung his glance upward. Gone tense, all the lines of his face broke queerly. He blinked, shook his head, and blinked again. Then a tight grin tugged his lips and he dragged one vast, relieved breath to his lungs. The cliff curled inward under the brink; wind and weather had cut away some soft spot here so that where he lay he could not see the cliff top—nor could the men grouped on it, peering down, see him.

"Well," Tularosa's voice said wickedly, "that's that! By Gawd, we got him!"

The cold satisfaction in the Towner man's words caused thin, silent laughter to roll across Marlatt's lips as he sank weakly back against the cliff's rough wall. An aching weariness flowed through him then, unstringing his muscles and leaving them jerking with an all-gone feeling that he knew for reaction.

A long while later Kane Marlatt got up and took stock of himself. His muscles still throbbed with a slow, dull ache, and each nerve of his racked frame quivered and jangled from the strain put on it; but he was still

entire and bore only one mark of the Towner gang's guns
—a crease in his scalp that he'd only just noticed. A faint
track left by some speeding bullet, more painful than
serious. Shaking the weed from his hat, he cuffed its torn
crown to some semblance of shape, readjusted its chin
strap and put it back on.

He stared across the valley to where, shaded with
mauves and ceruleans, the Tucson peaks loomed against
the sun. Afternoon was sliding into evening and, unless
he hurried, night would trap him on this ledge. Long
since, the diminishing thump of departing hoofbeats had
announced Tularosa's leaving, and Marlatt, unless the
man were a lot more subtle than appearances had given
evidence, was now free to discover if he might say fare-
well to this ledge which, in the final moment, had stood
between himself and death.

It was still between himself and death, yet if he could
not quit it the end would be just as certain as though
Tularosa's lead had found him. You could not hide from
hunger or fly by flapping your arms.

To the right, southeast by compass, the ledge angled
gently upward, and that way Marlatt bent his steps. The
grade's scant lift was extremely gradual, so insignificant
as to seem almost no raise at all. Then abruptly the tiny
ledge began narrowing.

Marlatt threw a quick glance upward. Where he stood
the wall curved away from the ledge, sloping gently east
toward the plateau's lip which, in this place, was twelve
long feet above him. Three feet wide the ledge had been
back there where he'd dropped onto it; where he stood
now it was only two.

With a grimace Marlatt continued, and the ledge continued to narrow. It shrank away to a foot and a half—to
one; and at this width, around some old erosion, drove
acutely upward at an angle of approximately thirty de-
grees. One bare slippery foot of treacherous shelf, and
beyond it a wild drop through space to the rock-littered
floor of the valley beneath. It was dusk down there and

the rocks were hidden in the curdled mark of approaching night; but even were it smoothest sand, certain death awaited the man who fell.

Marlatt jammed his belly against the wall. It was do or die. The dark gods laughed when a man stood still. They'd had enough laughing for one afternoon.

Marlatt twisted his head and peered downward once more. Water made a faint, muffled splashing, and an updraft off the flats below brought a damp, earthy smell; and a wolf's dim howl wailed through the stillness.

He spread his arms for greater balance and a nearer contact with the red cliff wall, and he moved one foot at a time, carefully testing each new surface before trusting his weight to it.

The plateau's lip was just above him now, hardly two feet—within easy reach should he raise his arms. He did not make that mistake, however. He was quite aware of what would happen should he trust his weight to that crumbly lip.

When the exploring fingers of his stretched right hand hooked into a crevice, he stopped; when he discovered that roughness would give him purchase, he solemnly lifted his left foot, bringing it up from the knee till he had its heel in his cupped left palm. Slowly then, and with infinite care, he worked the boot off, after which he stood utterly still till the reddening sun dried the cold sweat off him. Tossing the boot to the land up yonder, he commenced operations with the boot still on him. The sun was low when the second tossed boot sent its faint thump down, and Marlatt, with only thin socks between himself and the ledge, resumed the tortuous climb again.

He was a man whose muscles were stretched violin strings when he stood at last upon solid ground. Like a man gone blind he made his way to the adobe wall and dropped with his back muscles sagged against it. The smoke he rolled with shaking hands wasted more tobacco than was curled in its paper. But he got the thing built finally. It was the best cigarette he had ever smoked.

He could see two rock piles beyond the wall. He could

guess what they hid without going closer. Men he had shot. Considering them, he had one faint, quick twinge of pity; but he felt no regret for having pulled the trigger that had wound their ropes up. He had killed them deliberately, intentionally, but the fault lay elsewhere. It was not Marlatt's habit to confuse an issue. This was an old, a very old pattern that had had its beginnings away back in Texas. The passing of those two men was the natural and cumulative result of the manner in which they had done their living. Daily contact with violence had had its effect.

Marlatt got up presently and began his search. He was a methodical man, and his methodicalness rewarded him. Near timber's edge he picked a pistol out of the brush—a Colt's .44 with five shots in it. He felt a great deal better with that gun in his holster.

The sawtoothed crags of yon western mountains were edged with a fiery glow from the vanished sun when he struck off north, well back from the brink. He had no food, no horse, no rifle; but with tightened belt and his boots pulled on, he struck out for Tucson and the man Craft Towner had hired him to kill.

THREE

THE Tucson stage office, dingy, dim, thickly coated with dust, was about the last place a man would expect to encounter a pretty girl. Yet one was in there—a *damn'* pretty girl, if you accepted the view of the tall man lounged in its doorway. He had paused there, hipshot and idle, with big thumbs hooked in his gun belt and his bold eyes glinting approval. He was a slim-shanked man —actually gaunt in his slimness, and incredibly redheaded. His clothes held the grime of long hours in the saddle; and neither the girl nor the agent remembered having seen him before. He must, therefore, be a stranger, and as such of no special interest to either of them. They returned their attention to the business in hand, to the grip on the counter and the conversation his arrival had suspended.

"But I told you," the girl said firmly, "Ora doesn't want a receipt. He's not asking you to take this money on deposit—"

"With all due regard, ma'am, if it's a check your uncle wants I'm afraid you're going to have to go to the bank for it."

She said with quick challenge: "Is the Company tired of Ora Flack's business?"

"My dear young lady!" The agent looked shocked. "The Company regards your uncle with the highest esteem—"

"Then—"

"Unfortunately," the agent said regretfully, "I am not the Company. I have to follow instructions, and my instructions in this case are very plain—*very* plain. A receipt I can give you gladly. But no checks."

She stood and considered the look on his face. "Very well," she agreed, and pulled on her gloves. "I shall tell Uncle Ora you're—"

"Gosh sakes!" cried the agent hastily. "Don't you do it, ma'am! Don't you go puttin' it *that* way—*I* ain't got anything to do with it!" His countenance showed a most ludicrous alarm. "I got my orders straight from headquarters, ma'am—*no more checks!* If it was a little one you was wantin'—why, I'd take a chance an' make out like I'd forgot it or somethin'. But forty thousan' is a hellemonious passel of money, ma'am—"

He broke off, suddenly remembering the man in the door. The girl, too, swiftly turned to see if the stranger had overheard. But the fellow was gone.

The agent breathed a little easier. He mopped his face with a red bandanna. "You tell your uncle I'd like powerfully to oblige him, ma'am. But I'm plumb hogtied with these dingblasted regulations. I tell you, Miz' Ranleigh, ma'am, you can't hardly blame the Company, come right down to it. They been driven—"

Miss Ranleigh saw the talk freeze on his mouth; saw the mouth drop open, ludicrous in its dismay. Saw a wagon-sheet pallor cross the wrinkles of his cheeks. His popping gaze stared across her shoulder as though it viewed some slavering beast all crouched and cocked to spring.

The cold rasp of a voice just back of her said: "Reach—an' reach quick, brother!"

Statue still Miss Ranleigh stood, as though the words had rooted her there. Her shoulders shrank away from the sound; but even as they did so some remembered need changed the color of her glance and she brought the shoulders hard around, turning her head to see the lank black shapes that blocked the sunshine from the open door.

Two men stood there with lifted guns. Jerked up neckerchiefs hid their features, all but the hard, unwinking eyes that were surveying the agent for signs of resistance.

175

Then the taller man, a raw-boned ruffian with a battered horse-thief hat on his head, said coolly with a lurking humor, "Just hand me back that grip on the counter. . . . Thank you kindly, ma'am."

His bold eyes glinted a grudging approval. "You show good sense. No fuss nor feathers—that's the way I like 'em. If they's anythin' I hate it's a screamin' female." The hard eyes left her; bored the frozen agent. "Let's see what you got in that safe there, pardner."

The harried agent, very conscious of Miss Ranleigh's stare, flung a badgered glance from one to the other of them. The tall man's pistol joggled suggestively. "I'd shore hate to puncture such a puny worm, but if you don't git that strongbox opened right pronto, mister, you're goin' to make a new voice with the angel chorus."

The agent gulped. Pride forgotten, he backed from the counter like a man treading eggs.

"Well, now. That's more like it," the tall man drawled. "Just stoop over now an' spin that—"

The rest was lost in a jarring explosion that left Miss Ranleigh white and shaking. Having stooped, the agent had grabbed for his shotgun.

The tall man sheathed his smoking pistol. His pardner had already backed out the door. His voice called guardedly. "Okay, Buck," and the tall man nodded. The bold eyes swept Miss Ranleigh's face. "Better hightail it, ma'am—"

"You cowardly murderer!"

The tall man snorted. "'D you think I was goin' to let that little weakling shoot me?" He laughed harshly then and, with Miss Ranleigh's grip tucked under his arm, backed into the street and was suddenly gone.

Kane Marlatt rode into Tucson on a flea-bitten bay about nine-thirty of a cloudless morning. He saw the time on a clock in a saloon he was passing. There was dust in the weary creases of his high-boned face and his clothes were gray with it, but the touch of his glance was sharp as knife steel as he surveyed the signs whose faded letters were crudely painted on the walls of the buildings. He was searching for something, and when he found it he turned his horse into the Calle Real and jostled his way down its cluttered length till he came to the shaggy posts of Oliphant's Corral. There he stopped and got down

A long-haired man lounged out of the shade. "I'm Oliphant," he said. "How's Joe doin'? Still got his rheumatiz?"

"Joe?—Oh!" Marlatt grunted, following Oliphant's look. "Expect I got this bronc from Joe's range boss. . . ."

"That would be Hartsell."

Marlatt shrugged. "I was to leave the horse here—"

"Gear too?"

Marlatt nodded.

"Guess you'll be wantin' a complete outfit then."

"What have you got?"

"Well, I expect we could git together—*if*," Oliphant added cautiously, "you got the necessary wherewithal. This is a chancey country, mister, as mebbe you've found out. Lotta drifters—some of 'em right smart-lookin', too. But here t'day and gone t'morrah. Man can't invest in no credit—"

"I've got money—"

"I won't take no Tubac money—"

"I'm talkin' cash. Coin of the realm," Marlatt grunted.

"Good! I kin allus hear the voice of Cash. You go right ahead. Pick out any bronc you fancy; then we'll go look over the saddles. Go right ahead," he prompted.

Marlatt's look at the renters held little charity. "Let's get this understood," he said. "I'm lookin' for a horse—not crowbait."

The corral keeper thought that over. "A special horse, mebby?"

"It's certain-sure got to *look* like a horse." Marlatt squinted across the far side of the pen. "What you got in that shed over there?"

"Ummm . . ." Oliphant's tone was sly as his glance.

Marlatt got a roll of bills from his pocket and let the man see the ends of a few. Mr. Oliphant shed his coy-

ness pronto; flashed the smile of a man of business. Marlatt, inside of five minutes, was the owner of a blaze-
faced roan whose shape held promise of speed and endurance. "I'll be leavin' him here for a while," Marlatt
said, and went off afoot to explore the town.

He found little to attract him. It began as it ended in
desolation, a rolling range of mesquite and greasewood.
The metallic glare of the climbing sun beat down with a
headlong fury. The air was stifling, and sweat threw its
spreading stains across Marlatt's shirt; sweat's shine lay
on the faces of the passers-by. Most of the buildings were
single-storied; all were of adobe, brown and dusty. Dust
filled the streets hock-high to a horse, and people crossing were forced to plow through it.

He saw no sign of the famous wall; not even a crumbling trace was left to show where once its protection
had stood. This was a town of heat and squalor and
smells; a melting pot for all the scum of the Western
prairies. Thief's paradise, he thought, looking around. A
robbers' stronghold, and flapping with bustle. There were
lots of people dressed in all sorts of colors and conditions
of clothing. Burros and pack mules were moving everywhere, and the streets were raucous with the high-
pitched screams of naked urchins. With creaks and
groans and chain-clanking rattles, great lumbering wagons rolled hither and yon behind teams of oxen. Ponies
and wagons lined the hitch rails solidly. It was hard to
believe that in three hours' time these streets would be
left to the dust and flies—would be deserted, abandoned,
forsaken as Gomorrah. Many things the gringos had
changed, but tradition still claimed the middle of each
day.

There was a bank off yonder—big letters said so; but
Marlatt would have guessed it without the sign by the
number of beggars gathered round it. To the left of the
bank was a marshal's office, and next beyond was an immense saloon. A lanky man on its porch was extending
welcome; a frock-coated fellow who stood in the shade
of its wooden awning and sent his voice traveling up

and down the street. He was laboring under a considerable strain, for a crowd was gathering just beyond him, jamming up traffic and growing every second. A red-shirted fellow with a twenty-mule team offered a free education in the use of cuss words. A long-geared bullwhacker yelled: "Git the marshal!"

Marlatt tugged the leg of a halted horseman. "What's up?"

"Hell Crick, by the look. Miz' Ranleigh's claimin' them two fellers stole her uncle's money."

"Which two? Who's Miss Ranleigh?"

"Who's Miz'—Godfreys!" The horseman stared and spat. "You mus'—"

"Shut up!" snapped a bearded man fiercely; then, desperately, a girl's scared voice cried: "Stop them! They're the ones, I tell you! That tall man's the one who killed Mr. Dowling!"

It was no business of Marlatt's. He had all the trouble he could handle already. But he came from Texas and, to him, that meant something. He felt ashamed this girl had had to *ask* for help. He was white with anger when no man moved.

He went through the crowd like a knife through butter.

He could see her now—a tall girl in a bright red skirt with a parasol held above her yellow hair. He didn't think the parasol ridiculous; he wasn't thinking or he wouldn't have been there. He used his elbows harder.

"Ask him!" the girl cried. "Ask him what he's got inside his shirt!"

"I'll ask him!" Marlatt spun the last man out of his path.

FOUR

AND then Marlatt stopped—stopped short and still, with his eyes gone tight and narrow and the breath hard clogged in his throat.

"That's him—right there!" the girl cried, pointing.

It wasn't doubt that had stopped Kane Marlatt. There was only one man in that crowd she *could* mean—he had known that at once. A remote smile briefly touched Marlatt's lips, and it had nothing to do with either mirth or pleasure. Tall and saturnine, with a lock of red hair sweatily plastered across his forehead, bold eyes jade green against the raw brick-bronze of his cheeks, stood the last man Marlatt desired to see at that moment: Tularosa—boss of Craft Towner's gunslicks.

Shocked surprise jerked Tularosa's eyes wide open. His gaunt shape shrank as though he had seen a ghost. His face was ludicrous in its chagrined dismay. But only for a fleeting second; then crowding thoughts came to change its pattern.

There was irony in this thing for Marlatt. He had thought to help a frantic girl, and by that impulse had projected himself straight into the hands of the gang that had chased him across two territories and twenty-one counties—had resurrected himself right under the nose of the very man who had prosecuted that chase and had not quit till he thought him dead!

Marlatt's glance swept the tight-packed faces, briefly considered the swivel-jawed look of Curly Lahr at the gun boss' elbow; and there was in him a tumultuous urge to gunswift violence. But the glow died out of his eyes abruptly and left them blank, inscrutable, watchful.

There was the girl to be considered, and the discovered plans that had brought him here. He had to play this carefully.

These were his thoughts, but no hint of them disturbed the sun-darkened texture of his cheeks.

Trapped by his greed and this slip of a girl, Tularosa's plan had been to bluff this through, to convince the crowd that the girl was mistaken; that it had been someone else who had grabbed her money and killed the stage agent. But there'd been an uneasiness in his jeering scowl, a frayed edge of worry that he couldn't quite hide.

But those things were gone now, washed away by stronger emotions—by the malignant joy and the satisfaction that was curling his lips as he stared at Marlatt. There would be no mistake this time, his look said. He would cut Marlatt's string right here and now.

"Boys," he said, making his play for the crowd, "ef this young lady has lost some money, there stands the walloper thet's prob'ly took it! He's a—"

Marlatt said with a cold amusement, "You're wastin' your breath. The lady's already identified you, mister—"

"She's plumb mixed up, an' no wonder! Seein' a man git killed thet close to 'er! I say, by Gawd, *you* took 'er money! We seen you standin' there! An' when thet fool agent went an' shot off his mouth about there bein' forty thousan'—"

Marlatt, looking at the girl, said: "Seems right queer, ma'am, he'd be knowin' so much about it if he—"

"Hell," Tularosa snarled, "we was passin' the door when the agent said it—you all but run us down gittin' out! 'F we'd knowed what you was up to we would sure as hell've grabbed onto you; but I reckon it ain't too late right now. Grab 'im, Curly! We'll see, by Gawd, what he's got in his pockets!" His bony shoulders dropped to a crouch and he started forward, scowling, belligerent.

But Curly Lahr didn't mind his orders. He sensed the play, but he was extremely reluctant to force the issue in any such fashion. He stood his ground, scowling but hesitant to tackle a man whose gun he so dreaded.

The gaunt Tularosa swung round with an oath. "What

the hell's holdin' you? Crave to see this skunk git away with 'er money?"

"Mebbe," Marlatt suggested, "he's some bothered fearin' he won't get to spend his share of it."

He ignored them then. He looked at the girl. "If you think I took your money, ma'am, you just come right out an' say so."

"Of course you didn't!" she said vehemently. "*That* man took it—that red-headed man! And he shot the agent because he wouldn't open the safe!"

Marlatt walked up to him. "I guess you heard that. You're a sneak and a liar, Tularosa. Hand it over."

There were growls from the crowd. Someone yelled: "Get a rope!"

Tularosa, wild with rage, was yet cunning enough to know that rage would not serve him. He jumped to a wagon seat and flung out both arms. "It's a blasted lie!" he snarled hoarsely. "Excusin' my language, but that girl don't know what she's talkin' about—I say she don't *know!* How *could* she? We seen this fella in the stage office door. Jest as we come even with it, out he come hellity larrup an' went rattlin' his hocks up a alley. We was talkin', an' I never thought nothin' of it till I seen 'im again jest now. But I *did* think there was somethin' sort of familiar about him—an' there sure as hell was! They got his picture on telegraph poles clean acrost New Mexico Territory!"

A righteous wrath had hold of his cheeks. "You know who he is? Then by Gawd I'll tell you—*Kane Marlatt!* One of Kingfisher's right-hand men!"

An ominous silence followed' his words; a brittle, choked-up stillness through which Marlatt could feel the awed, black gaze of that entire crowd fixed on him. Tularosa had played an ace. That his words were a lie, that it was himself and not Marlatt who was Kingfisher's man, meant little or nothing—the damage was done. Those words had sown their wild havoc through this staring, excitable crowd. The rope enthusiast was yelling again; at the back men were pressing forward, deep growls in their throats, stealthy hands reaching back for their six-shooters.

Something was plain to Marlatt then. The girl and her money were clean forgotten, lost sight of entirely in the turbulent rush of this crowd's blind passions. Such was the power of Kingfisher's name. Marlatt knew he must act—and *quickly*, if he would save his life.

But it was no part of Tularosa's plan to have the tables turned again. He had Kane Marlatt where he wanted him now; he should not get loose of them *this* time. Knowing crowds, Tularosa was aware from past experience how the standards of conventional social conduct could most quickly and easily be stripped from them— how to fan blind lusts and hatreds to the point where these crazy fools would make an end of Marlatt for him, and do it on their own initiative.

He stood upon the wagon seat, gaunt, implacable—a god of doom. He towered above them, arms raised, fists clenched, eyes wild and flaming. "You men—you've worked damned hard for what you've got—fought drought an' floods an' the damn redskins fer a chanct to live—to raise your families here. You've sweated an' bled an' worked like dawgs to git a little stake together —to see thet your kids git the things you missed! You goin' to pass all that over to a damn cow-thief? You've heard of Kingfisher—you know what he does when he raids a outfit!"

He leveled a trembling fist at Marlatt. "I say this feller's a spy!" he shouted. "A low-down, stinkin', sneakin' spy! He's Kingfisher's scout come here to git the lay of things. Let 'im go, by Gawd, an' inside o' three weeks you'll have Kingfisher's men tearin' through this place like slaverin' wolves! Raidin', stealin', burnin'! Rapin' your women an' killin' yore kids!"

Tularosa knew what he was doing; he was launching a madness—a fear and hate that would lash these fools into headlong passion that would never ebb till they had Kane Marlatt draped from a limb. He chuckled deep in his throat as his wild eyes watched them. "You goin' to let 'im git back an' bring Kingfisher out here?"

The crowd loosed a roar; new voices swelled the rope-shouter's chorus. Snarls twisted men's faces. Fists and guns were brandished. The beast was waking. Just a few prods more, Tularosa gauged nicely, and he'd be done with Kane Marlatt, now and forever.

He was opening his jaws for that final lashing when a bearded man in a Jim Bridger hat shoved up to the wagon, spat and peered up at him. "You say they've put up his pictures all over New Mexico—this feller here?"

"Half the telegraph poles is sportin' 'em!"

"Damn' funny," the bearded man said, "I ain't seen any. Jest come back fr'm there, mister. The on'y pictures I seen was of *you!*"

FIVE

Tight, brittle silence clamped down on the street. There was no sound in that intense hush save the hoarse, jerky rasp of somebody's breathing. The bearded man's talk had caught Tularosa off balance. He still towered over them, but now his shape was some monstrous thing chopped out of gnarled wood with a blunt-bladed hatchet. His parchment cheeks were corrugated, flushed and bloated with an angry confusion. How could he have known that some fool in this crowd had been there? He cursed the man—cursed the mockery he saw in Kane Marlatt's gray stare. He was a slick-talking man when his wits were working; when they weren't, when as now he was stopped full-tilt by the unexpected, he had something else to fall back on. A thing that had never failed him—*violence.*

He fell back on it now. One lifted book took the wagon's driver square on the chin and pitched him headlong. His right hand rose with the glint of a sixgun. Flame spurted from it. The man in the Jim Bridger hat screamed and twisted; and everywhere, all about the wagon, white-faced men sprang swearing for cover.

The street was a scene of wildest confusion when Tularosa, bending, reached for the reins and saw Marlatt coming—saw his dark grinning face across the backs of the horses. He jerked his pistol around in an arc. When its bead was against Marlatt's chest, he fired.

But Marlatt kept coming. The gun was worthless—shot dry; its hammer point bedded on an empty shell. In a frenzy of fury Tularosa ripped the reins from the brake handle. One of Marlatt's boots was on the wheel now, his grinning face not three feet away. Tularosa swung his gun barrel at it. Marlatt's head jerked aside and he came

185

on up. Frantically Tularosa struck again. The wild blow slid off Marlatt's shoulder. Marlatt's hands closed tightly around his throat, and a red fog blurred Tularosa's vision. Again and again he struck with his pistol, driving its barrel into the dark mist before him, striving desperately to wrench himself free. The shouts and the swearing voices faded. With the last bursting atom of his strangled strength Tularosa tried for Marlatt again. The swing of his gun barrel stopped in mid-flight. Someone grunted; and Marlatt's fingers lost their traplike hold, clawed down his shirtfront and fell away from him. Tularosa drew one vast breath deep into his lungs. His blurred vision came back, and he saw Marlatt's shape falling backward, groundward; and then it was hidden in the billowing dust and he was lashing the squealing broncs like a madman.

Marlatt, stunned by the blow from that flailing gun barrel, became gradually aware of somebody fussing with him. As perception returned with an increased clarity, he grew conscious that the somebody had his head in their lap, was soothing his forehead with cool, deft fingers—was running those fingers through his black, tousled mane.

Remembrance then, disjointed fragments of a scene that yet hung to a pattern, clawed through the pain that was hammering his mind. With eyes jerked open, he struggled to rise; but the cool hands caught at his shoulders, restraining him. A voice said practically, "Better wait a bit, cowboy, till the world stops spinning."

Queer she should know that. It was spinning all right. And his head was splitting; but he twisted it round. "I—"

He stopped, surprised, and stared ludicrously at her. The hazel eyes staring back were quite friendly. But they were not the eyes of the yellow-haired girl who had lost her money.

That was what stumped him. Where had *this* girl come from? What had happened to the girl in the bright red skirt—the yellow-haired girl with the little blue parasol?

The hazel-eyed girl seemed to sense his confusion.

"She's safe," she assured him. "She's gone to the bank to lock up that money."

"Then I got it for her? I wasn't quite sure. . . . Seemed like I was reaching for it when that gun barrel caught me—"

"You got it all right." There was pride and approval in the girl's hazel eyes. "You mighty near choked the gizzard right out of him—I wish you had!" She stopped then, flushed, and took her hands from his shoulders; and Marlatt, looking up, scowled the grins from the faces of the half dozen hombres who were still hanging around. He got up and, stooping, helped the girl to her feet.

"Where's that mountain man that—"

"They've taken him down to Seth Ely's," one of the men said. "No use you goin' down there. He's deader'n a mackerel—that feller was sure chain lightnin' with a pistol. Can't see how he come to miss you—"

"Where's that fellow that was with him?" Marlatt asked. "The curly-headed one with the limp and—"

"He lit out hellbent when you jumped the other one. Some of the boys is huntin' him now."

"Don't see no one sittin' on *your* shirt tail."

The man's eyes scowled and the edge of a flush showed above his collar. "Ain't no call fer us to go chousin' after him. He ain't no business of ourn—"

"Me neither," Marlatt said; and thereafter ignored them. He turned to the girl. "Could I take you some place?"

She had carrot-red hair brushed rebelliously back from piquant features that were sunbrowned, faintly freckled, a little shy but not embarrassed. She returned his scrutiny with one as frank; laughed a little and said: "Why not? I expect Shirly-Bell's about ready to go. I'm to meet her at Oliphant's—you may walk that far with me. She'll want to thank you for saving Ora's money."

"Nothing to thank me for." They turned down the Calle Real. Marlatt asked: "Who's Ora?"

"Our uncle— Well, he's Shirly-Bell's uncle, really; I'm just his ward."

"Banker, is he?"

She showed faint surprise. Her hazel eyes peered up at him. "You don't *look* green—"

"Well, thanks," he smiled.

She laughed at him. "Haven't you ever heard of Ora Flack, the big cow—?" She gripped his arm. "What's the matter?"

"Nothin'," Marlatt murmured, drawing the back of a hand across his eyes. "The pain, I guess. That polecat swatted me harder'n I figured." His steel gray eyes roamed the way ahead. "You was sayin'?"

"I was about to say Ora Flack's about the biggest cowman in southern Arizona. You must be new in these parts—"

"I've heard of him," Marlatt told her, and let it ride that way while he got out the makings and rolled him up a smoke. He licked it; squinted up at the sun and said, "Don't suppose he'd be needin' any hands now, would he?"

She thought it over. "He's got a pretty full crew—but," she added, seizing his arm impulsively, "he'd be an ingrate not to hire you after all the risk you took to save his money."

Marlatt gave her a cynical smile. "My use was over when I got back the money. I don't reckon he'll let that influence him. Well, there's the corral up yonder," he mentioned, and made as though he would turn aside.

But she wouldn't let him. "Come on," she said, again catching his arm. "At least you'll let Shirly-Bell thank you."

He hung back a moment as though thinking it over. "All right," he said reluctantly. "No need to mention that job though—no sense embarrassin' your uncle."

She gave him an odd look, half indignant, half amused. Then she laughed, but her dark eyes watched him with a heightened interest. "Do you know," she said, giving his arm a squeeze, "I'm not at all sure that we've rightly met. . . ."

"I beg your pardon, ma'am." He dragged off his hat. "That hombre told at least half the truth; my name is Kane Marlatt certain-sure. It's my right name, too." He grinned down at her.

Standing there where they'd paused in the edge of a building's shadow, she saw him as a tall, dark man whose big-boned frame rendered the sinewy muscles of him inconspicuous. But strength was there; it was in the easy grace of him, in the taciturn quality of his steel-gray glance, in the way his white teeth flashed when he smiled. There was a hardness in him too, she thought; a bitter hardness that was like a wall thrust across every friendly impulse of him—a barrier he had raised against the world—or was it lifted only against himself? It might well be. The man was a fighter who would act, as she had seen him act, in the wink of an eye; but he would have to think about it after. He would think his way through every move he had made, for he was a thinking man, also. How else explain that lurking sadness which was so indubitably a part of him?—that brooding, bitter-almonds look that was crouched just back of his stare?

She flushed a little, wondering if he had sensed and read her appraisal of him. She made a restless gesture with her quick, strong hands. Then she smiled. "I—I'm sure it is—Kane. And I'm Corinne Malone. Cori's what everyone calls me," she said to let him know she approved of him.

"Cori Malone. That's a pretty name, ma'am. An' not one I'll soon be forgettin'."

Color showed on her cheeks for a little, and she held herself straight and still before him, giving him a chance to make his own appraisal. He nodded, selected a match from his hatband and put the hat back on his head.

There was a lessening of the warmth in Cori's eyes, and the corners of her mouth showed a little tight as she said, "Well—come on. I 'low you'll be wantin' to meet Shirly-Bell."

He did not at once move forward with her. He paused to haul a match head across his Levis, to bring its cupped flame to his cigarette. When he caught up she was smiling again. She took his arm with a gay little laugh. "Something to tell one's grandchildren about—tripping the streets with a Kingfisher man!" But he wouldn't enter into the spirit of it; his wide-lipped mouth remained sober. Cori shrugged and was taking her hand away when she felt him stop—felt his arm go stiff.

"Ain't that Miss Shirly-Bell yonder?"

She looked corralward toward where he stared; then nodded, puzzled, of a sudden uneasy. "Why— What do you— Yes! that's Shirly-Bell!" Then she had to break into a run to keep up with him.

Marlatt said: "What's the trouble here?" and both the man and Shirly-Bell wheeled on the instant. The man was a Mexican.

"This fellow's trying to steal our team!" Shirly-Bell's eyes were resentful.

"No, señor—no try for steal not'ing! Thees 'orse, she's belong for me! T'ree-four—mebbe five years!"

Marlatt looked at the horse. It matched in every particular save one the bay horse standing beside it. They were a fine-looking pair, well cared for and sleek despite the town's dust; as sleek as the vanished spring wagon back of them. "What's your uncle's brand?" he asked Shirly-Bell, though the brand showed plain on the horses' left hips.

"He has a separate brand for his horses," she said. "Spade, on the left hip. Everyone knows it."

Marlatt looked at the Mexican. Both horses were correctly branded. He mentioned the fact.

"But, señor!" wailed the man. "Ees got my brand on 'eem too! On other side— Mira! Look!"

Marlatt walked around the bay horse. "Lazy T on right shoulder. That your brand?"

"Si!—Si, señor!"

"Thought all you fellers used 'picture' brands," Marlatt commented skeptically.

"I 'ave bought thees bran' from *Señor* Tigh Martin. Eight-ten year ago. Me—Felix Gomez! Ees recorded, *señor*—"

"But your brand's been crossed out. There's a bar burned through it," Marlatt told him. "You can see it yourself. You must have sold—"

"No sell! No sell, *señor!* Ever' time, no sell! No sell *not'*ing!" He gesticulated wildly, his dark face sullen with anger. "Ees trick, *señor!* Ees trick for do me out—"

"I'll tend to this," a gruff voice said. A rough, heavy hand brushed Marlatt aside; and a big shape passed him at a rolling stride. He saw the Mexican cringe back from the man.

He was a bull-chested fellow with a muscular swell of neck and shoulder—a white-haired man, but not an old man. He said sharply, "What do you think you're doin', Gomez?" The Mexican dragged off his battered straw hat, and his eyes and his face got apologetic; but he said doggedly, defiantly:

"*Señorita* no got right for drive thees *caballo*—thees 'orse, she's mine! Mine, *señor!*" He seemed to gather courage, perhaps reassured by the sound of his voice. "*Mira*—look, *señor!* My brand! es right there on shoulder!"

As the newcomer's head turned to follow Gomez' pointing hand Marlatt got his first good look. He was young, as young as Marlatt, with burly shoulders and a bull-thick neck atop which sat a round moon face with bold and lively features set off by twinkling eyes that were at once good-natured and masterful. He wore a mustache and goatee that were white as his hair and immeasurably added to the commanding, distinguished appearance of him. Marlatt conceded the man was handsome. He was a man, Marlatt thought, rather used to having his way. Too used, perhaps.

"See there, *señor?* Weeth the bar through eet?"

The big man eyed the brand rather queerly, and considerably longer than Marlatt had done. It was plain he did not like it. But he shrugged and very coolly asked, "So what are you howling about? It's barred all right, and there's Flack's Spade brand right above it—"

"But I deed not sell Señor Flack thees caballo! I—"

"But you'll sell the horse to me, won't you?"

The way the big man put the question showed what answer he expected; and Gomez, nervously eyeing him, at last, reluctantly, nodded. "But—"

"Well, now," the white-haired man observed, "I expect a hundred dollars would probably change your views considerable, wouldn't it?"

Gomez, with his eyes like twin bugs on a stick, gulped audibly as the man drew a thick roll of bills from his pocket, peeled off one and extended it. "Some time when you're not too busy you can fix up a bill of sale and give it to my range boss next time he comes to town."

Leaving the Mexican still staring owlishly at the piece of paper he held, the white-haired man turned back to the others with a good-natured grin on his round moon face. "Well, there you are, ladies. Simple as A B C."

"You shouldn't have done that, Nick," Cori said; but the big man's attention was all for the other girl, though he was polite enough to "Tut, tut," a few times. He walked over to Shirly-Bell, leaving Cori regarding him thoughtfully. Marlatt, watching Cori, saw her shrug; and then her eyes came up and met his. She smiled, and said clearly with a cool, unbreakable dignity: "Shirly-Bell, this is Kane Marlatt, who saved Uncle's money for you." And when the yellow-haired girl looked round: "Kane, Miss Shirly-Bell Ranleigh."

Shirly-Bell came over then and held out her hand. Across her shoulder the big man regarded Marlatt with a livelier interest.

Shirly-Bell said, "I'm afraid, Mr. Marlatt, I owe you a great deal more than mere words can ever repay."

Marlatt dropped her hand quickly, obviously embarrassed. "Shucks—"

But whatever he might have said was lost, for Cori said quickly: "Nonsense! He needs a job, Shirly-Bell. You can tell Uncle Ora to give him one." Without waiting for Shirly-Bell's answer, she said to the big man back of her, "Nick, this is Kane Marlatt, a Texan man. Kane, Nick Bannerman."

Bannerman strolled forward, and gave Marlatt's hand a hearty clasp. There was a distinct air of power about Nick Bannerman; it rolled against Marlatt like a wave, all-engulfing and convincing. The man was a Somebody in this country. He said, cheerfully ironic: "Nuisance being a hero." He teetered his boots in the dust of the yard, considering Marlatt a moment. He said: "I'll give you a job if you're riding the grub-line."

"That's Ora's duty, Nick," Cori said coolly before Marlatt had a chance to say anything. "You've done enough for the Flacks, for one day."

Bannerman grinned. His blue eyes twinkled. "Don't ever argue with a woman, Marlatt. Looks like you're booked to ride for Ora whether you want to or not."

"And why wouldn't he want to?" Surprise looked out of Shirly-Bell's stare.

"Peace, woman!" growled Bannerman humorously and, taking her arm, helped her up into the spring wagon's seat. But Marlatt, too, wondered why he had said that. The man had laughed it off, but just the same Marlatt wondered if perhaps the adroit Mr. Bannerman had not said a bit more than he'd meant to.

He put the remark carefully away where he'd put that business of Felix Gomez and the twice-branded bay.

Cori, without waiting for anyone's help, had climbed into the seat and was unwrapping the reins. Shirly-Bell looked around. She said in her throaty voice, "Aren't you you coming?" And, with a shrug, Marlatt nodded.

"Of course he's coming," Nick Bannerman grinned. "He's got eyes, ain't he? I'll be coming out myself this evening; got to see Ora on a little business."

"Why not come with us?"

Bannerman looked tempted but finally shook his head.

"Guess not. Got a few things to see to in town first—"

"That girl in the Plaza?" Cori smiled sweetly.

Nick Bannerman chuckled. "The man that gets you's going to have his hands full. No," he said soberly, "I've got to see Doc Tompkins."

Marlatt cut in, "I'll be gettin' my horse. Be back in a second."

Bannerman was gone when he came out with the roan.

"You can ride with us," Cori said. "Tie your horse on back."

"Perhaps Miss Ranleigh—"

"Really, there's plenty of room," smiled Shirly-Bell, moving over against Cori and shaking out her skirt. "Come! Tell us about your adventurous life. Cori tells me you're one of Kingfisher's—"

"Cori," Marlatt said, "seems to have considerable imagination." He walked around to her side and reached up for the reins.

"I'll drive—I always do. You get in and talk with Shirly-Bell." Cori grinned at him. "Tell us about the man who tried to steal Ora's money."

There was a grim look about Marlatt's cheeks as he climbed up onto the seat beside Shirly-Bell. He said gruffly, "Don't even know him."

"Is that why you called him 'Tularosa'?" Cori said, swinging the team. "You *did*, you know—I heard you."

Drat the girl. Marlatt felt much as Bannerman must have when she'd thrown that Plaza girl at him. He found Shirly-Bell eyeing him queerly. "Did you really?"

Marlatt nodded. "Had to call him something—"

Cori said, "Is it true what he said about your pictures being—"

Marlatt laughed. "You heard what that mountain man said to that, didn't you?"

"But then how did he know your name was Kane Marlatt?"

Marlatt shrugged. "Better ask me somethin' easy, ma'am. I ain't much good at these riddles."

Shirly-Bell said, "You mustn't mind Cori, Mister Marlatt; she's an awful tease. She treats all the boys that way. Even Ora's range boss, Cantrell—"

"Don't you think, Mister Marlatt," cut in Cori, whipping the red hair back from her face, "that Shirly-Bell ought to be more reserved in the way she takes up with strangers? Not that Nick isn't the soul of honor, but—I mean, considering and all that we don't hardly *know* him? 'Course he's handsome enough and—"

"Cori!"

"Well, it's the truth. We don't know—"

"Now, Cori. I'm sure Mister Marlatt is not interested in our private opinions of other people. After all, you know, Mister Bannerman's a gentleman and has always been very friendly toward you. It does you no credit talking behind his back that way."

"Really, you've said quite enough, dear."

Marlatt grinned. "Who is this Bannerman, anyway?"

"A business acquaintance of Ora's," Shirly-Bell said in her mission-chime voice. "He's a ranchman from over in the Altar Valley—off there to the west beyond those mountains. He has a fine place, they say, though rather too isolated ever to be worth much."

"Too inaccessible," chirped Cori; and Marlatt laughed at the yellow-haired girl's exasperated sigh. She proved a good sport by laughing too.

"But really," she said, "Nick's a nice boy and I hope you'll like him. I'd like for you two to be good friends; if you take a job at Straddle Bug—that's the name of our ranch—"

"Ora's ranch," Cori said.

"Yes, dear," Shirly-Bell said; and to Marlatt: "You'll probably see quite a lot of each other."

"You'll get tired of him as I am," Cori assured him; and Marlatt, seeing the color edge Shirly-Bell's cheeks, felt an instant sympathy for her. He frowned at Cori. He could well imagine Shirly-Bell's feelings at being plagued this way in front of a stranger.

He found himself comparing the girls. They were as different, he thought, as night from day. Cori, red-haired and freckled, over forward and impudent, uncaringly clad in Levis and Stet hat with a boy's flannel shirt tightly showing her curves; a tomboy, and shameless, making fun of her betters.

There was no real comparison—might as well compare cheap rotgut with Bourbon, he thought a little impatiently. Shirly-Bell Ranleigh was a lady. Lissomely tall, a slim blonde goddess in a gay, flowered waist and bright red skirt with an absurd little parasol over her head. There was intelligence and breeding implicit in every line of her. She was beautiful! With dark, proud eyes and creamy throat, with deep yellow hair rippling richly back from features exquisite as—

Marlatt shrugged and gave it up. He could find no word that was fit enough. No word that was halfway adequate to describe the feeling she roused in him. Fresh and sweet as a prairie rose, he had never seen anyone like her; she was the quintessence of all the visions he had seen in his campfires. There was something about her that touched him deeply, disturbing the ordered run of his thoughts—driving from mind more pressing reflections. Admiration was strong in him for the control she had displayed through Cori's baiting. She was grave-cheeked now and strained and hurt, just a little bewildered, he thought, as though she could not understand Cori's attitude, Cori's malice. There was a sad, far-away look about her eyes . . .

"Well," Cori said a little tartly, "you might's well get out. This's the end of the line. We don't go no farther." And Marlatt, thus rudely jerked back to stern reality, looked up to find them stopped before the gypsumed walls of a low adobe ranch house. He helped Shirly-Bell down but would not look at her—*dared* not, lest she see or sense the dismal hunger in him. She was a woman who would some day make some man immensely happy. Would that man know his luck? Would he take her and keep her?—would he have the wit to thank God for his blessing?

Marlatt sighed.

She was not for him—nor for any other gun-throwing ranny who knew no home but the seat of his saddle.

He squared broad shoulders, and turned his wind-burned cheeks toward the man who stood watching from the ranch house doorway.

"Have a nice trip, girl?"

Cori said, "We damn near lost your money, Ora. You'll want to thank this fellow—he's the one that saved it."

"Mr. Marlatt," Shirly-Bell said, "this is my uncle, Ora Flack."

Marlatt stood there stiffly, eyes hard and bitter on the man Craft Towner had hired him to kill.

S I X

FLACK came off the porch with extended hand. But Marlatt appeared to be entirely occupied with twisting up a smoke, and the rancher, frowning faintly, put the snubbed hand back in his pocket. When his cigarette satisfied him, Marlatt looked up and met the cattleman's eyes. Something was plain enough to Marlatt then. This Ora Flack was a buggy boss. The quality and condition of his clothing shouted it, as did the smooth, uncalloused hand that now was a tight fist back of the sleek, groomed cloth of his trousers.

Ironic humor faintly twisted Marlatt's lips as he saw a darkness come into Flack's eyes. The cattleman was offended, and only the fact of Marlatt's being a guest here was keeping the man from retaliating; Marlatt read that in the fleeting narrowness of the man's surprised stare. Evidently his dignity was a much more serious thing to Flack than the dollars Marlatt had saved him. There was knowledge here, and Marlatt stored it while he considered whether he should offer amends or let matters ride.

Behind the high, dark planes of Marlatt's face was a toughness beaten into him by twenty-four years of hard living. Behind this toughness was the one soft streak that was his solitary weakness; the crazy urge that accorded his enemies as much chance to live as he gave himself; the same feather-headed chivalry that had brought him here across all these miles—the same brash impulse that had slammed him headlong to the rescue of Shirly-Bell Ranleigh.

"Glad to make your acquaintance, Marlatt. I'm in your debt, sir," Flack said; but the look of his eyes didn't match by considerable the hearty note to be heard in his voice. "In your debt both for saving my money and—"

"You owe me nothing," Marlatt drawled, coolly tossing his words across the other's speech. "What I did was done for your niece—entirely."

Flack's deep, wide chest showed a quickened breathing. But he smiled it off. "Then I'll thank you for—"

"Miss Ranleigh's thanks were entirely adequate," Marlatt said; and was at a loss to understand the antagonism Flack had roused in him. Their trails had never crossed before, he was sure; it made his antipathy to the man seem incredible. He saw amazement twist the cheeks of the girls.

It was Flack's hard-held calm, his control of himself that saved the situation. He bowed with a brief civility. "At least you'll not tear off till you've rested your horse—"

"Wasn't thinking of leaving," Marlatt cut in. "I came out here to wangle a job."

Flack hung poised by the porch with suspended breath. Then his shoulders loosened and a hard kind of smile cracked the lips away from his teeth. "For a job, eh? Well! I must confess I was beginning to wonder . . . However, we can talk of that later. You'll want to see my range boss, Cantrell. He'll be round some place come chuck time. Meantime," he said, and a faint hint of irony got its claws in his smile, "help your horse to some feed an' set comfortable."

Marlatt looked after him thoughtfully as Flack followed the girls into the house. Then with a shrug he climbed back up on the wagon and drove the team across to the stable. While he was unharnessing and currying them he tried to rationalize the perverse impulse that had governed him during his words with the rancher. His attitude had not made sense, and he knew it. Getting tough with Flack wouldn't buy him anything. He'd come out here, and at considerable risk, to warn the man. Not to browbeat him or start a feud with him, but to warn him of Towner's intentions. Even while clearing out of Craft Towner's country, he had deliberately turned his flight this way that he might drop by Flack's and warn the man. It had been just that same intention which had prompted his job-hunting talk with Cori Malone.

He pulled the saddle off the blaze-faced roan he had bought from Oliphant and rubbed him down with a wisp of straw. And all the time he worked with the animal he considered the craziness of his talk with Flack, from his deliberate refusal to shake hands with the man to that final suggestion of a job he didn't want.

He couldn't think what had got into him. Just the same he felt bound to admit that if he had it to do over he'd probably go right through the same rigmarole. Odd, he thought. Uncommonly odd.

The horses cared for, Marlatt crossed to the shade of the bunkhouse and put his back to the cool adobes. A smoke might help, he mused; and shaped one, tapering it up with a thoughtful frown. What was there, he wondered, about Ora Flack that should so rouse a man's antagonism? Was it something in the fellow's look? But no; it didn't hardly seem as if that could be it. Flack was personable enough—or seemed to be.

In Marlatt's memory the ranchman stood as sharply etched as a cameo, from his white and tall-crowned Stetson to the spurs on his fancy-stitched cowhide boots. Expensive black store duds covered his frame. Black silk made a flutter about his throat and a diamond glinted from his smooth left hand. But it was the man's face that Marlatt had looked at mostly; he could recall its every line and shadow, or at least every line he had seen. A thick black beard had concealed a part of it. Not a large beard though, and cropped short enough to show the bold, hard sweep of a blocklike jaw. But the rest of the face had been plain enough; an arrogant nose was the salient feature. Yet the man had treated him civilly enough—too civilly, perhaps, all things considered. A sight more civilly than most men would have.

Why? Why had he held himself in—been so courteous? Had some unknown need dictated that courtesy?

Marlatt snorted softly. Association with Towner appeared to have bred in him a vast suspicion of—

He broke off the thought. There was someone coming. It was Cori. She came round the corner as if she were hunting something, and when she saw him she stopped. There was considerable indignation in her look.

"What were you trying to do—start a fight?"

Marlatt grinned. "I expect it *did* kind of look that way—"

"Look that way!" Cori stared. Then, stormily: "Do you know what Ora ask—"

"Oh! Pardon me," exclaimed Shirly-Bell, rounding the corner and abruptly stopping. She stood looking from one to the other. A faintly apologetic smile swayed her lips. "Uncle Ora wants you, Cori dear."

"Damn!" Cori said inelegantly and, with a quick-flashing look at Marlatt's face, she went tramping off.

The back of the bunkhouse faced the corral, and from where he leaned Marlatt could watch the eight or ten horses penned there; but he wasn't. He was watching Shirly-Bell. A regard the girl appeared to be returning with a larger interest than she'd previously accorded him.

She was a reserved girl, even with those whom she liked, he guessed; and was by no means certain he fell in that category, though he hoped he did. She drew him strangely—as strangely and strongly as her uncle repelled him. There was a lure in her, an inexplicable something holding great attraction for a man like Marlatt. Bannerman felt it; Marlatt had seen that, watching him.

He said: "You've got a nice layout here."

"Do you think so?" She smiled, and all the lines of her face changed. Then the smile fell away and she asked soberly: "Are you really wanting a job with Ora?"

Marlatt shrugged. "Expect I could work for him as well as anyone."

"It isn't that. I mean—you talked so strange—almost as if you hated him, as if— But you don't, do you?"

"Why should I?" Marlatt dissembled. "This is the first time I ever saw him."

She was looking at him oddly, eyes darkly shadowed—twin pools throwing back the last light of dusk. Only there wasn't any dusk; and she was a slender shape, very near him, anxiously watching him.

She said at last, "I believe you do!" She took a deep breath then. "Why did you come over here?" Her eyes roved his faded gear as though she might find her answer that way. "Why?" Her voice was insistent now. "Don't tell me it was because we asked you."

Marlatt appeared to debate with himself. He said finally, wryly: "Why does a man do anything?"

But she brushed that away. "You don't want a job here. You came for something else." She reached forward swiftly and slapped at his pocket.

Marlatt's eyes shone coldly mocking. "You won't be findin' no stars pinned on me."

"You're no line-riding drifter!" She said of a sudden on an altered note: "You're a gun thrower!" and caught up her red skirt and ran for the house.

Gun thrower. Marlatt stood awhile, his unseeing glance on the dust of his boots. Queer how the ways of a man's life caught up with him. She must have sharp eyes.

"Gun thrower!" He said it over again—as she had; and wheeled impatiently with a lift of his shoulders. The crew was coming. He could hear the sound of their horses' hoofs whacking the yard, and the smell of the dust was a close, pungent thing.

He went around to the front of the bunkhouse and settled himself on a bench by the door. He was there when the crew came from penning their horses. Five of them, lathered and dusty, unshaved and uncaring. They came trooping round the bunkhouse corner, falling queerly silent when they noticed him sitting there. A stocky man well in front of the others came to a stop and put down his saddle. "Hmmm," he observed, looking Marlatt over. "New man?"

Meeting the man's inquiring gaze, Marlatt shrugged. "Dunno. I'm waitin' on the top screw now."

"You're lookin' at him. I'm the range boss here. Name's Cantrell."

"Glad to know you," Marlatt mentioned without getting up. "Mine's Marlatt."

"Where'd you say you were from?"

"Didn't say."

Cantrell's neck tipped a little forward. He regarded Marlatt with a narrowed stare. "Where are you from?"

Marlatt grinned. "You reckon that would affect the caliber of my work?"

Cantrell did not grin back. He seemed faintly bothered by Marlatt's words. He continued to stand there studying him. He was a bull-chested man with a blue, square jaw that ran flat to his ears and a nose that was hooked like an eagle's. There was a sledgelike kind of solidness about him—in the planted, far-apart set of his feet, in the ox-thick cant of his shoulders, in the unwinking stare of his pale yellow eyes.

Abruptly he shrugged and, without comment, strode past in the direction of the cook shack, in whose open door a man in an apron stood beating a dishpan. Three of the other men tramped along after him. The fourth, a small and hungry-looking man, tossed his hull on the kak-pole and winked at Marlatt. "Looks like chuck's ready. Better come an' set."

"Wouldn't want to make the rest of you short."

The small man stared after Cantrell and spat. "There's times," he drawled, "when it's plumb gratifyin' to be sho't. I'm Oxbow Rand—glad to know you, mister."

Marlatt got up and shook Rand's fist. "You must feel kinda lost in this outfit."

"A man," Rand observed, looking after the others, "can't always cut the herd he travels with."

"I expect that's so," answered Marlatt gravely. "Culls are mostly a matter of a man's opinion."

"I can see you been around," Rand said.

The others were eating when they entered the grub

shack. They took vacant places at one end of the long table. Food disappeared without much talk. Eating, here, was apparently regarded as a serious business. Several times, during the course of the meal, Marlatt caught the range boss covertly eyeing him; once, toward the end, his glance came up in time to meet Cantrell's fairly. The man's amber stare was cold and hostile. Marlatt's lips streaked a grin.

Their hunger satisfied, the men drifted outside to roll smokes and talk. Rand and Marlatt hunkered down in the shade of a tamarisk. The three other hands took seats on the bench beside the door. After a time Cantrell came out and stopped by them, listening. Their discussion seemed to center on the small events of the day's work. "I ain't been here always," Rand mentioned. "Used to be wagon boss for Miz' Cori's dad."

Marlatt said, "Kin of Flack's, was he?"

"Just a friend, I reckon, though there's some as claims they was distant relations. Anyway, in his will Ol' Tom named Flack her guardian." He squinted off across the blue-shadowed range. "She'll come of age nex' month, an' things'll be different."

Marlatt's quick glance at the man found Rand's dark eyes fixed upon him, bright with meaning. Rand said guardedly, "I ain't one to shoot off my mouth or tell any man how to play his hand, but I'd sure take it kindly 'f you could see your way to stickin' round here a spell. I—"

He let it ride, and commenced shaping a smoke. Marlatt, looking up, saw Cantrell approaching. There was something dark and suspicious in the range boss' regard. He observed then how the other men, the rest of the crew, had stopped their talk and were watching; and something clicked inside his head as he met Cantrell's stare with a bland regard.

"Rand," the range boss said, "go hitch up a team." And Rand, with a nod, got up and walked stableward. The range boss looked down at Marlatt then. "So you're wantin' a job on this spread, eh, bucko?"

Marlatt stood up. "Well," he said, hitching up his belt, "I could sure use some work."

"We're particular who we hire round here."

"Don't blame you—don't blame you at all," Marlatt smiled. "Fella's got to be with all this misbranded stock runnin' round." Fishing out the makings, he rolled up another smoke, pretending not to notice the quick, hard look the range boss gave him.

Cantrell said very softly: "What do you mean, misbranded stock?"

"Why, it looks to me like somebody's been almighty careless—"

"What're you gettin' at?"

"If you don't know, I'd say it's high time this outfit was hirin' a boss that come up to his job."

The rest of the crew had drifted over. They were spread out now just back of the boss, thumbs hooked to gun belts, shoulders tipped, eyes glinting, ready to back any play Cantrell started.

Cantrell's face was the color of liver. His bull chest swelled and a bloated look got into his cheeks. "Why, you damn sa—"

It wasn't Marlatt's look that stopped him. Marlatt's look had not changed in the slightest. Cold sweat made a shine across Cantrell's forehead. He licked stiff lips. But he dared not move with that cold, hard thing shoved against his belly. That quickly had his belligerence wilted. One moment he was a tough, burly shape tight cocked for violence; and then, in the bat of an eye, he was a dog, a dog with its tail tucked between shaking legs.

"No more nerve," Marlatt drawled, "than a jackrabbit."

Not even that—nothing, it seemed, could pry Cantrell loose of his belated caution. Rage and shame and a gouging fury thrust spots of fire in his fear-paled cheeks. He knew what figure he cut, frozen that way—bitterly sensed what his men must be thinking. Yet he stood rock still, scarcely even breathing.

Very drily Marlatt asked: "What was that you was sayin'?"

"I—uh—" New color flooded the range boss' cheeks. "Expect I was talkin' a—a little bit wild-like . . ."

"Why, that's comin' it down right han'some," grinned Marlatt. "Guess you was steppin' over to say I been put on the payroll."

Cantrell's eyes rolled. A pulse at his temple was swollen and purple. He might, with luck, catch a hold on his gun, but he knew in his bones he'd never get to use it. No hand could be quicker than a gun at your ribs; and that hard thing was making a dent in his belly.

He groaned; almost gagged when he swallowed. "I—uh—Yes! I was!" he whispered.

Marlatt laughed and stepped back. Both his hands were empty. He'd made a fool of Cantrell with nothing more dangerous than an index finger.

Out of the tail of his eye Marlatt watched the crew. An edge of his glance caught a new figure watching; swung a bit and then picked up another. He got out his Durham and shook some into a paper. Drawstrings gripped in white teeth, he was shutting the sack when somebody said, softly sighing: "Well!"

That was Rand. Marlatt knew by the vast satisfaction so plain in the word. He curled his smoke and looked at Cantrell. The man's face was livid.

"Out-thought an' outshot," someone summed up the situation.

And still another voice said: "Expect Cantrell will be seekin' new pastures." It was significant, Marlatt thought, of the range boss' changed status, that he had been referred to by name. The speaker had not called him "boss." Marlatt, seeing Cantrell's glowering eyes, grinned a little, maliciously. He was enjoying the man's discomfiture and would just as lief he knew it.

Obviously Cantrell did. His cheeks were black with fury and his twisted mouth made gasping sounds like a fish new-yanked from water. Abruptly Cantrell spun on his heel, and a rolling stride took him out of sight beyond the saddle shack corner.

A pants-scraped match lit Marlatt's smoke. He was comfortably inhaling, back propped against the tree, when Oxbow Rand drifted over. "You've got a hard way, friend," Rand told him.

Marlatt continued smoking, blandly appreciating the blue Rincon rim. The sun was down. Night would come when the afterglow faded. Cantrell had not showed himself again, and the crew was hunkered in low-voiced talk over by the bunkhouse, their squattered shapes forward-bent and earnest, mulling over that play with Cantrell. He saw them occasionally glance his way furtively.

He pinwheeled his smoke through the thickening dusk. "I find it pays to learn right away if a dog's all bark or got bite in him."

"Don't you make no mistake, boy. That vinegarroon's got plenty bite. Don't let him get behind you none."

"Shucks. Where I come from they wouldn't call him a baby frightener." Marlatt changed the subject. There was a wild idea roving through his head and, getting his back more comfortably against the time-roughed bark of the pepper, he said: "I've about made up my mind to oblige you. Air round this way is right salubrious. You said the red-headed girl was a ward of Flack's. How long?"

"Six-seven year."

"Mmmm. Didn't they never find out about her father's death?"

In the dusk Rand's glance looked peculiar. "How you mean?"

"Ain't they never found out who killed him?"

Rand took a long look roundabout. "Who told you Cori's dad was killed?"

Marlatt's grunt was expressive. "You can't tell wagon ruts from snake track here. If you want my help—"

"It ain't about that I'm wantin' it. You're off on the wrong foot, Marlatt. Cori's old man was killed by a horse—he always was a fool for buyin' bad broncs. He'd got six hundred miles to git hold of one no other guy'd touch with a ten-foot pole."

"Nice set-up. Where are they now?"

"Flack got rid of 'em when he took over—"

"An' what's become of the property? Where's her land?"

"Flack throwed it in with the rest of his holdin's—"

"Cattle, too?"

Rand nodded.

"What happened to her buildin's?"

"Flack's usin' 'em for a line camp—"

"An' you think the ol' man got killed by a horse?" Contempt and pity were in Marlatt's tone; anger and impatience, too. "Where the hell's your savvy, man?"

But Rand's voice was stubborn. "You can't go against the facts," he growled doggedly. "Lord sakes! D'you think for one holy minute—"

But Marlatt said: "With an outfit as big as that at stake—"

"Big as what? I never said—"

"You didn't have to. If it wasn't big you wouldn't be here; you'd not've hung round in this polecat's burrow—"

"Makes no difference," the short man muttered. "First off I had the same idea; I said, 'By Gawd, this business stinks!' But I'm tellin' you now, there wasn't one thing wrong. Tim Malone was killed by a outlaw bronc—"

He broke off and turned, shoulders stiffening.

A man said out of the blur of shadows: "Marlatt? The Ol' Man wants t' see you—up at the house. Right away."

SEVEN

FLACK's eyes traveled Marlatt's frame with a cold, hard scrutiny. They returned to his face without approval. "You show your trade, friend."

Marlatt shrugged but did not comment. This was a plain room—sparsely furnished, low ceiled, long and narrow and equipped very simply with a desk and three hide-bottomed chairs. A Remington print was tacked to the wall. There were no other furnishings or decorations.

"Not many, hunting a job," Flack said, "would have used your way."

Marlatt chuckled. "Got onto it, did you?"

"I watched you make a fool of Bob Cantrell in front of his men."

"I didn't make a fool of him—he was that already. All I did was let him prove it."

"I don't suppose," said Flack grimly, "it occurred to you that you might be undermining the man's authority—"

"That," Marlatt grinned, "was what I aimed to do."

"You've got gall to admit it."

"I got plenty gall."

Quick and black was the look of Flack's cheeks. "So you did it deliberately! Deliberately went out of your way to wreck the authority of a man I've been dependent on—"

"Shouldn't put your weight on such a weak reed. 'Course I did it deliberately. Allowed you'd be seein' that straight off."

"I see it now!" Flack snarled.

"Doubt if you do." Marlatt's look was insolent. "I don't do things just to be doin'. I broke Cantrell, mister, because I want Cantrell's job."

"You *what!*"

"You hear all right, Flack. I said I want Cantrell's job. You'll be needin' a range boss, an' here I am just shaped to your needs. Your move, ain't it?"

Flack's eyes took on a shoe-button polish. Marlatt grinned at him toughly.

The flare of the lamp was not kind to Flack's face. Anger was a stain on his cheeks, and their tightened skin showed his bones up like castings. He sat for perhaps six seconds motionless; then a kind of admiration stared from his eyes. "By God," he said, "you're efficient."

"Or I wouldn't be here now," Marlatt smiled. He thought to see a sudden glint in Flack's eyes, but he could not be sure. He said: "Efficiency's what you're lookin' for, ain't it?"

"Do you think I'd trust you after this?"

Marlatt shrugged. "You got to trust someone an' trust 'em damn quick."

"More of your riddles? What are you drivin' at now?"

"The riddle ain't mine till you've made me range boss —or if it is, it wouldn't need to be then." Marlatt met Flack's eyes straightly. "There's some curious things goin' on around here—a matter of brands, if you get what I mean?"

Flack's narrowed stare met his straightly. "Brands?"

"Brands," Marlatt smiled. He spoke of Gomez and the Mexican's remarks at Oliphant's corral. "The horse in question," Marlatt said, "was one of the pair your niece was drivin'. A bay. They were both bays—pretty good-lookin' ones."

"Well?" Flack said.

"I don't know whether it is or not. This fellow Bannerman paid Gomez for the horse. Seems to me though, if I was you, I'd be doin' some thinkin'."

Flack sat back in his chair and looked at him, his bearded face quite smooth and expressionless. "What do *you* think?"

"I haven't decided." Marlatt moved his right hand, absently rubbing his holster. "I'd have to know more about it before I made up my mind. Not sure I'm interested." He added reflectively: "I could be, though."

"I see." Flack said very softly: "You aim to be, don't you?"

A hard smile curved Marlatt's lips. "Your show, ain't it?"

A blackness was crowding Flack's glance again. His deep, wide chest showed a quickened breathing. He had a way of rubbing his thumbs with his next two fingers; he was rubbing them now, and there was a visible tautness in the cords of his neck. But whatever his impulse—whatever the thoughts that were locked in his head, he controlled them. "You're a brash and reckless man, friend Marlatt."

"Just the kind you need in your string."

Flack snorted and hauled himself up out of his chair.

"The time book's in Cantrell's shack. You can pay him off. . . . I'll go with you," Flack grunted.

It was full dark now, with the stars silver-streaking the deep purple heavens and the lamplight driving yellow bars across the loamy blackness of the yard. They were about to step off the porch, with the lamplit door standing open behind them, when a quick yell slammed across the yard and a rifle spoke out of the shadows. The bullet passed between the two stopped men, only missing Marlatt by inches; and a cowboy's boots somewhere hammered on the packed adobe. Through that noise Marlatt drove his shot, firing at the other man's muzzle flash. He stood then, forward tipped, for a long still moment before he put away his pistol and stepped off the porch.

Flack's hand reached after him. "Wait!—*wait*, you fool!"

Marlatt's head came round impatiently. "What for?"

"You might have miss—"

Marlatt's laugh was short. "I don't miss, Flack!" He strode off into the unrelieved gloom of the tree-thickened murk by the pole corrals.

211

"Get a lantern, somebody," Flack's lifted voice growled into the shadows; and when a member of the crew came with one he snatched it out of the fellow's hand and hurried corralward, the rest trooping after him.

By the poles they stopped. The circle of radiance cut across a man's boots.

"Rand," Marlatt's voice said out of the darkness, "you can unhitch that team. Cantrell won't be needin' it."

EIGHT

NEW shapes joined the group about the lantern. There was a muttered oath, and a man quickly said: "Better go on back to the house, girls. This ain't no kind of business for you to be looking at." A heavier, demanding voice growled: "What's going on here?" There was a swift flurry of movement, with some of the group giving away before it, and Shirly-Bell said with the right authority, "I've got—" and stopped there suddenly, choked and startled. While from close by Marlatt, Cori observed: "Feet first. With his boots on. I told him that's the way it would be."

Somebody raised the lantern. A broad, heavy shape bent above Cantrell's body. Silence clamped down on the gathering then, and thickened when the man stood up and raked it with a narrowed stare. "Who shot this fellow?"

"It's all right, Nick," Ora Flack said quietly.

The burly man replied: "I'll be judge of that. Which one of you shot him?"

Flack's men stood silent, dark faces expressionless.

"It's no good, Nick." Flack smiled at him faintly. "Bob got what he asked for."

"I'll decide that. You're takin' this mighty cool, ain't you, Flack? I always thought owners took up for their men." The big man leaned forward, his glance sharp and searching. "What are you tryin' to hold out on me, Ora?"

"Come off it, Nick. I've got nothing to hide—"

"Glad to hear it. Better tell me then—"

Marlatt said: "*I* shot him."

"So you've found your tongue at last!"

With the swing of his head, light from the lifted lantern struck full across the big man's face. It was a face Marlatt recognized. Bannerman's—the man who that morning in Oliphant's corral had paid for the Spade-branded bay.

Bannerman said: "I thought it would be you. What have you got to tell me, bucko?"

"I haven't got to tell you anything, mister. I don't even admit your right to ask questions. Who are you to be shovin' your weight around?"

Coldly and thoroughly the man looked him over, then brushed back his coat with the flat of a hand. There was a wink of light from the metal pinned there. "That convince you?"

"Okay—you're sheriff. Start spoutin' your questions."

"First off, bucko, I'll have your name—your *right* name this time."

Marlatt fell silent as he thought back across the years. In a way Bannerman was right to suspect him. There was no getting around the fact that he was a stranger in this country, that he had appeared in Tucson abruptly, without any heralding and on a horse borrowed in the night from a valley outfit. In the sheriff's place, Marlatt was forced to admit, he would have been suspicious also. The man's questions and attitude were entirely reasonable. This was a wild and sudden country, a place peopled in no inconsiderable part by folks who had quit more civilized regions for reasons they were not discussing. Moreover, Tularosa had told that crowd in the Calle Real that he, Kane Marlatt, was a Kingfisher man, a fellow high up in the outlaw's councils; and this white-haired sheriff would have heard of it. For all Bannerman could know they were both Kingfisher's men, a couple of thieves who had fallen out.

So Marlatt hung onto his temper, and when he spoke his reply was leavened by these reflections; by these and by the knowledge that there were *gaps* in his gunfighting past that he'd as lief were not brought up again. He said: "Kane Marlatt *is* my real name, Bannerman."

"Yeah?"

"You'll have to take my word for it."

"And what if I don't choose to?"

Marlatt shrugged. Folding his arms, he leaned against the corral's peeled bars and waited.

Cori Malone was watching him, and presently he grew aware of it and looked at her to find her eyes gone anxious, a fold of her dress tightly gripped in brown fingers. He noticed then that she wore a dress, a pale blue thing of yard-goods calico with tiny red and yellow circles on it; in town she had worn scuffed Levis, a battered sombrero and man's flannel shirt. He noticed other things—that she was young, with lips that were red and fetching across the wind-blown tan of her face. But she was only a child, just a puppy of a girl, with all a puppy's rash impulse.

His glance sought Shirly-Bell; found her close by. He observed then how the two complemented each other. Cori with her immature, boyishly slim figure, her freckles and rebellious red hair, made a perfect background for the older girl's full-bodied, imperious beauty. Shirly-Bell, tall, lovely and every inch a lady, was like a picture-book princess; a lithe blonde goddess, golden-haired and willowy, gentian-eyed, with a skin that was like spun flax in its paleness.

But Bannerman, it seemed, was talking again. Cutting loose of his thoughts, Marlatt gave him attention, discovering the sheriff had changed his tactics.

"I said—" declared Bannerman curtly.

"Hold on a minute," Flack interrupted, moving forward into the lantern light. "No need of the girls having to listen to this; take Cori into the house, Shirly-Bell." He looked around, then said abruptly: "No need of you boys losing sleep out here, either. Couple of you see to burying Cantrell; there's shovels in the harness shed and— Oh! One other thing! Till I say different, you'll be taking your orders from Marlatt now. I'm naming him range boss in Cantrell's place."

Bannerman's head came coldly round and he fixed a displeased stare on Flack. Marlatt saw a flush cross his cheeks, and the glint of amusement that brightened

Flack's eyes as Flack said, "We might's well be using my office for this. No harm being comfortable while we thrash this thing out. Come along, Nick. I've a box of cigars fresh in from the Coast and—"

Marlatt had to admire Flack's cool effrontery, the patent ease with which he shepherded Bannerman into the house and shut the door and, for privacy, barred it.

Scowling, Bannerman took the best chair, hitched it around and put his spurred boots on an edge of Flack's desk. Flack passed the cigars; held a match for the sheriff. The fragrant smoke thawed the man's mood a little. Bull strong and stubborn as Bannerman looked (and undoubtedly was), there was yet a suggestion of softness about him, of a mind that was not quite sure of its ground—a mind that could be shaped by others. Flack was proving it neatly. In Marlatt's thoughts Flack assumed new stature.

"Now," Flack smiled, "just what have you got against Marlatt, Nick?"

"I ain't got nothing against him—personally," admitted Bannerman, frowning. "I've no more against him than I'd have against any other gun thrower who came churning in here looking for trouble—"

"You been looking for trouble, Marlatt?" Flack asked, winking.

"I've got troubles enough without—"

"Exactly!" growled Bannerman, lowering his boots and setting his glass down. The slant of his cheeks showed a plain distrust. "I knew it! What are they? Who you running from?"

A stillness came on. Flack started to say something, but the sheriff waved him back. "You've cut in enough, Ora." His shoulders lifted and he eyed Marlatt darkly.

"Where you from, bucko?"

"Off east a piece—"

" 'East a piece' is a damn big country. *Where* east?"

"I don't see," Marlatt drawled, "that it's any of your business."

Nick Bannerman's stubborn jaw jumped forward. He

banged the desk with a heavy fist. "Mebbe," he said, "I'll make it my business!"

"Your privilege," Marlatt told him; and some wicked impulse made him add: "You won't be the first man tonight that's tried that."

Ruddy color pounded the sheriff's round cheeks. Temper slimmed his eyes to pale slits. "Meanin' Cantrell, eh?"

"Meanin' Cantrell, mister."

"I can lock you up for that little stunt."

"Think so?"

Nick Bannerman swore and started up from his chair, but Flack shoved him back. "Cantrell's out, Nick—"

"Who says so?"

"I do. You can't arrest a man for defending his life. Cantrell got in first shot. He was using a rifle—firing from ambush."

The sheriff's brows went up. He sat back in his chair, very calm, very thoughtful. "Well now," he said, "that's mighty interesting. Why would he be doing that, I wonder?" Glance suddenly sharpening, he said, "Bucko, where have you known Bob Cantrell before?"

"I didn't know him from Adam—"

"Adam who?"

"A figure of speech," Flack told him. "Marlatt means—"

"Suppose you let Marlatt talk for himself."

Marlatt said: "I never saw Cantrell till I came out here."

"People don't go round gunning folks just to be doing."

Marlatt shrugged. "I expect he had his reasons—"

"Exactly! What were they?"

Marlatt, about to remark that he hadn't inquired, caught Flack's warning glance. He said instead: "We passed a few words by the bunkhouse this evening. I guess Cantrell figured he'd lost face with the crew."

"And why would he be getting such an odd kind of notion?"

"He had it in mind to put Kane off the ranch, and Kane," Flack said, taking a hand again, "not only called his bluff but polished it off by compelling Cantrell to hire him."

"Mmmm. Compelling him, eh? How?"

Flack grinned. "He shoved a finger into Bob's ribs. Bob figured it was a pistol—"

"Very slick," drawled Bannerman. "Very slick indeed." He studied Marlatt with a narrowed stare. "In fact, the more I see of this drifter the slicker he appears to be." He said very softly, watching Marlatt: "What made you decide to come west so sudden?"

"Was it sudden?"

Flack growled: "Now listen, Nick—this kind of talk's gone far enough. There's no damn need of you two fussin'. I've always looked on you as a pretty good friend, but I'm not lettin' *anyone* tell me how to run the Straddle Bug. Marlatt's my range boss and I'm standin' behind him, *all the way*. Understand?"

Flack smiled, but there was a look in his eyes that made big Nick Bannerman hesitate. "Seems like you're settin' a heap of store by this fellow. I would think you'd want to know more about him—"

"If I'm suited, you ought to be," Flack said. "Any guy that can bluff a tough ranny like Bob with nothin' more terrible than a stiff finger is my idea of a man to tie to."

"*I'd* say a fellow like that was a damn good bet to keep your eye on," Bannerman differed, glowering at Marlatt. "In fact, I think I'll just take him on in—he's too damn slick to be honest!"

NINE

BANNERMAN'S lips had thinned below the glint of his eyes. Tipped forward he was on the edge of his chair, with a big fist curled tight round his gun butt. A breath, it seemed, would have touched him off, so cocked and gone dark was the look of him.

Marlatt said nothing, but his smile was derisive. It was Flack who broke the taut stillness.

"By God," Flack said, "I won't have it! You hear, Nick? Get your paw off that gun and act sensible!"

"I am actin' sensible." The sheriff's lips barely moved in that stiff, set face; dogged stubbornness stamped every line of it. "There's somethin' almighty peculiar here, and I aim to get to the bottom of it. This guy drifts in like a tumble-weed, plumb humpin' along out of nowhere. He shows up at Oliphant's on one of Joe's horses, which he claims he borrowed from Hartsell. I took the trouble to ride out there this morning, and they don't neither of them know hide nor hair of it."

He let his talk slough off, and a wildness threaded the room like fire because of the implied things he had left unsaid. He seemed to be waiting, as though for Marlatt to deny it; and when Marlatt refused the bait he drew a deep breath into his chest and a brighter light looked out of his stare.

"That ain't all. He buys a horse at Oliphant's, and leaves it there and walks up the street—afoot. Why? Who ever heard of a cowhand walkin'? Slick, that's what he is —so slick fresh butter wouldn't melt in his mouth. He went meandering up the Calle Real and just naturally pirooted slap-dab into the wind-up of that stage office stick-up—just like that.

"You know what I think?" Bannerman's voice was silky

soft now. "I think this whole damn business was a put-up job. I think him an' this Tularosa guy was working hand an' glove with each other."

"Now that's plain crazy," Flack cut in. "This murdering hold-up *stole* the money; Marlatt jumped him and got it back."

"*Exactly!*" Bannerman's eyes glinted satisfaction. "One of 'em stole it, the other got it back! Getting down to cases, don't that strike you as a little too pat? Don't it seem uncommon odd to you that neither of 'em jerked a pistol? That in the subsequent tussle the one got away and the other saved your money? That in the entire fracas neither one of 'em got hurt?"

"That hombre *did* jerk a pistol, so your whole case falls through," Marlatt quietly observed. "He killed a man, didn't he? Killed two men, in fact—Dowling, the express clerk, and that hide-hunter in the Jim Bridger hat. And if you don't think a gun-barrel hurts a man you better feel of my skull."

"That!" scoffed Bannerman, and snorted. "Didn't keep you from getting out here, I notice. Didn't keep you from playin' the hero and settin' yourself in solid with the Straddle Bug. Didn't keep Miss Shirly-Bell from getting Ora here to give you a job!"

There was a hard, hating light in the sheriff's narrowed stare, and Marlatt, striving to account for it, was caught off balance by the man's sudden move. With a rasp of steel on leather Bannerman got his gun out, and its focus took Marlatt's picture.

"Unbuckle your belt, friend, and get out of that hardware."

"Here—just a minute," Flack growled, beard bristling. "You're out of your depth, Nick; a long ways out—"

"He's got a damn suspicious mind," Marlatt muttered.

"Never you mind about my mind. Just get yourself shucked of that gun belt, mister."

"Now look," Flack said, "let's be reasonable—"

" 'Reasonable' is my middle name, Ora," declared the sheriff, grinning coldly. "If you can convince me—"

"I can," Flack said, and cursed the luck audibly. "I hadn't figured to say anything, but this pig-headed play of yours has forced my hand. Marlatt here is an undercover agent. I had to pull a lot of strings to get him here, and I'm not going to see you lug him off to no jail. You're a friend of mine, Nick, and I didn't want to hurt you, but when the law breaks down it's time for a man to take his own measures. Marlatt is the measure I'm taking. He's come out here to put a stop to whoever's smart wangling is trying to wreck this spread!

"Now wait! You've had your say; I'm entitled to mine. I admit your right to suspicion; I can show you, however, that the curious circumstances which have aroused it are nothing but a chain of coincidences.

"I sent for Marlatt three weeks ago—long before *I* could, or *he* could, have known anything about Shirly-Bell's trip with that cattle money. As a matter of fact, I only made up my mind to *buy* the cattle last night. The essential facts are there: somebody's out to bust up this ranch; the same somebody is not only stealing my cattle in wholesale numbers, but is taking steps to make me out a *cowthief* as well! Witness that Spade-branded bay you so kindly bought for me this morning, why I never *saw* that damned horse before! Where did it come from? How did it get into the corral with my own stock? Who is it that's being so generous to me with other people's animals?"

Flack leaned forward and glared at the sheriff. "That's only a patch to what's been happening. One thing has been clear to me a good long while. Whoever it is that's out to get me has got at least *one* man planted right here in my outfit—it's the only way any outsider could have known about me sending in that money this morning. And I think I know who the polecat was. He got wise to me some way—or got wise to Marlatt. He got rattled; made an issue of Marlatt's hiring when all he had to do was what he finally did anyway—squat down in the dark with a loaded rifle."

"You're talking about Bob Cantrell?"

"I am, Nick. Bob Cantrell, I'm convinced, has been drawing his pay from two different sources. I've had him now a little under a year. He brought fine references—I should have had the wit to check them—"

"Have you checked up on this guy?"

"Important people have vouched for Kane Marlatt."

"Yeah. That stick-up vouched for him—"

"Don't be a damn fool!" Flack said irritably. "I got in touch with these people, and they *suggested* Marlatt—"

"But how do you know this guy is Marlatt?"

Flack stared, looked exasperated and said with a scowl: "Now look here, Nick; I've argued the matter long enough. *You* know I been losing stock; the business of that bay should have shown you what sort of methods are being used against me. I've asked you to do something time and again. If these rustlers are too smart for you—too clever at hiding their tracks for you to flush 'em out into the open, then you've no complaint if I go outside for someone to put a stop to the business. You can't expect me to twiddle my thumbs and watch myself made a bankrupt."

He gave the sheriff an earnest regard. "Come on now; show you're a sport and shake hands with Marlatt. Between us, if we work together, we may be able to nab these polecats."

The sheriff said slow and consideringly: "So you think there's more than one of them, do you?"

"I don't know," Flack grumbled; "but I'll bust 'em up if it's the last thing I do! Nobody can run that devil brand on me an' expect to—"

"All right, trouble shooter," Bannerman grinned at Marlatt. "I'll shake your hand an' I'll wish you luck—I've an idea you're going to need it."

And Marlatt, looking deep in the star-packer's eyes, had a hunch that was no vain prediction.

TEN

MANY thoughts drummed for Marlatt's attention as he crossed the shadows of the starlit yard to take up his quarters in the foreman's shanty. But the thing intriguing him most just then was the remarkable defense Ora Flack had built for him. Why? What was back of it? A lot of fine words neatly woven together but without any truth to keep them that way—unless you counted Flack's mention of Marlatt as an undercover agent. He *had* been that when he'd wormed his way into Craft Towner's outfit; but Flack would not know that—he was making it up to hold off the sheriff. Could this, Marlatt wondered, be the result of those hints he'd let drop concerning misbranded cattle? Or was there something much darker, much deeper, behind it?

He was part way across the great tree-shadowed yard when remembrance of his bedroll stopped and turned him. It was in the bunkhouse. The place was dark; but Marlatt swung that way, walking slowly, still thinking. For this was habitual with him, this consideration of the obscure motives behind men's actions; an old and ever more strict kind of habit that was built on need and endorsed by experience. It was, he believed, one of the principal reasons he was still a part of the wild, tough life of this remote frontier. Only the strong and the quick survived. He felt no regret for Cantrell's passing; the man was a blundering, careless fool who had got what he asked for. If Marlatt's guess was right he'd been a crook, to boot. Which was not saying Flack's talk had been true when he'd called the man a crook to the sheriff. Marlatt had not made up his mind about Flack; nor about Nick Bannerman, either, for that matter. They were not careless fools—he was sure of that.

The bunkhouse door had been left open to lure what breeze later hours might bring. As he crossed its threshold, the sound of men's breathing brought up memories in Marlatt of pleasanter days, of things long forgotten. Familiar to him was the darkness of this room, with its reek of stale smoke, its horse smell and heat, and the acrid stench of the crew's unwashed bodies.

He had left his bedroll on the farthest bunk. He had crossed but a groped, scant part of that distance when he stopped abruptly, one foot still lifted. Some warning in the feel of this place had got through his thinking. Nerves cocked, he listened; and was that way, off balance, when the crew piled on him.

A smashing blow rocked the side of his head. A flying fist caught him hard in the ribs and drove him gasping against a bunk. Half blinded, sick, he was doubled there, retching, when a swung boot's heel gouged a path of flame across a cheek already laid open and bleeding. Some man's wild hope sailed across his shoulder and stopped at the wall with a meaty impact; that fellow's crazed yell sliced through the uproar like a knife through butter. And then Marlatt's hands found a hold on the bunk and he braced himself, stopping the next man's rush with a lifted knee. The man's shape dropped like a busted bag.

Marlatt pulled a deep breath and bent with both hands scraping the floor to find something he could use for a weapon, in his rage forgetting the belted gun at his hip. His search yielded nothing, but the bending saved him; for just as he stooped something thin, something glinting, whistled through the murk where he'd just been crouching. Window glass came down in burst fragments, striking the floor with a dry-paper crackle. Some fool then was letting a gun go off, filling the place with its smell of cordite, furiously spraying the walls with its bullets, the flame of those shots licking out like snakes' tongues.

Marlatt, low to the floor with a knee braced under him, kept their tally; and when the fifth blast drove its shot through the tumult he launched himself straight at the

224

man, coming off the floor like a bow-sped arrow. His hatless head took the man in the middle, smashing him solidly against the wall. Shock shook the building.

Eyes streaming from the smart of powder smoke, Marlatt whirled and ragefully waited. Somewhere a man shifted his weight on the floor's squealing boards, and off to the right some other man's groans grew fainter and fainter.

Then Rand's voice, thick with panting, said: "Marlatt?"

But Marlatt, with his back to the wall, stood tightly still and watched a man's shape come up off the floor three feet away and silhouette itself against the vague rectangle of the shattered window. Holding his breath hard, Marlatt waited till the man's wide shoulders came almost straight; then he yanked his gun and went diving forward. The wall-braced spring took the man in the chest and bowled him backward, folding him struggling and spluttering across a bunk's blankets. Marlatt's gun barrel took him across the head, and he went completely limp.

The fight was ended.

"Strike a light!" Marlatt growled; and out of the blackness came Rand's soft curse and the tramp of his boots as he crossed the warped planking. He got a bracket lamp lit.

The place looked as if a cyclone had struck it. One man lay tangled in a bunk's splintered wreckage. There was another one huddled in an angle of the wall, slackly sprawled there, chin on his chest, shirt in tatters. Wabbly braced on hands and knees, the third member of Cantrell's crew was by the overturned table, groaning and shaking and thoroughly sick.

Rand's stare found Marlatt. He was in the room's center, hunched there slump-shouldered, a battered shape in the lamp's yellow glow. He had a pistol still gripped in one down-flopped hand, and clotting blood was a smear on his face. He met Rand's look and shrugged tired shoulders.

Rand seemed about to speak but broke off, eyes narrowed. Marlatt, following that stare, wheeled and saw the group in the doorway. He grinned at them toughly. "Sorry, folks—the show's over."

Cori was there, her eyes round with fright. There was an odd sort of something crowding Shirly-Bell's look, and Flack's hooded stare was a cool thing, inscrutable. The sheriff said: "You've smacked your last man around this place, bucko. Drop that gun an' grab for the rafters!"

Marlatt said: "If you want the gun come an' take it, mister." He grinned derisively when Bannerman scowled.

"Resisting arrest—"

"Don't make me laugh!"

"You won't laugh," growled Bannerman, "when I get done with you."

Oxbow Rand took a hand. "Keep your shirt on, Nick. You've got no case against this fellow. It wasn't him that done that shootin'—"

The sheriff said: "No?"

"There's the gun on the floor that made all the racket. It was Turk done the triggerin'—he was tryin' to drop Marlatt. They had it all framed up to jump him, I reckon. When the going got rough Turk grabbed out his shooter."

Bannerman's head wheeled round, and his displeased look held thinly veiled anger as he raked Kane Marlatt with his willful stare. "You got a lot of friends, bucko; but one of these times they won't be around when your smoke blows away. You better not wait for that time. You better get on your horse and go while you're lucky."

ELEVEN

WITH bedroll slopped across his shoulder, Marlatt was presently threading the yard's deep gloom again. The stars winked gay from a blue-black sky, and the crags of a yonder mountain chain cut sharply across them with a weird kind of beauty. It was a night for things not compatible with violence, but if Marlatt noticed he gave it no thought. All his attention was claimed by the shadows. He wanted no more of this catch-as-catch-can.

It was hard, bitterly hard, to realize that once again he was doomed to play out a role stamped with turbulence. He had thought, when after discovering Towner's duplicity he had fled the man's ranch, to swing his flight this way and give Flack a warning. That done, it had been his plan to find some place where he could hang up his gun and forget the bad past. Only a fool could have hopes of that now. He had a duty here—an obligation. Not to Flack—he could do as he pleased about warning the rancher—but to Oxbow Rand who had asked his aid. It might be argued that Marlatt had made no agreement to help him; by the same token, though, his lack of refusal was tacit acceptance—and Rand had helped *him*. Just now. With his talk of Turk's gun. Marlatt was bound to repay that. But he knew in his heart he'd have stayed on anyway. The feel of this place had gotten into him. There was something going on here beneath the surface . . .

Eyes watchful, he hurried his step. There were a lot of loose ends that he'd got to sort out. He was behind on his thinking, and on this range it would be short shrift for the man who couldn't keep two jumps ahead.

He cut to the left and found the horse trough near the big corral's gate. He washed off the grime of the fight and cleansed the smarting cut on his cheek. A shallow slash, but painful. He made no attempt to improvise a bandage; in this country wounds healed best unwrapped. He ducked his head and combed back his hair with the ends of his fingers. It made him feel more human somehow, as if a bath were good for the feel of one's soul.

He pushed open the door of the foreman's shanty, closed it—and went coldly still as his hand left the latch. Someone was in this dark place with him. He had lived with danger too long to doubt the lifting hackles at the back of his neck. There was someone here, and—

"Over there to your right," a soft breath whispered. "You'll find a lamp on the table."

"Cori," Marlatt said coldly. "What are you doing here?"

"I've got to talk with you—"

"It can wait till morning."

"I must see you tonight," she said urgently. "Light the lamp—"

"Are you daffy? Go on now; get out of here—"

"Why?"

"Because I say to!" He started forward, but she backed off, softly laughing, mocking him.

"I'm not listed under the range boss' orders. Light the lamp—"

"Cori," Marlatt said, "get out of here."

"You aren't very gallant—"

"Gallant be damned! Haven't you the wit," he said quickly, "to think what they'll say if you're seen here?"

"That you're my lover?"

Marlatt cursed the girl's impudence, and she laughed —a gay little sound that was brimful with excitement and—it seemed to him—more than a little unabashed speculation. She said queerly: "Would you be?"

Marlatt stared through the gloom, trying to hold back his anger. After all, she was only a kid. He said: "I'm surprised at you, ma'am! A young lady—"

"I'm not so young! I'm old enough to—"

"You're a damn spoiled brat!" he snapped harshly.

"Talking like a honkytonk girl from the Plaza! You should be—"

"La!" she exclaimed; but he grabbed her and whirled her. A push of his hand sent her stumbling doorward. "Enough!" he growled. "You're going out of here—"

She caught her balance and flung round on him fiercely. "I won't! I shan't go a step till—"

"Cori! Are you inside there?"

Shirly-Bell's voice, gone tight and gone brittle. It came from the door, and the door stood open. They could see her, tall, straight and stiff. She stood in the opening, darkly silent, watching them.

Marlatt cleared his throat. "She just stopped by to—"

"Spare your lies." Shirly-Bell's voice was calm, very calm. It was cold as a knife blade. "It is no concern of mine why she stopped—nor what she was doing in there with the door shut." Some emotion broke through the disdain in her voice then. "You can explain all that to Ora when—"

"Shirly-Bell!" Amazed indignation was in Cori's tone. "Surely you wouldn't—"

"Wouldn't I?"

With a last dark look the yellow-haired girl swept around and was swiftly gone in the swirl of the shadows. They could hear the swish of her rustling taffeta, the quick, light tap of her high-heeled slippers as she hurried houseward.

"Kane!" Cori gasped. "What are we to *do*?"

She caught at his arm with frightened hands. "What have I—"

"We'll know soon enough," Marlatt answered grimly; and saw her go back from him—saw her back through the doorway. He followed.

She was just a pale blur in the gloom of the peppers; but black and bitter as his own thoughts were, he sensed her feelings, and some unguessed impulse of pity, of contrition, drove through the hard shell he showed the world, and he said more reasonably: "I'll go talk with him—"

"Please don't—don't bother! I wouldn't have you budge one step for me—not a step! Do you hear?"

The fierceness of her left him staring; and he was still that way, surprised and wordless, when Flack came striding out of the murk. Flack said: "Go to your room, Cori," and then, to Marlatt: "Inside, bucko—and watch your step."

Marlatt shrugged and turned, preceding the rancher in. He found and lit the lamp on the table, spun up its wick and wheeled and waited.

Flack shut the door and put his back against it. "Time we talked turkey."

"Go ahead an' talk."

"I aim to," Flack said. "These are your orders, and I won't repeat them. Stay away from my women."

"I know my place," Marlatt told him stiffly. "Cori just—"

"Leave it ride. And keep away from her. She's a young, inexperienced, crazy-headed kid and I won't have you fooling with her—I don't want you around her. I've acknowledged your favor by taking you on; but don't get above yourself. You had a smart idea, but it won't work —savvy?"

Flack's hooded stare was bland and bright. "No gun thrower," he purred softly, "is goin' to marry, into this outfit. When the bells get rung *I'll* pick the man."

He hooked big thumbs in his ornate gun belt. "When you need a woman—"

But Marlatt had quit listening. His eyes were like two polished marbles. His stomach muscles were convulsed, gone knotted. When Flack said: "Understand?" it took all Marlatt's will to get his glance above the rancher's belt.

He nodded mechanically.

"All right," Flack said. "I've a tough crew here—can't use no other. You may have more trouble with them. Do what you have to do, but don't take no gun to 'em. They know their work, and we can't replace them."

He studied Marlatt a moment longer, green glance slantwise. Then he jerked a nod. "That's all. Good night."

Some facet of the ranchman's parting cut through Marlatt's worriedly puzzled thinking, catching an edge of his sardonic humor. His long lips shaped a wry kind of smile as, stooping, he picked his bedroll off the floor and chucked it over on Cantrell's bunk. So that was all, was it?

All, indeed!

This Flack was a pretty cool customer. Very near as cool as Tularosa; and considerably shrewder. About as smooth as a miser's first ten-cent piece.

"*All*, says he!"

Kane Marlatt snorted.

Smart—that's what Flack was. Played with his cards hard-hugging his vest. He might have backed Marlatt up in their talk with Bannerman, but he wasn't explaining that talk to Marlatt. Let Marlatt think whatever he'd a mind to; what did Flack care what a drifter thought? Flack pulled the strings that moved the sheriff. Sly Flack, who knew that talk was for fools.

Marlatt's mind had a lot to think on: belts and looks and misbranded critters, the law of this country and the man who applied it, a girl's scared eyes—another girl's disdain. The whole odd feel of this Straddle Bug layout.

This was damned good range for a man to ride soft on. . . .

A step on the porch yanked Marlatt's head round. He was that way, cocked, when Rand came in.

Rand said at once: "What'd His Nibs come here for?"

"I don't rightly know," Marlatt told him, straightening. "He sort of talked around it."

Rand's glance raked the room, and he scowled at it irritably. "He's been actin' damn funny ever since he got back."

"Back?"

231

"Been away on one of his cattle buyin' trips."

"Oh." Marlatt crossed to the bunk. He stood there a moment looking down at it. Then he jerked Cantrell's belongings off and heaved them doorward. "You can take that junk out an' give it to the crew." He spread his own bedroll and sat down on it wearily. "How are they doin'?"

"I got 'em patched up," Rand said, "but they're feelin' ornery. Better handle 'em gentle—"

"These cattle buyin' trips—does he take them often?"

"So-so. There's times when he travels right frequent. Mostly, though, he's round pretty reg'lar. Why?"

"Just wonderin'," Marlatt answered indifferently. "What you think of the sheriff?"

"Ain't seen much of him."

"Well," Rand allowed with a twisted smile, "you prob'ly will if you stay on here. You'll prob'ly see quite considerable of him. He's got his mind set on marryin' Shirly-Bell."

"That makin' Flack happy?"

"Hard tellin'. Flack ain't one to peddle his notions." Rand paced the room, his look gone nervous. "You noticed anything since you been around here?"

"Quite a number of things."

Rand nodded, keeping on with his pacing. "Any one thing more than another?" He shot the new man a sharp, quick look.

"You mean the crew? Gun dogs, ain't they?"

"They're plenty tough—an' the rest is just like 'em. Fifteen guys ridin' for this outfit. An' every one of 'em a notch-cuttin' gun thrower!"

"Flack says conditions here make him keep a tough crew."

"Shouldn't wonder—but who makes the conditions?" Rand, turning, scowled at him.

Marlatt said: "Bannerman?"

"Bannerman's big, but this country's bigger—he can't watch every place. He does his lawin' pretty much where Flack tells him." Rand paused, and added thoughtfully: "Far as I know, though, Bannerman's honest. He's a rancher himself an' hates rustlers like poison."

Marlatt recalled what Flack had told the sheriff that evening about rustling. He told Rand about it.

Rand nodded. "There's somethin' queer goin' on all right. It goes deeper than Cantrell, though—a lot deeper. I saw that bay; he was with a bunch the boys brought up yesterday, I s'posed Flack had bought him. We got a lot of stock been vented that way."

"Be hard," Marlatt murmured, "to say which was stolen."

"Damn hard. We're runnin' upwards of forty thousan' cattle."

"That many?" Marlatt whistled. "I'd no idea this was such a big outfit."

"You're forgettin'," Rand said. "We're runnin' *two* outfits—Flack's an' Cori's. When Flack took over, Cori's Crescent had better than twenty-eight hundred cows under iron, an' the best range round here. Up till then Ora Flack was a two-bit cow boss."

Marlatt's hand rasped across his jaw. "An' Cori, you say, comes of age next month?"

The short man nodded. He eyed Marlatt darkly. "You beginnin' to get the drift of this business?"

"I'm beginnin' to see a vague light," Marlatt drawled.

Bow Rand stopped his pacing. He shook some Durham into a paper and rolled up a smoke, very slowly and carefully. "Ora," he said, "is pretty well satisfied just the way things stand. He's got a sweet layout here. Swings him a lot of weight in this county. He ain't goin' to take it kindly when Cori ups an' asks for an accountin'."

"You think she will?"

Oxbow Rand smiled dryly. "She likes him about the same way I like his crew. An' he knows it. I don't reckon he knows about me; I've kep' my trap shut. But he sure understands what *she* thinks of him."

"I don't see," Marlatt said, "as there's very much he can do about it. As her legal guardian he's bound to hand over her property when she comes of age—if she wants it."

"There's ways," Rand said darkly. "Ora's slick. She could take it to court when the circuit court gets here. But I doubt if they could do more than give her a judgment. Flack would laugh at it. He could drag it out over two or three years—"

"And by that time—"

Rand, blackly scowling, nodded. "She wouldn't have a cow left, or a horse, or so much as a saddle. If I got him figgered right, though, he'll play it smarter than that. He'll play the marriage game on her if he can't cut it no other way. He'll git her to thinkin' she can marry herself out of it."

"What have you told her?"

"I ain't told her nothin'. I keep plumb away from her. The first time Ora caught me talkin' with her would be the last day's work I'd do on this spread. I'm the only one of her dad's crew left. An' *I* wouldn't be here only I eat out of the same plate with the rest of the snakes."

Rand's face was bitter. "I've kep' my mouth shut an' I've done everything I been told—an' precious little it's bought me. I don't guess Ora'd even trust his own gran'-mother. I never git to go no place alone. There's been things goin' on, but you couldn't prove it by me. I been kept on here, but I might jest as well 'a' been shipped to Chi; there's times I ain't seen the bulk of this crew for eight-ten weeks hand-runnin'."

He turned his head and spat out the door. "Flack can talk all he wants about folks that's layin' for him; but you'll never tell *me* this spread's on the level. It may be —but *I'll* not believe it."

TWELVE

"THEN you think Flack's a crook?"

"I don't know," Rand muttered, "whether he is or he ain't. But there's *somebody* crooked around this outfit! I could—Hell! it all boils down to one of two things: Either, like Flack says, there's somebody out to coil his twine for him, *or* somebody's usin' a runnin' iron to pile up the Straddle Bug's profits faster. You—"

His voice trailed off.

Like a cat he whirled to face the door; a small shape crouching, heavy pistol at hip. Marlatt, too, had heard and wheeled, with his own hand spread tense and clawed above his gun butt. But that quiet, stealthy rasping of a shifted weight was not repeated and, though Marlatt prowled in the outside shadows while Rand took a careful look through the bunkhouse, the unknown listener got clear away.

Rand came up to Marlatt at the harness shed. The shake of his head was bleakly ominous. "They was all in their bunks. Turk was awake, though, an' if ever I saw hate look from a man—"

"Reckon it was Flack?" Marlatt asked him guardedly.

The short man shrugged. "But we're sure as hell goin' to hear more about this. Somethin'll break, an' damn sudden."

He stood a moment with his head tipped, listening. But no least sound came out of the dark that was not accounted for by the wind in the trees.

Again Rand shrugged, and thrust his gun back in leather. "There's a fella in town used to be on my payroll —when I was top boss at the Crescent. Cheto Bandera. A Mex—but white; an' come anythin' should happen— quick an' mean, d'ye see?—you git in touch with him.

Cheto cut his teeth at the same place you did an' he'd give his right arm if he thought 'twould help Cori."

"What about Miz' Shirly-Bell?" Marlatt asked; and the short man gave him a tight-faced look.

"Miz' Shirly-Bell," he said dryly, "can look out for herself. You tell Cheto I sent you. Cori's dad onct helped him out of a—"

"Hell. You ain't dead yet."

But Rand was not to be kidded out of it. "Never mind. You remember that, fella. If anything goes haywire, git in touch with Bandera." He swung on his heel in the gloom and departed.

Marlatt sat on his bunk in the foreman's shack with the light turned out and a gun in each fist. He'd got the extra pistol out of his bedroll and was of a mood to work both triggers if he heard any more prowlers sneaking around. He was tired—dog tired, but he'd too much to think of to feel at all sleepy.

Instead of reporting Craft Towner to the Grant County sheriff, he had quit New Mexico to come and warn this Flack of his danger. Towner had been trying to hire Kane Marlatt to gun Flack. Marlatt had said he would think it over, and that same night had cut his stick; and only barely in time at that. Tularosa's snooping had uncovered the knowledge that Marlatt was scouting for the Canadian River Cattle Association and that, more likely than not, he had seen through Towner's ranchman pose and knew him for the man he was, the notorious Texan, "Kingfisher"—tophand cattle thief and killer.

Marlatt felt no shame at having departed in such a lather. To have lingered so much as a few seconds longer would have marked him for a suicide's death. He would have had no chance with that killer outfit. Ben Thompson had been on the place; and Charley Basset and Luke Short, too; and Mysterious Dave Mathers had been looked for at any moment.

He was rather sorry, though, he had not cut over to

warn the sheriff. The Texas Rangers had been hunting Fisher, and would have given plenty to have had Marlatt's knowledge. But Marlatt's chief concern at the time had been to put himself beyond Towner's reach; and larruping hellbent through the gusty night it had come to him he had better warn Flack. He had swung this way with Towner's gundogs after him; and he had not drawn an easy breath till that ledge had tricked them in the Santa Ritas. Bitter surprise had been his portion when he'd found himself faced with the limping Lahr and Tularosa in the dust of Tucson's mob-crowded street.

But here he was now on Flack's Straddle Bug; and Flack had not had his warning yet.

He did not know himself why he hadn't warned Flack —why he'd kept putting it off. He'd felt odd about the man from the time he'd first seen him standing on the ranch house porch. He was intrigued by Flack, but he could not like him nor wish him well. Nor could he tell why he did not like him. Big and magnetic Flack certainly was; impressive in costly store clothes, fancy Hyer boots and silver spurs. Yet despite all this, something about the rancher had roused in Marlatt an almost instant antagonism. It had made him perversely withhold his warning.

He could not explain this queer reaction. Time and again he had probed it, weighed it, striving to find some answer to it. It must come, he thought, from some quality of mind or spirit inherent in the man which, while not directly manifest in either word or action, was nonetheless there—like the feel of red to the eyes of a bull.

He could not pin it down any closer than that. He had noticed the same thing, though, in Craft Towner; a kind of wildness, maybe. Like the faint smell of rankness that trails a wolf pack.

Thought of Towner brought Marlatt other thoughts till sheer weariness threatened to send him to sleep. Thought of Cori came to him, with her bright child's eyes and boyishly slim shape; and recalling the tempting red curve of her lips, he thought it too bad she was so spoiled-rotten. What had she wanted of him? A talk, she had said. Marlatt softly snorted. He knew what she needed—a darn good tanning.

Remembrance of Shirly-Bell's cool disdain pulled his chin off his chest; and he cursed his luck darkly, finding ready excuses for her thoughts and actions. She had been right to call him a gun thrower—for what else was he when you came right down to it? And her suspicions of their business in that unlit shack had been amply justified; if not by fact, by the kind of life she presumed he had led.

He sighed. He would like to have held her good opinion. Somehow she attracted him mightily, fully as strangely and strongly as her uncle repulsed him. But he could not blame her for the things she thought; like himself, she was what her environment had made her. She was a thoroughbred, a lady. Been strictly brought up—in a convent, probably. She saw the world's people in just two colors: jet black or snow white. There were no mixed grays in her category of values.

And it was just as well, probably. God knew Kane Marlatt had no right to be thinking of her—or of *any* good woman. Flack had told him. If he wanted a woman, he could ride to the Plaza. It was for the likes of him that they kept such places. Him and Ben Thompson and the rest of the toughs. . . .

Still skirting the thing uppermost in his mind, he came back to Flack, just as he had known from the start he would have to. To the glint in Flack's eyes. To the man's long fingers. To his clothes, to his boots, to his fifteen gun throwers.

Impatiently, scowling, he jerked his mind free. There were things more important that he'd better be thinking of. Such as who had been listening while he and Rand talked. . . .

But savagely, stubbornly, grimly defiant, his mind conjured up the image of Flack again—conjured up the man's ornate gun belt. As if they'd been etched in acid, he saw the wrinkled, bulged places Flack's thumbs had pressed in it. Many times Kane Marlatt had seen—

The crash of a shot broke the night's deep hush. It jerked Marlatt upright, weird thoughts forgotten. Frozen rigid, he crouched there, hearing the echoes smash against the buildings, strike and flatten, then fall away to sharp fragments that pulsatingly rolled out over the valley like the final burst of some distant clapping.

It had come from the bunkhouse.

Grim with foreboding, Marlatt came off the bunk. Dropping guns to the bed, he scooped up his hat and stamped into his boots. His mind raced ahead as he fastened his cartridge belt, deftly tying the whangs that held down his holster. There was going to be trouble— bad trouble; in his bones he felt it, and could not help but remember that piece of advice he had got from the sheriff. "You better get on your horse an' go while you're lucky!" That was the hint Nick Bannerman had given him; and remembering the latent hostility he had seen in the sheriff's blue eyes, Marlatt almost wished he had taken it.

Too late now. He thrust the extra pistol inside his shirt, felt it snug to his waistband. With his belt gun in hand, he went into the yard.

It was not nearly so dark as it had been. A faint line of gray edged the distant Rincons. A breeze which had sprung up whipped in off the desert; cool and sweet with the fragrance of yucca.

A lamp's yellow glow flowed bright from the bunkhouse. Stiff shapes stood black against the light from the door. They were facing the bunkroom, and the drone of their talk broke sharply as the sound of his boots came up with them. He heard his name spoken soft and bitter; and Flack's hunched shoulders came swinging round in a way that was purely wicked.

"That'll be far enough—just stop right there!" And Cori's voice cried sharply: "Where have you been?" And a queer look reached him from Shirly-Bell's eyes. The other shape belonged to the cook, and the pinched slant of his cheeks was guardedly wooden.

"Yes," echoed Flack. "Just where have you been?"

Marlatt ignored the man's ugly tone. He said: "I been in my shack tryin' to get some sleep—"

"I suppose you can prove that?"

"Sure," Marlatt said sarcastically. "I reckon the pants rats an' seam squirrels will furnish a testimonial for me—"

"If that's supposed to be humor," Flack glared, "you pick a damn poor time for it, friend. A man's been killed and—"

"You got reason to think I killed him?"

"If you want it that way—yes!"

Marlatt, stiffening, caught Shirly-Bell's imploring glance and grabbed a hold on his temper. After all, being the newest man here, it was not unlikely that Flack should suspect him. The wonder was that yellow-haired Shirly-Bell should place any trust in him; should, of all things, be extending him sympathy and appear to be siding him. It took trouble, he thought, to show a man who his friends were.

He got a rough-lock on his temper; and when Flack inquired how long he had been there, he said with forced calm: "Ever since you left."

"I don't believe it!" Cori cried hotly, and the glint in Flack's eyes gleamed subtly brighter. "You see how it is," he said, shrugging. "We've not a thing but your word for it."

"Are you callin' me a liar?"

But Flack just scowled and wheeled about to take a restless stride or two. And Marlatt's following glance observed again the quick, sure, springy reach of that stride. It was incongruous with the man's stooped shoulders and bearded face. With his back turned Flack looked ten years younger; and instinctively Marlatt's eyes flashed down to find that the ornate belt Flack had worn this evening was not about the fat waist now. He was not wearing a gun belt. But he was heeled; Marlatt saw, as the rancher swung round, the telltale bulge at his armpit.

"Let's see that pistol you're packin', Marlatt."

"What for?"

"You know any reason I shouldn't see it?"

"I've got no reason to think you should. This pistol's comfortable right where it is." Marlatt tightened his grip round the gun's worn stock, and the stare he gave Flack was as blank as the rancher's.

"You refuse to let me examine it?"

Marlatt, hesitating, saw the disturbed lift and fall of Shirly-Bell's breathing. "But, Oral!" she cried. "The gun was Ran—"

"Keep out of this, Shirly!"

"So the gun was Rand's, was it?" Marlatt grinned at him. "And what does Rand say—"

"Oh! To think you could stand there and play so in—"

"*Cori!* Go to the house—you, too, Shirly-Bell!" Flack ordered blackly. "Right now! Go—"

Marlatt had no chance to hear any more, for Cori was suddenly in front of him, her freckled cheeks paled and twisted with fury.

"You cheap, gun-packing murderer!" she cried; and stood, breasts heaving, ineffable scorn and contempt in her eyes.

The look of her shocked him. Alarmed, he was moving forward when her hand lashed up and slapped him, fiercely, again and again, till his cut cheek burned and the sound of her breath came in panting sobs. Going back a step, she flung her full anger at him. "I hate you —hate you—*hate* you!"

The singing silence that followed her words was bleak as the wind off Yukon ice; and the figures limned in the bunkhouse light were as still as things hacked out of marble.

Marlatt stood where her blows had left him, agate

glance locked with the glint of her blue one. The sound of her voice brittle as glass, Cori cried: "I hope to God Nick Bannerman kills you!" and whirled, running, half-stumbling into the clutch of the dark.

THIRTEEN

It was Flack who broke the silence. "Go find that little fool," he said, "and take her into the house, Shirly-Bell. And when you get her there, keep her."

He might as well have spoken in Greek for all Kane Marlatt heard of it. He stood wide-eyed, staring into the dark, with his tough face as blank as pounded tin. He had not known this yard was so cold, or that the echo of words could linger so drearily. He stood bathed in sweat in a world of ice. The coordination of muscle and nerve appeared to have left him—to have rooted him there, like the stump of a great oak blasted by lightning. Then a hand touched his arm with a soft, quick pressure; and Shirly-Bell's voice from the wind-swept yard said, "Never mind, Kane—*I* believe in you. . . ."

Her words broke the spell. Marlatt stirred like a big, shaggy dog coming up out of sleep and, warmed by the trust of this yellow-haired girl, felt the blood, dark and red, pounding through him again—felt his muscles swell with the lift of his anger.

When the dark had swallowed her, Flack said bitterly: "All right. Keep your gun. An' keep it off my men—"

"You know as well as I do I didn't gun Rand—"

"He wasn't gunned. He was knifed," Flack said. "An' you're the only one round—"

Brushing past him, Marlatt entered the shack. One look was enough. Rand had been knifed all right!

Marlatt saw something then that turned him rigid; and the cold came back to set his spine crawling, to lift the ends of the hair at the back of his neck. The headquarters crew were gone out of this shack. Their bunks were smooth. They had not been slept in. He was, there-

fore, aside from the cook, the only man round who could
have slit Bow Rand's throat—unless Flack had done it.

In the lamp's yellow glow Flack's regard was bland.

The cook, by the door, hadn't moved from his tracks;
only his head had swung round, darkly watching. His
bright, beady stare held the glint of plain malice.

"Where," Marlatt growled, "is the rest of this crew?"

Flack shrugged. The cook smiled thinly from a corner
of his mouth. "They had orders from Cantrell to go out
to Camp Two tonight. Since you gave no instructions to
the contrary, I expect they went." He said it smugly and
kept on grinning.

"Very neat," Marlatt breathed; and a lean formidable-
ness gripped his cheeks. "And just when—if you'd be
knowin'—did this exodus take place?"

"Right after chuck," the cook said through his teeth.

Marlatt carefully straightened. His glance swapped
the cook for Flack's bearded face. The rancher grinned
at him coldly. "If this is a frame-up—"

"Harsh words won't butter no parsnips, friend." Flack
put his hunched shoulders against the wall. "As I see it,
the play stacks up something like this. We've all of us
noticed one thing from the start: you an' Rand've been
too thick not ever to've known each other before. When
Cantrell interrupted you by the trees out yonder, you
was fixing up some kind of deal with Rand—some kind
of scheme to run off more of my cattle. Whatever it
was," Flack smiled thinly, "Rand got cold feet; or he
made up his mind he didn't want no part of it. He went
over to your shack later on an' told you so. More you
thought about it after he'd gone, the more scared you
got he'd be tippin' me off to it. So, quick's you reckoned
we'd all got to sleep, you honed up your knife an' come
over here an' skewered him.

"You made two bad slips," Flack went on, smooth as
velvet. "One was in picking the place for your killin'. It
was smart, in a way, and would prob'ly 've worked had
the other boys been sleepin' here—but they wasn't, as
you found out after you'd killed him. Your second slip

was in bunglin' the job—in letting him get to his gun before you'd done his business; that was what caught you. It gave you no time to remedy your first slip—it gave you no time to make sure he was done for—"

"Done for! With his throat cut like that?"

Flack shrugged, and smoothed the fancy vest down over his belly. "The shot spoiled your timing. You heard us coming. You had to cut an' run for it."

"An' so—?"

Marlatt's mind was racing. Even in the grip of temper's fury he was forced to admire the bearded man's artistry. Flack was a master of smooth deception. Who would have guessed he could have swapped broncs so swiftly! Barely five hours had passed since he had stood so squarely behind Marlatt against the sheriff. He must at that time have figured to have a use for him—else why all that dust he'd pawed up for Nick Bannerman? "Undercover agent," Flack had called him to Bannerman, thus neatly spiking the big sheriff's guns.

This slick-talking Flack had diddled him nicely. Marlatt could not even brand *that* tale a lie, for the rancher might very well have *sent* for an agent—might have sent, with fine irony, for *Kane Marlatt*, even. The Canadian River crowd would have recommended him well, if they'd not got wise he'd dropped the Towner case on them; and they probably hadn't.

Under his breath Kane Marlatt cursed softly. He'd never have believed he could so badly misjudge a man. And from the very start he'd been suspicious! But here it was. Not only had he underrated Flack, but he had grossly misjudged the speed with which this stoop-shouldered, pot-bellied rancher could move. The man was chain lightning! Barely five hours had fled since that scene in the office Flack had cleverly staged to lull his suspicions. Marlatt should have seen through it. If the man was a crook, no amount of fast gun-slingers could approach by a fifth the use Flack could get from Nick Bannerman's friendship—a star-packing sheriff eating out of his hand!

It was obvious enough to Marlatt now that Flack was aware of what Rand had said to him—was at least aware of the trend Rand's remarks had taken. And with macabre humor it was the plain intention of this pot-bellied rancher to get himself shut of the both of them, pronto. To play the one off against the other. Very sly.

Rand was dead. Therefore Marlatt had killed him.

Neat and simple—and indisputable. Once they were dead, who would give a whoop?

He saw Flack watching him with cool amusement.

"Where's the knife?"

"Hmmm—the point is well taken. Unfortunately," Flack smiled, "you took it away with you. Be a deal of bother to instigate a search for it, and not of much use if we happened to find it. You'd hardly be fool enough to leave it dirty, or to use a blade that could be traced back to you. I think we can do very well without it. The facts," he said blandly, "speak plain for themselves."

"You propose to cash in my chips for me, do you?"

Flack lifted protesting eyebrows. "They may do things that way where you come from, friend; but here around Tucson we try to act civilized. I shall hold you for the sheriff, of course—"

"You're not worried about what I might say to him?"

"Hard tellin' when Nick will show up here. Lots of things could happen between now and then."

"You must think I'm a fool!" Marlatt scowled; and a flick of his wrist set his pistol's barrel directly in line with the third silver button of Flack's fancy vest.

"Well—not exactly," the rancher said, blue eyes twinkling. "There's not very much you can do about it, friend. Shooting won't help you. You might drop me; but then there's Lanky behind you. A child couldn't miss with a sawed-off shotgun when its muzzle ain't hardly three feet from its target."

FOURTEEN

FLACK stood loosely watching him, cool as a well chain. He appeared to be enjoying this business. He was like a cat with a mouse, Marlatt thought; and rage rushed tumultuously through him. It took every ounce of will-power in him to keep from putting his luck to the test. He could drop Flack certainly; he might even manage to down Lanky. . . .

Cool reason came to crush the impulse; reason and re-membrance. The tempestuous urge of his roaring blood passed, and he saw with a sudden clarity how this slick-talking Flack might have tricked him again. The cook hadn't even a gun belt on—let alone a shotgun ready to hand. Flack had hoped with his talk to swing Marlatt's back around.

"Try again," Marlatt drawled, and grinned at Flack coldly. It was premature; for at that split second the lanky cook sprang. The lunge of his drive carried Marlatt off balance, drove him lurching floorward with the cook on his shoulders. His downthrust hands crumpled under the weight, and his chest came against the floor flatly. The pistol went skittering out of his fist, and from the tail of an eye he saw Flack coming; saw Flack's black beard and the gleam of his teeth—saw the wicked glint of a knife in Flack's hand.

Marlatt rolled, straining all his sinews against the cook's clutch. The cook's grip broke when he struck Flack's boots, and the battering force of his bony shoul-ders bowled the legs like straws from under Flack. The ranchman came down hard and grunted. He came down on the cook. Air belched from Lanky in one great *whish*. Teeth bared and cursing. Flack came afoot—and found Marlatt eyeing him above a cocked pistol.

"I don't suppose," Marlatt drawled, "that would be the knife, would it?"

For a second Flack glowered. Then a parched grin twisted the beard round his lips and he thrust the blade away in his boot. He said, "Don't push your luck too far," and started for the door.

Marlatt stretched an arm across his path. "You're not done with this yet." There was blood along the edge of his lips and his face was a fighter's, tough and reckless. There seemed to be no caution left in him. "You've started something, Flack, that I'll finish—"

"You'll wind up on a shutter if you don't get out of here!"

"Mebbe I will—but there'll be other shutters in the same procession. Remember that, Flack, when you see Nick Bannerman. You've stacked the cards well, but there's one or two you didn't have hold of. Better think of Craft Towner before you start yappin'."

He scooped up Rand's gun, got his own from the corner and went out of the bunkhouse—leaving Flack with his blue eyes blank.

He moved straight to the corral and roped out his horse, the blaze-faced roan he had bought from Oliphant yesterday morning. Yesterday! It seemed incredible so much could have happened in such a short time. He had come unheralded, unknown and unknowing; come seeking peace. He was apt to get it, but from a piece of lead, with his name carved on it.

He flattened the blanket on the horse's back, and a near sound of hoofs lent speed to the hands that reached down his saddle. With a grimace he heaved the hull on the roan. A lone wolf always, yet never had Kane Marlatt felt more alone than now.

He was tightening the cinches when Cori came over. Somehow he knew it was Cori without even looking at her.

"Where are you going?" she demanded.

He didn't turn nor bother answering. He stood coiling his rope. He put the rope on his saddle.

Cori said scathingly: "Quitter!"

When it seemed he would prove impervious, she cried hotly: "After all them brave words! Lettin' Flack run you out! I'd be *ashamed*—"

"All right. Nobody'll stop you."

He heard the catch of her breath; swung round and faced her. This cold dawn light was not kind to her. But he was in no mood to pity her. And the scorn and anger he saw in her eyes—

"I came out here," she said, "to ask your pardon. I've been thinking, and it's plain enough Rand's murder is a piece with the other things around here. I was wrong to think you had killed him—but I'll not ask your pardon!" she blazed.

All her hurt, all her scorn came tumbling out then in words that were sharp as the lash of a whip. "You haven't that much nerve! You haven't the spunk of a jackrabbit. Even a *coyote*—"

"Good night," Marlatt said, and reached for his saddle.

But he was not to be gone so swiftly as that.

He was swining up on the horse when a bull voice shouted: "Hold on there, you! I want to see you, bucko!"

It was big Nick Bannerman, the Pima sheriff.

FIFTEEN

This looked like it, Marlatt thought, and slewed a glance around for Flack. But Flack and the cook had not come in sight. The sheriff's long legs were nearing him rapidly.

"Me?" Marlatt said.

"I hope I got more manners than to talk at a lady that way." Bannerman, scowling, came to a stop with his left hand clamped to Kane Marlatt's bridle. "It may interest you to know I've got your gun-packin' pard safely locked in jail—"

"You must be mistaken, Sheriff. I've got no pard—"

"Your friend then. That hard lot calling himself Tularosa—"

"He's no friend of mine."

There was a leer on Bannerman's beefy face. "That's one point you're both agreed on, seems like. He says you engineered that stealin' and—"

"You're hopin' like hell to prove it, ain't you?"

"I'm *goin* to prove it." Nick Bannerman grinned at him. "You watch my smoke!"

"By that time," said Marlatt, "I'd have more beard than Flack's got. Sorry, Sheriff, but the chores of this ranch—"

"Ora can worry along with the ranch. You're goin' to jail, bucko. *Right now!*" With one swift sweep of a blurred right hand the sheriff had a six-shooter cocked and leveled.

Marlatt looked down his nose at it. "You'll get killed some day pullin' that stunt, Sheriff. Some fool will think you're in earnest, likely—"

A surge of red rimmed the sheriff's collar. "Go on," he said; "make the most of it, bucko. When you find yourself underneath a limb—"

THE TEXAS TORNADO

"The law requires evidence—"

"I'll furnish all the evidence anyone wants—"

"I'm sure of it." Marlatt held hard to his temper. "But in a case of this kind, the law—"

"The laws weren't framed to help the likes of *you!* Unbuckle that gun belt!"

Marlatt lounged in the saddle with his lean cheeks taut, with his eyes like steel. He said very softly: "I guess not, Bannerman," and like a flash his boot came up and stopped, hard and short, at the sheriff's chin. Bannerman's head went back as if a rock had struck him. His burly shoulders swayed and he staggered with his eyes rolled back; and suddenly crumpled.

Two spurts of flame bit the black rectangle of the bunkhouse door. Lead ricocheted from Marlatt's cantle. Hard on its heels came the crack of a rifle—twice—three times; and Marlatt fled with the creased horse under him going like a rocket.

Nick Bannerman, scowling hard after that speeding shape, swore bitterly. When convinced the man really meant to run for it, the sheriff too had flung up his gun and joined its bark to the blasts from the bunkhouse; but tumultuous passions unsteadied his aim. He had no better luck than the others were having. Choking with rage, he ran back to his horse and with shaking hands got the gear stripped off it. Lugging these things, he was passing the bunkhouse when Flack and the scowling cook came out. The cook had a rifle and his lips were twitching.

"I'm borrowin' a horse," Bannerman growled at the rancher.

Flack nodded. "Take the palomino."

"Hell with your palomino!" The grunted words came over Nick's shoulder. "How about that Morgan? I want somethin' with bottom—"

"Go ahead," Flack said; and followed him over. He stood by the gate watching Bannerman work. The cook went along to his pots and pans and was shortly sending

251

smoke up his chimney. "Better stop a bit and have some grub, Nick."

"An' let that bastard get clear away?"

"I've an idea he'll keep. Why don't you play this smart, Nick?"

The sheriff, cinching up, gave him one hard look. He slipped on the bridle. "Smart, eh? As how?"

Ora Flack considered. The glint of his eyes showed a secret humor, but he was thoughtfully sober when the sheriff turned.

"As how?" Bannerman's tone was impatient.

Pungently, concisely, the whiskered rancher outlined a version of Rand's killing; and the sheriff's look got blacker and blacker. Flack said smoothly: "Now look. I believe I know why he rubbed out Rand. . . ."

"Yeah?" Bannerman was plainly in a sweat to be gone.

"Yes," Flack said, and nodded thoughtfully. "I'm pretty near sure of it. I been thinking. This fellow and Rand have met before. They got thicker'n fiddlers about as soon as Rand saw him—got off by themselves where the rest couldn't hear them. They did a heap of talking—Marlatt, mostly; and it struck me first off he was cookin' up a deal to run off more of my cattle, or my horses mebbe."

"Now wait," he said as the sheriff would have spoken. "This ain't no time for a bull in the china shop. Any brash fool can go off half cocked; but the smart guy scouts where his boots will take him. When he jumps he knows where his boots will come down. This is a right good time to use your head, not your elbow—"

"Go ahead an' use it then," Bannerman growled. "I'm goin' to put *my* trust in a pair of hot spurs!" He said it wickedly and swung to his saddle; but Flack's quick hand caught the horse by the cheek strap.

"Just a minute!" Flack said. "He ain't skippin' the country. You better hear me out an' see what you're going up against. That fellow's no ordinary grubline drifter—"

"He's a damn gun thrower!" Bannerman cursed.

"He's a lot more than that," Ora Flack said quietly. "You're not any slough with a gun yourself—but if this guy's who I think he is, you'd have no more chance than a flea in hell's furnace."

The sheriff's quick look met the rancher's blue one.

"I've had one of the boys out looking around. He rode in from the east—from the southeast in fact. From off towards Texas—"

"Hell! I knew that already! 'Cordin' to this Tularosa, he come from over round—"

"New Mexico. Yes," Flack said blandly. "But before that I think you'll find he was getting his mail some place in Texas. I've lived in the Lone Star state myself, and this hombre—"

"Thought you knew all about him," said Bannerman acridly. "Didn't I hear you say important people had vouched for this Marlatt?"

"For Marlatt, yes. But you brought up an interesting point when I was telling you that. You asked how I knew this fellow was Marlatt. That's been the one weak spot in the entire business; and it got me thinking."

Flack's nod was grave. "I've about decided the guy *isn't* Marlatt."

"Then who in hell *is* he?"

"That's what I'm getting at. He's a Texan, certainly. So was Rand. Rand came, so he said, from Uvalde County. Rand's way of talking—his inflection—and this fellow's have a lot in common when you come to think of it. I've told you I believe Rand recognized him right away as someone he had known before. I am still of that opinion. I think it was *because* Rand recognized him that this—"

"All very well," Bannerman muttered impatiently. "But all this slick theorizin' ain't helpin' me get him locked up in no cell! Meantime he's larrupin'—"

"He won't larrup far. He came a long way to get here and, if he's the man I think he is—"

"For Gawd's sake," Bannerman rasped out savagely, "if you know—"

Flack smiled. "I think you'll find him described on reward bills as J. K. Fisher."

"Great God in heaven!" the sheriff cried. "*Kingfisher!*"

SIXTEEN

THAT had been a near thing, Marlatt mused as he lar-
ruped townward; and wondered for the twentieth time
why it was this white-haired sheriff should feel so hot
about him. He could think of nothing he had done that
would adequately account for it. He had known, of
course, that Bannerman, though giving in to it, had been
a long way from satisfied with Ora Flack's advocacy—
with that grand line of bull Flack had thrown last evening on behalf of Marlatt. He'd given in to it because
there'd been little else he *could* do; but it had been plain
enough he meant to go on probing, meant to pin the
deadwood on him if he could. And the hell of it was,
Marlatt grudgingly admitted, big Nick just *might* get
away with it!

One thing was certain. The sooner he got in touch with
this Cheto Bandera—

Right there Marlatt's thinking hit a snag again. For
after all, what could Bandera tell him that Oxbow Rand,
on the spot, had not already covered? The Mex hadn't
even been working for Ora.

But just the same Marlatt guessed he'd better see the
man. Rand had seemed to set considerable store by him.

He got to thinking of Shirly-Bell then, of her gentian
eyes and corn-yellow hair; and of the way she had stood
up for him. Not many girls would have had that much
courage in the face of Flack's displeasure. A splendid
girl. . . .

Marlatt stifled a sigh and then loosed a soft curse for
his folly. She *was* a fine girl—too fine by far for a rough-
neck like him; why, guys had been shot for such notions!

Just the same she was in his mind and she stayed
there, her image etched clear as a cameo. There was

something soft and gentle and appealing about her; and the run of his thoughts disturbed him. She was vivid and warm—she'd been *friendly*. She had got in his blood like a fever.

So engrossed was Marlatt in his thoughts of her that he reached and entered the dobe-walled town almost without being cognizant of it. To be sure, he was not unaware he was riding through town, and he smelled the town smells—heard the noise of it; he even hazily noticed the big-wheeled wagons, the bearded teamsters, the frock-coated gentry, the women with their baskets, the spur-clanking cowpokes, the urchins and dogs that were everywhere. What he failed to take heed of was the risk he was running in thus openly riding about Tucson. A good many people had witnessed his run-in with Tularosa, and some of those folks would remember him.

He was passing the bank when it happened.

Engrossed in his daydreams, he did not observe the black-hatted man abruptly stopped in its entrance, hard staring and still—nor the bloated look of his swivel-jawed face, nor the poisonous flush spreading over it.

Marlatt was just past the angle of the bank's open door when the bullet jerked at his neckerchief, and the sharp, flat crack of a pistol loosed its clattering echoes in the crowded street.

Marlatt's shape whipped round in the saddle and the glint of his eyes was like sunburned metal. His hard look raked the scared white faces that were frantically ducking for the nearest cover.

A long-haired urchin grabbed his stirrup and pointed. "Down there, mister! There he goes—*see 'im?* The purple-shirted feller in the Mex sombrero!"

But all Marlatt caugh was a fleeting glimpse of one spurred boot. That and the description were enough, however, to slam his own spurs into the roan; and they went racketing down the alleyway after him. There was only one man who limped that way, wore a purple shirt and a black sombrero. Curly Lahr, the Towner gun thrower who had helped Tularosa rob the stage office the day before!

But Lahr's luck was holding. He had got away yesterday and, inside of five minutes, he repeated the performance. He was a regular will-o'-the-wisp, Marlatt thought as, tight-lipped and furious, he rounded the corner and found the back street empty—there was not even a naked muchacho or a snoring paisano in the filth and dust of that fly-infested quarter. A solid block of doorless back hallways gave the only answer to the man's disappearance; and there was no way of guessing which hall Lahr had chosen, save that it must be one of these closest ones.

Piling out of the saddle, Marlatt dropped his reins and dived into the nearest. There were three shut doors opening off the dim corridor. Its far end terminated in an unkempt patio, hot, completely enclosed and completely deserted. Retracing his steps, Marlatt tried the doors, pounding on them vigorously with the barrel of his pistol.

But the action evoked no answer. The doors were barred and they stayed that way. Not even his growled: "Open up for the law!" got the least response for those back of them.

With a snort of disgust, Marlatt went back to his horse. He went back, that is, to where he had left it. But the blaze-faced roan was no longer there. It had gone as completely as Lahr had gone. There were no tracks, even, to prove it had been there. Marlatt glared, and said a few angry things swiftly under his breath.

He was still there, muttering, when a fat and wrinkled old woman, obviously very Spanish, came waddling into the passageway toward him. She had a black, lacy shawl round her head and bent shoulders and a colored straw market basket under her arm. There was a mole on her chin, and a figure of Christ was spiked to the crucifix bumping her bosom.

She eyed Marlatt brightly from under creased brows. Marlatt took off his hat. "You speak English, *señora?*"

"Americano? Sí! Si, señor!" A broad smile revealed white teeth, and she bobbed her rebozo emphatically. *"Muchas grande,"* she assured him.

"You can tell me, perhaps, how to find one who is named Cheto Bandera?"

She looked at him sharply. Looked again and, rolling her eyes, made the sign of the cross. She would plainly have departed save that Marlatt stood in her way.

"Bandera," Marlatt repeated the name, saying it louder. "Cheto Bandera—"

"Love of God—*hush!*" gasped the old lady nervously; and cast frightened eyes at the halls' dark rectangles. "The smallest pitcher can carry water. What good is a candle without a wick?"

Marlatt stared, took a look toward the hallways and regarded her dubiously. "Bander—" he started; and stopped, mouth open. The old lady had turned and, snatching her petticoats, had aimed for the street as if the devil were after her.

He let her go, shook his head and glared round more puzzled than ever. There was no one in sight. She was plainly daft.

He looked round again and finally shrugged. Clapping on his hat, he headed streetward himself. Lahr had got the best of him, but next time would see a different story told. At that, he'd been lucky; the Towner gun thrower might well have killed him with that murderous shot he had fired from the bank steps.

He fully expected to find a crowd round the alley. But there was none. Evidently daylight attempts at assassination were of all too common occurrence to rate more than passing interest in the walled town of Tucson. A robbers' roost the New Mexicans called it; and Marlatt conceded there was a good deal of evidence to support their opinion. Every man he saw—every white man, anyway—was armed to the teeth, and they were a rough, tough lot, to judge by their faces.

Yet the town was doing plenty of business. As he'd entered the street a shouting, whooping group of riders had come tearing around the bank corner, hilariously scattering dust and pedestrians without regard for life or property. There was plenty of cursing and a lot of black scowls, but no man lifted a hand in protest. There were more saloons in the town than stores, and honky-tonks and brothels appeared even more numerous, carrying on their business openly. "Not much better than Tombstone or Pearce," Marlatt mused, "only bigger."

The dust-filled air was hot and stifling; it made a gritty taste between Marlatt's teeth. There was movement everywhere, and the jostling walks were gay with bright colors, touched here and there with the faded blue of the Tucson military; horse soldiers mostly. A jolting stage swayed round a far corner; and up from the south came a line of wagons, creaking and groaning with their loads of lumber brought in green from the distant Cherrycows. Three boisterous cowboys came out of a saloon and laughingly emptied their guns in the air, and a monte man yonder deftly plied his trade at the edge of the walk on a three-legged table.

But the afternoon was wearing on. Marlatt had no horse and he'd not found Bandera; and hunger was beginning to make itself manifest. He found a hash house and went in and ate, afterwards taking a final turn round the plaza and heading for Oliphant's. He meant to find Bandera before he left, but it would do no good asking any of this crowd—

"Hail Mary! A little charity, *caballero!* In the name of Jesus, and God will repay you."

Marlatt's glance found the man on the steps of the bank. A deplorable beast with an unwashed face and a pair of cocked eyes that leered at him knowingly. A leathern dice cup in spatulate fingers was waggled wheedlingly. "Charity, *señor!* A trifle for the maimed, and the Mother of God will surely repay you." And he turned his cup over to prove it was empty. "Just a copper, *señor, en el nombre de Dios.*"

With a shrug Marlatt dug a coin from his purse, and the man caught it deftly, tried it with his teeth and pocketed it, grinning. "The gentleman is a friend to the poor. God preserve you." He ducked his black, shaggy head with a flourish; then indifferently wheeled it to look out for new prospects.

A sudden thought came to Marlatt and caused him to turn back to regard the man with a narrow inquiry. This fellow's true age was a matter of hazard, but he was Mexican obviously. An odorous wretch in a filthy dragoon jacket with nothing under it but a hairy chest and a twist of frayed rope precariously supporting ragged pantalones whose original color must have long been in doubt. A true scion, Marlatt thought, of the breed *pelado;* and the impossible angle at which a scaly left leg was doubled under him lent the crowning touch to a repulsive sight.

"A-a-ai-hé!" he exclaimed, catching Marlatt eyeing him. "Praise God! Your Excellency wishes to enlarge his gift?"

"Depends," Marlatt said. "I reckon you'd be knowin' most of your countrymen around here, wouldn't you?"

The beggar's cocked eyes dimmed a bit. "What the head knows, only the mouth can tell, *señor.*"

"Waggle yours then and be assured of my further patronage."

"Ai—not so fast!"

"While the grass is growing the horse may die," Marlatt said impatiently; and stared down the street as though casting about for a man more informed. It was getting late and, though Bannerman had every reason to think he had quit the country, the sheriff's bullish tenacity might nag him into making sure, and Marlatt had no wish to be trapped here. But he saw no sign of the burly sheriff, and there appeared to be no untoward movement in the steady traffic coming off the plaza. He brought his attention back to the beggar.

The man was eyeing him craftily. "What would your Excellency of poor Tio Felix?"

Marlatt said: "All I want is some information." He

nked a couple of coins in his hand. "An address. The
hereabouts—"

"Ai! Of a certain lady—"

"Of a man," Marlatt said, cutting short his leer. "A
quero who used to ride for El Rancho Crescent. Cheto
ndera."

The change in the beggar's look was startling. "Thun-
r and lightning! That one!" he cried. "That *picaro!*"
uttering under his breath, Tio Felix crossed himself;
d his regard of Marlatt held little favor. "His honor is
reckless man who throws such a name about the
reets. If a fool held his tongue he would pass for a
se man—"

"Look!" Marlatt growled. "Do you want this money
don't you?"

"Your Excellency asks a question."

"All right," Marlatt said, thrusting the coins in his
cket. "Someone else will tell me—"

"How true!" Tio Felix sighed. "He who would hide
ust hoodwink the devil. Does your Excellency know
hat manner of rascal he seeks?"

"If a hungry man has only two beans does he throw
em away because one is dirty?"

Tio Felix grinned. "After all," he shrugged, "though the
ell says no mass it may call up the righteous." A shrewd
eam brightened his cocked regard. "Did your Excel-
ncy say two golden eagles?"

Marlatt hesitated. "All right," he said. "Two golden
gles. Where can I find him?"

"No so fast. Not even God's angels could tell you that.
ut for two golden eagles I will myself show you tonight
here this *picaro* sometimes quenches his thirst."

Though Marlatt argued and threatened to find out
sewhere, Tio Felix could not be induced to say more
lightening than that; and in the end he paid the man
d the beggar named the place for their meeting.

"But how'll you get there?" Marlatt's puzzled glance
ened the beggar's bent leg. "And how'll I be knowin'
ou will even try?"

261

"Who cannot run can crawl. I am a man of honor. F
there yourself, *señor*, and you will find me waiting. F
two more eagles I will point out the man."

Tio Felix grinned as Marlatt vanished in the crowd.

SEVENTEEN

THE place Tio Felix had named for their rendezvous was a two-by-four dive off Meyer Street, in the *barrio libre*, not far from the southernmost edge of town. Clear across its cracked front with a bold red brush some imaginative soul long gone to his Maker had pretentiously painted: REGULAR PALOMA CANTINA. Right away Marlatt agreed with the first part—if it was no other thing the Paloma was "regular." Illumined with smoky kerosene lanterns, crowded and raucous as Bedlam, it was typical of its kind and reeked to heaven with cheap perfume, with tobacco smoke, sweat and garlic and a host of other smells not so quickly tagged; everything stank, including the patrons. The clamor was deafening. Flutes and fiddles, guitars and drums—all joined with the shrieks and laughter, the shuffle of sandals and click of high heels in making the most of each passing moment. The proprietor—a swart, squatty fellow with a cast in one eye and a curved steel hook where his left arm should have been—was shouting as bawdily as any of his customers. He had four or five hurdy girls passing round, snake-hipped and big-breasted, hawking their wares from table to table; but it was the patronage, mostly, that Marlatt took stock of. It would have been hard, he thought, if you had scoured the town, to have scraped together an assemblage more motley or vicious than the rogues and cutthroats so lustily cavorting in this tabernacle of Bacchus. A renegades' roost if there ever was one. Marlatt stood by the door and looked them over. For ten pesos, he thought, you could have hired the whole lot.

A girl came up to him, flouncing, lips smiling. She was plumply handsome, with flashing black eyes and a mop of black hair. She leaned toward him, hands on hips, and gave him the look there is no mistaking. But Marlatt brushed past her with a "Not now, sister," and wormed his way through the jostling crowd to where Tio Felix, true to his word, sat drumming a mug on the edge of his table. He looked contented and comfortable, with his cocked eyes dancing and his twisted leg on a greasy cushion that was stuffed with straw.

Marlatt could have sworn the beggar had not seen him coming; yet he must have. Dragging his interest from the flying bare legs of a Zincali dancer, he ducked his shaggy head and shoved out a stool with the heel of his hand. "Your Excellency honors our poor place. Be of the goodness to sit, *señor*," he bade, scowling around for a waiter. "A mug of pulque for the *don caballero*— Here, wait!" he called. "Make it two." And he grinned up at Marlatt. "It takes a wet whistle to make a sweet tune."

Marlatt dragged up the stool and rested his elbows on the table.

"Is he here yet?"

"Presently. Presently, *señor*." Tio Felix was not to be rushed. He waved an airy hand.

Marlatt kept his impatience from showing on his face; but it was not easy. Bannerman must have learned by now that he was somewhere in the town and, keeping in mind the stubborn streak of bullish tenacity which appeared to govern the man in all his actions, it required no strain of the imagination to picture the sheriff calmly turning the town on its ear to find him; and it might not be so calmly at that, Marlatt thought, remembering their parting.

He was of half a mind to quit the country; and would have save for favoring Rand. The man had placed an obligation on him. Too, there was Flack, and the riddle of the man's fifteen hired gun throwers—and a number of other things nagging Marlatt. Nor were Flack's intentions toward Cori's inheritance lightly to be thrown in the discard. There was that gun belt with its thumb-bulged creases; and the puzzle of why Craft Towner—who in Texas was rightly named John King Fisher—should try to hire Marlatt to gun Ora Flack. But the deciding thing that kept Marlatt here—kept him facing these odds that might swiftly overwhelm him—was the bitter-sweet memory of smiling lips and eyes as blue as Colorado lupine. A woman's trust; it was that which held him.

So he forced himself to sit here dawdling while the sheriff's search must be creeping closer; to sit here knowing that he had no horse—that if a showdown came he would have to steal one, or face Nick Bannerman across the smoke of pistols. He could not surrender; for once behind bars Flack would pin Rand's murder on him as sure as sunset.

"It was a brave thing—that. Does your Excellency not think so?"

"Eh?" Marlatt said.

The beggar laughed. "Who gathers wool must pay for the shearing."

"Afraid I didn't hear you. I was watching the dancers."

Tio Felix shrugged. "I said only the Son of God himself could afford to be so reckless. *Es verdad*—no?"

"I still don't know what you're talkin' about."

"About that *picaro*, Tularosa—who else? Has Your Honor not heard he is loose. again? Of a certainty! With my own poor eyes I have seen him walking the streets like an honest man. Si! Scarce twenty minutes fled."

Marlatt eyed him, startled. "Tularosa? The man who stuck up the stage office yesterday?"

"*Si. El hombre malo*. Ten riders have surround the great brick courthouse—it is all over town. With their rifles against his chest they forced the jailer to loose this fellow. He was in the first floor cell block. They took him out, and now he prowls through the town like a hungry lobo—"

"Who were these riders?"

"It is not known, Excellency. They were masked—but very bold, no?" Tio Felix shook his head and made clucking sounds in the roof of his mouth.

"What has the sheriff—"

"*Señor* White Head?" The beggar grinned and his

cocked eyes leered. "He was hunt for you. I think he will come here presently—"

He broke off, and Marlatt, following his glance, saw a scowling group bearing down on their table. In the lead was the hurdy girl, black eyes flashing.

"Mother of God!" Tio Felix cried. "What is this? What is this, eh, Rosita?"

The girl's outflung hand pointed squarely at Marlatt. "This hombre—"

She got no further. A commotion jammed the street door with figures. A cry went up. A jerked out scream went shrill and curdled—broke in the middle like a board snapped in two. There was an ominous roar; quick, angry curses. The crowd round the doorway swayed and staggered. The smoky light skittered red from knifeblades.

"Cuidado, hermanos! Los aguacil—"

On the heels of the shout a sixgun thumped swift crashes of sound that smashed like waves across the clamor; and one by one, with beautiful precision, the lanterns winked out in bursts of glass that mingled gunstench with the reek of hot coat-oil.

Marlatt's arm was caught in a grip of steel. With his free left hand Marlatt jerked a pistol and was bringing it round, tight-lipped and savage, when the beggar's breath fanned across his cheek. "Mercy of God—" Tio Felix hissed; "come quick—come quick! This way, *señor!*" and his fierce grip tugged at Marlatt frantically.

Straight back through the howling dark he led as if his eyes were a cat's; and Marlatt, stumbling, oft-swearing, followed perforce, for the beggar clung tight to his arm as though, knowing a good thing, he was loath to lose it.

What a rat's hole they followed! Through a hidden door in the Dove's back side, through the bricked-up walls of a musty tunnel that was dank underfoot and slippery with slime, through another thieves' roost and some kind of a warehouse that was jammed to the roof with sack-covered bales of what Marlatt guessed must be contraband. And ever the beggar's muttered tones gave warning—"A turn, *señor!* The roof drops, *señor!* Of

he head now be careful! Twist the foot to the left!
Vatch out for the barrels! God in heaven—have a care!
Now quick—this way!"

A crazy, wild and nightmare-like journey that carried
hem ever farther and farther from the man Oxbow Rand
had bidden him contact. It was galling! And bitterly, under his breath, Marlatt cursed the vicious run of luck
hat had dogged his tracks ever since he'd come here;
cursed his luck and this beggar whose procrastination
had lost them their chance. For Bandera had been right
here in the Dove. Deep in the marrow of his bones Mar-
att knew it. That strange sixth sense called the gun
hrower's hunch was all the apprisement Kane Marlatt
needed.

"Duck the head, señor—quick! Forward now."

They were out in the open under God's bright stars, in
a black, murky region of tumbledown houses whose
paintless slants leaned so far toward the alley their flimsy
palconies nearly rubbed railings.

With a quick, sure step Tio Felix led, and the panting
of his breath, the soft thud of their footsteps were the
only sounds in the black lane they traveled save, far to
rear, where a muted hubbub advised the Dove's
wings were still flapping.

"A near thing, that!" Tio Felix muttered, striking left
through the gloom. "It was the white-headed one—*El
Señor* Sheriff. But we have left him scratching—thanks to
the intervention of God's blessed Mother. He can scratch
till cock's crow and never guess where Your Honor's
gone. *Los ladrones* will hold him, never fear, *amigo*.
Many times he has hunt for Bandera before—"

"For Bandera!" Marlatt echoed. "You think he was
after Bandera?"

"But certainly! He would never think to find Your
Honor at the Dove—"

"But what would he want with Bandera?"

"*Carajo!* What, indeed!" Felix muttered, and made another quick turn in the night.

A pitch black cul-de-sac opened before them. In the

faint star haze Marlatt saw no outlet, but the beggar led
on; and presently Marlatt felt the man's hand on his
shoulder again. They passed through a door so narrow
Marlatt's shoulders scraped against the sides. There was
no squeak of hinges, so they must have been oiled or kept
well greased, Marlatt guessed; and saw to the right a
great oblong of lesser darkness and the vague outline of
a corral beyond. There was straw underfoot, and the
place smelled of cattle.

"We ascend to the roof," Tio Felix murmured, and
placed Marlatt's hand on the grip of a ladder.

"Not so fast," Marlatt said. He shoved his pistol barrel hard against the man's stomach. "I probably owe you
some thanks for gettin' me out of that; but if it wasn't
for you I wouldn't've been there, so that makes us even."

"To be sure, señor; but—"

"I'm not quite a fool," Marlatt told him softly. "What
you do, or what you're up to, is no business of mine. But
this evenin' you was a crippled beggar; it's been all I
could do tonight keepin' up with you. I think our trails
had better part right here."

Against the lesser darkness of the yonder oblong Marlatt saw the man's shoulders lift in a shrug. "As you
please, of course," Tio Felix said, "but if Your Honor has
business with this Cheto Ban—"

He broke off, head canted. Marlatt too, had stiffened.
Soft footsteps had paused in the dust of the alley; stealthy
steps that had stopped by the door.

There was an instant of quiet. Then the hush was
broken by a low, guarded call. "Cheto!" It was a girl's
voice—urgent. "Cheto—are you there?"

The men's eyes locked in the gloom of the stable.

It was Cori Malone who had called from the alley.

Tio Felix laughed softly. "To be sure, señorita. We are
both here," he chuckled.

But he chuckled alone.

Kane Marlatt stood like a rock in his tracks with the
snout of his pistol still against the man's belly. It was not
the reaction Tio Felix had looked for. Did the man not

nderstand that it was *he*, Tio Felix, who was Cheto Bandera?

Tio Felix, peering closer, felt his scalp suddenly prickle. Vith a hand streaking upward he whirled like a cat.

"Freeze, you lobos!"

The words came from the stableyard, three short steps istant. Bandera's shape went still as death.

"Now, damn your eyes, I've got you—*both* of you! Just link, by God, an' I'll let you have it!"

It was Bannerman, blackly crouched between them nd the pole corral, with a gun in each hand and his tin adge glinting.

EIGHTEEN

Cori's low gasp was startled—frantic.

Nick Bannerman's voice said: "Come inside, Cori, an
find me a lantern."

Marlatt stood with his warped cheeks twisted, askin
himself if there was any chance. There was always
chance, brash impulse assured him; but he recalled th
times when the wish had tricked him. There was no roon
for tricks in this cluttered sable.

The girl had not moved. Bannerman called again
harshly.

Balancing odds, Marlatt saw the issue. The whole pla
resolved on one tiny factor: *Could the sheriff see them*
If he *could,* to move would bring death hell-tearing. Bu
could he?

The ladder beside them was but a short step remove
from the broad rectangle giving onto the yard. The sher
iff's black shape was two strides beyond, in the lesse
gloom of the yard itself. Point-blank range—and the ma
showed clearly.

Desire pulled Marlatt's lip corners down; thrust a gun
barrel shine to the slits of his eyes.

Cold sweat beaded his forehead. If, in the murk of thi
stable, they were obscured from Bannerman, the guns the
sheriff was holding were little better than Marlatt's own
whose muzzle impotently stared at the floor. Surely if the
sheriff could see them as plainly as he would have them
think, wouldn't he have bidden Marlatt drop the gun?

Or was he playing this craftily, hoping Marlatt would
think just that and, so thinking, be lured into making a
try with the gun?

Marlatt's lip corners tightened. Resist of an officer in

270

pursuit of his duty would be all the excuse Nick Bannerman needed.

He peered through the gloom at the man's crouched position, and precisely then Nick Bannerman spoke. It was as though he had read Kane Marlatt's mind. "I've got this place surrounded, bucko. Better chuck that gun in a corner before it gets you laid out on a shutter."

Marlatt hesitated; and the chance was gone. Cori, coming in from the alley, said: "Nick, don't do something you'll be sorry for."

Bannerman's laugh was a harsh, rasping thing. "Never mind gassin', girl. Get the lantern. The quicker we have a light in here the safer it'll be for these friends of yours."

A match scratched through the sheriff's words, and Cori sprang into sharp silhouette, with the end of it brushing a lantern's wick. The wick flared. Cori pushed the lantern shut and hung it from a nail near the door. It was then Nick Bannerman's curse came slamming through the thump of his boots on the hard-packed floor.

"Where the bloody hell is that Mex?" He glared at Marlatt as though he would strike him with one of the pistols gripped in his hands. His wheeling glance struck at Cori bitterly. "*You* called to him—I heard him answer! Where is he?"

The girl's white cheeks showed nothing but wonder. "Perhaps—" began Marlatt; but the beggar's whine cut through his words. "For *dos pesos, señor*—wait! make it four; what lost and recovered becomes twice valuable! For four pesos then," Tio Felix leered from his crouch on the floor, "I will tell Your Honor where Bandera went—"

"Where?"

"It takes dinero to buy good pulque—"

Bannerman leveled a pistol at Marlatt's middle. "Throw that gun out the door!"

There was nothing else for it. Marlatt did as bidden.

With pale eyes flashing, the sheriff wheeled burly shoulders and made for the beggar.

In swift alarm Tio Felix cried: "He went out the alley as the girl came in!"

271

"Then my men will get him," The sheriff, losing interest, turned hard eyes on Marlatt. "I told you, bucko, that you'd better clear out. It's going to be a real pleasure to see your neck stretched. You should've cut your stick—"

"Never mind me. What do you want with Bandera?"

Nick Bannerman thrust his lefthand pistol into the waistband of his corduroy trousers. Twirling the other one by its trigger guard, he said, vastly pleased with himself: "Well, bucko, I don't mind telling you. It'll be no news to you Flack's been losin' cattle; none of this'll be news to *you*—but it's sure as hell goin' to startle Ora. Bandera, as you damn well know, has been helpin' you run off Straddle Bug stock. Bandera's been bossin' your rustlers for you. Rand's been tippin' you off to when an' where you birds can best grab 'em—"

Marlatt laughed contemptuously. "You expect to make that stick?"

"It'll stick all right—"

"I thought you was figurin' to arrest me for Oxbow Rand's murder."

"Nope." Nick smiled at him smugly, then turned so his smile could include the girl. "Some star packers might undertake to do that—but not me. When I go off I hit what I aim at. Remember that, bucko, case you think of tryin' somethin'. Nope; I ain't quite green enough to fall for that. I've got you dead to rights, *Mister John King Fisher!*"

There was danger here, and Kane Marlatt recognized it. If it was Bannerman's intention to pin that name on him, his guilt or innocence would make little difference. The crowd would take him out of Bannerman's hands. Just the same, he grinned; he could not help it. The satisfaction of the man touched his sense of humor.

"Kingfisher wears a mustache, Bannerman—"

"There's plenty of razors round this country."

"John King Fisher is a fancy dude. He—"

"Clothes don't mean nothing. Any guy can change 'em—"

"You'll never make it stick—"

"I won't have to." Bannerman chuckled. "It'll be up to *you* to prove you *ain't*. I won't have to turn a hand, even. You've switched the brand of your last steer, bucko. Skirts is what traps most of you polecats—"

"Skirts?"

The sheriff looked at Cori and laughed. "I been weaned," he said, "a long while back. Cori Malone ain't the first bit of calico that's tried her hand at this owlhoot business—"

"Have you gone off your head completely?"

"There ain't nothin' wrong with *my* head, bucko. It's—" He broke off, startled.

That was when Tio Felix became Bandera again. He came like a cat up off the floor with a knife pale-streaking from the blur of his hand.

An oath jarred out of the sheriff's mouth. The gun fell out of his hand with a clatter as the whistling blade skewered his wrist to a roof post. He stood there, rooted, with a vast surprise looking out of his stare as the beggar, shaking the twist from his leg, became straight-eyed and erect, with his white teeth flashing.

Nick Bannerman stared like a pole-axed steer. Rage turned his twisted cheeks black. With a strangled snarl he snatched for the knife that held him anchored.

He was like that, wheeling, with his free hand reaching, when a yell split the night and gun sound hammered the walls like sledges.

Marlatt spun in his tracks. One outsweeping arm caught Cori and flung her, stumbling, toward the ladder. "Up top—quick!" He dragged Rand's gun from his waistband and drove three shots through the stable doorway at the leaping figures diving into the yard. Bandera's swift reach snaked the second pistol from the sheriff's shell belt. "Up top! Up top!" Marlatt snarled at him hoarsely and saw the lawman's swung pistol maliciously stopped against the sheriff's head—saw the Mexican wrench loose his knife as Bannerman crumpled. Then the alley door was ripped from its hinges and he emptied

273

Rand's gun at the shapes coming through it, shattered the lantern and sprang for the ladder, crowding Bandera's bare feet up it frantically.

The stable was suddenly a screaming black bedlam stabbed and lanced with flashes of gunflame, bursting with shouts and rocked and shaken by the hammering concussions of exploding cartridges. It was, Marlatt knew, no place for a woman; and he caught the Mexican's shoulder roughly. "Ain't this damn rat hole got another outlet?"

Bandera, breathing heavily in the darkness, nodded. "Come—duck low," he muttered, and led them through a trap onto the roof, which was parapeted and, like most Spanish roofs, had hardly more than an inch or two's slope, just sufficient to carry the infrequent rains off. A short, running jump took them onto the next roof; another quick jump took them one roof farther.

Starlight flashed from Bandera's teeth. "Your Honor understands what men are these—"

"They're Ora Flack's!" cried Cori hotly.

"*Sabe Dios.*" The Mexican shrugged with Latin eloquence. "The sheriff will call them ours—*ladrones, bandidos.* Kingfisher's men—I can hear him sweat it—come to save Your Honor—"

"They *are* Kingfisher's men." Marlatt's tone was curt. "It was Tularosa who yelled back there; and I know Lahr's voice too well to m—"

"There they come!" gasped Cori; and Bandera growled: "Over the wall with you—quick, *señorita!* God's angels will watch for you—over now! *Muy pronto!*"

They ran to the parapet at the roof's far side, and Cori swung bare legs across it, agile as a boy, while Marlatt crammed fresh shells in his gun. Bandera braced himself and, catching the girl's clasped hands in his strong right one, let her down as far as he could. "Drop!" he bade her; and as her hands left his, Marlatt's gun roared twice.

A sharp cry came from off yonder; shrilly it sheared through the cash of gunfire. Hoarse shouts rose too, and malignant curses. Lead thumped and squealed and whistled about them, smashing bits from the wall just under them. Hoarse words welled out of Bandera's throat. "Blood of God—*jump!*"

NINETEEN

BUT Marlatt was not quite ready to jump. There was something he meant to do first. With chin-strapped hat on the back of his shoulders, he slid across the roof's low wall, and bracing his elbows, hung from its top on tense-clamped fingers. The strain was monstrous, but he kept his hold.

Bandera's urgent voice cried: "Drop! Quick, *señor*— let go!"

But Marlatt gave the man no heed. "Take care of Cori!" he muttered curtly, and kept his glance on the goblin shapes that, shouting blasphemies, were coming hellbent across the roof tops. It was like an avalanche, that bobbing, writhing waves of shapes that came roaring toward him through the swirling gloom. But only one shape was Marlatt watching. With black lids narrow, he watched that one with malicious interest—the gangling shape of the man snarling orders.

And then they were just short yards away, sloshing across the yonder parapet. With all his weight on one shaking arm, Marlatt loosed a hand and got Rand's pistol; thrust its barrel across the wall.

And then he did a crazy thing. Some soft streak in him —or pride, perhaps—made him give the man warning. "Sometimes," he called, "a man's wild ways catch him up, Tularosa!"

The words lost him his chance. Just as his finger squeezed the trigger the surface beneath his grip gave way—burst and crumbled under his fingers and dropped him crashing in a cloud of dust.

He struck on his boot heels and went over backwards.

Unhurt save in pride, and cursing bitterly, he scrambled up and stopped, shocked sober. The girl and Bandera had waited for him!

"You harebrained fool!" he swore at Bandera. "I told
u to get—"

A rattle of shots from above chopped his words off.
ri grabbed at his arm, and they raced toward where
e next house's corner thrust a vague gray angle through
e murk. They made it—rounded it in a burst of bullets
d falling plaster.

"God watches his own," Cheto muttered, panting.
Ve've slipped them—thanks to the Blessed Virgin! Quick
lown this alley! There's—"

His words choked off in a startled curse. The way was
ocked. Dark shapes were pouring into the alley ahead
them. The whistle of lead kicked dust up round them
gunfire spurted from the shapes running toward them.
arlatt's gun bit back, its flame stabbing whitely
rough the curdled gloom.

"Señor!" Cheto cried; and Cori pushed him after them
rough a door in the righthand wall.

Marlatt kicked it shut, and they found themselves in
tch black darkness; but it was some relief to have shut
ose sounds out. This appeared, Marlatt thought, to be
substantial building, oddly in contrast to the hovels
ound it. With quick, sure hands Cori shot the bolt.
e turned then, breathless, and Cheto's panting voice
sped: "Jesu! God's mercy only can help us now,
ala—"

"There must be some other door—"

"One knows it better than—"

Cori's tones said regretfully: "This is Bannerman's
wn house, Marlatt."

"Town house!"

"Sí. It was the house of his señora, prala."

"Señora!" Marlatt sounded all tangled up. An edgy
arshness scraped his voice. "Is the sheriff married?"

"Not now," Cori answered. "Lottie died last winter—
oor soul, she had her share of burdens. She was Spanish
d wildly in love with him. He broke her heart with his
arryings on; he never cared any more about her than
e cares for Shirly-Bell Ranleigh. Ambition is Nick Ban-

nerman's god—he's the friend of whoever best serves it
She said on a sudden, thoughtful note: "Don't underrat
him, Marlatt; he's smart and he's quick—"

In the darkness Marlatt snorted. "He was quick enoug
naming me Kingfisher—"

"It isn't that," Cori impatiently. "He thinks you're afte
Shirly-Bell—"

"I thought you girls hardly knew him—"

"You don't have to hug a polecat to know he's a pole
cat, do you?"

"What I mean—"

"I know what you mean." Perhaps it was Marlatt's lac
of denial that made Cori's tone so curt. "You're wonder
ing why he's so bent on Shirly when I'm the one that'
heir to the Crescent." She said scornfully: "I told yo
Nick was smart, Marlatt."

Marlatt saw it then, and whistled. But before he coul
say anything more something crashed against the ou
side of the door; and they all knew what was happenin
then. The gang outside had fetched a timber or somethin
and were going to hammer the door down.

"We've got to get out of here," Cori muttered.

Just like that pack of fools, Marlatt thought, to wast
time trying to break down a door when they could mor
quickly and easily have come through the windows
Perhaps if he smashed a window in some distant roon
they'd all rush round and forget this door. He decide
to give it a whirl; but he had not taken two strides whe
he came hard against Cheto's outstretched arm. A
though he had read Marlatt's mind, Cheto said: "All th
windows are barred, Your Honor."

Marlatt's head came impatiently round. "How well d
you know this house, Cori?"

"I've stayed here. Carlotta and I were friends be
fore—"

"There are no trick ways to get out?"

"I never saw any."

"Any way to get onto the roof?"

"That won't— Yes, there's a trap, but—"

"Roof flat or peaked?"

"Flat. This house has a tall, false front; it's a two-story house made to look like three—"

"Get up on the roof then—quick!" Marlatt snapped; and was wheeling off when the girl's hand caught him.

"Where—"

"On the roof," Marlatt growled. "Get up there before they bust—"

"Not till I know what you're going to do."

Impatience and anger made Marlatt's voice rough. "I'm goin' to try an' fool that gang away from here!"

"And if you don't?"

"You'll be no worse off on the roof than down here. And you won't be so likely to stop a bullet. Get her up there, Bandera, an' keep her there—"

Cori said: "Are you coming?"

"I'll come if I can," Marlatt growled, and went stumbling off into the darkness.

His plan was simple. If it worked, well and good. If it didn't, they'd be no worse off than they already were. There was no use hiding here unless they could give Tularosa's men considerable reason to think they'd got clear. If that thought could be sold them, any subsequent search of the building was bound to be more or less cursory; it might, anyway, exclude the roof.

In due course he found the house's front door and paused behind it, head canted, listening. He could still hear them battering at the alley door. There was no sound coming from the front of the house. Very quietly, carefully, he drew the bar and pulled open the door, slow fraction of an inch by fraction of an inch.

The night seemed light after the opaque blackness inside the house. He caught no sign of human presence in the unlighted buildings across the way and, sardonically, he considered the fact a pungent commentary.

Then, as he turned to scan the roadway in front of the house, he saw the bulk of a man's shape facing him in the obscurity!

TWENTY

THE loudest thing in Kane Marlatt's ears was the thump and pound of the heart inside him. There could be no doubt that the man had seen him; he'd been felinely waiting there for Marlatt's turning. Star's shine lay along the edge of his teeth. He'd a gun in his hand. It was cocked and leveled.

Why hadn't the fellow fired and dropped him?

And then, suddenly, he knew. The same impulse had held his fire that had held Kane Marlatt's back on the roof. This man wanted him to know he'd reached the end of his rope—wanted him to know who it was that had cut it; and with a kind of pleased surprise Marlatt recognized the man for Tularosa's pardner, the consumptive owlhooter, Curly Lahr.

Lahr said: "I been waitin' a long time for this," and fired point-blank.

The shot whistled air across Marlatt's left shoulder as, dropping cat-quick, Marlatt fired from his knees.

He saw Lahr jerk, lurch a half step backward. He hung there briefly with his gaunt shape tipping; then his knees let go. The bony shoulders catapulted forward. A streamer of dust trickled up from the impact and Lahr lay still with his pistol clutched in the hand doubled under him. Marlatt paused, looking down at him, shrugged, and stepped over him, a faint distaste curling the corners of his mouth. In death as in life Lahr had no dignity—sprawled in the road like a drunk in an alley.

There was no sound in the crouching night.

Abruptly then, noise came in plenty—the thump and clank of boots hard running. Marlatt stiffened as, above that tumult, harsh with fury, Tularosa's yell sailed high and clear. "Buck! Tim! Ed an' Wimpy! Git back to that door, you damn fools!" It was not in Tularosa's plans to be tricked by Kane Marlatt a second time.

In the open front doorway Marlatt paused, stooped, thinking fast, and ripped off his spurs. He turned and flung them, tinkling, as far out into the street as he could; then jerked off his boots and, with them in one hand and Rand's cocked gun in the other, stumbled off through the house on a hunt for the stairs.

He was just starting up them when he heard the sharp, flat crack of exploding rifles. In a ragged volley they swept the alley; and swift cries, a scream, sheared the racketing echoes. Above this din, hard with anger, came the bull-throated bellow of Sheriff Nick Bannerman.

Marlatt took the stairs three steps at a stride.

"Quick!"

It was Cori. She was at their top, and grabbed his hand in the curdled gloom and dragged him panting down a hallway and through an unseen door to the right; and Marlatt, as her hand left his, heard her softly close it. She was back in an instant, swiftly guiding him to where a chair loomed vague as a ghost beneath a patch of star-flecked sky that was squarely set in the ceiling's center. A man's hatted head blocked the stars for a moment; and Cheto's voice gave thanks to the Virgin.

Marlatt said: "Didn't lock that door, did you?" and Cori said angrily:

"Don't you think I've *any* sense?" Then he was boosting her up through the hole in the ceiling.

When she was clear he sheathed Rand's gun and pulled on his boots. "Can you pull me up, Bandera?"

"Are you hurt?" Cori cried; and Bandera, crouched in the trap, reached down a hand. He was strong as an ox. He grunted a bit. But a moment later Marlatt was with them up on the roof; and the chair they'd stood on was with them, too, for Marlatt had not dared leave it behind to be found, like an arrow, beneath the trap. He had brought it with him by thrusting a boot through its slatted back. Cheto settled the cover back down on the trap and followed them cat-footed across the roof to

281

crouch beside them in the shadow of the building's false front. Two windows in it faced the street, and Cori, curious, would have looked down from them had Marlatt not roughly yanked her back.

"Use your head!" he told her curtly; and was surprised when she hunkered beside him without retort.

Bandera said: "What now, Your Honor?" and Cori asked: "What's all the noise about? They're sure getting rid of a lot of good cartridges. Must be shooting each other by all that yelling."

"It's Bannerman," Marlatt told them quietly. "He's taken a hand with a couple of deputies." He turned his narrowed glance to where Bandera squatted. "Rand's dead. Somebody knifed him in the bunkhouse last night —Flack, I think, though I ain't real sure. Told me yesterday if anything happened to get hold of you. Any idea why?"

Cori said: "Then he *did* suspect it!"

Cheto nodded.

"Rand was bossing the Crescent then," Cori said to Marlatt. She kept her voice low lest they be discovered by the men they could hear ransacking the house. "He was off on a deal for some cattle when it happened. Cantrell wanted to fire him like he fired the rest of the Crescent hands when Flack took over, but I raised such a riproar they let him stay—I guess they figured he couldn't know anything anyway; but they've never left off watching him. They've never left me alone with him since. They never pretended to keep me away from him, but Cantrell always had somebody round."

"I still don't get it," Marlatt told her, puzzled.

"*Señorita* speaks of the horse, Your Honor—"

"Didn't you know my father was killed by a horse?"

Marlatt thought back. "Yes . . . I believe Rand did say—"

"Flack engineered that," Cori said bitterly. "The horse—"

"I thought Rand said the horse was one your father had got from some outfit—"

282

"Out of this country? It was," Coir said. "Nick Bannerman told Dad about it. Bad broncs were a sort of weakness with Dad—everlyone knew it. Bannerman said there was an outfit up around Trinidad had the worst damn bucker he'd ever heard of. Nothing would do but Dad must have it. He wrote to this outfit and they made a deal—that was where Cantrell came into the business. He was the man who brought the horse down here."

"But he never went back," Bandera said. "He hung out in town—"

"And after Dad was killed and Flack took over the Crescent on order of the court," Cori broke in, "the first thing Flack did was hire this Bob Cantrell to rod the combined outfits. Cantrell got rid of every Crescent hand but Rand; but— Tell him about the horse, Cheto."

"*Seguro.*" Cheto said very softly: "Your Honor will be surprised to know I saw this *caballo* in Flack's corral three-four weeks before that time—*es verdad.* Blood of God, yes!"

"But I thought Cantrell—"

"He did," Cori told him. "This famous bucker, according to Bannerman, was at Trinidad. Dad wrote the outfit at Trinidad and got a reply from there. They agreed to sell and said they'd send a man down with the horse. Cantrell showed up with it; Bannerman said that was the horse all right, and—"

"Cantrell," Marlatt said, "was a Texan."

"You knew him?"

"I know Texans." Marlatt said to Bandera: "Sure this was the same horse you saw in Flack's corral?"

"Same *caballo.*"

"Did it buck?"

Cori nodded. "But nothing like Bannerman had led Dad to expect. Dad was so disgusted with the horse he said he was going to make it earn its cost and keep—"

"But it really was bad?"

Cheto said: "Crazy, *señor!* No sense—*muy malo*—a notchtail killer—"

"What happened?"

"Dad was riding it after some spooky steers," Cori said, "and the horse went down and rolled on him."

"Kill the horse, too?"

"Killed now," Cheto said, and grinned at him. "Not killed then—"

Cori said bitterly: "It fell on purpose."

So it had been Flack, after all, Marlatt mused. Some way, sly Ora had wangled Cori's father into naming him executor of the Crescent and guardian of Cori and then, snake-cold, had cut the old man's string.

Thinking back over what he knew of the man, it was with a distinct sense of shock that Marlatt realized suddenly just how deadly Ora Flack really was. That bland, whiskered face Flack showed the world hid a savage cunning that would balk at nothing which might hinder the maturing of his own desires.

And what were Ora Flack's desires? Greed for money was probably one of them. Like enough, greed for power was another; the two, Marlatt reflected, usually tramped hand in hand. Abruptly then a preposterous notion caught at Marlatt's attention—a crazy kind of nightmarish thought that sent cold chills up and down his spine till reason came to scoff it away. It could not be; Flack was slick all right, but not *that* slick. Only one other man did Kane Marlatt know who could stand in Flack's class— Craft Towner; but not even Towner could be *that* damn sly!

It just wouldn't wash, Marlatt's reason told him. There was a limit to cunning, to trickery and pretense. Such things could be carried only just so far. No sane man would dare dream—and yet— The size was too close to right to be laughed off. And there were bolstering details that brought cold sweat into Marlatt's palms as, one by one, his mind recalled them. There was—

He found himself trying to visualize Flack behind the blur of those short-cropped whiskers; and another wonder laid its hold on him. Why had Towner tried to hire him to gun Flack?

Reflectively Marlatt said to Cori: "Rand seemed pretty well sold on the idea Flack's been layin' pipe to steal your outfit—"

"He's already stolen it—"

"That's the kind of rash statement will lose your case if you ever bring suit against Flack—"

"I'll bring suit!" Cori said fiercely: "I'll fight him through every court in the land!"

"And probably get a sight less out of it than you've got right now—"

"I've got nothing now, so what could I lose?"

"What could you fight with? Lawin'," Marlatt told her drily, "costs a heap of money—"

"I'll find someone to back me—"

"An' if he wins, how much do you reckon will be left time you've paid him?" Marlatt said shortly. "If it comes to a fight in the courts, you're licked. No matter what the outcome, you'll not get a nickel—"

"You sound—"

"Never mind. I'll do what I can for you—"

"I don't want your help!"

"That," Marlatt drawled, "sums you up very nicely."

Even in the gloom he saw the glare of her eyes. She was coldly furious. If she'd had a quirt she would probably have hit him. Maybe, he thought, she had some right to feel that way; but a lot of her troubles were of her own devising. She was a sight too brash; too impulsive and headlong. Needing help, she had a knack of embarrassing those who would help her at every turn. Her presence here now was a first-class example. Why couldn't she be like Shirly-Bell—stay in her place and behave like a lady?

The thought of Shirly-Bell sobered him; brought him sternly back, face to face with what they were up against. Sounds from below were getting louder and louder. Searchers were combing the second floor now . . .

Nick Bannerman's voice just below them said: "No use, boys. They've got clear, I reckon. His gang held us up."

"What *I* can't get," another voice broke in, "is wha they were doin' all that shootin' for. 'F I didn't know better, I'd've thought they was fightin' amongst them selves—they was tryin' to break in that door when w jumped 'em."

"A dodge," Bannerman said, "to make us think the weren't connected with 'em. Those were Kingfisher's men all right; an' Kane Marlatt's Kingfisher, no two way about it. While they was puttin' on that show for us Marlatt an' Bandera was makin' themselves scarce. You notice—"

"What about that bird we found out front? *I* didn't drop him—Buck didn't neither! He's the one helped Tula-rosa hold up the stage office."

Bannerman said: "There's no gaugin' the ways of a bunch like that crowd. Kind of guys run with Kingfisher's apt to do anything. They're a pack of wolves. Probably had a fight over some of their spoils. Well," he said, abruptly brisk, "we're wastin' time here. I'll get back to the office an' set things movin'. We may catch them yet. There's not many roads headin' east towards Texas. . . ."

The sound of their boots moved toward the stairs.

Cori sneezed.

TWENTY-ONE

No PLACE, Marlatt thought, in all the world could be as still as this house had grown. It was an utter quiet, uncanny, breathless, brittle with import. He could almost hear the turn of men's heads as the trio beneath them stared at the ceiling.

A man's voice said: "By God!" and right on its heels, another cried: "Where does that hatch go?"

Bannerman said: "On the roof. Fetch a chair."

Marlatt heard the words and did not move. Cori, too, was like a statue, her dark eyes probing Marlatt fearfully, anxiously. Only Bandera showed life or movement. He got the makings out of a pocket and, with the smoke half rolled, let it flutter away from him. He turned in the starlight to inspect his gun, and threw a quick searching look to where Marlatt squatted. Marlatt gave no heed; and Cheto sat there, fidgeting.

Marlatt made a tired, beaten shape in the shadows. His shoulders sagged and all the lines of his face had let go. There was no use fooling themselves any longer. This was it. Without the girl— But she was here, as usual, right in the thick of things; barging round like always, a bull in the china shop. There was just one chance. One thin, thin chance . . .

He locked tired arms about his knees, settled back on his haunches and grimly waited.

A chair creaked protest in the room below them. Bandera, growling, lifted his pistol.

"Sit down," Marlatt grunted, "and put that gun up."

Cori, turning, reached a hand out timidly. "Kane . . ."

"Well?" Marlatt did not look at her. This whole play hinged—

"I—I'm sorry, Kane."

"I guess we all are, Cori."

She swallowed hard; they could plainly hear her. "We could fight—"

"We been fightin'. You can't lick the law—"

"Nick Bannerman's—"

"I know. It doesn't change things. He's still the law; all the law we've got here."

"Law!" Cori's laugh was scornful. "I'd sooner trust an Apache Indian! So you *are* a quitter. I was right after all."

Marlatt eyed her blackly. "What do you think I should do? Put a gun on Bannerman an' blow his head off?"

The lid came off the hatch with a clatter. Above it showed a hatted shape, and Marlatt threw his voice at it swiftly. "Your pot, Nick. Never mind the gunplay. We're yellin' calf rope."

A thin, startled silence spread across the roof. The shape in the hatchway climbed out warily. Burly shoulders pushed a head through the opening, and stars' gleam faintly winked from a pistol. "You're quittin'? Givin' up?"

Surprise was plain in Bannerman's voice, surprise hardedged with a cold suspicion. "What's the dodge?" he growled.

"Has there got to be one?" A heavy kind of patience timbered Marlatt's tones. "Do I seem so damn hard to convince?"

Bannerman peered through the gloom with a fishy stare. "There's somethin' wrong with this picture, bucko. You're up to somethin'—"

"If suspicion was doughnuts you'd be a bake shop, Sheriff—"

"Mebbe I would; but it ain't in reason for your kind of guy to kink his rope that way. I wasn't born yesterday! You're a Texas man, Fisher. It ain't in Texans to lay down like that. I've met a few of the breed, and they'd charge all hell with an empty bucket. What kind of rusty you tryin' to cut?"

"Would it make sense if I told you we'd a heap rather be locked in your jail than dead on this roof?"

"It might if I could believe it."

Marlatt shrugged and, with a sigh, got up. The deputy's gun followed every move, and Bannerman's eyes were hawk-sharp, watching. "That's a chance you got to take, I reckon," Marlatt drawled and, appearing indifferent to what they might think of it, unbuckled his gun belt and tossed it over near the edge of the roof. "You been wantin' to lock me up," he said. "Here's your chance—hop to it."

The deputy started for the rolled-up belt. "Look out!" gritted Bannerman. "That may be a trick to get you over here an' shove you off—"

Marlatt's curt laugh fired the sheriff's cheeks. "Go on," he snarled. "Laugh hearty, bucko. When you're all through I'll do *my* laughin'." He looked at Bandera. "All right, sport. See how far you can heave that hogleg."

Bandera chucked his gun beside Marlatt's.

"Search 'em, Ed. Take Fisher first."

There was a bulky bandage around Bannerman's gun wrist. His pistol was awkwardly held in his left hand. A thought clicked over in Marlatt's head. He remembered something then. This white-haired sheriff was ambidextrous; the awkward display he made of that pistol was bait, pure and simple. Like his talk. He *hoped* they would try something. The wish was plain in the twist of his shoulders as he called some muttered word down the hatchway to the deputy waiting in the room below.

Marlatt grinned to himself. This sheriff's ambition was riding him hard.

He stood with raised hands while the sheriff's man Friday slapped him over for a hold-out gun. He showed a weary indifference which was entirely deceptive; it barely concealed the relief he felt when the man stepped back, grunting: "Nothin' on him."

"Try his boots."

A hard grin twisted Bannerman's jowls as the man straightened up with the six-shooter Marlatt had got from his bedroll.

The chance was gone.

TWENTY-TWO

MARLATT paced his cell, trying hard to think where he'd made a wrong turn. What had he done that might better have been left untried and forgotten? Not surrender, certainly. He'd had no alternative. Fight? He snorted softly; took six steps, swung, took six back again. Not with Cori so likely to get hit.

They had almost cut it. Then Cori's sneeze had queered the deal. After that, to have fought would have been sheer madness. Even if, by some freak chance, they had downed the sheriff and the deputies with him, it would have gained them nothing. At the first burst of gunfire Tularosa and Company would have come hell-tearing. It seemed wisest to surrender, and it still seemed so; for this way, at least, they had staved death off a bit. Cori's life was safe, anyway—though why that fact should afford him satisfaction was beyond Marlatt's guessing.

Even if—as Bannerman claimed—he believed the girl to be in league with outlaws to defraud her guardian, no court in this land would dream of jailing her for it. Like it or not, Nick would have to loose her. She would not have been loosed had Tularosa caught her.

These were the thoughts which had influenced Marlatt; these, and the one slim chance of that boot-cached gun. Had the pistol—

Marlatt shrugged. It hadn't. The sheriff had outguessed him. It was time to consider the future. Two things were likely. The townfolk, scared of their shadows from talk of Kingfisher, might—if properly managed—come storming the jail with the demand Kingfisher and Cheto be turned over to them. Bannerman would like that. So would Flack. Either, or both, might attempt to arrange it. It would solve a lot of things.

On the other hand, there could be no mob action unless the sheriff made public news of their capture. Such news entailed a serious drawback, for the sheriff, if an honest man, could hardly fail to realize what Kingfisher's men would do in such a case. This jail was vulnerable. If Kingfisher's men could spring Tularosa—

The thought called others to Marlatt's attention.

Everything hinged on one small point: the sheriff's official and personal integrity. If Bannerman were honest, just a blindly ambitious and headlong fool, he would keep the news of this coup to himself for a while. But if the sheriff was a rogue—

The sound of boots running down the narrow corridor drew Marlatt round to face the door. But it was only a jailer with Marlatt's breakfast.

"Has the news got out?"

The jailer said nothing. He pushed his tray underneath the grating, gave Marlatt a scowl and went tramping off.

Marlatt shrugged. He commenced his breakfast with a hungry man's relish. He was halfway through when boot sound again came down the corridor. "Visitor," his warden growled, and hauled off a ways to stand with a hand wrapped round his pistol, stiffly alert and suspiciously glowering.

It was a girl who came slowly up to the grating and stood with her cheeks pressed against the bars. A girl of plump curves and hard rouged features. Her fingernails were painted red. She had bleached yellow hair and dark eyes that were haunted and sullen as they swept over Marlatt from black hair to boot heels.

"So you're the sport Nick's callin' Kingfisher!" Her red lips curled in a short, hard laugh. "Do you know who I am?"

Marlatt shook his head. He had a good idea though; and the girl gave it confirmation.

"I'm Blonde Mary—the one the Malone kid calls Nick's 'Plaza Girl.'" Her lips kept moving, but without sound now: "You want to leave this dump?"

"Yes?" Marlatt said; but the jailer strode forward, eyes bright with suspicion. He caught the girl's shoulder, whirled her wickedly round, and with brutal savagery slammed her back from the cell.

"Now, you slut—do your talkin' from there!"

Eyes black with hatred, the girl straightened the flutes of her stand-up collar. Then a cold reserve smoothed her cheeks inscrutably and, fingering the beaded cross that hung from a necklace bright against the black of her dress, she walked down the hall with composure; and with dignity let herself out.

Swearing under his breath, the jailer tramped after her.

Ten minutes later the sheriff came visiting.

Marlatt's cell was one of the last in the first-floor block; he'd no idea where they'd taken Cori or Cheto Bandera. He could not see them, nor had he heard them since his arrival here. He asked Nick about it.

Nick was packing a shotgun and, by his look, was in high good humor. "Never mind," he grinned. "A man's first worry is for himself; an' you better get at it. The news is out."

"The news?"

"That I've got Kingfisher locked up in this jail." Sly humor looked from Nick's blue stare. "It's too bad, bucko. I'd hoped to prevent it; but one of my deputies had to shoot off his jaw. I tied a can to him, but the beans are spilled now, and it's too late to move you. If you know any prayers you better start sayin' 'em, because"—a feline grin tugged at the sheriff's wide lips—"at the first sign of trouble I'm takin' care of you."

He patted the barrels of his shotgun significantly. "Nobody's takin' *you* out of my custody."

Marlatt said nothing. He sat down on his cot with his lips tight clenched.

The jailer tramped up with a chair from the office. "That French dame from the Plaza was here a while ago—"

Was she now? You mean the blonde one—Mary?
nin' up to our prisoner, was she?"

I dunno. I threw her out. She was actin'—"

Tch, tch," the sheriff clucked. "You shouldn't have
ie that, Louie. I get a lot of good tips—"

An' one of these nights you'll be gettin' a knife!" the
er said sourly, and clanked on out to the office, mut-
ing.

3annerman chuckled. "Louie's soured on women." He
ped back his chair, braced booted feet on the bars of
grating and sat regarding Marlatt with a vast satis-
tion, the shotgun handily cached in his lap. "How was
t breakfast? Pretty good, wasn't it, bucko? It oughta
en; I told 'em to send you the best they had. Helll"
grinned; "I aim to treat you right, Fisher."

Marlatt eyed him with a frozen calm. "Did you ever
the Kingfisher, Bannerman?"

You bet your sweet life—I'm lookin' right at him!"

Blonde Mary—"

You don't want to pay no mind to her," Nick said
ily. "She's got a mad on at me. Jealous of Shirly-Bell.
w *there's* a woman that'll bring a man somethin'l
u're smart all right; I could see that when you first
d eyes on her—"

If you've anything to do, Sheriff, don't let me keep
u."

Don't be so modest, bucko. You're the most important
siness ever stepped in this office. I'm stickin' right
re till your gang tries to spring you. Got your prayin'
ne yet?"

He laughed at the dark glint in Marlatt's eyes. "Tch,
l You shouldn't take on so. You'll strain somethin'
e. As I was sayin', you showed good sense in pickin'
ll Ranleigh. She'll be a damn rich woman when Flack
ks off. But you made one mistake. For a brand artist,
her, you show almighty poor at readin' sign—"

"You're crazy in the head."

"No so damn crazy I don't know a claim jumper when
pot onel I filed on Ranleigh a long time back. When

that girl marries she'll be marryin' *me*—that's a thoug
you can mull on while you're takin' the jump."

Marlatt said nothing; but a turbulence was in hi
hotly churning his blood. He could not sit still. He g
impatiently up and bleakly tramped the confines of l
cell with Bannerman watching him, smugly grinning.

Stopping by the window, Marlatt stared through
bars.

"Hear the pounding, bucko? That's your gallov
They'll have it done by noon. I've got the rope all boug
—a brand-new, stout one. 'Course," Bannerman wink
slyly, "you could make a break for it likely if you g
religious convictions against stretchin' hemp. Tell y
the truth, I'd just as lief you would. 'S what I'm pack
this sawed-off for—eighteen buckshot lookin' right at yo
nine in each barrel." And he laughed deep down in l
throat, maliciously.

Marlatt said: "Have you got any smokin'?"

"Sure thing, Mr. Kingfisher. Anything you want. A
you got to do is name it." He tugged a Durham sack o
of shirt pocket, tossed it through the grating, then fish
papers and a match out of his hatband. "You can ke
'em," he grinned. "Light up an' smoke hearty, buck
Compliments of two or three hundred outraged citizen:

All the ground-floor windows of the building we
open, but it was built of red brick and was hot as a fu
nace. Sweat made streaks of shine on their faces. Ba
nerman had on a baggy tweed coat to uphold, perha
the dignity of his office. It increased Marlatt's discor
fort just to look at it. He drew the back of a sleeve acro
his forehead. It came away soaked.

"You mustn't mind this heat," the sheriff taunte
"You'll find it rightdown cool 'side of where you're goin

Bannerman's badgering talk drifted off, faded to
hectoring, monotonous mumble behind the knife-edg
churnings of Marlatt's desperate thoughts. Again ar
again he reviewed the events that had brought him
the end of his string. He could find no place where l
might have done differently with resultant profit. H

dwelt particularly on last night's affair but was forced inevitably to concede his surrender justified. How *could* they have fought on with Cori so handy to the path of wild bullets? It was the girl's impulsive character that had licked them; if she'd not been there they might have cut it. Yet he could not honestly despise her; she was a heap too blunt and forthright to suit him—too impulsive, brash and boylike. He did not condemn her for these traits, but they concealed from him the girl's true worth.

Marlatt, like most Texans then, regarded women as beings set apart to be protected, to be shielded with men's lives against the harsh realities of rude existence. There was a place for women in this life, but if they would retain their high position in men's esteem and affections they had to keep to the place allotted them; they must not cross its boundaries, which were definite and strict. This wild Arizona country was man's domain —and man's only; man's notions shaped its code and were the guide to woman's destiny. Thus was Shirly-Bell Ranleigh an admired and proper lady, while Cori, by this rigid view, was a heedless, headstrong rebel who had no one to blame for her troubles but her own tempestuous self. What court would give a second thought to the claims of such wild baggage in the face of the quiet restraint and suave assertions to be expected from Ora Flack?

Marlatt's temper writhed and boiled with remembrance of the sheriff's allusions. He had spoken of Shirly-Bell as though she were a piece of ground to be staked by the first man sighting it; as though she were a horse to be bought, or a harlot. Marlatt's locked white fists were clenched with rage as he stared unseeingly through the bars of the window. Bannerman's tone and remarks were unpardonable—doubly so, linked as they had been with the name of a common tommie.

There was a high roan flush on Marlatt's cheeks, but the sheriff misconstrued it. "Tut, tut," he drawled with a leering chuckle. "You may be tough over in Texas, Fisher, but it takes a real hombre to be tough here. We use fellers like you for baby fodder; an' that loud-mouthed pard of yours, Ben Thompson—shucks! he wouldn't last two seconds here."

With Marlatt helpless in his power at last, Bannerman was malignantly set on enjoying himself, on paying back with compound interest all the things he held against him. He took a vast delight in the Texan's predicament, a keen satisfaction in baiting him. He harped upon the gallows theme. He guffawed long and loudly over the prospect of what his shotgun could do if Fisher's men or the townsfolk found guts to rush the jail for him. "The boys out front'll hold 'em off long enough for me to un-ravel these buckshot, bucko. I wisht your gang *would* try it on; I'd like to see your face, my friend, when this load rips through your belly!"

It was half after nine by the slant of the sun when Louie yelled, "Nick!" from the sheriff's office. "Your Plaza skirt's out here again—come a-runnin' before she wrecks the place. I've stood all her yap I aim to!"

The slam of a door brought the sheriff's chair down. A black scowl creased his cheeks; and he shoved the chair back away from the grating, carefully laid his shotgun down on it and, muttering balefully under his breath, went stamping off down the corridor.

"Marlatt!" Just a whisper of breath, but plain enough, the call pulled Marlatt back to the window. He squeezed his bronzed face hard against the bars and saw Oliphant peering up at him.

"You still got that roll you was flashin'?"

The stableman's meaning was plain enough. He referred to the currency Marlatt had shown while dicker-ing for the blaze-faced roan. He still had it, for this was a hard-money country that had little use for the fluctuat-ing paper currency put out by faraway banks in the East.

Marlatt nodded; and Oliphant—the horse-trading Yan-kee—said quickly: "Pass it out an' I'll—"

"Head for Missouri, eh?"

"Wouldn't be out much if I did, would you? Won't be

din' much change to spend it in there—nor where
u're goin' if you don't flit pronto. Chances are I can't
lp much anyhow; but cash talks, mister, if you want
should try. But think fast. She can't keep him there
rever—"

"Got a pistol on you?" Marlatt tossed him the green-
cks.

"Here you are," grinned the stableman, and handed it
.. "Louie's gone out, but Ed's here some place. Buck's
the Mexican's lappin' up booze. I'll be watchin' my
ance. Quick's Bannerman starts for your cell again—"

"He's startin' now," Marlatt muttered; and Oliphant
nished. But this gun was enough. A vast exultation
elled Marlatt's arteries. With this gun in his hand he
as ready for anything. He'd been a fool to give up his
eapons last night.

He turned from the window, folding his arms in a
ay that hid the gripped pistol behind his left elbow.
steely glint showed its flash in his eyes at the jingle
d clank of Bannerman's spur rowels.

The sheriff hove into sight, scowling. "Damn strum-
t!" he snarled, and bent by the chair to pick up his
otgun.

Oliphant's hail came out of the office, and Oliphant's
ots rolled sound through the corridor. The sheriff,
rprised, lashed round in a fury. One spur caught a
air leg and sent the chair crashing. The double-
rreled Greener hit the floor with a clatter, stopped
ith its stock just beyond the cell's grating.

"Flack said to tell—"

The nasal twang of the stableman's voice was lost bend the sheriff's bull bellow. "What the hell you mean
min' out here! You—"

"Flack said—"

"Git!" That one purred word was soft and wicked.
he sheriff's left hand was wrapped round a six-shooter.

Oliphant, still coming, said: "Flack—" and stopped.
is staring eyes bugged out like saucers. "My Gawd—
ook out!"

Like a snarling cat the sheriff spun. Black fury rolle across his cheeks and the lifting muzzle of his gun spa flame when he saw the pistol in Marlatt's hand. But th shot went wild, ricocheted off the grating. With a savag grin Marlatt squeezed the trigger.

The grin fell away. His face went blank. Again an again he triggered frantically. But the hammer kicke down without result.

The stableman's pistol was loaded with empties.

TWENTY-THREE

MARLATT knew one moment of ice-cold fear. He crouched, blank of eye, dismayed and frozen, while a million thoughts whirled through his head and he heard no sound but the thump of his heart.

Rage grabbed him then. "You greedy bastard!" he said through clamped teeth, and hurled the gun at the tricky tableman with every ounce of strength he could summon.

The man let out a frightened bleat, and the smug grin shaping his cheeks went twisted. The whistling pistol took him square in the chest and knocked him sprawling with a groan of terror.

Marlatt sprang on the instant, floorward and doorward, the roar and crash of the sheriff's firing banging round through the jail like a third alarm. Marlatt's mind knew one thing only a raging desire, a white-hot urge to get his hands on that shotgun—and use it!

Bannerman was knowing a need, too—a fierce one. Face streaked with sweat and eyes like gun steel, he stood spraddle-legged twelve feet away and drove his shots with a vicious cursing that neither helped his aim nor temper. His lead slapped the bars of the iron grating, whistled and thwacked and ricocheted whanging—but it did not drop nor stop Kane Marlatt.

It did not seem, in so short a space, that a man so good could so consistently miss; but the sheriff was doing it, blaspheming wildly. He stood with his square chin ragefully jutted, with the bones of his cheeks standing out like castings. Malevolence, and the tumult lashing him, made cracks of his eyes—cracks bright as gun flame; and every time he missed he swore, louder, more sav-

agely—like a mad bull bellowing, with the following sho
going wilder than ever.

Perhaps it was that knife-slit wrist that made his firing
so unnaturally faulty; he was doing his shooting left
handed, and Marlatt was not standing still for him
either. And now Marlatt's hand was through the grating
—was reaching for the sheriff's dropped shotgun.

Bannerman realized suddenly what was going to happen if he didn't get to that shotgun first

Marlatt saw the jerk and leap of his muscles; saw the
big form crouch—saw the big form leaping. Bannerman's
boots looked like housetops coming. With a grunt from
the strain, Marlatt stretched tense fingers and touched
the sawed-off gun, touched the butt of that double-
barreled Greener. But he couldn't catch hold of it,
couldn't quite budge it. His desperate fingers were an
inch too short.

The sheriff's leap landed him full-tilt on it; his weight
and momentum drove it out from under him—drove it
hard at the grating of Marlatt's cell. Bannerman struck
on his hip with a solid thump. The pistol went skittering
out of his hand, his gleaming cheeks grimaced at the
pain to his wrist, but his stubborn mind was locked on
his purpose and he flung all his weight over hard on the
barrel.

Marlatt cursed at the pain to the fingers ground under
it; jerked them free and saw Bannerman, quick as a cat,
slide clear and lock both hamlike hands round it. He
meant to yank the weapon clear. He *yanked* it; but Marlatt caught a flying hold on the stock and kept it,
though both strained arms were dragged through the
grating and his heaving chest was against the bars.

He kept his hold but he couldn't better it, and Bannerman, snarling, twisted round on one knee and braced
a boot on the grating—braced and tugged, with his sweat-
streaked face gone knotted and purple, with the burly
shoulders of him bulging his shirt.

Teeth bared and clenched, Marlatt put all the strength
he could get in that grip. But it wasn't enough. The stock

as slipping. His wet palms greased it. He could feel
the thing oozing out of his grasp and then, like an eel,
was loose from him—gone!

When Blonde Mary connived with the stableman, Oli-
hant, in the crackpot plan to get Marlatt free, she was
doing it, not from a sense of high moral principle or because she knew Marlatt wrongly accused, but from a
purely and personal resentment of Bannerman. He had
used her ill and, unless he were prepared to right mat-
ers pronto, it was Mary's intention to even the score. For
some reason Nick set a deal of store by having this
stranger locked up in his jail. Very well! She cared not
at all what scheme might be tucked up the stableman's
sleeve; he was offering her a chance to get even with
Nick and she meant to take it. If Nick wanted to do the
right thing by her—

With her first look at Nick it was plain he didn't. He
grinned at her hugely; patted her shoulder. "Well, well,
Mary—how you doin' these days? They tell me you've
opened a—"

"Never mind that!" She threw his hand off, angry eyes
bright and hating. "You know what I'm here for!"

"An' you know what I told you last time." There was
nothing complimentary in Nick's dark look. "The past is
past an' damn well done with. I paid you off—"

"Look out I don't pay *you* off! I think I'll ride out and
talk with Bell Ranleigh— Nick! You're hurtin' me—"

"I'll hurt you! You slut!" the sheriff snarled, and three
times his cuffing hand went across her cheeks; then he
grabbed her shoulder, roughly shoving her doorward.

"I'll tell Bell Ranleigh—"

"You go near Bell Ranleigh an' I'll tear your damn guts
out!"

She called him something entirely unprintable and
tried to get out when he suddenly jumped for her, but
her whirling skirt got stabbed on a bill spike that was
bolted to the top of his desk. Bannerman's huge hands
caught her. The next thing she knew she was out in the

street, on her back in the dust, with her fancy dress torn
almost up to her thighs.

There were six men in sight, and all six were laughing, great uproarious guffaws, as Blonde Mary yanked
down her skirt and righted her hat. But their catcall
ceased as a pistol cracked inside the courthouse; by the
time the third shot blasted the silence Blonde Mary had
the street to herself. She reached a hand down inside
her bodice. In considerable hurry Oliphant passed her
in the courthouse doorway; neither one of them ever
glanced at the other. As Blonde Mary reached the cell
block doorway she removed the hand from inside her
dress. The dim light glinted from the barrel of a derringer. Kicking off her slippers, she crept cat-soft down
the high-ceiled corridor. She saw the shotgun jerked
from Marlatt. She was two yards behind him when Bannerman, with his lips drawn back from the sheen of his
teeth, reversed the shotgun and reached for its trigger.

"Don't believe I'd do that, Nicky."

The soft drawl of her voice stopped Bannerman cold.
He looked rooted, with his eyes blue slits and his grip
on the Greener gone whitely rigid. Her tone must have
told him she had a gun on him; and the give and take of
their past relations must have held some strong signifi-
cance to have kept the man so stiffly still. He hardly
seemed to breathe, Marlatt thought. It was as though he
suspected she *wanted* to shoot.

Blonde Mary said: "Use that good left hand, Nick, and
get your keys out. . . . Careful! That's right. Now toss
them to Marlatt."

Marlatt caught them. Four on a ring. The largest
looked like the one he wanted. He was reaching his arm
through the bars of the grating, had the key in the lock
when the derringer spoke. The lock clicked sharply as
Bannerman swore; then the door swung open and Marlatt
was at him, both lunging hands clamping hard on the
gleaming double barrel of the sheriff's weapon.

Bannerman still had a finger caught in the trigger
guard, and all the strength of his massive shoulders was

behind his effort to bring that murderous, gaping muzzle up.

Marlatt fought with a silent fury to keep himself alongside of the weapon; and that was the way things were, at a deadlock, when the girl ran in behind the sheriff and began beating at his head and shoulders with the empty six-shooter she had snatched from the floor.

Cold sweat stood out on the sheriff's clamped cheeks. The end came suddenly, sharp and decisive. Trying to get away from that clubbing pistol, the sheriff lurched sideways and got a spur hung up in the leg of his trousers. He tripped and fell with the shotgun roaring.

TWENTY-FOUR

Marlatt pulled clear with a sense of nausea. He dragged a shirtsleeve across his face. He did not look at the sheriff again but said, still panting, to the white-cheeked girl: "Wait here!" and, grabbing the keys, dashed out to the office. His belt and gun were hung from a peg, and he snatched them down and hurried back to the cell block, buckling them round him as he did so. He found Bandera in another wing of the steel-barred cages, and the Mexican's eyes popped when he saw him. He unlocked the grating. Blonde Mary ran up as Cheto stepped free. "You better leave by the back," she told them breathlessly. "There's a crowd collecting out front of this place—"

"We ain't leavin' yet!" Marlatt grabbed the pistol she was holding, and shoved it at Bandera with a handful of cartridges jerked from his belt.

She caught his shoulder. "If you don't leave quick you won't *be* leavin'—"

"Find Cori—"

"There's no use hunting these cells for that girl. Bannerman let her go first thing this morning—right after he'd locked you up—"

"What's that?" Marlatt cried; and then went stiff as the implications swept crowding in on him. "So Nick *was* a crook, after all!" he growled.

"—and a big bunch of riders left town right afterwards," Blonde Mary rushed on as though he hadn't spoken. "They lined out south on the trail toward the Straddle Bug and—"

Marlatt swore; described Tularosa.

"Yes. He was leading them."

Marlatt shoved the ring of keys at Cheto. "Go through

this jail an' loose every man who's willin' to fight—send 'em down to the office to collect their hardware!"

In Bannerman's office three minutes later Marlatt faced eighteen astonished and curious men. His questions revealed no felons among them; all had been jugged for minor offenses and one of them, oddly enough, was the Mexican, Gomez, Bannerman had bought the bay horse from. They were mostly youngsters, salty and reckless, who had been locked up for too much celebrating. None of the town's riffraff was here. Marlatt judged them with a quick, hard stare.

"Boys," he said, "I'm in a jackpot. I been booked in this boardin' house as John King Fisher, the Texas outlaw, an' by the looks of the crowd pilin' up outside—"

"We get it," one of the cowboys grinned. "You're wantin' us to help you git out of here—"

"That's part of it. The rest of the play's apt to be more lively. There's a passel of gun throwers whackin' up dust on the Straddle Bug trail. I've an idea they're after the Crescent beef cut—"

"Which is what to you?" a lanky man asked.

"It's nothin' to me, except I won't stand by an' see a girl stole blind—"

"What's the matter with Flack's hired gun fighters?"

"They may not be out there. Or they might be surprised—they might be a lot of things. I don't propose—"

"Where's the sheriff? An' what was all that shootin'?"

"Bannerman's dead. He accidentally shot himself—"

"He sure used up a heap of ca'tridges!"

Marlatt said coldly: "The point is I don't want that herd stole. You boys want to help me, or had your rather stay nice an' safe in jail?"

Several of the men scowled. One or two muttered. The lanky man said: "There's somethin' queer here. Ain't you the gent they call Kane Marlatt? Then what's your connections? You a lawman—"

"I'm an operative," Marlatt said, "of the Canadian River Cattle Association—"

"That's a stockman's outfit. You acquainted with John W. Poe?"

"I been workin' with him up till just recent. We're wastin' time," Marlatt growled impatiently. "Are you or ain't you wantin' chips in this fight?"

"Speakin personal," the lanky man said, "I don't buy into a thing like this blind. I—"

Marlatt said to Bandera: "Put him back in his cell. Mebbe we better put 'em *all* back! We've got the wrong place, Cheto; we've blundered into a convention of parsons!" He swept them a caustic, contemptuous glance. "Where I come from men will *fight* for a woman."

Flush-faced, the lanky man growled: "You got no call t—"

"Shut up!" And to Bandera: "Get him back in his cell! Get 'em all back—pronto! We'll go down to the *barrio libre* an' see if we can round up a few of them one-armed beggars that mebbe ain't scared to bust a few snivelin' laws—"

"Hey—wait! Hold on," muttered a lantern-jawed runt whose legs were so bowed he looked like a wishbone. "How about it, boys? We goin' to let this galoot make talk like that at us? We goin' to pine away in this damn jail when he's offerin' us a invite on a silver platter to jamboree that'll mebbe make hist'ry? C'mon, you curly wolves—let's heah yo' howl!"

He heard it.

The crowd outside must have heard it, too, for when, rearmed and with hats cuffed low across hard, squinted eyes, they sifted silently out into the sun-drenched street, there was not one bystander within sight of the courthouse. Not a team, not a dog—not even a gopher.

Ten minutes later, mounted on horses from Oliphant's corral, they took the south trail at a headlong gallop.

They rode grimly silent, rode hard and rode steady. Some of their number had at first yipped and yelled in the sheer exuberance of being free and on a trail again; in the excitement and anticipation of the action they

resaw when they came up with the rustling sons who
were out to steal the Crescent beef cut. But those who
ode nearest the front, close to Marlatt, were swiftly
influenced by his own grim mood; and shortly the shouts
nd the horseplay were left behind and the pace settled
own to an easier lope.

Marlatt's blue glance was opaque with his thinking.
There must be no more mistakes, no more blundering
lindly. These things followed patterns; all this violence
uddenly got afoot was no mere vagary of chance. Like
Bandera's role of Tio Felix, there was a purpose back of
:; need, an object. Bandera had been forced to hide his
identity because of Bannerman. Bannerman had been
fter the Mexican because Bandera held the key to
what had been assumed the natural death of Cori's
ather. The sheriff would never have felt secure as long
s Cheto was free to tell what he knew of the killer horse
that had caused Malone's death.

A lot of knowledge was to be drawn from Bannerman's
onnection with that horse. What interested Marlatt was
he hook-up with Flack. The events leading up to old
Malone's death conclusively linked the sheriff with
Flack. The sheriff had brought Malone news of the
orse. Malone's death had brought Flack control of the
Crescent. Control of the Crescent had made Flack
owerful, and friendship with Flack kept the sheriff in
ffice.

Flack was crooked. Bannerman must have been
rooked also. He had clearly been in league with Flack—
ad been aiming to strengthen his hand by marriage
with Flack's niece. The whole atmosphere of Flack's out-
it smelled of intrigue and crookedness. There were too
nany cattle; not even the rustlers Flack claimed were
working on him had kept the range from being over-
grazed. This slick talk of rustlers must be more of Flack's
lyness. Only one man in Marlatt's memory had been
alf as slick as this smug Ora Flack. That man was
Craft Towner—born John King Fisher! Suave Craft
Towner, rail thin and lightning fast on the trigger.

They were uncommonly alike, Craft Towner and Flack
Only Flack was fat and Towner lean. Marlatt remem
bered the ornate belt Flack had fingered, that cartridge
belt with its odd gun contrivance. Not many men packed
a gun that way. There was no creaking holster on Flack's
fancy belt; a plate of metal with a slot riveted onto it. A
pin-headed screw, replacing the regular hammer screw
of his pistol, was fitted into the slot and caught in a
niche at its lower end, thus allowing the gun to hang
open and swinging. All Flack had to do to set it smoking
was squeeze the trigger. It did not have to be drawn.
There was nothing to draw it from.

It was a pretty sure bet, Marlatt thought, that Flack
had been operating the combined Crescent and Straddle
Bug spreads as a "distribution" ranch: a holding ground
and shipping point for cattle stolen out of Texas and the
Nations; out of New Mexico Territory also, probably. A
place where doctored brands could heal while the critters
fattened on Santa Cruz grass. The coming of the railroad
to this mountain-ringed valley would have been the last
neat touch to Flack's consuming greed for ownership of
Crescent. Marlatt doubted if there was a better layout in
the whole Southwest. No wonder the man was slavering
for it!

Marlatt's lean jaw tightened as a new thought clicked
through his mind. The *connection*—at last he had it! The
reason Craft Towner had tried to hire him to gun Ora
Flack! Flack and Towner had been working together—
Flack and Kingfisher, rather, for Towner *was* Kingfisher.
Flack, grown important and powerful, grown fat with
pride, must have thrown Fisher over—gone in for himself. Locked away in this fastness, hemmed by mountains
and deserts, he had thumbed his nose at the Texas outlaw
—had lounged back to pocket the profits himself! This
was why he paid wages to so many gun throwers!

Neat. Very neat. Ora Flack was a jackal laughing at a
wolf.

But his laughing days were about over. Even now

gfisher's men would be cutting out the Crescent
f. . . .

nother thought clicked into place. More than once
Marlatt wondered why Tularosa's men, when they'd
night rushed the stable, had not killed Bannerman,
sheriff. He could see why now. The answer was so
ple he felt a fool for not having guessed it sooner.
gfisher's men had not killed Nick because as sheriff
d been playing Kingfisher's game; he had been a
ded part of this elaborate Tucson set-up. Here was an
lanation also for the cat-slick ease with which Fisher's
boss, Tularosa, had been sneaked from that almost
regnable jail once the sheriff's need of the man was
e with.

hey'd been smart—give them credit. They'd been
ker than whistles. But as old Abe Lincoln had once
nted out, you can't fool all of the people all of the
e. They had cut their strings a little short, and now
y would pay for their crimes, for their thievery. With
se reckless riders Marlatt would force a showdown;
would break this gang up once and for all. Even as,
ady, he had set in motion the rumbling wheels that
uld rush the Kingfisher to a felon's death. For while
men he had taken from Bannerman's jail had been
vn at Oliphant's gathering horses he—Kane Marlatt—
d been at the depot sending a wire to the Grant
unty sheriff, tipping him off to Craft Towner's identity.
a few short hours the New Mexican authorities would
ve the Kingfisher behind stout bars.

And then a vague uneasiness got into Marlatt, an inex-
cable premonition of disaster he could neither explain
shake.

t had to do with Cori in some fashion—that much he
derstood at once. In these last few hours they had,
h of them, grown much closer to the other. He real-
d this with a sense of shock—of disloyalty to Shirly-
ll; of surprise and almost of consternation. It startled
n to realize the new respect he had conceived for Cori.
alysis would have revealed that the experiences, the

common peril, they'd so recently shared had much to
with the strangeness of his feelings toward Cori; b
Marlatt was too upset with discovering that he cared
all to go into the matter so deeply as that. All he realiz
now was worry, and an oddly uncomfortable sense
guilt.

Cori!

Again and again in his mind her name repeated itse
The throbbing rhythm of the horses' hoofs seem
measured to the cadence of that name. Co-ri! Co-ri! Co-
it cried, until there was no peace in Marlatt anywhe
Never Bell Ranleigh but always Cori; it hammered
his subconsciousness over and over and over until he w
imbued with a wild and fantastic urge for speed.

Dire were his thoughts and bleak his mood as th
pelted on beneath the boiling sun, with the stifling wi
whipped up off the desert cuffing their hat brims, score
ing them, blinding them, plastering their gritty clothes
the fronts of them. All natural moisture seemed bak
clean out of them. Their tongues were lumps in mout
lined with cotton; their eyeballs seemed bedded
cactus-spiked sand.

When they paralleled the last notch of the Tucs
Mountains, Marlatt signaled a brief halt to breathe th
horses; and all the time they were resting there Marl
tramped the burning dust of the trail with hands lock
behind him, his dark face scowling and a devil of wor
in the looks he kept swinging at the lowering sun.

Bandera attempted to reassure him. "Be at peac
amigo. We will catch them—if not here, then before th
reach the Empires, surely. They will make poor time wi
all those cattle."

"An' there's the question of water," declared t
lantern-jawed man. "They'll have to gear their pace
the variance in miles between the known waterholes—"

"I was not thinking of the cattle." Marlatt raised
arm for the group's attention. "I'm goin' to leave y
yonder. You'll take your orders from Bandera, boys. I
used to ride for Crescent an' knows this range like th

palm of his hand. When you come up with Tularosa's bunch they'll be usin' their rifles—don't be scared to use yours. There ain't a man in that crew but what's a thief an' outlaw. They're all renegades—plain border scum."

"Then we'll turn off now," Bandera smiled with a lower lip caught between his teeth. "A draw I know of will be just the place to stop *los coyotes*. No other way can the cattle pass. Come, *amigos;* we will wait there for them, and with the kind permission of God's blessed Mother—"

With a shrug he grinned, and the more reckless of them grinned back at him, chuckling.

They went to their horses and began tightening cinches. Out of a deep understanding Cheto looked at Marlatt and slowly nodded. He asked no questions about Marlatt's intention, nor where he was bound for—just held out his hand. "Go with God," he said when Marlatt shook it.

TWENTY-FIVE

MARLATT had about made up his mind, when in the dusk he rode through the Straddle Bug's gate, that he'd been all nerved up over a far-fetched notion that had no foundation in solid fact. He almost regretted not having gone with the others—not that they needed him, but for the personal satisfaction of settling with Tularosa. There would, however, be some compensation in telling sly Ora the game was up; and Flack was here. Cracks of light outlined the shade-drawn windows of his office.

Marlatt felt a little better now. He had tracked his uneasiness down at last and knew it had sprung from Blonde Mary's information that Cori had been released from Nick's jail. There was no reason why she shouldn't have been. The sheriff had arrested her out of caution, out of his need for misleading Marlatt and the Mexican till he should have them safely housed behind bars. There was nothing sinister about it. All that talk of bandit queens had been so much hogwash; Bannerman had never believed her in league with outlaws. With Bandera and Marlatt in jail, the sheriff had had no further need of Cori, and so had turned her loose.

Marlatt stopped his horse by the veranda and got stiffly out of the saddle. Almost at once Shirly-Bell was before him, coming out of the house and pausing, rather queerly, in front of the door. She wore riding togs now—short skirt and boots, with a thin print blouse and a felt hat's strap beneath her chin. She was picturesque and wholly desirable; and Marlatt was amazed—felt guilty, almost —that he could regard her with so much detachment.

"I thought you were in jail," she said, and there was something very like resentment in her voice that brought Marlatt's brows up sharply.

"You sound like you might be sorry I'm not—"

"Did you come here to make a quarrel with me?"

"You know—"

"I know someone's been killed every time you've been ere! Poor Uncle Ora's been worried—"

"Too bad about poor Uncle Ora. You tell him I've got message—"

"I'll take your message. What—"

"Thank you, ma'am; I think I'll take it myself—"

That was when Bell Ranleigh dropped her sweet, emure fine-lady airs and became a real flesh-and-blood erson. Marlatt heard her gasp; saw the blur of her arm; lt the sting of her gloves as they struck his cut cheek. e stared, astounded, while she struck again. Smiling ryly, he put out a hand and caught her wrist. "You eap, gun-toting bravo!" she cried. "Let go of me, damn ou! Get off this ranch—"

"I expect I better see Ora first."

Gone savage, primitive, panting foul names at him, e fought with a vicious headlong fury to keep him way from the door behind her—fought like a crazed, ommon barroom hellcat.

Sudden remembrance of the trail's foreboding lashed larlatt with an urge for haste. He flung her from him, pped the screen door back and went down the hall like e wrath of God. He kicked Flack's office door wide pen.

Lamplight trapped him blinking there, stopped cold nd frantic by the sight before him.

Cori, with her man's woolen shirt peeled down to her aist, sat roped to one of the hide-covered chairs, bound ght and brutally but in such fashion her hobbled right and could reach without effort the pulled-up table and e pen, ink and paper so confidently laid there. Handy nd lazy in a chair beside her sprawled Tularosa with a er on his face, booted feet on the table.

A small fire glowed on the hearth nearby. From its eap of coals a length of metal protruded, a slender bar of iron—a running iron, illegitimate marker of stolen cattle, cherry-red at the end shoved into the fire. Above it crouched Ora Flack with his devil's lips smiling as he told the girl with reflective tolerance: "It's entirely up to you, my dear. If you'd rather have your little pink hide all decorated up than sign over something you haven't got anyway, you'll soon have a—"

That was when, with a crash, the office door flew open. For one split second the tableau held while a clatter of heels rushed sound from the hallway. Tularosa gave one strangled shout and leaped from his chair with both hands clawing.

They never touched leather; never brushed his gun butts. Two explosions belted the air of the place. Both shots struck Tularosa hard and smashed him, goggle eyed and gasping, three backward, lurching, nerve breaking steps that finally dropped him, like a log, on the fire.

Flack had instantly whirled and stood now, crouched with his cheeks sheet-white, with his spraddled hand empty. And because Flack's gun, with its ornate belt, lay plain on the table a good seven feet from the ranchman's hand, Marlatt held his fire. He couldn't drive slugs through an unarmed man—could only glare like a fool and curse the luck that must give this fiend the final laugh. For how could the law cope with sly Ora Flack? The man's power and his influence would laugh in his face. He would hoot to scorn every story they told; and the courts would believe him.

With a bitter oath Marlatt sheathed his gun. "Untie Miz' Co—" He was stopped in mid-speech by the gleam in Flack's eye. But like Cori's scream the look came too late. Even as Marlatt's hand swiped hipward another hand closed round his gun butt. He realized with shock it was Shirly-Bell Ranleigh's.

The girl's hand had the gun clearing leather when Marlatt's fist slapped down on its barrel. But the girl was too shrewd—too quick for his purpose. A backward lunge ripped the weapon away from him. He had to wheel or let her gun him.

He spun and, cat quick, struck it savagely. Yet even as the six-shooter flew from her grasp he heard Flack spring.

With frantic haste Marlatt dropped to his knees and tried to throw himself sideways. The rancher's weight slammed into him headlong. He tried to roll free, but Flack's leg blocked him. "Smash the lamp!" Flack gritted; and that was when Marlatt saw the knife—eight inches of steel honed razor-sharp coming pellmell toward him in Flack's left hand.

Marlatt writhed, and brought a knee lunging up at that driving hand. It caught Flack's elbow, wringing a snarling groan from him as the knife fell clattering from his nerveless hand and the light snuffed out in a burst of glass.

Flack had rolled clear—was on his feet, his tall shape outlined against the shadows, when Marlatt's searching hand found the knife. All his bottled rage was in the leap that sheathed the blade in Flack's fat belly. But it was Craft Towner's voice that said: "By God—"

And everything went completely black.

How long she'd been calling Marlatt didn't know; but it was Cori's voice that finally roused him. His opened eyes saw a blinding light that gradually dimmed to the pale yellow glow of one lone lamp; and he realized then that, once again, he was stretched out prone with his head soft-pillowed in a woman's lap—in the same woman's lap!—in Cori Malone's!—in a room plumb filled with grinning faces!

He struggled to rise but, as they'd done before, her hands restrained him. As in a dream he heard her say: "Better wait a bit, cowboy, till the world quits spinning."

And wait he did. He felt weak as a kitten, and mighty foolish till he heard her say: "You mavericks clear out of here. Mosey over to the cook-shack an' favor a lady by shakin' up some supper."

Bandera snickered but filed out with the rest. When

they were gone Marlatt opened his eyes again. Cori had her shirt on properly once more, but the room still looked pretty much of a wreck. He asked: "What happened? What'd they do with Flack's body an' where's Bell Ranleigh?"

"She's gone off with Flack's body—"

"Gone *what?*"

She let him get up. "You better get this straight. They've both lit out—"

"What do you mean 'lit out'? I put that hawg-sticker—" He broke off to look scowlingly where she pointed. Then he saw the feathers, and a great light washed all the questions out of him, as he remembered Craft Towner's voice shouting: "By God—"

It was all mighty plain now that he saw all those feathers strewn over the floor. No wonder Ora Flack had reminded him of Towner—Ora Flack *was* Towner! Behind whiskers and a feather-padded belly. And Towner, of course, was Kingfisher—John King Fisher—wiliest brain in the whole Southwest, the trickiest outlaw that had ever quit Texas.

No wonder sly Ora had kept ahead of him. He had known all the time who Marlatt was. But it was as Craft Towner he'd pulled his slickest stunt. Trying to hire Marlatt to gun Ora Flack! That had been *real* cute!

Marlatt saw it all now. Kingfisher, seeing the game up as Towner unless his men finished Marlatt, had made that offer to discover if Marlatt knew him as Ora Flack also. When he found Marlatt didn't he had hit the trail, leaving Tularosa to deal with Marlatt. As Ora Flack he must have been pretty startled when Marlatt showed up with the girls that day. He must have been equally startled when Marlatt showed up tonight.

Well, he'd got away.

Marlatt looked at Cori. He said lugubriously: "Go on—let's have it."

"Think you can stand hearing the truth about Shirly? She was Ora's mistress—"

"Yeah," Marlatt said; "we can forget that dame with

316

rofit. I been taken in all around. The guy we've known s Ora Flack was Kingfisher, the Texas outlaw. What appened after the lights went out?"

"You jumped for Ora and he hit you with a chair. He nust have been pretty scared of you—"

"Never mind smoothin' it up for me. Did the boys save hem cattle?"

She nodded, watching him. He started to run his hands hrough his hair, winced and tramped the room, scowlng darkly. Abruptly he stopped and faced her, frowning. Cori," he said, "I been a damn fool— Oh, I don't mean bout Kingfisher. I'll get the last laugh on him yet; they'll rab him quick's he shows in Grant County. I mean bout *you*. I been a—"

And that was when Cori grinned up at him. "I been uite a fool myself," she said. "Do you reckon we could tart over even?"